ANNE M

Caelinn Largey has worked as a teacher in France and Nepal, and as a refugee aid worker in Thailand. Now living back in Dublin, she is married with two sons. This is her first novel.

Caelinn Largey

Anne Marie
in the City

POCKET BOOKS

TownHouse

First published in Great Britain and Ireland by Pocket/TownHouse, 2002
An imprint of Simon & Schuster UK Ltd,
and TownHouse and CountryHouse Ltd, Dublin
Simon & Schuster UK is a Viacom Company

Copyright © Caelinn Largey, 2002

This book is copyright under the Berne Convention
No reproduction without permission
® and © 1997 Simon & Schuster Inc.
All rights reserved
Pocket Books & Design is a registered trademark of Simon & Schuster Inc

The right of Caelinn Largey to be identified as author of this work has
been asserted in accordance with sections 77 and 78 of the Copyright,
Designs and Patents Act, 1988.

1 3 5 7 9 10 8 6 4 2

Simon & Schuster UK Ltd
Africa House
64–78 Kingsway
London WC2B 6AH

Simon & Schuster Australia
Sydney

TownHouse and CountryHouse Ltd
Trinity House
Charleston Road
Ranelagh
Dublin 6
Ireland

Oh the Places You'll Go © 1990 by Dr Seuss Enterprises, L.P.
All rights reserved. Used by permission of HarperCollins Publishers Ltd.

Extract from *Birds of America* by Lorrie Moore
reproduced by kind permission of Alfred A. Knopf.

A CIP catalogue record for this book is available from the British Library

ISBN 1 903 65002 X

This book is a work of fiction. Names, characters, places and incidents are
either a product of the author's imagination or are used ficticiously. Any
resemblance to actual people living or dead, events or locales is entirely
coincidental.

Typeset by SX Composing DTP, Rayleigh, Essex
Printed and bound in Great Britain by Clays Ltd, St Ives plc

Acknowledgements

Thanks first of all to my husband, Patrick O'Sullivan, for allowing himself to be repatriated to the land of his forebears and for being the sole breadwinner while this book was in the writing. His support means everything. And to our sons Brian and Fintan for not complaining that I spend more time with a whole host of imaginary characters than with them.

To my Utterly Brilliant Brother Ciarán for all his practical assistance, especially where computers are concerned.

To Joana Murphy, whose careful reading of early scripts and unfailing encouragement helped set me on the right track.

To Barbara Barry, ex-Oncology Sister, Mater Hospital; Malachy Kelly, Assistant Chief Officer, Mountjoy Prison; Clare Gavin Maguire, ex-Special Branch; Gillian Kelly, Barrister; Lisa Gaughran and Michelle Kelly, ex-*U Magazine* for generously giving of their time and expertise. I take full responsibility for any inaccuracies in the presentation of the information they provided.

In memory of my mother and father

Dublin, Here I Come

'Well, this is it, I guess.'

The whistle had sounded. Anne Marie's mother handed her a small, slim package, hugged her and stepped back onto the platform.

'Bye, kiddo,' said her father. 'Be good some of the time. Work hard, play hard and show those Dublin jackeens a thing or two.' He put his fist to her chin, then pulled her face down and kissed her on the forehead. The guard came along and closed the door. Anne Marie's parents waved and turned away.

She watched them go. They were holding hands like lovers, fingers interlocked. Her father walked from the hips with his feet turned out and knees bent, as though he had just got off a horse or a ship and still had to find his land-legs. Her mother was obliged to shorten her stride to stay with him. They wore identical jeans: real American working denims that were loose at the bum and tapered to a neat boot-hugging fit at the ankle.

From the back they look like sister and brother, thought Anne Marie. She wished she didn't mind that they hadn't waited to see the train leave.

The platform began to slide past. She caught a last glimpse of her parents as they reached the exit. They had moved closer together and put a hand into each other's back pocket.

Anne Marie returned to her seat clutching the package to her chest. She sat down, then got up again and transferred to the opposite side so that she was facing the direction of travel.

'Dublin, here I come,' she whispered.

Nineteen years old – it was about time she flew the nest. Before she got pushed out? No, that wasn't fair! They just wanted her to be independent, to have a life of her own.

She had a sudden vision of her parents back in the bungalow, pulling off each other's clothes on their way to the bedroom. From now on it wouldn't matter if they didn't make it that far, since she wasn't going to be around to barge in on them. She looked for the bright side and found it.

At least you won't have to cover your ears at night any more, she told herself.

With that ounce of comfort, Anne Marie turned her mind to what lay ahead. Dublin: the Fun Capital of Europe. Boom Town. The Happening Place.

Anne Marie sighed. After New York, where she'd spent part of the summer with her parents, it was hard to imagine Dublin as a city of thrills and excitement. She had only been there twice in her life, the last time when she was twelve and had been taken by her grandmother to do Christmas shopping. Jurys and Grafton Street, that was all she remembered.

Thinking of Christmas reminded her of the package from her mother. Obviously a book. Anne Marie believed she knew which one. She tore off the wrapping paper and held it up, smiling. *Oh, The Places You'll Go!*

Her parents were big fans of Dr Seuss. She opened the title page to see what messages they had inscribed. On one side her mother had taken a quote from the end, *Your mountain is waiting*, and in brackets underneath, she'd written *Up! Up!* – Anne Marie's first words. On the opposite page, her father's inscription was *Walk Tall!* Anne Marie automatically squared her shoulders. Her father had started telling her to be proud of her height even before she had turned sixteen and topped six foot. It was thanks to him that she didn't have a stoop.

God, she was going to miss them!

Blinking a tear from her eye, Anne Marie wished she wasn't such a homebird. With parents like hers, she should have been a fearless adventurer. An Antarctic explorer or something. Yvonne and Seán must have travelled the world several times over by now, but they gave no indication of wanting to stop. As a child, the sign for Anne Marie that summer had arrived was their rucksacks being taken down from the attic. For as long as she could remember, they had used the two-month break from their teaching jobs to travel to wild, unusual places like Borneo and Greenland. Anne Marie would be packed off to stay, along with her cousins, in her grandmother's big house near Limerick. After a few months she would be picked up by a pair of tanned, weather-beaten travellers who slowly meta-morphosed back into her father and mother.

Now she was the one leaving them behind. It felt strange, making Anne Marie wonder if she was ready for this big step towards independence. After finishing her secretarial and computer course, she could have gone on to find a job in Tralee, which was near enough to her hometown of Killorglin to commute every day. But everyone had seemed to expect that she would head for the capital.

'Plenty of opportunities in Dublin, and you'll have the pick of the crop,' her course director had told her after she had come first in the exams.

'You'll be off up to Dublin now. We'll see you at weekends for the first few months, then you'll forget all about us,' her friend Maggie had complained. 'I know the way it goes. The bright lights will dazzle you so we'll seem like real hicks when you do come home. You'll be a city girl in no time!'

Anne Marie was not so sure. Cities didn't appeal to her in general. She thought she would continue to prefer the quiet and beauty of the country to the buzz of the metropolis. But she didn't know. That was the problem: it was new territory she was entering. Fortunately, her cousins, who were all students at Trinity College, would be there for her. They had been in the capital for the past two years and more. Anne Marie was looking forward to living with them. She had always loved the summer holidays in Nano's big house; two whole months spent with Gerald, Darina and Cornelius had more than made up for her parents' prolonged absence.

It was true that she hadn't seen much of her cousins of late, but they couldn't have changed very much since those blissful summers, could they? Gerald had sounded pleased on the phone when she had told him she was coming up to Dublin and needed a place to stay for a few nights. He had insisted that she come and live with them in their flat in Rathmines. Anne Marie had welcomed the offer, but she had no intention of staying with the cousins indefinitely; she had assured him that it would just be until Christmas at the latest. By then, she should have found her feet in the capital and saved enough for a two-month deposit on a flat of her own.

As the train arrived at Limerick Junction, Anne Marie settled down to fantasise yet again about the gorgeous pad she was going to find, dead cheap and really central. Today, it was a garden flat with a bedroom, a living room, a bathroom and a dinky kitchen that looked straight onto a flowerbed.

'There's a little courtyard, then some steps up to the garden,' she imagined herself telling her mother over the phone. 'When I do the washing up, I can smell the roses that are practically climbing in the window!'

By the time the train reached Heuston Station, Anne Marie had moved from the garden flat to a penthouse overlooking the Liffey, and from there to a house in the suburbs that she was sharing with three hunky guys. A medical student, an artist, and a mechanic. She couldn't make up her mind which one she liked best.

The house in Belvedere Square

Anne Marie took a taxi from the station to Rathmines, an area not far from the city centre made lively by a large population of young people in rented accommodation. The cousins lived in a square of tall, elegant Victorian houses set around an enclosed park. *Private, Residents Only* the sign said. Anne Marie hoped that would include her.

She paid and got out of the taxi. The driver made no

move to help her with her luggage. Maybe Dublin was going to be like New York after all, Anne Marie thought wryly as she struggled to lift her suitcase onto the pavement. She carried her two small bags up the steps to the hall door, then went back for the case. She'd reached the top again before it occurred to her that she could have got one of her cousins to help.

But when she looked, she couldn't see a bell with their name on it. Timidly, she pressed the bell in the middle of the door, hoping that it wouldn't bring all the residents to answer it together.

A minute later, she was obliged to press it again. Still nothing. Anne Marie stepped back and looked up at the windows. She thought she saw a curtain twitch on the floor above. It was well after five o'clock; surely someone should be in! She pressed the bell a third time. At length, she heard footsteps in the hall. The door opened and she found herself staring at a woman in a plaid dressing gown with a green face out of which two bulbous eyes regarded her with suspicion. Anne Marie couldn't help thinking that she bore an uncanny resemblance to the Wicked Witch of the West. And not just because of the green mask.

'Excuse me,' she said nervously. 'I'm looking for the Davenports. Two brothers and a sister – they're supposed to be at this address.'

'And who might you be?' The apparition scowled, creating two cracks in the green mask.

'My name is Anne Marie Elliot. I'm their cousin.'

'Are you here on a visit for the weekend?' She peered past Anne Marie. 'That's a very big case you've got with you.'

'No, I'm coming to stay. This is the right address then?' Without wishing to seem rude, Anne Marie was anxious to get past the strange woman who had answered the door but seemed determined to keep her from entering.

'Oh you're at the right house all right. Two boys and a girl, isn't it? They live downstairs in the basement. They have their own door, down the steps and round to the side. But I'll let you in this way, just this once.'

The woman opened the door wider and jerked her head towards the back of the hall. 'Stairs through the door at the end. Mostly it's kept locked. It's not for normal use. Security reasons, don't you know.'

Anne Marie dragged her case into the hall. 'Are you the landlady?' she asked doubtfully.

The woman gave a high shrill laugh. 'Me? The landlady? Saints alive, no! I'm your upstairs neighbour. Vera Meaney's the name. I've been in the house the longest – eight years, believe it or not.' Suddenly, she grew suspicious again. 'You are staying with your cousins the Davenports, aren't you? You haven't made any arrangement with His Nibs upstairs about the rooms here, have you?' She stepped back and spread her arms protectively in front of the first door to the right of the hallway.

'I'm sorry, I don't know what you mean. If you don't mind, I'd just like to go downstairs and let my cousins know that I've arrived now.'

'Of course, of course . . . I'm sorry, I should have realised: he'd never let anybody new have them. They're the best rooms in the house, you know – or they will be as soon as he has them renovated. I'm sure he'll offer them to me first. It's only right after all.'

Anne Marie gestured towards the door at the back of the hall. 'Please, I've had a long day, I'd really like to get settled.'

'Yes, yes, don't mind me! Down you go – would you like me to come with you – to help you with your case?'

'Thank you, but it's all right, I can manage it on my own,' said Anne Marie, who had seen enough of Vera Meaney to be able to tell that she would be glad of any excuse to see her cousins' flat. While Vera held the door open for her, she hoisted her case high enough to prevent it from bumping on the steps down to the basement. 'Well, goodbye now. I'm sure we'll meet again,' she said when she reached the door at the bottom.

'Oh, we will indeed,' said Vera as she, regretfully it seemed to Anne Marie, closed the door at the top of the stairs.

Cousins, Cousine

Suddenly, Anne Marie found herself in darkness. She hoped that her cousins would hear her knocking on the connecting door; she didn't fancy being stuck in limbo between the two floors or having to go back up and call on Vera Meaney for help. In fact, when she tried it, she found that the door in front of her wasn't closed.

She turned into a long passageway. There were three closed doors along one side, but at the end, she could see through to a kitchen. She heard voices and music playing. Leaving her luggage at the bottom of the stairs, Anne Marie went to announce her arrival.

The cousins were all in the kitchen. Gerald was leaning against the sink, smoking and jerking his head in rhythm with the music. Darina was sitting at a table with her back to the door. Cornelius was at the other end of the table, his hands wrapped around a mug of tea. He was the first to spot Anne Marie, just before she said, 'Hello, everyone!' He jumped up, sloshing tea on to his hand.

'Oh, ow! It's yourself, is it? You're here! That's great!' He came over, stuck out his hand for her to shake, but then remembered it was scalded and drew it back again. He stood and grinned at her sheepishly. 'God, but you've got awful big!'

'Shut up, Corny,' said Darina as she twisted around on the chair. 'Nice to see you, coz. We've been expecting you – the kettle's on for a fresh pot. How did you manage to get in without ringing the bell?'

Anne Marie explained about the strange-looking woman who had let her in.

Darina made a face. 'The Meaney one. Well, she was bound to buttonhole you sooner or later. Better to have got it over with.'

'She seemed to be afraid that I was going to move into the rooms on the ground floor.'

'Did you hear that, Ger?' said Darina. 'Vera's angling for the empty flat upstairs.'

'That figures,' said Gerald. He turned to Anne Marie. 'The woman who used to live there left last month. Her name was Helen. She was a French teacher.'

His sister narrowed her eyes and smirked at him, so he continued hurriedly, 'How was your trip, Anne Marie? You're looking well. And your folks – how are they? It must have been sad for them, saying goodbye to their only child.'

'Oh, I don't know,' said Anne Marie. 'It'll probably seem strange having the house to themselves for the first few days, but it's not like I've emigrated. Sure I'll be going home every month or so.' She kept quiet about how she imagined her parents would console each other for her absence in the meantime.

'Tea's made,' said Gerald. 'Con, stop gawping at her and wash a few mugs, would you? And give the table a wipe before Anne Marie sits down. We want her to think this is a classy establishment, don't we?'

'It does seem very nice.' Anne Marie looked around the kitchen, which was far bigger than any that she had imagined for her dream flats. It had fitted pine units on two walls, a huge table in the centre of the room, and a window that gave on to the front garden at eye-level.

'Oh, the kitchen looks right onto a flowerbed!' cried Anne Marie, marvelling that one part of her fantasy had been fulfilled. She surveyed the small paved area, the steps up to the lawn and, in spite of the dearth of roses, she decided that it was a good omen for her life in Dublin.

Over tea, the cousins caught up with each other's lives. It was almost three years since they'd last met, so there was plenty to tell.

As they chatted, Anne Marie examined each of the Davenports in turn. Gerald was twenty-two but she thought he looked much older. His hair was receding and he was thinner than she'd ever seen him. His eyes were veiled and kind of sleepy and he seemed to be permanently smiling to himself at some private joke.

Darina looked . . . *weird* was the word that sprang to mind, but Anne Marie thought it a little harsh. *Distinctive*, she decided. Her cousin had dyed her long, formerly brown hair a strange shade of red. Her ears were pierced in several places and displayed an assortment of silver rings and studs. Anne Marie thought back to their last meeting at their grandmother's house, just after Gerald had finished his Leaving Certificate. Darina had been a plump, sulky teenager with braces on her teeth. She was slim now, but her face was pale and she had an ugly crop of spots on her chin that she kept fingering.

Only Cornelius was as Anne Marie remembered him. Except more so. Dark hair, high colour and a perpetual expression of surprise. Unlike the others, he had put on weight. He gets more like Uncle Dan every time I see him, she thought, picturing her mother's portly elder brother, owner of a shoe factory specialising in sensible footwear.

Having completed her mental inspection of the cousins, Anne Marie couldn't help wondering how she appeared to them.

The look, the face

'You have got even taller than last time we saw you,' said Darina, looking critically at her cousin. 'Huge, in fact. You must be six foot, are you?'

'Six-one-and-a-half last time I checked.'

'You could be a supermodel!' said Cornelius.

'No, she couldn't,' Darina contradicted him.

'Why not?' Her brother sounded wounded.

'She hasn't got the face for it, that's why.'

'Now, now, what are you saying?' Gerald smiled benignly at Anne Marie. 'I think she has a grand face.'

'I didn't say she was ugly, did I?' said Darina hotly.

'She just hasn't got the right bone structure to be a model. Her face is too round; there's no definition to it. Her eyes aren't big enough or blue enough, and her hair's more mousy than blonde.'

'Actually,' said Anne Marie in a small voice, 'I've never even dreamt about being a model. It's not something that would appeal to me at all.' She swallowed and told herself she didn't mind the way they were talking about her. She was a cosseted only child; she needed to develop a thick skin. Staying with the cousins was going to be good preparation for Life.

Gerald stood up. 'Well, enough of that. I'm sure Anne Marie would like to be shown to her room. She'll want to unpack.' He turned to his cousin. 'In honour of your coming, we decided we'd eat out tonight.'

God, he really is emaciated, thought Anne Marie as he stretched his arms over his head and yawned, causing his sweatshirt to ride up and reveal a concave stomach covered in light brown fuzz.

'Darina forgot it was her turn to shop, so we've no food in the house anyway,' said Cornelius, who must have had the hide of a rhinoceros to be able to ignore the look his sister gave him, thought Anne Marie.

'Come on, I'll show you where we are.' Darina got up from the table and led the way down the corridor. 'This is the boys' room,' she said, opening the first door. Anne Marie didn't have time to see anything before it was closed again. 'And that's their bathroom beside it.' She stopped outside the third door. 'Here's my bedroom – ours, I mean. That's your case and stuff there, is it? You might as well bring them in out of the way. Here, pass me one of the bags, I'll give you a hand.' She opened the door and slung the bag inside. Anne Marie winced, and hoped the bottle of Bailey's she had brought as a present for the cousins hadn't come to grief.

'I'll let you have the top bunk,' said Darina. Anne Marie glanced around. The room was quite big; surely there was enough space to have two beds on the floor? Darina was doing her no favours – the ceiling was so low that she doubted if she'd be able to sit up in bed.

'What's in there?' she asked her cousin, pointing to a door at the back of the room.

'Just our own *en suite* bathroom. Bath and shower, what's more. Not bad, eh?'

'It's great!' said Anne Marie after she'd taken a look. 'It's a really nice flat. Everything in it looks brand new; it must have been done up recently. But why are there two bathrooms? And the kitchen – it's very big, isn't it? With the bunk beds and all, it reminds me of a hostel.'

'That's because it was supposed to be one. The landlord was going to turn the whole house into a sort of a New Age backpackers' place, but he didn't get the planning permission. He'd already done the work down here, though.' She paused, then added carefully: 'Which is why it's a bit more expensive than other basement flats in the area.'

'Yes, you'll have to tell me how much the rent is, and what you do about electricity and food and all that. I suppose there's a kitty, is there? I can give you some money tonight, in advance, like.'

'That would be good,' said Darina quickly. 'The rent works out at a hundred a month. Electricity, heating and all the rest is usually another fifteen on top of that. We have a kitty for food, we put in about twenty-five quid a week each. I think it's kind of low just now, so if you could put your contribution in today, we'd be able to go shopping tomorrow.'

'I can give it to you here and now,' said Anne Marie, and she took out her purse.

At the Café Firenze

'Where are we going to eat?' Cornelius looked from Darina to Gerald.

'I don't know. What do you fancy, Anne Marie?'

'She doesn't know what restaurants there are in the area,' said Darina. 'So there's no point in asking her.'

'I'm easy anyway,' said Anne Marie.

'I'll remember that!' Gerald grinned wolfishly at her.

Anne Marie smiled uncertainly back.

'How about a Domino's pizza?' suggested Cornelius.

Ignoring him, Darina turned to Gerald. 'There's that new place, the Café Firenze. You know the one? It's near the canal. I was there once for breakfast – they do great cappuccinos. We could try it for dinner. It got a good write-up in the *Irish Times*.'

'Sure, whatever.'

'If Anne Marie is agreeable, it's fine by me.' Cornelius took his jacket off the back of the chair and went to stand beside his cousin.

Darina made a face. 'Pass the sick bag,' she muttered to Gerald on her way out of the kitchen.

It was a fine autumn evening. Anne Marie was glad to be out walking, even if it was only to reach the restaurant. It was nice that the canal was nearby; she would be able to go out every evening for a stroll. That way, she might not miss the wide-open spaces of home quite so much.

Darina and Gerald had linked arms and gone on ahead. Anne Marie was walking with her youngest cousin. She knew that he was happy to see her, but he seemed unusually shy in her presence. 'How are the studies going, Cornelius?' she asked, trying to put him at his ease.

'Not so bad, thank you, Anne Marie,' replied Cornelius formally. 'I'm going into second year now. I don't mind telling you that I found it hard to adjust to living away from home. Dublin can be very unsettling at first. There are a lot of temptations that you don't get in Limerick and I'm afraid I allowed myself to be distracted when I arrived. But I took myself in hand and knuckled down to the books in the last term and I'm glad to say that I got very good results in my exams.'

'Congratulations!' said Anne Marie.

'Thank you.' Cornelius gave a little bow. 'Those two now,' he continued, jerking his chin at Gerald and Darina, 'they seem to think life's one long party. They've both changed courses at least once and they still don't know what they want to do. The repeats were a fortnight ago and it wouldn't surprise me if they failed again. It's not lack of ability, you know. They could do just as well as me if they put their minds to it. But no, it's the pub tonight, a club tomorrow, the pictures the next day and never a thought for the money that our parents are spending on their education.'

'I thought there were no fees for undergraduates any more.'

'Only as long as you pass your exams. Gerry's after repeating a year, so his fees have to be paid. That's nearly two thousand pounds! Darina's on her last chance. If she doesn't pass all her exams from now on, hers will have to be paid too. Then there's maintenance money for rent and food. Dad and Mam don't want us getting jobs during termtime because it would be detrimental to our studies. So you see, it all mounts up. I believe that we owe it to our parents to study hard so as we can get good jobs at the end of it all.'

Anne Marie quickened her step. Darina and Gerald were almost out of sight. She was fond of her youngest cousin, but he could be hard going at times. She turned to him as he trotted beside her.

'What are you planning on doing when you graduate, Cornelius?'

'I'm going back to Limerick to work with Dad in the shoe factory. I'll be like an apprentice at first, even though I'll have my Business Studies degree. If you want to succeed, I believe you have to know every stage of the process, from the factory floor to the marketing and distribution of your product. I intend to spend time in each one, not as the boss's son, but learning my way just like any other worker. Of course, I wouldn't spend more than six months in any one section, that would be counterproductive—'

'Hey! Down here, you two!' Anne Marie stopped and looked down the narrow laneway they'd just crossed. To her relief, Gerald and Darina were standing in front of a tiny, bistro-style restaurant.

'This is it,' called Darina. There were four or five stainless steel tables and chairs outside the restaurant, but as far as Anne Marie was concerned, the evening was nowhere near warm enough for pretending they were in Florence.

Gerald was looking at the prices on the menu fixed to the door. 'Hmm, it's a bit more than our usual

Friday night takeaway, but I suppose as we're celebrating the arrival of our dear cousin,' he winked at Anne Marie, 'we can rise to a tenner a head, can't we?'

It was early enough that despite the fact that they hadn't made a reservation, they had no trouble getting a table for four.

'I'm glad it's not busy,' said Anne Marie. She was trying unsuccessfully to fit into her seat by the wall. 'There are a lot of tables for such a small place, aren't there?' She stood up again. 'I'm afraid I can't get my legs under. Do you think I could I sit on the outside, please?'

Reluctantly, Darina swapped with her.

'What are we going to drink?' Gerald held up the wine list brought by the waiter.

'I don't think we can afford wine,' said Cornelius, who didn't drink.

Darina looked at the menu. 'Depends on what we're going to eat. We won't bother with starters, I presume. The main courses are all between six and twelve quid, dessert's another three. We could go for a carafe of the house red. How much would that be, Gerry?'

'Eight quid. What do you think, Anne Marie?'

'Well, as it's my first night in Dublin, I'll get it. To say thanks for having me.'

'Oh, well!' Darina looked up. 'That's very nice of you, coz.' She opened the menu again. 'In that case, I think I will have a starter. The mussels are supposed to be very good.'

Sex drive in the older generation

The bill came to sixty-seven pounds fifty-six. Handing over her credit card, Anne Marie decided she needed a course in assertiveness. It was her own fault: she should have said she meant just the wine.

They went into The Station on the way home. Gerald bought the first round. 'Bacardi and Coke for Darina, and two glasses of sparkling water for Con and Anne Marie.' He set the glasses down. 'Do you not drink, Anne Marie? You hardly touched the wine back in the restaurant.'

'I do, now and again. Mainly weekends, I suppose. If we're at home on a Saturday, Seán always opens a bottle of wine at dinner.'

Cornelius sat up. 'Who's Seán?'

Darina cast her eyes upwards. 'Uncle Seán, of course. Did you not know that Anne Marie calls her parents by their first names?'

'Oh, right. I'd forgotten.' He relaxed again.

'They asked me to,' Anne Marie said apologetically. 'When I was twelve.'

'Speaking of names, tell me again why you all have different surnames,' Darina said. 'Seán Hughes, Yvonne Davenport and Anne Marie Elliot. Kind of weird, isn't it? I mean, nobody would ever know you were related if they saw your names written down. Is yours different from theirs because your old dear was a feminist and didn't want you to have your father's name?'

Anne Marie took a sip from her drink. She was unduly sensitive about this subject but she didn't want to show it. Her parents had explained to her many times that she had been given the surname Elliot because she was born soon after the death of a cherished American friend. Privately, she often wished that they could have found some other way of commemorating a man whom she, obviously, could never know. She might have minded less had there been other offspring called Elliot, but as an only child, Anne Marie regretted the fact that in her small family, there was no common last name.

She told her cousin about the dead friend and, in answer to Darina's blunt enquiry as to whether she minded having a different name to both of her parents, she merely shrugged and said that she had got used to it.

'Got used to what?' Gerald had gone back to the bar for his pint. He pulled out a stool and placed it near enough to Anne Marie for their knees to touch while Darina explained what he'd missed.

'Oh, right. Your folks always do things differently, don't they? How are the lovebirds, anyway?' He nudged his sister. 'Do you remember that time, Dar, when we caught them snogging behind the rosebushes down at Nano's?'

'Don't be embarrassing Anne Marie like that!' Cornelius said severely.

'She's not embarrassed. Sure you're not,' Darina said without looking at her cousin. 'Anyway, she must be used to seeing them at it. They're a touchy-feely couple, always have been. Isn't that right?'

'Yes . . . I suppose,' said Anne Marie, who found she would rather not hear her parents discussed like this.

'Better that than the way ours are.' Gerald drank from his pint and set it down. 'They don't even sleep in the same room any more.'

Cornelius paled. 'What do you mean, they don't

sleep in the same room? How do you know that?'

Darina sighed exaggeratedly. 'God, Cornelius, you really are the limit. How could you not have noticed? What do you think the junk room was cleared out for? You were there in the summer when the bed came and all.'

'But . . . I thought that was for guests.'

'Guests! Who ever visits them? Only us or Gran, and she always has the box room. Come on, Corny, you can't be that thick! Even you must realise that they haven't done it for years – probably not since you were born. She finally kicked him out of their bedroom around Easter, and he slept in the study until the other place was decorated.'

Hunched over his mineral water, Cornelius said nothing. He looked so shocked and pained that Anne Marie felt sorry for him. She cast about for a new topic of conversation.

'Tell me, Gerald, what's the landlord like? Is he nice?'

'Brandon? Yeah, he's OK. He's Irish-American, but to look at him you'd think he was Indian. Indian as in Cherokee. He lives upstairs on the top floor. We'll have to bring you up to meet him – he likes to get to know all his tenants.'

'What do you think of him, Darina?' Anne Marie asked after another worried glance at Cornelius, who seemed to be on the verge of tears.

'Mmm, he's quite striking, I suppose. Very blue eyes, which is strange for someone who claims to be part Indian. He looks at you meaningfully and asks if you're happy with your life. He's into Buddhism and the Eanneagram, and all sorts of New Age stuff. And Gerry's right, he likes to know what's going on in the house. We really ought to have brought you to meet him as soon as you arrived. He'll be down now first thing in the morning to check you out. With a face on him like we've just murdered his mammy, but he's prepared to forgive us.'

'We'd better give him the rent when he comes down, Dar,' said Gerald. 'We were a bit late with it last month, remember?'

'Do I what?' She turned to Anne Marie. 'We got lectured for half an hour on how money isn't important, but trust is. He didn't care about the money at all, he said, but it hurt him to think that we could break our agreement just like that.'

'Speaking of money,' said Anne Marie, 'I've given you the twenty-five for the kitty, but you'll be wanting the rent as well if he's coming down in the morning. I haven't got a hundred pounds on me now, but—'

Cornelius's head shot up. 'A hundred pounds?'

Gerald leaned back to blow smoke away from the table. Looking at his sister from half-closed eyes, he smiled his private smile. Darina hung her head, her expression hidden by her hair.

Cornelius glared at her. 'How come Anne Marie has to pay more than us? That's not right.'

'Well, it's . . . em . . . You see . . .' Darina glanced up at her cousin. 'We – or I, thought you might like a room of your own, and we were going to give you the double room, but then we – I mean I – decided it was better to keep the double room for, you know, guests, so he's right, I forgot. You'll only be paying eighty pounds, the same as the rest of us.'

Cornelius snorted.

Anne Marie looked confused. 'What double room?'

'Oh, didn't you see it? At the bottom of the stairs

you came down, just in front of you. It was supposed to be a common room in the hostel Brandon didn't get permission for. We use it as a sitting room and for, em . . . overnight guests. It's kind of like a conservatory at the back so it's a bit cold in winter, but it's lovely when the weather's warm. I'll show it to you tomorrow.'

Anne Marie had the feeling that she was missing something, but she let it go. It was her first evening, after all, and she couldn't expect to fit in at once. She remembered that the summer holidays had always started out the same way: the three cousins seemed to have a secret code that made it hard to work out what was going on between them. It would take the best part of a week before she would feel that she had mastered it. That was one of the problems with being an only child: she had no experience to help her deal with complicated family dynamics.

As soon as she had finished her drink, Anne Marie said she was tired and wanted to go back to the flat. Cornelius jumped up to accompany her and, after a moment's hesitation, the other two joined them.

It was obvious to Anne Marie that Cornelius was still upset by what had been said about his parents. Walking back along the Rathmines Road in the same formation as before, she did her best to cheer him up. 'Look, don't mind what Gerald said back there,' she said, taking his arm the way Darina had done with Gerald. 'Lots of couples sleep apart and it doesn't mean they don't love each other any more. I think it's just to do with getting older. Seán and Yvonne are still only in their early forties, remember, so it's different for them. Uncle Dan is . . .' She stopped. He was only five years older than her mother, which made him forty-six. Her aunt was a bit older than her husband;

late-forties maybe. But as long as Anne Marie could remember, they'd been a middle-aged couple, whereas it seemed that as she got older, her own parents got younger.

'It's all her fault!' Cornelius suddenly burst out, startling her.

'Sorry – whose?'

'Ever since she set up her own business, she's been different. She dresses like a young one and she's had her hair dyed blonde. She's even gone back to using her maiden name! And she's after buying her own car and she goes all over the country for days at a time. Dad comes home in the evening to an empty house; no fire lit, no meal cooked. No one to look after him. It's a disgrace, that's what it is!'

Anne Marie didn't know what to say. Poor Cornelius was incapable of making a joke, so she had to assume he meant it. But how could he? It was the start of the third millennium; the battles had all been won long ago, hadn't they? Way back in the 1970s, people like Yvonne had fought for and achieved equal status for women. The few who still called themselves feminists were regarded by Anne Marie's generation as dinosaurs. That made her cousin positively primeval!

'Cornelius,' she ventured, 'I don't think Auntie Barbara's setting up in business is the problem. She's obviously got a great flair for it, and it's nice that she was able to make a new life for herself when all of you were gone, so—'

'And where does that leave Dad? How do you think *he* feels? The factory isn't doing as well as it was ten years ago. That's why I'm in a hurry to get my degree – I'll apply my knowledge to turning it around again. But to make matters worse, there she is, flaunting her success in front of him! It's very demeaning for a man, you know, that sort of thing.'

'Oh,' said Anne Marie weakly. The problem with post-feminism was that you didn't have the arguments at your fingertips. She knew them, naturally, but they were buried deep in her subconscious along with stories about Princess Smartypants and old pirate women. This was pathetic! Yvonne, she knew, would have torn strips off her nephew by now.

'Well, I'm sorry if Uncle Dan is unhappy,' she said placatingly, 'but I'm sure he'll come to terms with the change of lifestyle in time. It might even be good for him in the long run. You'd never know what hidden talents and ambitions he might discover!'

Mentally, she apologised to her mother. I'll read *The Second Sex* again, promise. And this time I'll finish it.

Bedtime thoughts

By midnight, the four-storey house on Belvedere Square was quiet. Down in the basement, the cousins had said good night. Gerald was lying on the couch in the sitting room. The television was on, but he wasn't watching it. With his hands clasped behind his head, he was staring at the darkened ceiling, where the flickering images made pale patterns that didn't impinge on his thoughts.

It was late July. The cousins were down on their grandmother's estate. He'd wandered off by himself, crossing into a field that was leased to a neighbouring farmer and was therefore technically out of bounds to the children. There was something sensual about the heavy heat that made him throw himself on to the grass with his arms outspread, ready to embrace the earth and drink in the scent of summer.

After a while he turned onto his back to stare up at the dizzy blue sky. Every sensation seemed to be heightened; the burbling of the stream, the taste of the blade of grass he'd been chewing, the smell of the hay, the beetle he'd felt crawl across his stomach. Its little legs tickled exquisitely as it climbed up and down the hair that had begun to grow around his navel.

That was probably what had made him undo his belt and lower his jeans around his hips. He'd been stroking himself lazily for some time – there was no urgency to his pleasure – when he first became aware of her presence. He couldn't see her, but he knew she was there. The thrill was so powerful that a replay of the experience had for many years been Gerald's most effective erotic fantasy.

But now it was over. As soon as Anne Marie had walked into the kitchen, Gerald had known that she would never again appear in his dreams. How could he lust after someone who stood six-foot-three in her shoes and could probably knock him flat with one hand?

In the girls' room, Darina was doing mental arithmetic in bed. Eighty quid for rent, twenty-five for the kitty, thirty-five for the second-hand books she was buying from that student who always got Firsts – that left how much? Eighty-five? OK. She'd spent sixty on – what? Booze, fags, what else? A couple of magazines, junk food, a card for her mobile and some photocopying. Was that all? Oh, and that leather jacket in the charity shop. Bugger! The dry-cleaners – it was still there, which meant another fifteen before she was clear. Damn it, she wasn't going to be able to get those funky boots in Zerep this week either.

Darina sighed. I wish I could save, she thought, or that there was someone I could borrow from. Anne Marie? No, not after this evening. That little shit Cornelius: if it wasn't for him, she'd have had an extra twenty.

Darina stared at the bottom of the bunk in which her cousin was presumably sleeping. It was good to have another person to share costs, but she wasn't sure yet how she felt about Anne Marie living with them. It was different now they weren't kids any more. She remembered the summers they'd spent together, the way they used to walk with their arms wrapped around each other. Like bleedin' Siamese twins. Well, those days were dead and gone. She'd better be nice to her cousin for a day or two though, to make up for the business with the rent. Anne Marie was obviously loaded – credit card and all, so it would be as well to keep in with her.

Turning on to her side, Darina closed her eyes and began to dream herself a lover.

In the bunk above, Anne Marie's last sleepy thoughts were how different things were in real life to what you imagined. She'd been right about the kitchen looking onto the garden, of course, but she couldn't have predicted how different her cousins were going to be. Different from what? From what she remembered, she supposed. Or from what she'd been expecting? What had she been expecting? She couldn't remember. Oh, this was getting too confused.

I know I'm glad to be here anyway, she concluded,

as lines from the Dr Seuss book passed through her mind. *Congratulations! Today is your day. You're off to great places! You're off and away!* Her new life was just beginning. It was exciting, really. Anything could happen. *And when things start to happen, don't worry. Don't stew. Just go right along. You'll start happening too.* What a nice thought! Just before sleep overtook her, Anne Marie wished very hard that things might start happening soon.

Down the hall, Cornelius lay on his stomach with his head buried under the pillow. He was dreaming of the dispensation from the Pope that would allow him to marry his first cousin.

Two floors up, Vera Meaney from Borris-in-Ossory lay in her virginal double bed and beseeched God not to leave her on the shelf. She would be thirty-one next month, she reminded Him, and time was running out. She didn't threaten to lapse, or even to miss Mass on the odd Sunday if He continued to ignore her, but He must be made to realise that her patience, unlike His, was not eternal.

Across the landing from Vera, a man called Sylvester Reed thought about the young woman at the door. He'd been standing well back from the curtain when she looked up so he was fairly certain that she hadn't seen him. The face had been a shock: so round, trusting and familiar. The face of innocence. If only he'd seen her when she'd arrived, he'd have had a couple of minutes to get over his emotion, to compose himself. Perhaps he might have answered the door.

Was there still time? Maybe her coming was a sign. He'd wait a day or two and see.

In the illegal attic conversion above his second-floor apartment, Brandon O'Kane was sitting in the lotus position on a silk prayer mat from Indonesia. He was naked. On either side of him, scented candles floated in burners filled with coloured water. He was meditating on the message in the medicine cards, which lay spread on the floor in front of him. But the arrival of a new person in the house had changed its energy balance and he couldn't concentrate. He wouldn't be able to relax until he had found out what she was like.

A few hundred miles away in Killorglin, Seán Hughes switched off the bedside lamp and reached for his wife's hand. 'So, how do you feel?' he enquired.

'Don't know yet,' Anne Marie's mother replied. 'It doesn't seem real. I mean, I can hardly believe it's twenty years since . . . you know. Where did the time go? I feel exactly the same—'

'You look exactly the same, too.'

'Oh sure! So do you, then.'

'Flatterer! But it is true in a way: we haven't changed that much, whereas Anne Marie has gone from being a twinkle in . . . in—'

'*Our* eyes.'

'Yeah. Thanks. From a twinkle in our eyes to an independent young woman starting a new life on her own.'

'Amazing, isn't it? She's practically the same age we were when we met. You know, now that she's gone, I can't help feeling guilty that I wasn't a better mother.

I wish I could have been a bit more maternal or something.'

'Don't be silly, look how she turned out. Isn't she a credit to us?'

'Yes, yes, of course she is. That's mostly thanks to you, though. You're the most wonderful father she could have had – kind, loving, infinitely patient and great fun as well. You know, I never thought I'd hear myself say this, but . . . in a way I'm very glad that things turned out the way they did.'

Seán was silent for a moment. Then he turned and buried his face in Yvonne's hair. When he spoke, his voice was choked. 'Thank you, love. Thank you.'

Yvonne lifted his head and kissed him gently. 'I'm sorry it's taken me so long. It's not something that came to me in a flash; it's slowly been growing over the years. Anne Marie leaving today just made me see the big picture more clearly.'

'Are you sure we shouldn't have told her before she left? We did say when she was eighteen, remember.'

'I know, but . . . no. You'll have to trust me on this one, Seánín. She's not ready to hear it yet. Let her find her feet in Dublin first. Once she's got a life that's totally separate from us, then we'll tell her. For now, she needs us to be the same as we've always been.'

Seán grinned. 'What, you mean totally out of control like this?' He growled and raised himself above her. 'Urrgh! Wild beasts with disgusting and unnatural urges – sex-mad deviants that just can't get enough of it! Is that what you mean?'

'Exactly!'

Yvonne scissored her husband's legs to make him fall back on the bed and then twisted herself round so that she was on top. 'How did you guess?'

Cappuccino and confidences

It was Saturday morning, the day after Anne Marie's arrival in Dublin.

Uncharacteristically, Darina was up first.

'How about I treat the two of us to breakfast at the Café Firenze, then we go shopping together? I could show you around town if you like,' she said to her cousin as soon as Anne Marie came out of the shower.

'That'd be very nice, thanks. I need a few things all right. I'll have to photocopy my CV at some stage, so if you know of—'

'Read's of Nassau Street. It's the cheapest place in town.'

'Great! You're all ready, I see. I'll get dressed, so . . . I won't be a minute.'

Anne Marie clasped her bathtowel around her and waited for her cousin to leave the room. How else could she get dressed? Was it going to be like at the seaside when she was a kid, holding her towel between her teeth while she pulled on her knickers? Maybe Darina was like Yvonne and Seán, who used to wander about the house in the nude when she was small, before the extension was built. Then they'd got a new bedroom with bathroom *en suite*. Lying in bed, Anne Marie would hear their giggles and the slap of a hand on wet flesh.

'I'll just check I've got my bus pass and things and meet you in the kitchen,' Darina said at last.

Anne Marie sighed with relief and closed the door.

Darina dragged a chair out from the kitchen table and sat down. Gloomily, she lit a cigarette. She hadn't realised her cousin was such a prude. If Anne Marie was that uptight about nakedness, what would happen when Darina brought someone home – would Anne Marie go all holy on her? Darina decided she'd better sound her out over breakfast.

'Cappuccino?' The waiter held out the fat cup with its frothy head of milk.

'There,' said Darina, pointing to her cousin. 'The espresso's for me. So,' she began after the waiter had gone, 'did you leave anyone behind in Killorglin?'

'Leave anyone behind?' Anne Marie looked blank.

Good Christ, I don't believe this! Darina made herself smile conspiratorially as she leant across the table. 'Like a boyfriend?' she whispered.

'Oh, a boyfriend. God, no!' Anne Marie realised that her cousin was trying hard to be friendly. She wished she had some confidences to offer as a reward. But she hadn't, so she smiled ruefully instead. 'I'm afraid there's nobody pining for me back in Kerry. Or anywhere else, for that matter. What about yourself? Have you met anyone up here?'

Darina shrugged. 'Not really. A few one-night stands and a fling with a married man. That didn't last long – all he wanted to do was talk about his wife and what a bitch she was.'

'Oh,' said Anne Marie.

She looked more uncomfortable than outraged, noted Darina, who had made up the bit about the married man. That was a relief. It wouldn't do to have Anne Marie running home to Kerry with tales of debauchery. She smiled, prepared to be nice. 'So coz,' she began, 'tell us – what's your type?'

'My type?' Anne Marie looked around the restaurant as though expecting to find the answer on the walls. 'I

31

don't know, really.' Her eyes came to rest on the waiter. He was leaning on a chair, staring out the window at nothing. Anne Marie examined him as a male specimen rather than as a bearer of food and drink. He wasn't bad. In fact, he was rather good-looking. Black hair, dark skin, brown eyes. She remembered he'd spoken with a pleasant English accent when taking their order last night. He was tall too, she noticed. Yes, she liked the look of him.

'Well? You must have a type. Come on, tell me!'

But Anne Marie didn't. The Café Firenze was too close to home. She'd be teased every time they came in for coffee. Anyway, she wasn't so sure she liked him after all. Something was missing. She glanced over once more. He looked so . . . what? Preoccupied? No, it was more than that. Sad. She realised that in the four hours she must have spent here between last night and this morning, she hadn't seen him smile once.

No, he was definitely not her type.

'I'm not fussy about a fella's looks, so long as he's got other qualities,' she said finally. 'A sense of humour, for instance. Good manners. And I like someone who can talk, who's kind of witty, you know? He'd have to be generous too; I can't stand meanness. A sense of responsibility is important to me as well.' She smiled at her cousin and spread her hands deprecatingly.

Neither she nor Darina realised that Anne Marie's description was one that matched her father in every respect.

The waiter idly watched Darina and Anne Marie as they stood putting on their jackets outside the café. He wondered why some women seemed to go out of their way to make themselves unattractive. The one with the brassy red hair, for instance – did she imagine she looked good? It wasn't just the hair, which was bad enough, but the clothes she had on too. A purple cotton skirt with fringes.. Doc Marten boots with yellow and black laces. A sloppy jumper and a black leather jacket. Nothing looked good in its own right and the combination was downright ugly. As Darina cupped her hands to light a cigarette, he turned away in disgust.

The other one was far nicer. She had a pretty face that reminded him of a famous Madonna – he wished he could remember which one – and she was neatly dressed in a tan jacket and beige trousers. Her ankle boots were polished and her hair was tied back with a chiffon scarf. You could tell she cared about her appearance. Which made it even more of a shame about her height.

Anne Marie gets tough

After pointing out the Jewish bakery and the charity shops on Camden Street, Darina figured she'd done her bit as far as showing her cousin around was concerned. She wished now that she hadn't committed herself for the morning. Especially as it transpired that Anne Marie wasn't as loaded as she'd seemed. She had less than four hundred pounds in her bank account, and that had to cover rent and other outgoings until she got a job. So lunch of a pint and a salmon sandwich in Neary's was not on. Too bad, thought Darina as they passed the Royal College of Surgeons on their way to Grafton Street. Then something occurred to her.

'Oh shit!'

'What?'

'Brandon – we left without talking to him.'

'Brandon? Oh yes, the landlord. What's the problem?'

'He'll be looking for you. Maybe we should go back.'

'Darina, I only arrived yesterday evening. Why all the fuss? It can't matter if I don't see him this morning. I'll be there later on.'

'It matters.'

'Why? Is he some kind of bear that you're all so scared of him?'

'Of course we're not scared! You just don't see what's at stake here. D'you think flats like ours are easy to come by? And at the rent we're paying? Well, for your information, they're not! You should have seen the place in Ringsend where we lived before. The walls oozed damp, the carpets stank and the kitchen was a tiny alcove with nothing in it. When we saw the new place, we couldn't believe how nice it was. We'd have jumped through hoops to get it. Brandon's got his own ideas about what sort of tenants he wants. I don't even know what criteria he uses – all I know is, he had turned down about ten people before he met Gerry in a bookshop and decided he'd give us a try. We were bloody lucky that he took a fancy to us. If he decides he doesn't like the look of you, that's it. He couldn't evict us, but he sure as hell could make life unpleasant. So we'd appreciate it if you would just go along with this.'

The cousins faced each other at the corner of St

Stephen's Green. A man coming out of the shopping centre knocked into Darina. She glared at him when he said he was sorry.

Be assertive, thought Anne Marie. If she gave in now, she'd be setting a dangerous precedent. She steeled herself. 'Look, Darina, I'm sorry. I really have got a lot of things to do in town today. But I promise that as soon as I get back to the flat, I'll go up with you to meet the landlord. If he doesn't like me, I'll leave. All right?'

Darina reluctantly agreed. She said she was going back to the Swan Centre in Rathmines to do the shopping. On her own she wouldn't be able to carry much so Anne Marie would have to make another trip mid-week. By herself.

Anne Marie said that was fine by her. Flushed with victory, she crossed South King Street and joined the crowds on Grafton Street. She knew her cousin well enough to realise that Darina would walk all over anyone who let her. But it takes two to tango, Anne Marie reminded herself. And she was pretty sure that her cousin would respect her all the more for not lying down like a doormat.

Bewley's was packed, so she continued walking towards the Liffey, which she knew divided the city into Southside and mysterious Northside. Standing on O'Connell Bridge, she looked west towards the Phoenix Park and the chimneys of the Guinness brewery. That way lay Heuston station and the Naas dual carriageway – the road home. Directly in front of her was the Ha'penny Bridge; she had a vague memory of crossing it or a similar footbridge when she was very small, her hand held in a reassuring adult grip as she gazed down into the brown water that flowed beneath her feet. She headed that way now, drawn first by the memory and then by a sign advertising a bookshop-café on the north bank.

The Winding Stair was aptly named, she discovered as she followed the stairs through the shop and up to the café on the first floor. It was a cheerful place, with big windows overlooking the Liffey and a mural depicting famous Irish writers painted on the back wall. She treated herself to a slice of carrot cake and sat by the window with her latte, wondering as she looked down on the passers-by how long it would take her to come to regard Dublin as home.

In order to belong, she needed to establish her own pathways through the city; routes that would become so familiar that she wouldn't have to refer to landmarks as she came and went. At the moment she was a tourist, squinting at street names and unsure where to turn next. She needed destinations; places to go to that would be uniquely hers. Her office, her doctor's, her sports club. Her boyfriend's? Yes, that too, in a little while. It would be nice to meet someone, but for now, Anne Marie had more pressing needs.

Taking out her copy of Friday's *Irish Times*, she unfolded it at the *Appointments* section. She pushed her plate to one side, clicked on her ballpoint pen and began to peruse the advertisements for the job that was going to launch her into adult life.

The cousins had been surprised by her decision not to go on immediately to third-level education. Cornelius had asked her outright if she'd got enough points in the Leaving Cert. She'd told them she had got five hundred and fifty. 'But that's more than any of us!' he'd exclaimed.

Anne Marie herself sometimes wondered why she

felt so strongly that university was not for her. Not now, at any rate. She didn't rule out doing a degree later on, she'd told them; as a mature student, or by night. 'But if you went as a mature student, you'd be ancient when you graduated!' Darina said. 'Twenty-five or twenty-six at least!'

Twenty-five: a quarter of a century. Anne Marie hoped that by then she would feel grown-up. Eighteen had been a big disappointment. She'd got her full driver's licence and the vote all right, but her birthday hadn't made her feel any more adult than when she was seventeen. Maybe twenty-one was the significant age. People still had big parties for their twenty-firsts, so it must be a rite of passage to something. She hoped that having a job would help. Girls in offices always seemed older and more wordly-wise than students of the same age.

She looked down at the pages of ads for sales executives with their offers of high salaries and fringe benefits. Do you have what it takes? they demanded. Anne Marie didn't. She wasn't aggressive enough. Because she was tall, people assumed she was bursting with self-confidence. Whereas I'm actually quite meek and easily browbeaten, she thought. She smiled as she thought of the scene with Darina. Most of the time!

The bear in his lair

It was late afternoon when Anne Marie got back. She'd bought something small for the flat, just something she'd spotted while browsing in Habitat, she would say to Darina, that she thought they could do with in the hall.

It was a doormat, made of coconut fibres. She kept a straight face as she explained to Darina that it wasn't too thick, but would be better for wiping feet on than the piece of carpet tile they were using at the moment.

Darina said that Brandon had dropped in a note. He wanted to see her. She should go up on her own. At once.

Anne Marie went out the basement door and round to the front. It seemed silly to her that they each had a key to the hall door, but not to the connecting door inside. It was all right when the weather was fine, but what about in winter? Would they have to kit out in rain gear or overcoats just to go up and get their post? Bicycles would be kept in the main hall, too; the basement corridor was far too narrow to house them. None of the cousins had one, but Anne Marie thought she might buy one for getting around the city. She decided that she would ask the landlord for a key to the inside doors.

Sylvester Reed saw her come up the front steps. Was it possible she had felt the connection between them? Could she be coming to him of her own accord? So soon? He went to his door and opened it a crack. A few seconds later, Anne Marie appeared.

He hadn't realised how tall she was. Strong too, no doubt. That might be a problem. He watched her sprint past his landing and on up the next flight of stairs. Too bad. He closed the door again and went to sit on his bed.

Everything was ready. He could do it on his own as originally planned, but her arrival had to have a meaning. He could listen out for her on her way down, talk to her. Invite her in, maybe? No! Not this time. He just had to find out her name. That was all he needed.

The door to the landlord's apartment was wide open. Sitar music was playing somewhere in the background. Anne Marie wondered if this was a test. If she walked straight in, she passed. But that wasn't in her nature. Without crossing the threshold, she knocked softly on the door.

He appeared almost immediately. He must have been waiting just the other side, thought Anne Marie in alarm.

'Come in,' he said, spreading his hands in a gesture of welcome. He was dressed in a long Eastern shirt and loose pants; the kind of thing Imran Khan wore. His hair was tied in a ponytail, and yes, he did have the strangest eyes. He was smiling, but there was something odd about the way he looked at her feet rather than her face.

She glanced anxiously down at her shoes. 'Em, should I take them off?'

'Oh no, that won't be necessary. Not down here.'

Down here? They were on the top floor! She stepped over the threshold and followed him inside. It was a big room – must be two or three knocked into one, she thought. The floor was made of smooth, polished wood. There was very little furniture; only a low table and a few floor lamps of different heights. There were several pieces of sculpture, however, and some woodcarvings. Over the mantelpiece hung a couple of scimitars, their crossed blades disturbingly untarnished. There were a lot of fearsome masks on either side of them.

'Please, take a cushion and make yourself comfortable. I'll put on the kettle for tea. Which would you prefer – jasmine, Chinese green, or rosehip?'

Anne Marie opted for Chinese green only because it sounded more like proper tea than the flowery ones. She took a brightly-patterned flat, square cushion from a pile that Brandon had pointed out to her and went to sit near the table. It was only then she saw what he'd meant by 'down here'. Almost half the ceiling had been cut away. A spiral staircase behind the door led up to the attic. She could see a sloping roof and a large Velux window. So that's his lair, she thought.

Penis gourd

Brandon came out of the kitchen carrying a tray. He set it down in front of Anne Marie and went to fetch a cushion for himself. He sat opposite her, crossing his legs and pulling each foot until it rested sole uppermost on the other thigh.

Ouch, thought Anne Marie.

'Your name is Anne Marie Elliot. You are nineteen. This much I know,' said Brandon. 'Now tell me the rest.'

Anne Marie gulped. Why hadn't Darina warned her about this? What was she supposed to say?

'I'm . . . their cousin. The Davenports', I mean,' she told him. 'Their father is my mother's brother. I'm from Killorglin. That's in Kerry. Maybe you know it? I came to Dublin to get a job. And, well . . . that's about it, really.'

Brandon smiled with closed lips. Anne Marie

thought he looked like a cat. He had high cheekbones and a long, sallow face. His nose was long and narrow, his lips thin. It was the expression that was most feline, though; he reminded her of Scar in *The Lion King*, playing with the mouse he was about to eat.

'Let us take tea. Later, I will ask you some questions.' He lifted the pot and began to pour from a height into two tiny, handleless china cups. To Anne Marie's dismay, the tea really was green. Large leaves floated on its surface.

'So good for the digestive system, this Yunnan ming cha, don't you find? Of course, for optimal effect it's best drunk earlier in the day.'

He was gently chiding her for having made the wrong choice, she realised. The tea was bitter and slightly smoky. Anne Marie was glad the cups were so small.

'You have a lot of interesting . . . artefacts,' she said, hoping that was the right word.

Brandon turned and allowed his gaze to travel around the room as though he were seeing the objects in it through Anne Marie's eyes. He smiled his cat-smile.

'Everything in this room has a particular significance for me. Each object belongs to, or reminds me of, my past lives.'

'Yes, I can see you've travelled a lot.'

Brandon looked pityingly at her. 'I was speaking of my past lives. Before I was reincarnated in this one.'

'Oh.' Anne Marie thought hard. 'So all the stuff in this room comes from your previous incarnations? Is that it?'

Brandon bowed his head as though she had paid him a compliment.

She looked around once more with interest. 'What, you mean even the lamps?'

'No, of course not the lamps!' he snapped back.

Anne Marie, who hadn't meant to be facetious, looked at him in surprise. But Brandon O'Kane was not about to let a negative emotion get the better of him. He pulled himself straight, closed his eyes, and with one finger on the side of his right nostril, inhaled deeply. He held his breath for about ten seconds, exhaled, then did the same with the other side. When he opened his eyes again, he was smiling.

'Would you like me to tell you something about them?' he asked kindly.

'Yes, please,' said Anne Marie, and her eyes strayed to a strange twisted horn on the mantelpiece, just beneath the scimitars.

Brandon followed her gaze. 'That's a penis gourd,' he said. 'I would have worn one like it when I was living in the highlands of what is now called Papua New Guinea.'

'Oh.' Anne Marie swallowed. 'Em, when was this?'

'Difficult to say. Time is irrelevant to the soul, but if you insist . . . perhaps three to five thousand years ago.'

'I see,' said Anne Marie, although she didn't. She looked around for something easy to enquire about. 'I like that mask,' she said, pointing to the least savage-looking one.

Brandon was pleased. 'Ah yes, that definitely belonged to me. My ceremonial mask. You can see it's Native American, of course, and you've probably guessed that many of my ancestors in this existence were what you called Red Indian when you were a child.' Here he paused, perhaps in order to give her a moment to reflect on the great hurt she'd inflicted on his people.

'My first memory of being a Native American is older than that, but it's an important one. I was the son of a chief,' he continued. 'When the *Mayflower* landed, my people helped the newcomers survive. We showed them how to grow corn – at that time, European farmers used to scatter seed, wasting most of it – whereas we had perfected the art of agriculture. First, we prepared the ground, then we drilled holes with sticks and placed the seed in them along with a fish-head for fertiliser. We grew beans and squash among the corn; that kept down the weeds as well as providing a perfectly balanced diet.'

Anne Marie knew all this. She'd seen it on American TV during the summer. *After the Mayflower* was the name of the series. She was trying to remember who had presented it. The actor with the gravelly voice – what was his name?

'. . . but then I was murdered by traitors who were in cahoots with the white men.'

'What? You were murdered?' Anne Marie tuned back in.

Brandon smiled at her. 'Many times.' He gave a sad smile. 'Just think how different world history would have been, had I been listened to back then. We'd have wiped out those first settlers and prevented any more from landing. The white man would never have got a foothold in America.'

The landlord told Anne Marie about some of his other lives. He'd been a courtesan in the time of Louis XIV (yes, of course he could be a woman!); an executioner for Henry VIII – but not the one who cut off the heads of his wives; a brave with Geronimo – that was when he'd owned the mask she'd asked about; and finally, a dancer with a can-can troupe that had toured the Wild West in the 1920s.

'How does one get to remember one's previous lives?' Anne Marie asked politely. She said 'one' because she didn't want him to think that she was doubting his word.

'Practice,' said Brandon. 'I meditate every day for three to four hours. I also use some mind-expanding substances that allow me to connect with my former selves. Of course, I wouldn't recommend that method to others. Most people don't have the discipline for it.'

'You mean . . . drugs?'

'As I said, it's not for everyone. Naturally, I only use the purest ingredients; leaves I picked and dried myself.'

'I see.'

Brandon reached over and patted her on the knee. 'You're a young soul. You haven't been on this planet long. Maybe two or three times before, no more.'

'Oh,' said Anne Marie. She wished she hadn't got such a baby face.

'Come, I'll show you upstairs.' Brandon rose to his feet in one fluid movement that to Anne Marie was as extraordinary as anything else she had seen or heard so far.

At the bottom of the stairs, he turned. 'Now you may remove your shoes,' he said.

Sylvester's tryst

It was another fifteen minutes before Anne Marie left the landlord's apartment. Sylvester, who had been listening intently for her footfall on the stairs, came out of his room at once. She had her head bowed and didn't see him on the landing. She started when he spoke.

'Good evening.'

'Oh! Hello.'

'You're new here.'

'Yes. I just arrived yesterday. I'm staying down in the basement with my cousins. My name's Anne Marie.'

'My name is Sylvester Reed. I live in here.' He gestured to the half-open door behind him. 'You're very welcome.' He held out his hand and stared at her fixedly.

'Oh, thank you.' Anne Marie shook his hand. It was dry and cool.

'Well. I won't keep you. Perhaps you will have tea with me some time soon?'

'That would be nice,' said Anne Marie.

He took a step back, stared at her again, then disappeared into his room.

What a strange little man! Anne Marie shook her head with a smile and continued on down to the basement. She opened the connecting door on the ground floor with the key Brandon had given her. She was dying to tell the cousins about her strange interview with their landlord.

Upstairs, Brandon congratulated himself on having at last found another Number Nine. Because she was so young, her spiritual side was not well developed, but that would come. Perhaps he could teach her. He probably shouldn't have offered to initiate her on the water pipe; not so soon, at any rate. She had looked shocked, as though she suspected him of wanting to seduce her. Innocent child! Little did she know how far beyond the transitory pleasures of sex he had progressed.

Eanneagram, eannyone?

'So, what do you think of our loop-the-loop landlord?' said Gerald with a sly grin as soon as Anne Marie came into the kitchen.

'Why didn't you tell me what it was going to be like?' she said, laughing. 'You're all so mean!'

'What? And spoil the surprise?'

'He likes us to be virgins,' explained Darina.

'What happened? What did he do?' Cornelius looked alarmed.

'Keep your Y-fronts on, Corny. I was speaking metaphorically. So you got the whole shebang, did you? Past lives and all?'

'Can-can dancer, executioner, Indian brave, courtesan – that's all I can remember.'

'Oh, they're not the ones I heard about.' Gerald tilted his chair on to its back legs and leant against the wall. 'An Aztec human sacrifice, an Egyptian pharaoh, a Roman soldier in Gaul – that's what he chose for me.'

Anne Marie giggled. 'We shouldn't laugh, but he's quite a character, isn't he?' She frowned suddenly. 'He asked me all these questions, and wrote the answers down, or ticked them off, because they were nearly all "yes" or "no". What was that for, do you know?'

'That was the Eanneagram,' said Darina.

'The what?'

'Eanneagram,' said Gerald. 'It's Greek. Means –
well, I've forgotten what it means, but—'

'Nine drawing,' supplied Darina.

'Right, because there are nine points on this circle,
and each one corresponds to—'

'You've heard of painting by numbers? Well, this is
personality by numbers.'

'Sorry, Dr Davenport, please go ahead. Forgive me
for talking while you're interrupting.'

'Piss off, Gerald!' Darina turned to her cousin.
'Basically, people are divided into nine personality
types. You have the good and bad traits that go with
that type, but you're also influenced by the types on
either side – your neighbours – and by the types at the
other end of the arrows in the star-shape that point to
you – your wings. But they're the refinements, you
don't have to bother so much with them. It's your
basic number that counts. I'm an Eight: that means
I'm bossy, into power and getting my own way.'

'QED,' said Gerald under his breath.

'Gerald's a Seven. That's about pleasure. He likes
the good life. He's all for instant gratification and has
no sense of responsibility.'

'Life and soul of the party, the Optimistic Epicurean
– that's me!'

'What number are you, Cornelius?' asked Anne
Marie, trying to draw her youngest cousin into the
conversation.

'He's a Six,' said Darina. 'Loyal, hard-working, law-
abiding.'

'Oh, that's a nice one.' Anne Marie smiled at him.
'Of course, you probably don't believe in any of this.
Do you?'

She suppressed a smile as Cornelius cleared his

throat and puffed himself out exactly as she'd seen her uncle do at family gatherings.

'Actually, the Eanneagram has become quite respectable. The Vatican ran a seminar on it a few years ago. And the CIA uses it to study the behaviour of world leaders. It would have distinct uses in business, of course. Hiring employees, sizing up competitors, that sort of thing.'

Anne Marie was impressed. 'Is that a fact? I'd better find out a bit more about it, so. I wonder what number I am?'

'A Nine!' Three voices answered together.

'Oh.' Such unanimity! Was she that easy to pigeon-hole? No mystery at all? Anne Marie was disappointed. 'So, what's a nine like? Dare I ask?'

'Hold on.' Gerald crashed his chair on to all its legs, got up and left the room. He came back with a magazine, which he handed to Anne Marie. On the cover was a star-shape inside a circle and the legend *Inside: The Eanneagram explained. Twenty-four page supplement*. 'Happy bedtime reading,' he said.

Space cadet

Next morning, Anne Marie got up early with the intention of exploring the outskirts of the capital city. The sky was clear and the forecast good – maybe she'd go to the coast. She could take the DART to Howth or Bray and spend a day by the sea.

Nobody else was up. Last night, Gerald and Darina had gone into Temple Bar at ten o'clock and they hadn't come home until nearly morning. Cornelius had retired to his room to finish reading a book. His light had still been on when Anne Marie went to bed at midnight.

Before going to sleep, Anne Marie had read all about Number Nine on the Eanneagram. The Mediator: patient and stable. That much was true; she hated conflict and she was quite a calm sort of person. She hoped she didn't have to accept the negative aspects that went with this personality type – she wasn't lazy, or repressed, or unable to prioritise, was she? It was interesting, though, how well her cousins seemed to match their numbers. If they all read about each other's good and bad points, that might help them to live together in harmony. The magazine article had described how communities of nuns used the Enneagram to this end. Maybe she would mention that next time there was any sign of friction, she thought as she wrapped her sandwiches in tin foil.

The toilet flushed in the boys' bathroom. Someone sniffed loudly. Must be Cornelius, she thought as bare feet approached the kitchen.

But it was a strange young woman who came in. She glanced over at Anne Marie as she made her way over to the counter. 'Howya. Any chance of a cuppa tea? I've a mouth on me like the inside of a cement mixer.' She felt the kettle. 'That's just after boiling, is it? Great stuff.'

Anne Marie stared at her in open-mouthed amazement. The girl had pink hair. Blue streaky mascara. Purple nail varnish. She was wearing a T-shirt of Gerald's that barely covered her hips. As she stretched to open an overhead cupboard looking for a mug, it rode up to her belly button.

'Underneath, the press on the left,' Anne Marie said

faintly. The girl was wearing nothing under the T-shirt. Her pubic hair was the same colour as the hair on her head.

'Tanks. Where d'youze keep your sugar?'

'It should be on the counter beside the teabags.'

'Righteo.' She sniffed again. 'I suppose I'd better make one for your man as well. Does he take sugar?'

'Who?'

'Your brother.'

'I haven't got a brother.'

'Jaysus, whatever! Ah here, I'll give him two spoons. If he doesn't like it, I'll drink it meself.'

The girl squeezed the teabags with her fingers then dumped them in the sink. She picked up the mugs and nodded to Anne Marie. At the door she hesitated. 'Eh, what's his name again?'

'Whose?'

'The fella I was with last night.'

'What fella?'

'For fuck's sake, what are you on? I thought you lived here and all!'

'Oh. You must mean Gerald. Sorry, I—'

'Gerry. That's right. Good stuff.' As the girl pulled the door closed with her foot, Anne Marie heard her sniff and mutter something. It sounded like, 'Bleedin' Spacer!'

Ten minutes later, the young woman with pink hair stormed out of the basement flat.

'Is she gone?' Gerald poked his head warily around the kitchen door.

Darina was making herself a cup of tea. 'It's all right, bro. She's outta here. And so am I. Back to my bed.'

'Thanks, Rescue Ranger. You really saved my bacon that time.'

'Your bacon? More like your sausage roll!' Darina lunged for his crotch as she passed him on her way to the bedroom.

'Oh, ow! Don't, please.' Gerald winced and limped over to the table. He collapsed onto a chair and held his head in his hands. 'There's no part of me that isn't sore,' he groaned.

Anne Marie was too embarrassed to comment.

Sylvester Reed heard the door of the basement flat slam and ran to his window at once. Seeing that it wasn't Anne Marie, he turned away in relief. Pink hair didn't interest him. He finished what he was writing, sealed it in an envelope and hid it. Taking another envelope, he silently opened his door and crept downstairs. He left the hall door ajar while he scurried down the steps and round the side. The door to the basement flat had no letterbox. He pushed the envelope under the draught excluder and disappeared back the way he had come.

He'd just closed the hall door again when Anne Marie left the flat. She checked she had her keys and swung her day pack onto her shoulder. By the time Sylvester was back at his post, she'd already turned the corner on to Leinster Road.

Preserving Innocence

'Well, how was it? I suppose you know the city like the back of your hand by now.' Gerald was leaning against

51

the counter, cigarette in hand, coffee beside him, when Anne Marie came back after her day out.

'Oh no, of course not. Sure I nearly got lost trying to find the DART station. I meant to go to Tara Street but I ended up in Connolly instead. I didn't even know which side of the Liffey I was on! I'm hopeless when it comes to directions. But I had a grand day altogether. Howth's lovely. I did the cliff walk. 'Twas gorgeous weather and all. I saw the high-speed ferry come in and go out, and another boat, a really beautiful old-fashioned yacht—'

'That would have been the *Asgard II*.'

'Is that what it was? I wish I'd had my camera, but then again, a photo couldn't have captured the magic of it. 'Tis a pity you all didn't come too. I feel it was selfish of me to have had so much pleasure just for myself!'

Gerald smiled fondly at his cousin. She'd no idea how lovely she looked at that moment – cheeks flushed, eyes bright – a fine country lass. He loved her Kerry lilt, particularly strong when she was animated. His Limerick accent had been diluted by three years at Trinity; now it only made itself heard when he was tired or stressed. Darina's was gone entirely; she'd worked hard at eradicating it from Day One. Only Cornelius spoke as though he'd never left home.

Gerald wished Anne Marie could keep her precious freshness, her wide-eyed wonder and childlike simplicity. Of course, it was impossible. The city would change her. Life would. He sighed. Sometimes, it would be nice to be able to preserve people exactly as they were. If he could, he would choose to preserve her the way she was right at this very instant. Smiling and shaking out her hair as she came round the table to get the kettle.

The Invisible Man

It was while they were all eating dinner that Anne Marie suddenly thought to mention her encounter on the second landing. 'Oh, I meant to tell you, I met another of the residents on my way down from the landlord's yesterday. Sylvester. He seemed nice.'

A stunned silence met this piece of information. Spaghetti paused en route to three mouths. Anne Marie looked at each of her cousins in turn. 'What is it? Why are you all staring at me like that?'

'She's seen him,' Gerald said wonderingly. 'She's only been here a day, and she's seen him.'

'What are you on about? Is this another of your jokes? Come on, lads, tell me!'

'Ahem,' said Darina pointedly.

'What? Oh sorry, lads and lass, then. I thought 'twas only my mother objected to that sort of thing.'

'Hey, never mind the feminist bollix, if you'll pardon my figure of speech, this is important! Anne Marie has seen The Invisible Man!'

'What d'you call him that for?' laughed Anne Marie. 'He was pretty visible to me.'

'We've been here over a year and I've never seen him,' said Gerald.

'I saw him once, in the street. But it was winter and dark, so I didn't really get a good look at him,' said Darina.

'I've seen him from the back, going up the stairs after picking up his post. I said "hello" once but he didn't look around. Of course, he may be hard of hearing.' Cornelius believed in giving people the benefit of the doubt.

'Oh! That is strange.'

'So tell us, what does the mysterious Sylvester look like from the front?' Darina asked.

'Brown,' said Anne Marie.

'Brown? Just – brown? What kind of a description is that?'

'That's the way I see him. He makes me think of a small brown animal. He's got brown hair, a brown moustache that's quite thick but very clean-cut, if you know what I mean. No straggly bits. I can't remember what colour his eyes were – brown too, I suppose, but . . .' She frowned and stopped. There had been something odd about his eyes. A lack of expression. She'd noticed it when they'd shaken hands.

'So, did he say anything?' Darina was all agog.

'Yes, he asked me my name, welcomed me to the house, then invited me for tea.'

'He did what? By God, Anne Marie, you're a fast worker.' Gerald poured more wine into his cousin's glass.

'Stop, Gerald! I'm not used to drinking like this.'

Darina slid her glass over to her brother. 'Go ahead, I am.'

'Is it not very expensive, a bottle of wine nearly every night? I'd have thought that as students, you wouldn't be able to afford to splash out very often,' Anne Marie said without thinking.

Her cousins' reaction made her realise she'd put her foot in it. Darina scowled, Gerald looked away. Cornelius, however, was triumphant.

'You're quite right, Anne Marie. I'm fed up trying to tell them. They gang up on me. Now that you're here, it's two against two.'

'Oh, but I didn't mean to start a row! I'm sorry, it's not really my business.'

'Of course it's your business!' Cornelius was being unusually forceful. 'You pay into the kitty, same as myself. It's supposed to buy food for all of us, not keep that pair in wine and cigarettes.'

'All right, all right.' Gerald raised his hands soothingly. 'Point taken. Let's not come to blows over a few quids' worth of drink. We'll start the new régime next week when term begins. But this is the last day of the holidays, so let's celebrate. Pour yourself another lemonade there, Con, I want to propose a toast. Everybody, lift your glasses.' Four glasses were raised. 'To The Invisible Man.'

'The Invisible Man!' The cousins clinked glasses and cheered.

A cry for help

Although it was only Freshers' week, the Davenports all went into Trinity on Monday morning.

Left on her own in the flat, Anne Marie decided to do some housework. She wanted to atone to the cousins for the friction she imagined her presence was generating. It didn't occur to her that they'd been squabbling and making up for the best part of twenty years and would continue to do so whether or not she was there.

After tidying the room she shared with Darina, Anne Marie dusted and hoovered the sitting room, stripped the divan bed where Gerry and the girl with pink hair had slept and put the sheets in the wash, cleaned the kitchen and emptied the dishwasher. She stopped for a cup of coffee, then tackled the bathrooms. Her last job was to sweep down the hallway. Anne Marie started at the back stairway and brushed all the dust down towards the entrance. She stopped when she reached the new doormat and opened the door.

It was only when she lifted the mat to shake it outside that she saw the white envelope on the floor. It had her name on it. The writing was small and even, and Anne Marie guessed at once that it had come from Sylvester. Her invitation to tea had arrived! Putting the envelope in her back pocket, Anne Marie finished her cleaning. She knew what was in the letter, but she enjoyed the ritual, unconsciously picked up from her mother, of having everything done before she sat down to read.

The note was from Sylvester, but it wasn't what she'd been expecting.

Dear Anne Marie,

You have a kind face. Please help me, I need to talk to someone. Come as soon as you can. I will be waiting.

Yours,
Sylvester Reed

There was no time or date on the note, but Anne Marie knew it must have been left the previous day. She stared at it in dismay. The poor man – he sounded desperate! And he was going to think that she'd ignored his appeal. Would he be in on a Monday morning? Hardly, unless . . .

Anne Marie didn't let herself think about the 'unless'. Armed with pen and paper to leave a note in case Sylvester was out, she ran up the stairs to the second floor. When she knocked on the door, it yielded.

'Hello?' she called irresolutely.

There was no answer. She pushed the door harder and it swung open. In the middle of the room was an old-fashioned iron bed.

Sylvester was lying on it.

Anne Marie didn't need to enter the room to know that he was dead.

Hornblower and the Atropos

Detective Inspector Declan Martin was not a misogynist. He just thought women had no place on a police force. 'They haven't got what it takes,' he maintained to his cronies down at his local. Meaning: balls. But even DI Martin had to admit that it was useful having a *banner* around in situations like these.

Garda Brenda Clarke had been in the squad car sent from the station in Rathmines. Now she was sitting on the stairs with her arm around the girl, asking her if there was anywhere they could make a cup of tea. Good, he was gasping for one himself. The girl didn't answer. She was sniffling and shredding a paper handkerchief. Going over and over her part in the incident.

'I feel so guilty. If only I'd seen the note in time, I could have prevented it. He must have been terribly lonely. It's awful to think he was waiting for me as his last hope. When I didn't come, he obviously assumed I didn't care, that nobody cared whether he lived or died.' She started sobbing again.

Poor kid. It was probably the first time she'd seen a dead body. Must have been a shock, all right. The head twisted towards the door, eyes staring at you as you walked in.

DI Martin looked around the room once more. Clear-cut case of suicide. There'd be an inquest; they'd take away the cup and analyse the dregs to see what it was that he'd taken, but that'd be an end of it. Not DDU business really, but the local inspector was on holidays and his sergeant-in-charge a lazy bollix. Martin didn't mind. It got him out of the office.

Although it wasn't a suspicious death, long habit made the detective register the details of the dead man's surroundings as though they were vital evidence. The man had been obsessively tidy. The sparsely furnished room was spotless. Unbelievably clean, in fact. Why?

His curiosity roused, Martin nosed about a bit more. There had to be some dirt, somewhere. He even pulled out the cooker in the little kitchenette to look for grease stains, but found none.

The man must have scrubbed and scoured no less than a day before he committed suicide. Why go to such bother? And where was all the cleaning stuff? Martin opened presses and pulled out drawers. Most of them were bare. Curiouser and curiouser. He stood in the centre of the room and clicked his tongue. The girl had gone downstairs with Brenda. He'd have to ask her a few more questions. The other residents too. That meant coming back this evening. Meanwhile, what else was there? The bookcase, with its collection of C.S. Forester books. Martin smiled. His father had been a great Hornblower fan. This character too, by the looks of it. He had the whole set – all in chronological order, naturally. Martin ran his finger along the spines of the books and thought fondly of his father.

Hornblower and the Atropos. He remembered that one. His dad had made him look up in the Encyclopaedia to find out what Atropos meant. Imagine, he could still remember. It was the name of one of the goddesses in Greek mythology who controlled men's destinies. The third Fate; the one who cut the cord. The book was also the third one in the series, after *Mr Midshipman Hornblower* and *Lieutenant Hornblower.* Funny, the stiff had it in fourth place, after *Hornblower and the Hotspur.* Now that was strangely careless of him.

Or was it?

DI Martin reached for the book with a mounting sense of excitement. He knew by the rising of the small hairs on the back of his neck that he was going to find something.

It was in the middle of the book. A slim white envelope, sealed but with no name on the outside. He tore it open. Inside were two pages of small, even handwriting, with double spacing between the lines.

Martin began to read. After the first few lines, he gave a low whistle. At the end of the first page, he took a deep breath. He held it while he turned to the second page and quickly read to the end. Then he let out the breath in a rush. He looked over at the body in the bed as though seeing it for the first time.

'Well, fuck me!' he said slowly.

The archivist

The *Evening Echo* ran the story the following day. DI Martin stared gloomily at the two-inch-deep headlines. SOUTH CIRCULAR STRANGLER SUICIDE. A junior reporter – 'the hackette with the hair', he called her – had managed to get her story in before the official garda press release. Martin wondered who had spilled the beans and what she had done for the information. He grunted in disgust. Why couldn't she have used him as her source? He'd have strung her along with a few tidbits – nothing close to home, of course – and fucked her silly for them. A symbiotic relationship, wasn't that what you called it?

At least she hadn't got the full story. He turned the page and skimmed through the article again. It concentrated on the original murders – three girls aged between ten and fifteen strangled over a period of six months – and on the failure of the police to catch the culprit. Thanks be to Jaysus he hadn't been directly involved in that investigation; a certain superintendent Martin knew was going to have egg on his face when the psychological profile done at the time came to light. Martin had a copy of it in front of him.

A loner, unobtrusive and mild-mannered. Probably works in an undemanding clerical job that involves little interaction with others. The man had been an archivist. *Obsessed with cleanliness.* You betcha. *May have tics such as constant hand-washing, polishing his desk.* Cleaning behind cookers. *He is repulsed by the idea of sex.* More fool him. *His victims are virgins – untouched, pure.* Poor kids. *His mission is to preserve them that way.* Bloody wacko.

But how could someone else have known what was

going on in your man's mind? Scary stuff when you came to think of it. Martin remembered sitting over a pint in the Garda Club with Fahy, who was now Superintendent Fahy, but at the time was the DI leading the investigation.

'Shaggin' academic,' Fahy had said bitterly of the criminal psychologist who'd done the profile. And a woman to boot. Of course, Fahy had dismissed her conclusions. Flying in the face of the facts, he'd insisted that the culprit was a local pervert linked to recent rapes in the area. Martin had sympathised. Back then, criminal psychology had been in its infancy. Now Joe Public was doing night classes in it, for Jaysus's sake.

Martin got up from his desk and stretched. Sylvester Reed's confession would close a few cases for the Murder Squad. Not for the families of the victims, however. They'd just go on suffering. Anne Marie's face came into his mind. Nice young one, that. Just as well she'd never know what a lucky escape she'd had.

They'd found enough of the date rape drug Rohypnol in the teapot to fell an ox. Your man had been planning on taking her with him.

Vera's fifteen minutes

Vera Meaney had never been so happy. There it was, on page two of the *Evening Echo*. Her name! A little story about her! Well, not about her exactly, but still . . . it was so exciting! She read it again, although by now she knew the few paragraphs in which she featured by heart.

SHOCKED

Vera Meaney, 29, from Borris-in-Ossory, shared a landing with the killer. 'I'm shocked,' she said. 'He always seemed like such an ordinary man. Very quiet, kept himself to himself. I can hardly believe it!'

Vera lived next to sinister Sylvester in the house in Belvedere Square for eight years. Reed may have been planning his suicide for some time: Vera heard him taking bags of rubbish downstairs late at night. She also noticed that there were extra black plastic sacks out for the last two bin collections. Gardaí found no personal belongings in the dead man's room.

'Nobody could have guessed from looking at him that he was the South Circular Strangler,' said Vera. 'It's scary to think that a killer could look so normal.'

The Evening Echo *spoke to some of the other residents, but none of them knew Reed. American landlord, Mr Brandon, was unavailable for comment last night.*

Vera was pleased that the reporter had put her age at twenty-nine. She hadn't told a lie exactly; she had merely said that she was a year off thirty. Obviously, the girl had thought she couldn't possibly be more.

What a pity they hadn't used the story she'd told the nice reporter about the time she'd asked Sylvester for milk. He had just moved in and it seemed the best way to get to know her new neighbour. He'd opened the door an inch and told her he hadn't got any. Of course Vera knew it was a lie. He looked frightened, she remembered. At the time she'd assumed he was shy.

Over the next few weeks she'd made a point of smiling at him when they met on their way to and from the bathroom. Then she'd begun to notice that he was going earlier, before she was up. She hadn't told the reporter that bit.

A shoulder to cry on

'How do you feel?' Gerald appeared inside the door of the girls' room with a mug of tea.

Anne Marie sat up carefully to avoid bumping her head against the ceiling. 'Oh, Gerald. Is that for me? You're awful good. D'you know, I think I'm OK. A bit wobbly inside, maybe. But not as bruised and battered as I was feeling last night. When I woke up there a minute ago, I even felt happy. Then I suddenly remembered everything. It wasn't a nightmare, was it?'

'Sorry, Am. It all happened.'

Anne Marie turned on to her elbow and smiled. 'Am. You used to call me that when we were kids.'

'And you called me Ger-lad.'

'Yes, I thought that was your name. Ger-lad. It kind of suits you.'

'Thanks – I think. Go on and drink up now, it'll get cold.'

'Are the others up?'

'Up and gone. Darina's meeting a student to buy books, Cornelius is gone to the barber's.'

'Is it late?'

'Nearly ten o'clock.'

'What! How could I have slept that long? Eleven

63

hours! I thought I wasn't going to get a wink with all that went on yesterday.'

'The excitement, that's what it was. And the sleeping tablet. You were out like a light, Darina said.'

'I still can't believe it, you know. It was bad enough finding the body. Knowing I could have stopped him killing himself if I'd got the note in time. Then to learn that he was a murderer! And that he wanted to confess to me. That's obviously what the note meant. Though why he chose me, I can't imagine.'

'Your kind face, remember?'

'I don't know about that. I'm not sure I could have taken it. His confession, I mean.'

'I'm glad you didn't have to.'

'So am I. And by the way – thanks.'

'Thanks for what?'

'For . . . you know – last night.'

Gerald put his finger to his lips. 'Shh, we wouldn't want anyone to hear about that, now would we? But tell me – was I good?'

Anne Marie blushed and reached over the edge of the bunk to cuff him. 'You know what I mean! Thanks for being there. For taking charge. For getting rid of that reporter. For lending me your shoulder to cry on.'

'Hey, that's what shoulders are for!'

On yer bike

After Gerald left for college on Tuesday, Anne Marie's parents phoned. She'd spoken to them the previous night, of course, but she'd had to cut short the conversation when the detective returned. Now they wanted to talk at length about her ordeal, and Seán kept asking her if she was sure she was all right. He even offered to come up to Dublin for a day. Anne Marie was touched. Her parents didn't normally worry about her. She told them she was fine, and that she'd rather they didn't come up. She would go home for a weekend before the end of the month, she promised.

It was a surprise to discover that she really did feel all right. Everyone had been so nice: Brenda, the garda who'd made her drink hot sweet tea and didn't mind when she kept bursting into tears; the detective, who'd come back to ask her questions and was very patient when she didn't know any of the answers, and Brandon, who'd invited her upstairs for something to calm her nerves right in front of the guards.

Then the cousins had arrived in; first Gerald, who'd put his arms around her and held her tight; then Cornelius, who'd fussed and clucked like a mother hen and tried to get her to eat; then Darina – well, maybe not Darina, who'd acted as though she couldn't care less. But Anne Marie decided she wasn't going to let one cousin's attitude upset her. She had enough to think about without that.

Gingerly, as though probing a rotten tooth with her tongue, Anne Marie approached the events of the previous day to see how well she could stand the memory. She remembered her concern when she read the note, and how the thought had crossed her mind that Sylvester might be suicidal and that she might be instrumental in saving him. That was why she had taken the stairs three at a time to get to his room. Now she couldn't help feeling slightly ashamed of the way she had pictured herself as the Good Samaritan rescuing a poor soul from the depths of depression.

She went on to the moment before she'd pushed open the door, when she knew in her heart that it was already too late. As she was being entirely honest with herself, Anne Marie had to admit that along with dread, she'd felt a little thrill of excitement. What if there really was a dead body in there?

It was funny how her attitude had changed as soon as she'd seen it. There was nothing titillating about the sight that had greeted Anne Marie when she opened the door. She winced. This was the most painful part; the scene that she was afraid would haunt her in flashbacks for the rest of her life. Sylvester's face twisted towards the door as though he'd been waiting for her; his bulging eyes; the way his swollen, discoloured tongue protruded from his mouth. The smell too – she still had it in her nostrils.

Anne Marie shivered and began to brush her teeth more vigorously. She needed to get out of the house, preferably until evening when the others would be back. Although the body was gone and Brandon had spoken about a cleansing ceremony he was going to perform in Sylvester's room, she half-felt that the dead man's ghost might be lurking reproachfully nearby.

The fine weather looked set to continue for some time. Remembering her plan to purchase a bicycle, Anne Marie decided today was the day. She bought a *Buy and Sell* and took it into the Café Firenze. It was mid-morning and she was the only customer. The waiter smiled at her when she came in.

'Cappuccino?' he asked.

'Yes, please.' Anne Marie was chuffed. He'd recognised her! Four days in Dublin and there was a place she belonged! Her mental map of the city had got its first coloured pin. It was another good omen, she was sure of it. And the waiter did have a nice smile after all.

The *Buy and Sell* had an advertisement for a lady's racer, ten gears, hardly used. Anne Marie went to the restaurant payphone and rang the number. A woman answered the phone and said yes, the bicycle was still available. Anne Marie almost dropped the phone, however, when she heard that the address was the South Circular Road.

Omens were silly, she suddenly decided. All in the imagination. She gave her name and said she'd be there at the appointed time of seven o'clock.

She spent the rest of the morning photocopying her CV and the afternoon being interviewed by the Alfred Marks and Manpower employment agencies. She ate an open sandwich in the Winding Stair, deciding that it too merited a pin on her map when the woman serving behind the counter opened her eyes wide at the height of Anne Marie and gave her an extra-large serving of egg mayonnaise.

At twenty past six, Anne Marie set out along the Quays towards Kilmainham. She knew that the South Circular Road began somewhere around there. At ten to seven, she checked her little map to see why she hadn't yet reached it. But her map ended at the Four Courts. She asked for directions and set off again.

Eventually, she found the number of the house she was looking for in a street of terraced Corporation houses. Some of them had nice gardens and sparkling white net curtains on the windows. Others looked a bit neglected. This one had an overgrown garden that was full of rubbish, including the wreck of a car and an old fridge. There were no curtains on the windows, which were so dirty that it was impossible to see through anyway. Anne Marie picked her way up to the door. She could hear shouting inside. She rang the bell and it stopped. Someone stomped into the hall and bellowed through the door.

'Fuck off!'

Anne Marie took a step back in confusion. That wasn't very friendly! She was tempted to leave, but she really wanted that bicycle.

She rang the bell a second time. The footsteps sounded again, but this time the door was thrown open so violently that it almost came off its hinges.

'I thought I told you to fuck off!' He was a big man, red of face and large of fist.

Anne Marie backed away. 'It's about the ad in the *Buy and Sell*.'

'What fuckin' ad? We're not selling anything. Now get the fuck out of here.'

'But it's here, and I rang this morning.' Anne Marie held up her copy of the paper.

The man took a step towards her. 'Are you deaf or wha'? I've no ad in no shaggin' paper. Now fuck off with yourself!'

Anne Marie retreated as far as the gate. 'Look,' she began. 'I only want—'

'On yer bike!' roared the man.

Which under the circumstances, Anne Marie found particularly galling.

Victor

Walking back along by the canal, Anne Marie realised her mistake. The road she was on was not the South

Circular; it was called Dolphin Road. Somewhat cheered by this discovery, she stopped someone and asked again for directions. It was now half past seven.

At eight o'clock, Anne Marie gave up in despair. She had been as far as Conyngham Road and back and still hadn't found the address in the ad. Now she was completely lost. Her feet ached, her stomach had begun to growl again, and she had no idea how to get home.

Home! She thought of her parents' bungalow on the outskirts of Killorglin, of the fields around it that she knew like the back of her hand, of the town where people greeted her by name, and wished with all her heart that she could be transported there instantly. Tears of frustration welled up at the corners of her eyes.

'Excuse me, are you lost?'

Anne Marie started and looked around.

A tall black man was looking at her with concern. 'I was visiting a friend. I saw you go past some time ago. I think you must be walking in circles. Can I help?'

Anne Marie sniffed and rooted in her bag for a tissue. It was embarrassing to be offered assistance by someone who was so obviously a foreigner.

'I was looking for an address on the South Circular Road, but I didn't find it,' she mumbled. 'It's all right. I think I'll just go home now. If you could point me towards the River Liffey, I'll be OK from there.'

'But the South Circular Road is very close! I'm going that way myself. Shall I show you?'

Reluctantly, Anne Marie allowed herself to be led away. He was probably very nice, not an axe murderer or anything, but having found Sylvester's body only yesterday, she felt she was justified in being a bit wary of encounters with strangers.

Her rescuer walked fast; Anne Marie had to run to keep up with him. He seemed disinclined to make conversation, but Anne Marie felt awkward trotting alongside him in silence.

'Are you a refugee?' she asked.

'The correct term is asylum seeker,' he said stiffly.

'Oh,' said Anne Marie, who hadn't known there was a difference. 'How long have you been here?'

'Too long!' He sounded bitter. 'I am a lawyer for Human Rights. I thought the Irish might have some understanding of what that means. After all, your ex-president was for a time UN Commissioner for Human Rights. But it would seem I was wrong. Mary Robinson is not your average Irish person.'

'Where are you from?'

'Many places. I carry a British passport, among others. Most recently, however, I have come from Congo Brazzaville,' he said.

'I see,' said Anne Marie untruthfully.

'You're so pleased with yourselves, you Irish!' he suddenly exploded. 'You think you're great! Warm-hearted and hospitable. Ireland of the hundred thousand welcomes. That's a joke! I've just come from a house that has been attacked three times. The woman who lives there has been spat at, called vile names and told to go home. Her husband has been beaten up twice. These are people who've suffered torture in their own country and fled to this supposed haven. I'm trying to move them to a safer area of the city before it's too late.'

'I . . . I didn't know it was so bad.'

'Well, it is. I work with ARASI, the Association for Refugees and Asylum Seekers in Ireland. I deal with cases like this every day.'

'I'm sorry,' said Anne Marie humbly.

He suddenly smiled. 'Yes, I can see that you are. I am being unfair. I shouldn't be taking my anger out on you. You are lost in a strange city. I know what it's like; that's why I came over to you.' They had reached a crossroads. He turned to her. 'This is the South Circular Road now.'

Anne Marie looked around. 'But I've been past here twice before! I walked for miles and couldn't find the right house.'

'You went straight on?'

'Yes, of course.'

'Ah, but that's where you went wrong. The South Circular Road turns left here. Let me show you on my map.'

He took out a street guide to Dublin and traced the course of the road with a long brown finger.

'Oh, I see,' said Anne Marie. She felt defeated. The city had conspired against her, sending its streets swerving slyly off in unexpected directions. 'Thank you.'

He gave a slight nod. 'That's all right. You may keep the book.'

'Oh, but I can't! I mean, I shouldn't. It's yours; you need it too. I can get one for myself.'

'So, send it back to me when you've finished with it. My address is inside the cover. Now excuse me, there's my bus.' He gave a brief wave and ran ahead of the number 19 that had stopped at the lights.

Anne Marie looked inside the cover. His name, surprisingly, was Victor Mackenzie.

Caelinn Largey

Guilt trip

By the time Anne Marie arrived at the right address, it was almost half past eight. She went up to the door of a Victorian redbrick house and pressed the bell. There was a scurry of feet, followed by the squeals of childish voices.

'I'm opening it!'

'No, I am. You did it last time.'

'Ow!'

'Aah! Mammy – he's pulling my hair!'

'She bit me first!'

Listening to the screams of rage and pain coming from the other side of the door, it occurred to Anne Marie that there were certain advantages to being an only child that she had tended to overlook when she'd longed for a little sister or brother.

At last, the door opened. A solemn-looking girl of nine or ten gazed up at Anne Marie without speaking. Behind her, two smaller children were fighting on the floor with concentrated ferocity.

'Hello,' said Anne Marie. 'I've come about the bike that's for sale. I know I'm late, but I couldn't find the house.'

The girl continued to stare at Anne Marie in silence. Then she turned and ran down the hallway, neatly side-stepping the fighters' flailing limbs on the way. Presently she came back, bringing with her a woman wearing an apron and rubber gloves.

'Are you the Anne Marie that rang this morning?' said the woman. She looked to be in her late twenties, though there were faint lines around her eyes that might mean she was older, thought Anne Marie. She was petite and attractive, with dark corkscrew curls and an elfin face.

'Yes, I got lost, that's why I'm late.'

'It's gone! My mother-in-law took your call; she left a note to say you were coming at seven. I did hold onto it until half-past,' the woman added defensively, 'but then I assumed you weren't coming and sold it to the next buyer. I'm sorry.'

Anne Marie was bitterly disappointed. She'd set her heart on getting a bike today. Not just any bike, she realised as she fought back the tears, but this bike, from this woman. The journey had been like a fairytale quest, complete with its maze of streets, an ogre in the first house, and a good fairy who'd shown her the way. Now that she had reached the castle, she was entitled to her reward.

'In any case,' the woman went on, 'it wouldn't have made any difference if you had come on time. Sure, look at the size of you! Your legs must be up to my waist! The bike would've been way too small for you.'

'Oh. Yes, I see what you mean all right.' Anne Marie made a brave attempt at a smile. She thanked the woman and turned to go.

'Hold on a minute.'

Anne Marie stopped halfway down the path and turned around.

'Look, I'm sorry you had a wasted evening. I don't suppose you'd be interested in an old-fashioned bike, would you? You know, a big black sit-up-and-beg thing? There are a few of them out in the garage if you'd like to have a look.'

Anne Marie said she would.

'Where are you from?' the woman, whose name was Roz, asked as she led the way through the house. The children followed, including the pair that had been laying into one another on the floor a minute earlier.

'I thought I recognised the accent,' Roz said when Anne Marie told her. 'We love that part of Kerry, we go down every summer. At one point we even thought of buying a house, but we left it too late. Everything sky-rocketed. We couldn't afford a garden shed at today's prices. Still, I suppose it's a good thing in a way. If we had a holiday house, we'd have to make use of it by going down every long weekend, and when you've got small kids, that journey's no joke.'

'They seem quite a handful. The younger ones anyway,' said Anne Marie, who had just had an arm grabbed on either side.

'Jake, Ruth – stop that! Leave Anne Marie alone!'

'Whee!'

'I'm flying!'

Anne Marie staggered as the children began to swing out of her.

'That's enough, you two! Come on, time for bed. I'll be up in a few minutes to read you a story.' Roz pulled the boy away from Anne Marie and tried to usher him towards the stairs. He slipped out of her grasp.

'Are you a giant?' he said to Anne Marie.

'No, she's the beanstalk!' the girl said. They took a fit of giggling.

'I'm sorry about this,' said Roz. 'Listen, why don't you have a look in the garage while I get rid of this pair. I don't know what state the bikes are in, so you'd better take them out and try them in the garden. I'll put on the kettle for a cup of tea after.' She gave Anne Marie a key and showed her where to go. Then she turned and let out a bloodcurdling snarl, much to the delight of the two small children who squealed and raced ahead of her up the stairs.

There were three men's bikes in the garage, two big black antique models and a more modern red one. They were dusty and in need of oil. Anne Marie tried all three. The old-fashioned black ones appealed to her sense of aesthetics, but reluctantly she rejected them as too uncomfortable and hard to pedal. The red one had three gears and was light enough to be carried. It was also the most nondescript of the three, and therefore the least likely to be stolen. She was busy wiping off the dust with a tissue when Roz rejoined her.

'Peace at last! I see you've made your choice. The older ones belonged to my dad, but I think that one's Stephen's – my husband.'

'Oh, do you want to check with him first? He might not want to sell it.'

'Not at all. He's never used it in all the time I've known him. You're welcome to it.' Roz led the way into the kitchen. 'Now how about that cup of tea? I'd offer you something stronger only I'd be forced to keep you company. And then I might not be able to stop!'

Anne Marie said tea would be fine.

Roz continued to talk over her shoulder while she busied herself with the teapot. 'So, you're new in Dublin? I hope you don't mind teabags, I've got the real stuff somewhere but I hate washing the pot out after so I don't normally bother. There are some biscuits in the press behind you; maybe you could get them down? God, it must be great to be so tall, I have to get a stool to do that. Are you studying up here? It must be hard, living in a city after the beauty of Kerry. If I won the Lotto, I'd retire there tomorrow. Where did I put the sugar, is it there on the table? It is? Good. I normally keep it away from the twins; they eat it out

of the bowl with their fingers. Right, that's everything, I think. We'll just leave the tea to draw for a
minute. I'm sorry, I know I talk too much! I'm going
to shut up now and you can tell me something about
yourself.'

Anne Marie smiled. Roz was her exact opposite in
many ways – small, voluble, and full of nervous energy,
but Anne Marie had taken an instant liking to her. She
told the older woman that she'd been born in America
but had grown up in Killorglin where her parents, both
originally from Limerick, were teachers in the local
secondary school. She explained that after leaving
school, she had decided she wanted to work, so she
had done a computer course in Tralee and now she was
in Dublin looking for a job.

Not much to tell, she thought when she'd finished.
Apart from having been born in America, there was
little of interest in her first nineteen years. Except for
the events of yesterday, and she wasn't about to blab
about them.

'What sort of a job were you looking for?' asked
Roz.

'Oh, any kind of office job, really. I've done a course
in office administration and computers. I'm familiar
with most of the software that's out at the moment.'

'Do you know anything about desktop publishing?'

'Oh sure! I produced a magazine as part of my
assessment.'

'Hmm. What a pity you weren't here last week. I
work for a women's magazine; we were looking for
someone with your skills when our Editorial Assistant
upped and left without warning. You could have come
for an interview. There's a new person supposed to
start tomorrow, but I'll tell you what – why don't I

take your number just in case something happens? It's a small team and we all work very closely together. If someone doesn't fit in, it can be awful. The last one didn't, which is why she left in such a hurry.'

'That's very nice of you, thanks.'

'I can't guarantee anything, you realise.'

'Sure, I understand.'

While Roz poured tea, Anne Marie sat back and looked around the kitchen. It was a big room, obviously an extension, with a tiled floor and French windows leading to the garden. The table was covered in a waxed cloth with a still-life pattern of fruit in a bowl. The Shaker wall units were the same pale green as the bowl on the cloth. Children's artwork adorned one of the walls.

'This is a lovely house,' she said. 'It doesn't seem like much from the outside – I mean, it looks just the same as all the others in the terrace, but the inside is beautiful. You've obviously done a lot of work to turn it into a real family home.'

'Blood, sweat and tears, that's what it took. Plus a phenomenal amount of money and ten years of our lives. But I suppose it was worth it. We work hard, Stephen and myself, so when we come home we want to relax in pleasant surroundings. Of course, with kids it's impossible to have a really beautiful house. That's not the point anyway, is it? They live here too. We keep the sitting room locked so that it stays nice for us and our occasional visitors. I try to have the kitchen relatively presentable, but you wouldn't want to see the living room and their bedrooms at the end of each day!'

'Who minds the children while you're at work?'

'Stephen picks them up from school and brings

them home most days. He's a journalist with the *Irish Times* and works evenings. When he leaves for work, a young one from a few doors down comes in. She gives them their tea and oversees homework. When I get in at around six, I have quality time with my children until it's time for them to go to bed.'

'Sounds like a good system.'

Roz rolled her eyes and gave a short laugh. 'If only! That last bit was sarcastic.'

'Oh?'

'*The Working Mother: A Study in Guilt*. Guilt for not being there for them all the time. Guilt for wishing it was Monday when I am with them at the weekends. Guilt for having to take time off work to see their school play. Guilt for knowing none of their little friends' names. Guilt for not being Superwoman. Guilt for wanting to *be* Superwoman. Guilt for feeling guilty.'

'That's a lot of guilt!'

'Too right, it is! And that's even before we get to the marital relationship. Would you believe I have to make an appointment to see my husband at lunchtime twice a week? Our paths wouldn't cross otherwise. As for You Know What – I can't remember when we did it last. Sometime in the last millennium!'

Anne Marie blushed, then giggled.

'Seriously though,' Roz went on, 'I sometimes wonder what it's all for. How did life get to be so crazy? It wasn't like this in our parents' time, that's for sure.'

'Did your mother stay at home?'

'Well . . . she died when I was ten, but up to that she was the traditional mother all right.'

'Oh, I am sorry. Ten – that was very young to lose

her. Have you got other family? What about your father?'

'He's still around. He married again. Lives near Drogheda. We go up the odd Sunday, but he never comes down. Debbie doesn't like kids.'

'What about sisters and brothers?'

Roz shook her head.

'So you're an only child, just like me!'

Roz gripped her mug. 'I had a sister. She died along with my mother. Car crash.'

'Oh, God! How awful!'

Roz stared straight ahead. Her voice lost all inflection, becoming flat and emotionless. 'Twenty-five years ago this December. Drunk driver. Big shot now, owns property all over Dublin. He got off scot-free. Swapped seats with his wife; said she was driving.'

'That's appalling! But . . . how do you know that's what happened?'

'I was in the car too. Nobody would listen. I was a child, remember? Naturally unreliable. I was con-cussed, so my memory couldn't be trusted, they said.'

Anne Marie gazed at Roz in awe. So bouncy and bubbly – you'd never guess there was any tragedy in her past. People really were extraordinary! Anne Marie wished she could do something heroic for Roz. A grand gesture that would somehow wipe out the past. She realised that her own life had been blissfully uneventful; even the Sylvester episode paled to nothing by comparison.

Roz took a tissue from a box on top of the micro-wave and blew her nose. 'Ever since having kids, I've felt the need to grieve all over again. It's so unfair that my mother isn't around – she'd have been a wonderful grandmother. And Ellie, my sister – she'd have had kids too. We'd have gone on holidays together, our children would have grown up like one family. That's the way it was supposed to be! I keep meaning to take time to go off on my own some place and howl about it. But I've been too caught up in living day-to-day. And that's so frenetic there's no time left for anything that really matters.'

Roz spread her hands apologetically. 'I'm sorry for unburdening myself like this to you. With Stephen working nights, I'm starved for adult company after six p.m. Work is great, of course, but I'm the only one with children, so we tend not to discuss our home lives much.' She suddenly grinned at Anne Marie. 'You poor thing! You came for a bike, and you got an earful instead! I have to say, you are a good listener.'

Before Anne Marie could say that she didn't mind, she found it fascinating in fact, the door opened. The eldest child came in, dressed in Laura Ashley pyjamas and Eeyore slippers.

'Mammy, I finished the book myself. Can you come and tuck me in now?'

'Eleanor, sweetheart – I'm sorry. I'm coming right away.'

Anne Marie stood up. 'I'll go. Just tell me how much for the bike.'

'For heaven's sake – take it! I'm delighted to get rid of it from the garage. If you wouldn't mind bringing it in yourself while I go upstairs with Eleanor. I'll be with you in a few minutes. And don't forget to leave your phone number – put it on the whiteboard, will you? I'll write it into my address book after I've let you out.' She took the girl's hand. 'Say good night to Anne Marie, Eleanor.'

The child looked up at Anne Marie. Her eyes were

like deep brown pools: unfathomable, thought Anne Marie.

'Good night. Sleep well.'

''Night,' said the child, but she didn't smile.

Anne Marie gets a job

By the end of her first week in Dublin, Anne Marie had been interviewed for three jobs. The first was with a computer firm in Tallaght. She liked the MD, an attractive man in his early thirties who told her that his firm was going places. Seeing the hunger in his eyes, she'd had no trouble believing him. Regretfully, because she knew that he liked her too, she turned down the job when he offered it to her. The salary was too low and Tallaght was too far out.

The second job was with a fashion house. The woman who interviewed her had black hair scraped into a bun and skewered with a silver pin. Her Katharine Hepburn mouth turned down at the corners when she heard Anne Marie's accent. From the way she said she'd be in touch after the interview was over, Anne Marie knew not to hold her breath.

The third job was in a new hotel ten minutes' walk from the flat in Rathmines. The Personnel Manager skimmed through her CV while two women took it in turns to ask her why she thought she was suitable for the job. They all appeared terminally bored with the proceedings; twice, the Personnel Manager yawned without bothering to hide it. Anne Marie decided she didn't want to work in a hotel.

On Friday afternoon, she was in town looking for a

second interview suit – she'd noted the raised eye-brows the woman in the fashion house had directed towards her conservative navy A-line skirt and plain jacket – when she came across an employment agency she hadn't seen before. It was situated above a fashion-retail outlet at the back of the Powerscourt Centre. There were two windows, one with the name *Lucinda O'Brien* written on it in gold letters, while the other read *Employment Bureau*. She went up the stairs and found herself in a modest one-roomed office. There were several filing cabinets, a telephone and an electric kettle, but no computers or any of the other essentials of a modern office.

Lucinda O'Brien was sixty-nine if she was a day, decided Anne Marie, but it appeared that she wasn't prepared to admit to the last three decades of her age. She was pencil-thin and contrived to show it by wearing a narrow skirt with a large belt. Her face had the bland smoothness of an egg, and her permed, white-blonde hair was artfully styled to cover any traces of the scalpel.

Lucinda O'Brien greeted Anne Marie with a brief smile and gestured her to a chair while she went through her CV. Noticing how she held the file, Anne Marie was convinced that she could make out very little of what was written in front of her. But vanity prevented the older woman from reaching for the glasses that were on the desk. She wore a lot of jewellery, including several heavy gold bracelets, and many rings on her fingers. But the backs of her hands were liver-spotted and trembled as she turned the pages. Anne Marie felt a sudden rush of pity for the pathetic creature who couldn't bear to grow old.

'I'm very good with computers,' she began. 'I know

all the software that's come out in the last few years. There's a copy of the reference I got from the director of the course in Tralee at the back, if you'd like to take a look at it.'

Lucinda O'Brien made a great show of turning to the last pages in the folder that Anne Marie had given her. 'Yes, yes. I can see you've got good qualifications all right. What about your typing skills – are they up to scratch? Do you know how to set out different kinds of business letter? Shorthand has gone, of course, but can you spell? So many girls nowadays can't. They expect a machine to do it for them.' She sighed and shook her head. 'I would have been mortified to send out a letter with a misspelling when I was a secretary,' she said. 'But some of the application letters I get are full of them. People just don't care any more.'

Anne Marie said she'd always been good at spelling. 'My father's an English teacher,' she explained, which seemed to reassure Lucinda O'Brien about Anne Marie's suitability for employment more than anything in her CV.

'Splendid! Splendid!' she said. 'I may just have something on my books for you. If you wouldn't mind going for a cup of coffee – there are lots of nice places in the Powerscourt Centre across the way, I'll see what I can do.'

Anne Marie turned at the top of the stairs in time to see the older woman put on her glasses and take up the folder once more. She didn't realistically expect anything to come of her unplanned visit to the Lucinda O'Brien Employment Bureau, but after half an hour, when she duly went back up to the little office on the first floor, to her surprise, Lucinda handed her a piece of paper with an address on it.

'Mr Desmond Dunne, the well-known property developer, is looking for a Personal Assistant. His office is in Fitzwilliam Square. You're to go for interview straight away. He's expecting you,' she said.

Dunne Investments was on the first floor of an ivy-covered house in Fitzwilliam Square whose door Anne Marie was sure she'd seen featured on a poster of Georgian Dublin. A languid receptionist buzzed her in and directed her through the glass doors to the stairway at the back of the hall.

There was nobody in the office marked *Reception* at the top of the stairs. The desk was bare except for a flip calendar of South Africa and an ashtray full of paper clips. The computer and other office equipment on a desk by the wall had dust covers on them. Anne Marie realised with a not unpleasant lurch that she was looking at what could be her office if she got the job. Immediately, she began to imagine the little touches that would make it cosy and reflect her personality. A spider plant on the shelf, a photograph on the desk, a picture or two on the walls . . .

A door at the back of the office opened. A large, handsome man whom Anne Marie judged to be in his late forties came out with his arm extended and a wide smile of welcome.

'Anne Marie, isn't it?' He took her hand and squeezed it in his massive one. 'Desmond Dunne. Come on in.' He held the door and stood back to allow her through. The office was a large sunlit room with three windows that looked out onto the square. She could feel her feet sinking into the plush carpet as she approached a huge leather-topped desk with a matching swivel chair that was probably the biggest she had ever seen.

'Sit down, sit down,' said Dunne, pointing to the chair facing the desk.

As he took his seat in the swivel chair Anne Marie examined him more closely. First impressions were important. He looked nice, she decided. For such a big man, he dressed well. Not that he was fat, but he had a rugby player's build – massive from the neck down – and such men often looked like gorillas when they were got up in suits. Dunne looked well in his. It was a restful shade of grey and the jacket fastened without straining the fabric, which looked soft and expensive. Under it he wore a white shirt and a grey tie with a discreet black design. It was clipped in place by a gold tie-pin. Anne Marie approved. She disliked flashy ties and bright shirts. Office wear should be conservative, she believed.

'Now, Anne Marie – we'll get down to business. Tell me, what part of the Kingdom are you from?'

'I grew up in Killorglin.'

'I knew it! I'm a thoroughbred Dub myself, but there's not many accents that I can't place. Killorglin – lovely town. I was at the Puck Fair a couple of years ago. Great bit of craic! You must enjoy it.'

'Actually, we nearly always go away around that time of year. It gets very crowded, like.'

'I see, I see. So – are you long in Dublin?'

'A week today.'

'Is that all? Well, well! Is this your first interview then?'

Anne Marie reddened. 'No, I've been to a few but the jobs didn't really appeal for one reason or another. And . . . I suppose, I wasn't suitable for some of them.'

She stopped. You weren't supposed to say things like that; you were supposed to sell yourself. Trouble was, she felt completely unprepared mentally for this interview. She was wearing the wrong clothes too: casual trousers and her boots.

She decided to be upfront and to hell with the consequences. 'I'm sorry, Mr Dunne. I wasn't expecting to have any interviews today, so I'm not dressed for the occasion or anything.'

Dunne smiled and shook his head. 'Never mind. I told Miss O'Brien I needed someone to start right away. She said you've got a good CV, plenty of summer jobs – I like that. I'd say you're a hard worker, aren't you?

'Well, yes. I—'

'Of course you are! I've never met a Kerry person who didn't know the value of hard work. And the value of money!' He winked at her. 'You're no exception, I see. Salary in excess of fifteen grand you're looking for, is that right?'

'I believe I'm worth it,' said Anne Marie, trying not to squirm in her seat. It had seemed like a lot starting out, but Seán had advised her not to sell herself cheaply. If she valued herself highly, other people would too, he had said.

'Oh, I'm not disputing that. If you're the right person for the job, you'll be earning far more in no time at all. But in order to find out if you *are* that person, I have to ask you a few questions about yourself. Is that all right?'

'Sure,' said Anne Marie. That was what an interview was about, wasn't it?

'Where do you stay in Dublin?'

'I'm in a flat in Rathmines.'

'On your own?'

'No, I'm sharing with my three cousins. They're students.'

'Oh.' He looked disappointed. 'The job would involve a fair bit of overtime, and possibly some travel. Would that be a problem?'

'No, not at all.'

'You've no . . . commitments, then?'

'Commitments?'

'Like a boyfriend. Fiancé.' Desmond Dunne grinned and winked at her again. 'I wouldn't want to deprive any man of your company. One of the best girls I ever had was doing a line when she started this job, but after she'd been a year at it your man broke with her. It was all my fault, apparently. For keeping her out too late at night and whisking her off to foreign parts at the drop of a hat.'

He neglected to mention that the woman in question was his current wife, and that lately he had begun to notice that she was becoming disconcertingly like the first one in the shrillness and frequency of her recriminations against him.

Anne Marie told him that she had no commitments that would prevent her from doing her job. He reached out his hand to shake hers and told her she had it.

Anne Marie was nonplussed. 'But don't you want to see my references? And I don't even know what the job is yet!'

Dunne apologised and said he'd assumed that Miss O'Brien had dealt with the practical details like references, job description and all of that. As far as he was concerned, she could start on Monday, he said.

After Anne Marie had left, Desmond Dunne rubbed his hands with glee. She was perfect! The size of her – almost as tall as himself! She'd look a bomb once she was dolled up. A good-looking PA was a great business asset; set her in front of a group of rivals and they'd be so busy looking at her legs they'd sign anything. He frowned. Her legs – he hadn't seen them. Tall girls often had disappointing legs – no shape to the calves, thick ankles. He hoped that wasn't the case with Anne Marie. The rest of her was fine – curves in all the right places. Her tits weren't that big, but they looked high and perky. They would fit neatly into his cupped hands. Desmond Dunne stood up and pulled at the darts in the trousers of his Louis Copeland suit. 'Down, boy!' he admonished. 'This one's going to take a lot of warming up!'

The Big Chill

Roz McDaid lay on her side at the edge of the queen-size bed in the house on the South Circular Road. Four feet away, her husband Stephen was lying with his back to her. She knew by the quality of his stillness that he wasn't asleep. It was the fourth night of the Big Chill that had turned the centre of the bed into a no-go area. Roz was close to tears. She hated it when he withdrew from her like this. Roz believed in talking through differences, in bringing everything out into the open. Being argumentative by nature, she dealt with problems by teasing and worrying at them until they surrendered. But that was not Stephen's way. 'There is nothing to discuss,' he would say, and retreat into wounded silence for up to a week at a time.

It didn't help that Roz knew she was in the wrong. She should have asked before giving away his bike. No matter that it had been gathering dust in the garage for eight years; she ought to have checked with him before getting rid of it. She'd said sorry. She'd even offered to get it back – only to find that someone had rubbed Anne Marie's number off the whiteboard before she'd had a chance to write it into her address book.

Roz thought back to the evening that had been the cause of all this and wished she wasn't so keen on sorting other people's lives out for them. A bike for Anne Marie, and possibly a job. Must be because I've made such a mess of my own, she sighed.

For some time now, Roz had felt that her life was off track. The trouble was, she had no idea why. It was a very good life in many ways, and she honestly didn't see how she could make it better. What aspects of her life would she change if she had the chance? Her job? No way – it was what kept her sane! She loved the magazine, her own position as Editor, the buzz of working with other creative people. She got to travel as much as she wanted, and she had interviewed lots of famous people that she admired. So, definitely not her job.

Her family? Roz crossed herself superstitiously and muttered a prayer for their safety before she allowed herself to think about what changes she would make if she could.

It wasn't hard. The twins: if only they weren't so wild. If only there was someone who knew how to control them. If only those aromatherapy oils had worked. Put a few drops in their bath, a mother at the school had advised; it'll calm them down. She could have drowned them in the stuff for all the good it did. They were unmanageable; she freely admitted it. It was some small consolation that even her mother-in-law had acknowledged herself beaten before the twins' second birthday. The old battleaxe had found that Good Old-fashioned Discipline was no more effective than aromatherapy in dealing with their high-spirited antics. Yes, if she could change the twins, make them more tractable – just a little, mind, not as extra-ordinarily good as Eleanor, for instance – she'd be happy.

Roz sighed inwardly. Three kids: how had that ever come about? She still found it hard to understand how she'd gone from her declared intention at the start of her career: 'maybe one child, at the last possible moment' to a family of three before she was thirty.

It was Stephen's fault, of course. Very soon after they'd moved in together he had persuaded her that their life would be made complete by a child, so they'd had Eleanor. Three years on, he'd pointed to the success of that enterprise and so, more reluctantly this time, Roz had given in. She'd been hoping for another girl, even though she ought to have known that Eleanor couldn't be repeated. On the other hand, she knew that a boy would please Stephen. But twins! She'd laughed, thinking the obstetrician was having her on. Seven years later, she wondered if she'd ever get over the shock.

At least there's no danger of any more, she thought as she surreptitiously pulled more of the duvet over to her side. Stephen had finally got the job done at the beginning of the summer. She smiled: the prospect of no nookie all the time they were on holiday in Kerry had put the skates under him. That was almost six months ago – soon they'd be able to give up using condoms altogether. Won't that be nice, thought Roz, and she turned to snuggle into her husband's back.

Then she remembered that they weren't talking. She hesitated. Sometimes he rebuffed her efforts at re-establishing friendly relations. Sometimes he fervently welcomed them. Which would it be? Tentatively, Roz reached her hand across the great divide and laid it on the small of Stephen's back. The springs groaned as her husband instantly rolled into the middle of the bed and enfolded her in his arms.

The eyes have it

Vera Meaney was first onto the minibus that was taking her home to Borris-in-Ossory for the weekend. She took off her dark glasses to greet Joe, the driver, who was reading a newspaper in the front passenger seat with his feet resting on the back of his own chair. He nodded and went back to his paper. Vera was disappointed. She'd been hoping it would be his brother Frank this weekend. Frank would have known about her adventure. He'd probably have put his hands to his own throat and gagged as she was getting onto the bus just to show that he'd heard all about it. She wondered if the rest of the regulars read the *Evening Echo*, then thought again how it was a shame that none of the other papers had sent reporters of their own to follow up the story. Naturally, RTÉ had covered Sylvester's suicide on Wednesday's 6:01 news, but the cameras had gone to the South Circular Road where he'd committed the murders instead of to Belvedere Square where he'd died.

Vera decided to sit nearer the front than she usually did. That way, everyone would have to pass her when they got onto the bus. All of Borris-in-Ossory would have heard, of course; her mother would have seen to that. Vera had rung as soon as the detective left on Monday so that her mother, who ran a newsagent's, would be able to tell all the customers as they came in the next day to be sure and get their copy of the paper. Vera thought she might offer to serve in the shop on Saturday, or maybe after Mass on Sunday. Usually she refused point-blank, telling her mother that she came home at the weekends for a rest, but this was different. People would want to see her. They'd be expecting her to relive the adventure for them. Vera experienced an anticipatory *frisson* as she pictured herself the centre of attention, describing how she had firmly but kindly fought off the unwelcome attentions of the lonely bachelor who had shared her landing. I always knew there was something odd about him, she would finish. You could see it in his eyes.

The Godfather

Brandon O'Kane knew there was no such thing as luck. Every single happening in the entire universe was the effect of a cause. Apparently random events became inevitable once you untwisted the strands – which often stretched back centuries – that led to their occurrence. Most people failed to understand this. They lived their lives entirely unaware of the far-reaching consequences of even the most insignificant act. Brandon, however, was acutely sensitive to the implications of cause and effect because he'd raised himself to a higher plane of consciousness. He even exerted a certain amount of control over events that were likely to impinge on his life.

Take the whole business with Anne Marie and Sylvester Reed. He'd approved of Anne Marie from the first, intuitively knowing that she was going to be good for the spirit of the house. After his first interview with her, he'd smoked his water-pipe a little and meditated.

Anne Marie's aura was healthy. Aquamarine predominated, showing that she was calm and reliable, but also imaginative. A tinge of yellow indicated optimism, and there was precisely the amount of red he would have expected for someone of her youth and energy. While he was meditating, however, the colours of Anne Marie's aura had begun to change. Something outside of her was blackening its outline. Sylvester Reed's face had floated before Brandon.

Sylvester, along with Vera Meaney, had been a sitting tenant when Brandon had bought the house four years previously. It had only taken one look at his aura, which was a sludgy brown-grey hue, for Brandon to want him out at once, but Sylvester had proved remarkably stubborn for someone who presented such a meek and inoffensive exterior.

When his face had come to interfere with Anne Marie's aura, Brandon had assumed it was doing just that – interfering – and had banished it. But when the image kept returning, Brandon had accepted that his unconscious was trying to tell him something and had concentrated on it instead. That was how he'd learnt that Sylvester had it in mind to harm Anne Marie. Brandon had been able to frustrate his intentions by using the full force of his powers to reinforce Anne Marie's aura. He'd concentrated until it had recovered its original sheen, then he'd reinforced it with an invisible shield of his own.

But even Brandon couldn't have predicted that his victory over Sylvester's dark side would result in his tenant's destruction. It was not something that Brandon would ever have willed, but the fact that it had come about in this way certainly was convenient. Brandon couldn't help feeling grateful to Anne Marie. Sweet child! He would have to continue to take an interest in her development. The Universe had clearly appointed him to the role of spiritual godfather whose duty was to watch over and guide Anne Marie as she took her first faltering steps towards enlightenment.

Designer doll

When Anne Marie arrived for work on her first day, she found the doorway to her office blocked by a rail with a dozen or more women's suits hanging on it. They all had labels from the top Irish fashion designers on them.

Desmond Dunne came out of his own office and welcomed her. He pointed to the clothes on the rail. 'Your uniform – pick three that you like and try them on. Don't worry if there's a problem with the size, that can be sorted out later.'

'But Mr Dunne, I can't afford designer clothes!' protested Anne Marie.

'I know you can't. Like I said, this is a uniform provided by the job. You'll need something a bit dressy for evening functions too, but let's start with the day wear. Come in and show me when you've got them on.' He went back into his office and closed the door.

Anne Marie was taken aback. She'd never heard of a boss providing designer clothes as a uniform before. Three outfits – that must be two thousand pounds' worth at least. But Mr Dunne was not someone you argued with; he'd made it clear at the interview on Friday that he expected her to look good, so if this was what he meant, she'd better go along with it.

She spent the next half an hour in the Ladies trying on all of the suits on the rail. How did he know her size, she wondered as she pulled the skirts up over her hips and found that they all fitted perfectly. However, some were a bit on the short side. Anne Marie was used to wearing trousers; having so much leg on view made her feel naked. In the end, she disregarded labels and style and chose the three outfits that had the longest skirts.

She wore the most sober of these, a black jersey Richard Lewis suit to show Dunne. He made her twirl round and walk the length of his office before he pronounced himself satisfied. 'What about the others?' he said.

Anne Marie brought them in and held them up. 'I thought this one for everyday wear,' she said, showing him a light grey worsted John Rocha, 'and the one I'm wearing for meetings as it's a bit more formal. Then this green Louise Kennedy one is kind of . . . I don't know, like for Fridays or something? I thought I should pick one light colour, just for contrast.'

Dunne nodded. 'Right you are. I'll have someone get rid of that yoke from your office as soon as I can. In the meantime, maybe you could go out and get something done with your hair?'

'My hair?' Anne Marie reached up and touched the

back of her head. Maybe her chignon had come undone while she was trying on the clothes. No, it was still in place.

'Could you not get it jizzed up a bit? Not that I'm criticising your style or anything, but it might be nice if you had a bit of – you know, a kink or something in it.' He waved his fingers at the side of his head to show what he meant.

'Oh. Sort of Julia Roberts, you mean?'

Dunne grinned. 'The very thing.'

Anne Marie was wondering if she had the courage to tell him that she rather liked her hair as it was when the phone on the desk rang. Dunne picked up the receiver and grunted into it. He cupped his hand over the mouthpiece and nodded at her.

'Take your time,' he said. 'I'll see you back here after lunch and we'll run through a few things together.' Then he swivelled sideways in his chair and resumed his conversation on the phone.

Back at the flat later in the evening, Anne Marie had trouble recognising her reflection each time she caught sight of it in the mirror. She looked like no one she knew. Everyone around her seemed to approve of the change, however. When she had come back from the hairdresser's, Dunne had told her she looked smashing. Funnily enough, it was her legs he'd been looking at as he said it. When she got home, Cornelius declared that he didn't care what anyone said; now she definitely could be a supermodel. Darina was less admiring, but she did go so far as to say that Anne Marie no longer looked like a country lass, which her cousin assumed was intended as a compliment. Surprisingly, of all the cousins it was Gerald who seemed least enthusiastic about the change in her appearance. He agreed that she looked very sophisticated, but she could tell that he preferred her as she was before.

This would not have bothered Anne Marie so much if she hadn't been feeling something similar herself.

Party plans

It was Gerald's idea to have a party. 'How about it? Start the academic year with a bang,' he said to Darina one evening about ten days after Anne Marie's arrival.

'What's there to celebrate?' Darina wanted to know.

'Well, we passed the repeats – scraped through in my case – that's one thing. Anne Marie's presence in our midst–'

'I thought we'd already celebrated that.'

'All right then,' said Gerald, who was beginning to be irked by his sister's attitude to their cousin, 'we could celebrate the fact that she got through the ordeal of finding a murderer dead in his bed upstairs without flipping her lid. Or have you an objection to that too?'

Startled, Darina looked across at him. Anne Marie was a minor source of irritation, no more. A quick examination of her conscience told her that she might have been less than welcoming to her cousin, but she hadn't expected to be taken to task for it by Gerry. He was her ally, always had been. At that moment, she really did feel a stab of jealousy. No way was Anne Marie going to come between them!

She forced herself to smile and said that she'd certainly be on for a party at Hallowe'en. 'Were you thinking of fancy dress?' she asked.

'Could do. Let's wait and see what the others say,' said Gerald. 'I saw Anne Marie carrying her bike up the steps a minute ago. Con is studying, but he'll be in for his tea as soon as he hears her.'

Darina sniggered. 'Puppy love, eh? I wonder does Anne Marie mind.'

'I'm not sure she notices,' said Gerald, who had seen nothing odd in Cornelius's attachment to their cousin.

Anne Marie was definitely in favour of the idea. 'A party – great! Can we dress up?' Her eyes were bright with excitement.

'Postman's Knock and Rice Krispie buns too, if you like,' said Darina before she could stop herself.

'Hallowe'en? I'll be going home that weekend,' said Cornelius. 'But that's OK, I'm not so fond of parties anyway.' He turned to his brother. 'I hope you were planning to ask Brandon for permission first?'

'*Naturellement*. We'll invite all the residents. And yes, I think it should be fancy dress. Brandon could come as one of his previous incarnations – the can-can dancer, that'd be a good one! What's-her-name from Borris-in-Ossory could be . . . could be . . .'

'Herself,' said Darina. 'Have you seen the way she dresses? She must make her own clothes – you'd never find anything so awful in the shops. The other day I saw her going out in a suit made from a pair of curtains. I swear it's true – it was the same pattern as in the bathroom of the house in Ringsend. Remember? Lime with orange flowers. And she had green shoes to match. The amazing thing is, she thinks she's gorgeous!'

'What about you with your dingy skirts and big clumping boots?' said Cornelius. 'What do you think you look like?'

Darina was startled. Cornelius had never commented on her appearance before. Not that she'd put any *meas* on his opinion, but it rankled all the same. Lots of students dressed the way she did; it was ridiculous to compare her to the Meaney one upstairs.

'How about a theme party?' Anne Marie broke in hurriedly. 'Black and White, or maybe Famous People in History?' She had been to a party like that when she was ten. She'd wanted to go as Marie Antoinette with a wig and beauty spots, but her mother had persuaded her that she'd be better as Grace O'Malley, the pirate queen. She had worn a scratchy woollen blanket and a belt with a real dagger that all the boys had wanted to unsheath.

'Yeah, a theme's a good idea,' said Gerald. 'That way you know at once who the crashers are. Let's do a revival – we could have the music to go with the era. Who's got a favourite decade?'

'Not the sixties, please,' said Darina. 'They've been done to death.'

'How about the seventies?' said Gerald. 'There's lots of good music and the clothes are sort of back in fashion, aren't they? For women anyway. You know, platforms and flares – that sort of thing.'

'Or we could go way back,' said Anne Marie. 'They do a Roaring Twenties festival in Killarney every year. We went last year – it was a great bit of gas.'

'Flappers and jazz? No, thanks!' said Darina.

Nobody knew much about the decades in between. By default, the 1970s won.

'LSD, bell-bottoms and Horslips,' said Gerald. 'Way to go!'

Caelinn Largey

Chocolate Sensation

Jacqui Dunne parked her BMW on the west side of Fitzwilliam Square and took a compact from her Gucci handbag. She adjusted the rear-view mirror so that she could see her face in it and began to dust powder lightly over her cheeks. She had applied her make-up with particular care this morning but after the drive in from Meath, there was a slight sheen to her complexion that made her look as though she'd been exercising. She repaired the damage and freshened her lipstick, then checked herself from every angle. Was her chin beginning to sag again? Surely not! It was only six months since she'd had it done. Her man was the best in Dublin; he'd guaranteed her it would last several years. Must be a trick of the light.

Jacqui Dunne was a handsome woman. That was how she'd been described in the society pages of a woman's magazine recently. Handsome: funny how the word was different when it was applied to a woman. It didn't just mean good-looking, like for a man. It meant you were big, but carried yourself well. Jacqui wasn't sure whether to regard it as a compliment or not. Not like Junoesque. If ever she was called that, she'd kill herself. Or better still, the person who said it.

My legs are still as good as ever, thought Jacqui as she stepped out of the car. Well, maybe a bit beefy at the top, but who's to know? The parts on view are what count. She wished she could see herself from the back. High heels and sheer tights showing off her shapely calves, and the bulges round her middle out of sight. Today she was wearing an elegant Jen Kelly outfit that made the most of her assets while cleverly playing down the bits she was not so proud of. Her shoes were Italian, with heels that added four inches to her already significant height. Yes, she felt more than ready to deal with the latest threat, this kid from Killorglin who was barely out of nappies. What was her name? Anne Marie Something-or-other. Jacqui opened her Gucci bag again and took out an envelope. Inside was a white card with ten lines of print on it. Ten lines that had cost Jacqui three hundred and fifty pounds to acquire. She considered it money well spent. Elliot – that was it: Anne Marie Elliot.

Anne Marie was typing from a dictaphone when the visitor arrived. The receptionist downstairs hadn't phoned up to announce anyone, so the sudden appearance in Anne Marie's office of a large imposing woman with a mane of carefully coiffed chestnut hair came as something of a shock. Anne Marie hurriedly took off her earphones and stood up.

'Hello, may I help you?' she said, trying in vain not to appear as flustered as she felt.

Jacqui waved a hand regally and headed towards her husband's office. 'Carry on,' she said. 'I just need to see Des for a moment. I'm Jacqui, his wife.'

Anne Marie relaxed at once. She held out her hand and smiled. 'Mrs Dunne! How nice to meet you. I'm afraid Mr Dunne isn't in at the moment. He's at a meeting, but he's due back at half-past twelve. Would you like to wait in his office? I could bring you a cup of coffee. Oh, I'm sorry – I'm Anne Marie, the new secretary.'

Jacqui Dunne took her hand and pressed it lightly. 'Anne Marie, a pleasure. How silly of me – of course, Des told me he wouldn't be in the office this morning. I was on my way to Magills to pick up some truffles –

we're entertaining tomorrow – but I suppose I have got time for a coffee. Let me just check.'

Jacqui made a show of consulting her watch, a diamond-encrusted Cartier that had cost as much as her BMW. She would take it off her wrist and hide it on a chain round her neck as soon as she left. The watch was part of her contingency plan: if the worst came to the worst – which Jacqui was doing her best to ensure never happened – this watch, along with many other expensive pieces of jewellery she had acquired over the last fifteen years, would help keep her moderately well off for the rest of her life.

Having decided that she did have time for 'a quick cup' Jacqui sat herself in one of the armchairs that formed a circle round a low table in her husband's office. This was where he conducted informal meetings – the ones where his clients didn't realise they were being screwed, reflected Jacqui with a smile. While Anne Marie made coffee, Jacqui surveyed the scene of her former glory. That desk . . . if it could talk! How long had she been working for Des before they'd ended up on it? Fifteen minutes, maybe? She'd known at the interview, of course. He'd been far less interested in her secretarial skills than in her other attributes – tits and legs mainly – which Jacqui had then helpfully contrived to allow him to glimpse.

Possessing neither the capacity nor the desire to go into business for herself, Jacqui had long ago decided that the shortest route to the lifestyle she wanted was marriage to a wealthy man. She was twenty-five and aware that her assets wouldn't last for ever. By the time Desmond Dunne's eyes had fastened onto her breasts, Jacqui's sights had already been fixed on the mansion in which they now lived.

It was ironic that the price she'd had to pay for achieving her goal was her consent that it could all end very quickly. Dunne's divorce from his first wife had been bitter, messy and expensive – so she would understand why he was asking her to sign a pre-nuptial agreement, wouldn't she? Smiling, he had handed her a pen, just before they'd left their Palm Springs hotel for the wedding ceremony. Jacqui had understood only too well. It didn't matter that divorce was not yet legal in Ireland – that hadn't prevented the ending of his first marriage – and Jacqui had no faith in lawyers. She understood from the start that what her husband wanted, he got. If he were to decide that it was time to trade her in for a younger model, she would be history, courts or no courts.

In order to put off the evil day for as long as possible, Jacqui had quietly gone about making certain that no gold-digging little trollop would ever repeat her story. The private detective she employed was discreet and efficient. If her husband sometimes wondered why Jacqui's better-looking successors lasted no more than a few months, he never said. And it was simply amazing the dirt you could dig up on people when you wanted. All those skeletons tucked away in closets; Jacqui had quickly learnt that everyone, but everyone, had something to hide.

Anne Marie brought in a tray and set cups, milk-jug, sugar-bowl and a pot of freshly-brewed coffee on the table. She sat down opposite her boss's wife and poured for them both. Mrs Dunne refused sugar, using two Sweet 'n' Low that she took from a tiny gold box in her handbag instead. She asked if the milk was reduced fat and, when it wasn't, opted to take her coffee black. So why, Anne Marie wondered, did she then eat two of the Snack Fingers that Anne Marie had bought for her elevenses?

But Mrs Dunne was nice, decided Anne Marie. For the first few minutes the boss's wife quizzed her about all sorts of things including what her long-term goals were – something that Anne Marie hadn't even begun to consider – but after that she relaxed. She insisted that Anne Marie call her Jacqui and chatted in a friendly manner about her children, their house overlooking the River Boyne and the difficulty she'd had in getting good caterers for tomorrow night's dinner-party.

Although it was well after twelve when she got up to leave, Jacqui declined to wait the extra few minutes for her husband. If anything, she now seemed anxious to be gone before he arrived. At the door, she stopped and confided in Anne Marie that she'd rather Mr Dunne didn't hear about her visit. He'd just think she was silly to have forgotten that he wasn't going to be in his office when he'd told her only yesterday that he would be out at a meeting all morning.

Then why did she come – just to get a look at me? Anne Marie, who was not entirely gullible, guessed that Jacqui had planned her visit deliberately to coincide with her husband's absence from the office. But the idea that she was the object of the exercise seemed too preposterous to entertain. Shaking her head at the incomprehensibility of it all, Anne Marie put on her earphones and resumed her interrupted letter-writing.

Jacqui returned to her car in rare good humour. Anne Marie was wonderful! A complete innocent! Surprising that Des had even considered her. She was pretty enough in an insipid sort of a way, and very tall – which she knew he liked – but the girl had zero sex appeal. The designer suit was wasted on her; she wore it as though it was on temporary loan and she was afraid to crease it. Was her husband losing his touch? Or was he so bored that he felt he needed a challenge? Anne Marie was certainly a new departure. Maybe the tarts he brought to the Baggot Street apartment satisfied his needs so that he didn't have to have it permanently on tap in the office any more. Well and good! Jacqui was more than happy to turn a blind eye to the procession of exotic call-girls – about which she kept herself well-informed – if it meant that her husband was less likely to fall into the clutches of a younger version of herself at the office.

It was a huge relief for Jacqui to know that she didn't have to worry about Anne Marie. As she got older and her waistline grew thicker, Jacqui found she was becoming increasingly insecure about her hold on her husband. They'd stopped having sex years ago, by unspoken mutual consent, and lived more or less separate lives most of the time. It was a relatively harmonious arrangement, except when Jacqui allowed her fears to get the better of her and gave her husband the third degree about his involvement with other women. He retaliated by pointing out that she was turning into a lump of blubber in spite of the fact that they had an indoor swimming pool, a sauna, a gym and acres of grounds to walk in right outside the door. He himself swam, lifted weights and jogged every day that he was at home, he reminded her, while she sat on her fat arse and ate chocolates.

Having concluded that she could spare herself the

expense of sending her private detective down to Kerry to check up further on Anne Marie, Jacqui felt she was entitled to a little treat. Bewley's? Their handmade chocolates weren't bad. She'd been very good for almost a week – just one teensy-weensy little *torte* in the new café in Slane – and those two Snacks just now. Cheap, nasty chocolate – she shouldn't have bothered – but when they were there in front of her it was so hard to resist. The craving for the real thing grew as she drove round Stephen's Green looking for a parking space. Lir had nice stuff too. But what she really fancied was a box of Butler's truffles, obviously as a result of what she'd invented when she was talking to Anne Marie. What were the other kind of truffles anyway? Some sort of expensive nuts? Edible acorns? Pigs liked them, she knew that much.

Fortune continued to smile on Jacqui as she turned into South King Street and a car pulled out at the far end of the street. She nipped into the parking space and smiled to herself as she took her ticket from the Pay and Display. What a good day this was turning out to be!

Anticipation of the pleasure ahead lit up Jacqui's face as she strode past the Gaiety. A senior executive from Eircom on his way back to the office stepped aside to let her pass. The sight of her flushed cheeks, parted lips and sparkling eyes made him wish with gut-wrenching fervour that she was what he went home to at night. But Jacqui was oblivious to her effect on him and on the several other, younger men who cast approving glances in her direction as she reached Grafton Street and made straight for Butler's Chocolate Café.

The moment of supreme delight was at hand and it had nothing to do with sex.

The Man for the Park

Desmond Dunne had also had a good day. Driving home to Meath that evening, he smiled to himself as he thought back on some of its highlights. He'd made a killing on an investment in Beirut – a 400 per cent increase on shares he'd bought in a construction company fifteen years ago when the war was at its height. He would put it into more property; not in Ireland – he had enough trouble concealing the holdings he already had from the Revenue Commissioners, but there were plenty of other places he could buy. Hong Kong, for instance. He already had money there, looked after by a businessman with an outlook and needs similar to his own. Dunne had helped him purchase a castle in the Midlands; your man was due over next month to look at it and see a firm of architects about its conversion to a luxury hotel. He himself would have to make the journey to Hong Kong at some stage – and Anne Marie would come along too.

The thought of Anne Marie accompanying him on a trip abroad caused his heart to flutter. Must be getting soft in my old age, he thought. She was a lovely girl all right, the sort any man would be proud to have as a daughter. Not that he'd want her for his daughter, mind, because then he couldn't have those other feelings for her. He grinned. She'd been so sweet this afternoon when he'd come back, blushing and avoiding his eyes while she said no, there'd been no messages while he was out. Dunne had only to open the door of his office to know that his wife had been on the prowl again. The room still reeked of her Chanel No. 5.

It amused Dunne no end that Jacqui was terrified he would abandon her for a younger woman. The truth was, he never made the same mistake twice. And why would he be tempted to change the current set-up? Didn't he have the best of all possible worlds? The wife in her big house in the country, and he with his bachelor pad in town where he did what he liked. Nor did it bother him that Jacqui was responsible for the abrupt departure of several of his PAs; the girls quickly lost their novelty value so his wife was actually doing him a favour by getting rid of them before he had to find a reason for doing it himself.

He wondered what Jacqui had made of Anne Marie. She was different. Younger than the others and not as sexy. Funnily enough, that was part of the attraction. He liked her air of innocence, the way you could tell that she was incapable of hiding anything. She made him think of simple things: baby soap, April skies, skipping games. Maybe she was a virgin. If she was, he could be her first! At this thought, his trousers bulged once again. 'Jaysus, it's like being sixteen again!' he exclaimed as he accelerated to overtake a line of cars stuck behind a tractor on the narrow road outside Ashbourne.

By the time he reached home, Desmond Dunne's good feeling about himself, his financial affairs and life in general had given rise to an extraordinary ambition – to be the next president of Ireland.

When he went into the living room, he found his daughter Tiffany lounging on the couch. She was watching television and chewing bubble-gum. 'How would you like to live in the Phoenix Park?' he said, tweaking her hair as he passed the couch and picked up the remote control.

'Ow, stop it, Daddy,' she said, then: 'Hey, what are you doing? I was watching *Buffy*. Turn it back!'

'Not on your nelly! You've homework to do, haven't you? And I bet your room's a mess.'

'Our teacher's out sick, so I don't have any new homework for tomorrow. And we pay someone to clean the house, don't we? So what's the point of me having to tidy my room. You don't clean yours, do you?'

'Less of your lip, Missy, or you might find yourself living in the Phoenix Park for real – under the trees! Now git – I want to watch the news. You've got your own TV, haven't you? Go and watch that.'

Tiffany slouched off, muttering about tyrants.

Dunne was in such an expansive mood that he even told his wife about his dream. 'Well, why not?' he said over the chicken chasseur dinner she had prepared herself, as though to compensate for the fact that she had been spying on his latest employee. 'I'm a success-ful businessman, pillar of the establishment and all that crap. And a fine figure of a man to boot! The cameras would love me. Just you wait and see – people will have had enough of the Marys by the time this one's term is up. She'll get out if she's any sense at all. I think I'll be in with a very good chance indeed.'

'Don't you have to have done some sort of community service to run for president? And be nominated?'

'Yeah – so? There's still a few years left to get in with the County Councils, open parks, kiss babies and all the rest of it. No problem there.'

'What about your private life? Nobody would nominate you if they knew the truth about that!'

Dunne scowled. 'What's the matter with you? Don't you want to be First Lady? My private life is neither here nor there. All you have to do is smile and keep your mouth shut. Look at Clinton, for Jaysus's sake.'

First Lady! Jacqui lay in bed that night saying the words to herself. Oh yes! She could see herself in that role all right. 'Good evening, President Clinton. So nice to meet you. And Bill. It's a pleasure to welcome you once again to *Áras an Uachtaráin* . . . Yes, I have made some changes since you were here last. It was all rather dull when I arrived. A bit of colour to liven it up, I thought . . . Thank you, yes – I suppose it does say a lot about my personality . . . It was lucky for you, Hillary, that you had taken care of the alterations in the White House when Bill was president . . . it must have felt like coming home. Perhaps I could show you the rest of *Áras an Uachtaráin* later on; the master bedroom is particularly impressive, if I say so myself . . .'

Noodle soup

It was only the second week of term but already Darina was fed up. University was turning out to be far more like school than she had bargained for. She had told herself that her second year would be better than her first, when she had switched halfway through the year from Irish to French. She had had to work harder than she liked just in order to scrape a pass in the exams.

But so far, being a Senior Freshman was no more exciting than being a Junior Freshman. Russian was still too much of a slog to be enjoyable. Having discovered Dostoevsky at sixteen, Darina had decided there and then that she would one day read *Crime and Punishment* in the original. Further reading of the Russian classics had confirmed her love of the literature, but it was taking longer than she had imagined for her to become proficient enough to read novels without having to stop and look up every second word.

But at least she still had her love of Russian to sustain her. French was different. Already, Darina regretted her change of subject. Thanks to years of family holidays in France, she was fluent in the language. She had hoped to shine without much effort, but to her dismay she found that nothing about the course stimulated her. And for Darina, boredom was lethal.

But quite apart from the academic side of things, Darina was deeply disappointed by college life in general. Where were the exciting people she had hoped to meet? What had happened to her visions of passionate late-night discussions with some of the great brains of the land? All she had encountered up to now was mediocre teaching and smug fellow students focused on the lucrative jobs they would walk into when they had completed their courses. And she had yet to see a single male who took her fancy.

So it was that, disgruntled with life in general and finding herself with a few free hours, Darina turned her back on the Lecky Library where she ought to have been researching an essay on Simone de Beauvoir and headed back to Rathmines late on the Thursday morning. She had picked up a new Liza Cody crime novel in Oxfam the other day and was looking forward to stretching out on the couch with a cup of coffee and a fag. Her enjoyment of the moment would be heightened by the knowledge that everyone else in the house was out working or at lectures.

But when she got home, she found Gerald lying on the couch in the living room.

'What are you doing, skiving off lectures?' she asked with mock severity. 'A bit early in the term for that, isn't it? I thought you were turning over a new leaf after your miraculous pass in the repeats.'

'No, this is legit. My nine o'clock was cancelled, but I'm going in for the afternoon. I thought I'd have a bite of lunch first. Are you hungry? I'll do us some noodles if you like.'

'Yeah, sure.'

Darina dropped onto the couch and took out her cigarettes.

'Did you hear that we're not being allowed to smoke in the kitchen any more?' said Gerald on his way out the door.

'I did not. Who says so, anyway – Brandon?'

'No, Con and Anne Marie. Well, Con mainly, but he's got Anne Marie's full support, he says. I suppose he has a point, and now he can't be out-voted any more.'

Darina shrugged. Gerald, who'd been expecting an outburst, looked at his sister in surprise. 'What's the matter, Dar? You seem a bit down in the dumps. Is anything wrong?'

'Oh, just life,' his sister said with a sigh.

'Want to talk about it?'

'Nothing to tell. No money, no boyfriend, and college sucks. That's about it.'

'You too? I thought it was just me. Except for the boyfriend bit.'

'God, and this is only Michaelmas term.'

'Maybe Anne Marie has the right idea; a mere fortnight in the city and she's got a plum job, new clothes, the lot. There's times when I wouldn't mind swapping this student lark for a nine to five and plenty of money in my pockets.'

'But that's what's waiting for you after you've got your Economics degree. All you have to do is pass your exams for the next couple of years.'

Gerald made a face. 'Exactly.' He pointed towards the hall. 'Right, I'm going to see about those noodles.'

Waiting for the water to boil, Gerald reflected ruefully that exams were the least of his worries. Unfortunately, his troubles had nothing to do with his academic performance. The kettle gurgled and switched itself off. As he poured the boiling water over the bowl of Magi-noodles, Gerald's hand shook.

He was in deep shit and could see no way out.

Homeward Bound

After she had been working for a week, Anne Marie decided it was time to take a trip home. She told herself she was going because her parents would be dying to hear all about her new job, and of course, to see for themselves that she had not been permanently traumatised by the events surrounding Sylvester's death.

The real reason was that she could not wait to see them again. So much had happened since she had made the journey in reverse that she could scarcely believe it was only a fortnight since she had left home for the capital. Seán would put his arms around her and ask her gently if she wanted to talk about the terrible experience with Sylvester. She did. She wanted to relive it one more time for them, then put it out of her mind for ever. Yvonne would listen without asking questions. She was not your typical mother; she didn't fuss and never intruded into Anne Marie's life. But Anne Marie knew that her mother was there for her if she needed her, always.

The train from Dublin was crowded. Anne Marie sat beside the window, next to a teenage boy whose leg frequently knocked accidentally-on-purpose against her own. Opposite Anne Marie was a nun dressed in civvies who smiled sweetly at her every time she caught her eye.

Anne Marie took out her book, a fat paperback that demanded little mental effort. She read steadily until Limerick Junction, where the longer than usual stop broke her concentration. Excusing herself, she left the carriage and went to get a cup of tea, which she drank standing up in the restaurant car. She waited until the train had started up again to return to her seat, but once she had squeezed past the unobliging boy to her place by the window, she found it impossible to get back into the story that had held her interest since Dublin. To discourage the nun from starting up a conversation with her, however, she kept the book open in front of her as she allowed her mind to wander.

Was Dublin everything she had hoped it would be? Anne Marie recalled the dreams she had had before leaving home and matched them against the reality. In many ways, things had turned out better than she had hoped. Her job was far better paid than she had expected, and Mr Dunne was lovely to have as a boss.

The cousins' flat was very comfortable, and the rent was reasonable. She would be able to save most of her salary and pretty soon she would have enough to be able to rent a place of her own, if she wished.

In that case, why was she so happy to be going home to Kerry? Why did she feel that something was missing in her new life? She'd got what she wanted, hadn't she? And if what she had was not what she wanted, then what did she want? Words from the book her parents had given her came to mind. She had read it so many times now that she knew it off by heart.

> *You'll get mixed up of course,*
> *as you already know.*
> *You'll get mixed up*
> *with many strange birds as you go.*
> *So be sure when you step.*
> *Step with care and great tact*
> *and remember that Life's*
> *a Great Balancing Act.*

She had got mixed up with strange birds all right. Sylvester was one, Brandon another. It was reassuring to know that according to Dr Seuss, it was normal to feel mixed up and fearful when you were starting out on your own. And to be told that in spite of all the hurdles, you would succeed. *(98 and ¾ per cent guaranteed!)*

When the train pulled into the station in Killarney, her parents were on the platform. Yvonne had spotted her at the window as the train pulled in and raised a hand in greeting. Seán opened the door and waited impatiently for the other passengers to alight. When Anne Marie appeared, he stood back in mock

115

astonishment. 'But who ees zis?' he said in a put-on French accent. 'She ees so glamorous! She must be a film star! I take you straightaway to your hotel, Mademoiselle!'

Anne Marie laughed and stepped into his embrace.

Yvonne smiled, gave her daughter a quick hug and picked up her bag. 'We're parked up the town. Are you hungry? Seán was going to prepare a light supper for you at home, but if you'd prefer, we could have dinner here in Killarney instead. What do you think?'

'Let's go straight home!'

Seán could not get over how changed she was. He told her she looked a million dollars and that he really had thought for a second that she was some Hollywood film star when he saw her in the train. Yvonne said that the new hairstyle and colour made her look very sophisticated, all right, but Anne Marie noticed that her mother kept stealing thoughtful glances at her that suggested she might not entirely approve of the change.

Her friend Maggie was less reticent. 'God, Anne Marie, what on earth have you done to yourself?' she exclaimed when she opened the door to her on Saturday morning. 'I mean, you look fantastic and all, but I just can't believe it's you!' She pulled a mesh of Anne Marie's hair and let it spring back into place. 'Great colour too; blonde really suits you.'

Later, when they were sitting in Natterjack's café sharing a pot of tea, Maggie turned to her friend. 'What did I tell you, girl?' she said accusingly. 'Didn't I say that you were going to turn into a city slicker? Now, was I right, or wasn't I? Mind you, I didn't expect it to happen so soon. Sure you're hardly a wet day gone! I'm left wondering what else has been going on up in the Big Smoke. What have you been getting up to, girl? Who's all the blonde bombshell bit for anyway? Out with it! I want a name and a full description, please.'

'Don't be silly, there's nobody.'

'Then why have you gone red all of a sudden? C'mon, tell me!'

'Maggie! There isn't anyone, I swear. You said it yourself: I've only been gone a fortnight. What do you expect? I'm still the same old Anne Marie, you know. I'm hardly going to grab the first man I come across, am I?'

'Well, I suppose you always were a bit of a wallflower. I just thought . . . well, never mind. Tell me about this new job instead. What's the boss like? Is he young? Handsome? Available?'

'Maggie!'

Anne Marie was relieved to be able to talk about the safe topic of her PA job. There was nothing to tell her friend on the romantic scene, and she certainly didn't want to discuss the Sylvester tragedy. Discretion was not Maggie's best point; in fact it didn't come into her make-up at all. She would have it broadcast around the town in minutes that Anne Marie had found the body of a serial killer in her house in Dublin. It was bad enough being recognised as the daughter of two teachers in the local school; if word got out about that gruesome incident, Anne Marie's notoriety would know no bounds.

Going home later that day, Anne Marie reflected that in spite of her protestations to Maggie, she had changed since leaving the town. Maybe it was because she was now a visitor in Killorglin that she noticed things she had never noticed before. How inward-looking people were, for instance. Even her best friend was not immune to the small-town mentality. She was far more interested in relaying the latest local gossip than in hearing about anything that happened as far away as Dublin. When Anne Marie had tried to tell Maggie about Brandon, thinking that her account of the landlord's quirks and esoteric beliefs would make her friend laugh, Maggie had instead grown impatient and eventually interrupted Anne Marie with the news that she had picked out the dress that she intended getting married in whenever Packy, her childhood sweetheart, got around to popping the question.

Rock 'n' roll chick

That night, Seán opened a bottle of champagne to celebrate Anne Marie's job success.

Over dinner, she regaled her parents with tales of her first two weeks away from home. The previous night had been spent talking about Sylvester's suicide, so she still had plenty to tell. Unlike Maggie, they were interested in everything, particularly her relationship with Brandon. He had taken her under his wing, she explained to them, because they were both Number Nine on the Eanneagram. Seán couldn't help wondering whether his interest in Anne Marie was more than spiritual, but she laughed and repeated Brandon's words of reassurance to her: 'Like an angel, I am a non-sexual being.'

After dinner, Seán took out his collection of 1970s LPs and his old record player. Anne Marie had told them about the cousins' forthcoming Hallowe'en theme party and he was thrilled to have an excuse to revisit what he referred to as his 'glory years'. He pulled Anne Marie onto the floor and for the best part of an hour, they danced to the music of Supertramp, Pink Floyd, The Rolling Stones, Queen and The Eagles. Then Yvonne came into the room from the kitchen, where she had been washing up. Lifting the needle from the record, she substituted her own choice.

'Oh no, it's the Sound Police!' Seán said, putting his arms around her from behind. 'What's wrong, Officer – don't you like my taste in music?'

'What taste? You never had any!' Yvonne twisted round and kissed him on the lips. The doleful voice of Leonard Cohen began to issue from the speakers. Holding Seán's hand, Yvonne shuffled backwards into the centre of the floor and began to slow dance with him.

Anne Marie flopped on to the couch and watched them. They were holding each other close, resting their heads on each other's shoulders. Seán, who was a good two inches shorter than Yvonne, had his arms around her waist, while she had hers clasped behind his neck. Gerald's words in the pub came back to her. She could see what he meant; it was odd the way her parents still behaved as though they had just met. It had never bothered her as she was growing up, but now that she was no longer living under the same roof, it felt uncomfortable. She didn't like being excluded, and it troubled her that her parents were behaving just as they would have if she hadn't been there.

Seán must have guessed her thoughts because he

suddenly smiled down at her and held out one hand. Yvonne too, turned and held out her hand. Shyly, Anne Marie got up from the couch and went to join them. As they swayed together to 'So Long, Marianne', Anne Marie was overwhelmed by mingled feelings of happiness and sorrow. Her first departure had been in the nature of an adventure; she had felt a little sad, yes, but also excited at the prospect of the new life ahead. In her heart, she still belonged here at home.

Now, only two short weeks later, she was part of that new life. Her eyes stung with the effort of holding back the tears as she realised that from now on, she would return to this house only as a visitor. When she left tomorrow, she would be leaving behind her childhood.

Sweet Dreams Are Made of These

Oscar Bari was dreaming. Leaning on the back of a chair in the Café Firenze during a lull in business, he stared unseeingly through the window and imagined himself in a field of clover. Around him, the gentle hum of bees gathering nectar was a pleasant augur of the rich, dark honey he would soon be harvesting.

For as long as he could remember, Oscar had loved bees. High in the tower block of his windy northern-English hometown, he had fed his passion with books from the library and videotapes from the National Geographic and the Bee Research Association. That had kept him going until summertime, when he and his family made the annual trip to the small Tuscan village where his father had been born. It was there that Oscar's grandfather had first introduced him to the wonderful world of the bee.

'What is the most useful animal in the world?' the old man had asked him one day. They were walking in the meadow above the farm that Oscar's father confusingly called home, even though they only came to it for a holiday.

'The cow,' four-year-old Oscar had replied.

'Oh, the cow is very useful all right,' agreed his grandfather. 'She gives us milk. And cream and cheese. But if she was not there, would we die? No! We could get milk from the goat or the sheep, could we not? No, the most useful animal in the world is much smaller than the cow. Try again.'

'The rabbit?' Oscar suggested, thinking of the appetising stew that his grandmother had made the day before from a pair of rabbits snared by one of his big cousins.

'No, smaller still.'

Oscar couldn't guess. His grandfather sat down and made him lie beside him in the warm meadow grass.

'Close your eyes. Now, what do you hear?'

Nothing, thought Oscar. But he didn't want to disappoint his grandfather, so he lay still and began to concentrate. The grass made no sound, because there was no wind. There was a bird singing, but it was far away in the trees. Nearer to him, he could hear nothing. Except insects. But insects weren't useful to people. Nasty creepy-crawlies and buzzy flying things. Some of them had stings that really hurt. Once he'd been stung by a wasp in a park. Wasps weren't nice. They didn't make honey like—. In a flash, the answer came to him.

He sat up. 'Bees! It's bees, Grandad, isn't it?'

'That's right, *carissimo*. The little bee is the most useful creature in the whole world. And do you know why?'

His grandfather explained to him that honey was just one of the many useful substances that bees provided. There was also wax, for making candles and polishing furniture, and propolis, a kind of glue that bees made from the sap of trees and was good for fighting germs. And what about honeycomb? Had he ever broken off a piece of honeycomb and eaten it straight from the hive? No? Well, he would soon. And royal jelly – did he know that it was a superfood given to the future queen bee to make her big and strong? He could eat it, too – it would help him survive the winters in that far, cold place his father had taken him to.

Oscar listened, entranced. The bee that to him had been a striped, flying menace was shown to be a gentle, hard-working creature without which many of the earth's other inhabitants would not survive.

'If the bees didn't carry pollen from one flower to another,' said his grandfather, 'there would be no new plants and trees. You wouldn't have the almonds, apricots and cherries you love to eat when you come here. Many of the vegetables which you will one day learn to like also need the little bee to help them make seeds that we can plant again.'

'But if bees are good, why do they sting?'

'They only sting to defend themselves or their hive. And a bee-sting is not so bad. It hurts a little, but sometimes a little hurt can prevent a big one. When Grandmama gets pain in her joints, I put some bees on the back of her hand and let them sting her. That makes her feel better.'

*

The door opened and a couple of cashiers from the local supermarket came in. With a sigh, Oscar returned to the present. He took a cloth and began to wipe the espresso machine while they debated whether to have tiramisu or Black Forest gateau with their cappuccinos.

Life was never as simple as you imagined when you were a child, thought Oscar sadly. He had always planned that he would return one day as a beekeeper to the village where his grandfather and all the generations before him had lived and died. Like many exiles, he had idealised the simple life of the home country. But when he had returned for the funeral of the old man three years earlier, he'd been shocked by the changes. One of his cousins had sold the meadow above the village to a property developer. It was now covered with holiday chalets and apartment blocks. The bees had gone.

Oscar's dream no longer had a resting-place, so he carried it with him in his head, taking it out when he arrived somewhere new to see if it fitted. Was this where his bees belonged? So far, the answer had always been no. But Oscar believed that one day, he would come to a place and his dream would tell him that this was home.

For now, such a day seemed impossibly far off. First he had to return to England and finish his Engineering degree, but before he could do that, he would have to persuade his uncle to sell the restaurant, or at least to take on a manager. The first heart attack was a warning, the doctors had said: if he didn't alter his lifestyle, Giorgio Bari wouldn't see sixty-five. The family had convened as it always did when there were matters of grave import to discuss. If poor, childless

Giorgio wouldn't retire, then one of the family would have to go to Dublin to live with him and ease the burden.

Oscar was not sorry to have been chosen. Sometimes the old ones knew what he needed better than he himself did. Back in England, the melancholia that had begun around the time of his grandfather's death had steadily been getting worse. There seemed to be nothing he could do; he felt as if he were stuck in a photograph from which the sun was slowly leaching colour. During last year's dreary winter, when the world around him had finally turned to monochrome, Oscar had begun to suffer from blinding headaches.

Seasonal Affective Disorder, normal at this time of year, the doctor had said. Yes, Oscar had thought, he's right. I am sad.

Coming to Dublin had helped. The restaurant was packed every evening, and now that he had some help, Giorgio was talking about doing lunch as well. Oscar was too busy to feel despondent. He also enjoyed the company of his uncle, a quiet man much pitied by the family for his single status. Oscar was familiar with the story of the fiancée tragically killed a week before the wedding was due to take place, but if his uncle was still suffering from the loss, he didn't show it.

The supermarket girls left and the café was empty once more, but before Oscar could return to his inter-rupted reverie, the bell on the door pinged to announce the arrival of another customer. Oscar recognised the tall girl who had been in three or four times in the last few weeks. He smiled at her. It was nice when people came back; already there were quite a few regulars that he knew by name. He would like to know her name too; she would be a welcome addition to the clientéle.

Anne Marie returned Oscar's smile and sat down at a table near the window. She put her bags under the table; the travel bag she had taken home to Kerry with her and a carrier bag from her parents that contained Seán's homemade bread and her costume for the Hallowe'en party. She ordered a cappuccino and a ciabatta sandwich, took out her diary and began to fill in the details of the last three or four days. It was not a large diary, so she didn't have room to write down her innermost thoughts and feelings, but by keeping her writing small and using a form of shorthand code that she had developed over the years, Anne Marie was able to fit in pretty much everything she wanted to say about the weekend at home.

Before she left, there had been a couple of surprise announcements: the first was that Seán's brother Éamonn and his American wife Gloria had adopted two Russian babies and were bringing them home to Colorado next month. Having always assumed that they were childless by choice, Anne Marie was surprised to learn that this was not the case. It was Gloria's steadfast opposition to adoption once it became obvious that they were not going to have a family of their own that was responsible. Anne Marie had not been told what had occasioned the change of heart, but according to her father, the new parents were over the moon with their instant family.

The second announcement followed on from the first. To celebrate the new arrivals, Seán and Yvonne were going out to spend Christmas and New Year with Éamonn and Gloria.

Anne Marie was going to her grandmother's.

It was not that she minded being left behind, Anne Marie thought as she read over what she had just written. (The bare facts, without any telltale under-linings, exclamation points or dots to indicate her reaction to the news.) She was delighted that her parents were going to the States to share the joy and no doubt lend a hand with the babies too, and she herself was looking forward to spending Christmas with Nano.

So why had she felt the need, when the train had deposited her at Heuston Station, to go somewhere other than back to the flat in order to mull over the news before she passed it on to the cousins? It was because she wanted to present it to them as a perfectly satisfactory arrangement in which she had played a deciding part, but she knew that she needed to see it that way herself first. Darina was very sharp at picking up what was going on under the surface and Anne Marie didn't want her leaning on any vulnerable spots.

Hence the stop-off at the Café Firenze for a bite to eat and a chance to get used to the idea that her parents had barely waited until she had left home before they started making plans for Christmas that didn't include her.

It's supposed to be the other way round, Anne Marie thought ruefully. But I'm the one that behaves like a doting parent, and they're like the teenagers who can't wait to escape from the oppression of family gatherings.

Distracted by these thoughts, Anne Marie was halfway back to the flat when she realised that she had left behind the bag with her fancy-dress costume in it. She turned and hurried back to pick it up, hoping that nobody would be interested in stealing a blue satin pants suit and matching platform boots that had once won first prize for her mother in an Abba contest.

Oscar signalled her with his eyes as soon as she walked in the door. He was serving a customer, which took some time, but as soon as he had finished, he went behind the counter and produced the bag.

'I tried to catch you after you left,' he said apologetically, 'but I couldn't see which way you went and I didn't want to leave the restaurant for long. I hope you don't mind – I had a look inside to see if there was a telephone number or anything.'

Anne Marie turned pink. 'Oh! So you've seen my Hallowe'en costume. It's . . . very seventies, isn't it?'

Oscar smiled. 'Are you going to a fancy-dress party?'

'Yes – no. I mean, the party's at our place. I share a flat with my cousins not far from here. Thanks for holding on to the bag for me.'

'The bread smells good, too.'

'Oh yes. That's Seán . . . my father. He bakes wonderful bread. I was at home for the weekend and he gave me some to take back. It's very good.' Anne Marie hesitated for a second, then coninued in a rush, 'Em . . . I was wondering . . . about the party, I mean. If you weren't doing anything on Hallowe'en night, you could come along – if you like, that is.'

'Thank you, I would like that very much. I'll be working of course, but if I could come later, say around midnight, or half past? And I'm afraid I won't be in fancy dress.'

'Oh, that's OK. I'm sure plenty of other people won't bother dressing up. Here's the address – it's only ten minutes from here. So, thanks again and . . . see you at the party.'

'*Ciao*.'

Anne Marie came out of the restaurant with her heart thumping. I didn't know I was going to do that! she thought. Imagine, I invited a guy to a party. And he said yes!

For the rest of that evening, both Anne Marie and Oscar wore smiles that they would have been hard put to explain had anyone enquired as to the cause.

Hash Brownies

At half past ten on the night of the party, the fun still hadn't begun. A few guys from the flat next door were in the living room discussing the music with Gerald. Darina was taking a shower. Anne Marie was in the kitchen wondering if she'd last until midnight without falling asleep. She'd spent the whole day preparing food, with very little help from her two cousins. For her chore, Darina had chosen cleaning the flat before the party – which had taken her all of one hour – and Gerald had volunteered to do the clearing up afterwards. They'd both been out for most of the day.

Thinking that a shot of caffeine might help, Anne Marie took her little Italian coffee-maker out of the press and put two heaped spoons of ground coffee into it. But before she had time to add water, Vera Meaney arrived in the kitchen carrying a bottle of Blue Nun. She was wearing psychedelic green bell-bottoms, a loose orange shirt and a headscarf with metal discs sewn along its border. She gave a little wave when she saw Anne Marie.

'Hello, it's only me! Here's my contribution to the

celebrations. It was very kind of Gerald to invite me – I've never been down here before, you know. Very nice, I must say. You must pay a lot of rent for it.' She paused significantly, but when Anne Marie didn't oblige, she glanced around the room then sidled closer to her. 'I'm glad it's just the two of us,' she said conspiratorially. 'I always meant to have a chat with you about You Know Who. In a way I feel responsible for what happened. I should have known. You see, he tried it with me when I arrived.'

Anne Marie looked at her blankly. 'Sorry, I'm not following you. Who are we talking about?'

Vera lightly slapped the back of Anne Marie's hand. 'Oh now, you know very well who I mean! The maniac upstairs – Sylvester! To think that I lived beside him all that time unawares – it gives me the shivers. Of course, Anne Marie, I don't mind telling you that I knew there was something not quite right about him from the start.' She tapped the side of her nose and winked. 'I have the nose, you see.'

You certainly do, agreed Anne Marie silently. Vera's most distinguishing feature was sharp and hooked, with a tip that seemed to be trying to meet the hairy upper lip thrust towards it by prominent front teeth. Immediately, Anne Marie was sorry for the uncharitable thought. You're getting to be like Darina, she admonished herself.

'Oh yes, my nose rarely lets me down,' Vera went on. 'That's why I feel I ought to apologise to you, Anne Marie. I do feel sort of responsible for what happened to you, or nearly happened, should I say.'

'What do you mean?'

'Well, he approached me first, you see. It was a long time ago, just after he arrived in the house – before

129

Brandon bought it. I'm the only one left from that time now, imagine! Anyway, he came to my door pretending he wanted to borrow some milk but naturally, Anne Marie, I knew it was just an excuse to get to me. I gave him the cold shoulder – politely but firmly, you understand. He tried talking to me a few times in the hallway after that, but I kept it up until he got the message. So you see, Anne Marie, he was on the lookout for someone new when you arrived. Just imagine! If I'd been as friendly and unsuspecting as you are, I'd be mouldering in my grave by now!'

Anne Marie gave a nervous laugh. 'Oh, you've got it all wrong – Sylvester didn't mean me any harm. He wanted to confess. I think the memory of the terrible things he'd done was just too much for him. That's obviously why he committed suicide. But he wanted to tell someone first.'

'You mean you don't know – oh, Anne Marie, I'm sorry, I shouldn't have opened my big mouth. Now you're going to be upset!'

'Upset? About what?'

'No, no, my lips are sealed. I'm sure it's better for you not to know. Besides, my informant would be very annoyed if she could hear me. I wasn't supposed to spread it round.'

'Look, I don't know what you're talking about, but if it concerns me, I think I'm entitled to know.'

'Wild horses wouldn't drag it out of me.'

'I see. In that case, if you'll excuse me, I need to see Gerald about—'

'Oh, all right then, Anne Marie. But you're not to say I told you. Sally'll have my guts for garters if she finds out.'

'Sally?'

'The reporter from the *Evening Echo*. She came back to interview me again a fortnight ago. She's going to write a book about Sylvester's life and she needed to talk to the person that knew him best: me. Anyway . . .' Vera put her mouth to Anne Marie's ear as though they were surrounded by eavesdroppers and lowered her voice to a whisper. 'She told me that they found a knock-out drug on the table with the tea-things. It's clear what that means, Anne Marie: he was planning on slipping it into your cup! Then he was going to murder you! So you see—'

Anne Marie suddenly felt weak. She moved away from Vera and leant back against the microwave for support. Was it true? Surely not! And yet . . . Oh no, she'd thought it was all over, but now she was going to have to relive the whole episode in the light of this dreadful new information.

Brandon came into the kitchen carrying a tray covered in tin-foil. He replied to Vera's gushing welcome with a nod and made his way over to Anne Marie. He stood before her in silence for a couple of seconds. 'Your chi is unbalanced,' he said finally. 'Trouble around the third and fourth chakra. Would you like me to restore it?'

Anne Marie managed a weak smile. 'No . . . no thanks. I'll be fine.' All she wanted was to be left alone.

'So be it. I have made some brownies for the party. I'll leave them here, shall I?' He placed the tray on top of the microwave and removed the tin-foil. 'Perhaps you'd care to try one now? They are very mild and might do you good.'

'All right, I will.'

Anne Marie took one of the squares from the tray and bit into it while Brandon waited for her verdict. It was moist and chocolaty. 'Mmm, this is delicious,' she said. 'Thank you!'

'Enjoy.' Brandon smiled and bowed with joined hands as he backed towards the door.

'Oh, aren't you going to stay?' said Anne Marie, dismayed at the prospect of being left alone with Vera again. 'The party should be starting any minute now.'

'No. I always meditate for an hour or two at this time of night.' He extended his right hand, palm out-wards, towards Anne Marie. 'Be well,' he said. Then he was gone.

Vera snickered. 'Who does he think he is – Mr Spock? I'm glad he's not staying, aren't you? I don't mind telling you, Anne Marie, he gives me the creeps. What was I saying before? Oh yes, Sylvester. I wonder what made him change his mind? About murdering you, I mean. He must have decided against it at the last minute, otherwise you wouldn't be here now, sure you wouldn't.'

'Stop!' Anne Marie's mind had leapt to the envelope lying hidden under the new doormat. What if she had found it on the Sunday? She would have rushed upstairs at once. The cousins, thinking she had gone out for the day as planned, wouldn't have missed her until night. By then, it would have been too late. She shuddered and put her hands over her ears. She was alive and that was all that mattered. It was even possible that Vera was making the whole thing up. 'I really don't want to hear any more,' she said. 'Here, have a chocolate brownie.' She thrust the tray at the neighbour from upstairs.

Vera turned her face away. 'Get thee behind me, Satan! My waistline, don't you know. It's all right for you, Anne Marie, you've got the height to carry off an extra few pounds. The rest of us have to learn to say no. What's in them, anyway? They look very rich.'

'Chocolate, nuts, and . . . I don't know. Something else. Molasses, maybe? Or some kind of spice. They're very nice, whatever he put in. Are you sure you won't have one?'

'No. But you go ahead, Anne Marie. Don't mind me.'

While Anne Marie ate another brownie, Vera told her all about their landlord. He was filthy rich, she said; his father was president of a huge corporation that owned banks and multinational companies all over the world. Brandon had never had to do an honest day's work in his life. Instead, he'd spent years travelling the globe, living in India and Bali and strange places like that. Vera knew all this because her mother's uncle was a parish priest in New York and he was very friendly with a bishop who knew all the prominent Catholics in the city. At Vera's request, her mother had written asking for the lowdown on the suspicious American who was her daughter's new landlord.

After a while, Anne Marie found she was able to tune out Vera's prattle. Chewing on her fifth brownie, she noted too that the shock of what Vera had told her was wearing off. She could consider the whole Sylvester incident as though it had happened to her in another lifetime. She was still here, wasn't she? Some benevolent spirit had decided it wasn't time for her life to be snuffed out.

But to be saved by a doormat? Her spirit minder was a practical joker! She giggled to herself. Brandon must be getting to me, she thought. But that was all right; maybe there was something in what he said.

In fact, Anne Marie was beginning to feel that she

was on the edge of some great universal truth; any minute now it would reveal itself to her in a fantastic burst of light. Already, she was beginning to see things around her with great clarity: a hairline crack where the light fixture was attached to the ceiling; the deep purple of the cabbage in the salad she'd prepared; tiny beads of perspiration clinging to Vera's moustache. She saw all this clearly, but from a great distance. She felt as if she were drifting high above her surroundings, looking down on it all through the wrong end of a telescope. Maybe this was what higher consciousness was all about. Maybe I'm being enlightened, she smiled. I'm having an out-of-body experience and it's wonderful!

Gerald came into the kitchen to get a bottle opener. He stopped in amazement at the sight of his cousin grinning vacantly to herself. Then he ran back to tell Darina. She looked at him in disbelief. 'Anne Marie stoned? No way! This I gotta see!'

Hard men

Some hours later, Gerald was having a quiet smoke in a corner of the living room when his sister came to get him.

'So this is where you are – I was looking for you everywhere. You'd better go down to the kitchen. There's a couple of yobs after gate-crashing. They say they know you, but I don't like the look of them.'

Gerald met the two men in the hallway. The bigger one was dressed in black leather trousers liberally adorned with chains. His head was shaved and his forearm covered in tattoos. The smaller one had greased-back hair and an earring in one ear. He wore an Armani suit, dark glasses and carried a cellphone. They were so like caricatures of the hard men employed by criminal bosses to do their dirty work for them that they might not have been out of place at the fancy-dress party. Until you saw their faces and realised that they were the real thing.

Gerald swallowed and glanced nervously around. Darina had stayed in the living room and Anne Marie was nowhere in sight. If he could just get rid of them now no one would be any the wiser. He'd sort it all out somehow – just let them go without creating a scene, please!

The bigger man nudged his companion and pointed to Gerald. 'There he is, Deco.'

The smaller man removed his dark glasses. He smiled and held out his hand for Gerald to shake.

'Gerry, my man! You're having a party. That's nice.' Without letting go of Gerald's hand, he spoke over his shoulder. 'A party. Nice. Right, Nailer?'

Nailer grunted.

'Yeah, it's good news for us an' all, because if Gerry here is having a party, it means he's got money, right? Now, we don't mind him not inviting us – we won't hold that against him will we, Nailer?' He squeezed Gerald's hand, making him wince. 'No, we'll let that pass. Even though it wasn't very friendly, like. Our feelings could've been hurt an' all. But like I said, we won't hold that against him. Not when he's got money for us. Money he didn't have last week. D'you remember how broke he was last time we saw him, Nailer? Fifty quid is all we got. That right, Gerry?'

'Ah Jays, lads,' said Gerald, trying not to cry out

loud as the pressure on his hand increased. 'I can't pay you now. I don't have it, honest to God. The party was my cousin's idea. She's staying with us and she's working . . . she's not a poor student like me. She paid for it all out of her wages.'

'Well now,' said Deco, 'where is she? We'd better have a word with her – see if she can come up with the two-and-a-half grand you owe The Man. Plus interest. I nearly forgot about the interest. Did I mention that he's getting a bit tired of waiting on you to pay him? Because he is. So let's go have a word with this rich bird.' He pulled Gerald to him and caught him in a head lock. 'And you'd better pray she's got the cash, because we're not going away without it.'

'No!' Gerald pulled out from under the restraining arm. 'Leave her out of it. I'll . . . I'll think of something.'

The two men advanced on him until he had his back to the wall.

'Your time for thinking is over, mate,' said Deco. 'We warned you an' all. Remember when I told you what happens next? Nailer's been getting ready for it – working out in the gym every day, haven't you, Nailer?'

Nailer grinned and put one hand around Gerald's throat. He began to squeeze. Gerald gagged and tried to prise the fingers away. Nailer squeezed harder. When he finally let go, Gerald, gasping for breath, slid down the wall until he was sitting at their feet.

'I . . . have no cash,' he wheezed. 'But I might be able to come up with something else. Just . . . just gimme time, all right?'

Deco kicked him. 'No more fucking time, I told you. And what d'you mean, no cash? You think we're going to take a fucking credit card? Hear that, Nailer?

He thinks The Man accepts Visa and Mastercard!' He drew back his foot to kick him again.

'Wait, wait,' pleaded Gerald.

Through the legs of his tormentors, he could see that the party was going well. In the living room, people had started dancing to Blondie. A couple swayed into the hall, arms around each other. They tried the handles on the bedroom doors and laughed when they found them locked. They staggered down the hall, bumping into Nailer as they headed for the kitchen. The girl looked down curiously at Gerald on her way past.

'I might be able to get you something that's worth more than what I owe,' said Gerald. He put his hands on the wall behind him and pulled himself up. 'It's a ring, value at least five grand. Tomorrow – I'll try and get it tomorrow. I swear.'

Deco put his face close to Gerald's. 'For a fucking university student, you're very fucking stupid,' he said. 'We want what's owing and we want it now. Not tomorrow – now!'

'All right,' whispered Gerald. 'I'll get it tonight. A few hours, that's all I need.'

Deco checked his watch. 'You've got until two o'clock. The usual place. Be there.' He jerked his head to Nailer and led the way to the door. They left without looking back.

Thief in the night

Gerald checked up and down the corridor to make sure there was no one around to see him as he reached up to the lintel above the girls' bedroom door and felt around for the key. He slipped it into his pocket and went back to the living room. Darina was close dancing with a guy from her class and it looked like she was going to be occupied for the next while. Anne Marie was still spaced out in the kitchen. That was a worry. She might suddenly decide she needed to lie down.

Gerald went in and put his arm around her. 'How's it going, Anne Marie? Are we having fun yet?'

Anne Marie turned and smiled at him dreamily. 'Oh, Gerald. 'Tis yourself! 'Tis a lovely party altogether. I'm having a lovely time. The people are all lovely. The food is lovely. These cakes are lovely – you should try one. Oh dear, it looks like they're all gone. That's a shame. They were lovely, you know.'

'Yeah, that's great, Anne Marie. You're enjoying yourself, so. You're not feeling tired or anything, are you?'

'Oh no, Gerry, not at all. It's a lovely party.'

'All right, Anne Marie. Stay where you are. I'll just make you a cup of coffee.'

'Oh thank you, Gerry. That would be lovely.'

As soon as he had sat Anne Marie at the kitchen table and put a cup of strong, black coffee into her hands, Gerald made his escape. He let himself into the girls' room and locked the door behind him. His hands were shaking as he rifled through Anne Marie's drawer.

She had a lot of nice things: delicate silk tops and matching panties, French bras, sheer tights. They were neatly folded and smelled of roses from the bag of pot pourri that lay on top of them. Gerald felt as though he were violating his cousin by touching her things like this. I'm sorry, Anne Marie, really I am, he said over and over in his mind as his fingers hungrily scrabbled for the ring that was going to give him his life back.

Never again, I swear! It's the straight and narrow for me after tonight. Just let me get away with this, God, and I'll turn over a new leaf.

Gerald did not really believe in a deity, but in moments of great stress, he addressed his pleas to a sort of a supernatural version of himself: a bored, unpredictable god playing an eternal game on a pinball machine. If the game was going well, this god might throw an unexpected gift to Gerald, like the time he had arranged for him to bump into Brandon in a bookshop, on the very day that the washing-machine in the grim Ringsend flat had flooded the kitchen. They had got talking and within five minutes Brandon, who did not believe in coincidences, had offered Gerald the flat in Rathmines provided, as he put it, that none of the prospective tenants displayed an unhealthy aura when they came to be interviewed by him.

Tonight must have been a high-scoring night for Gerald's god because at last, hidden in a box of pantyliners at the back of the drawer, he found what he was looking for. It was wrapped in tissue paper, inside an envelope that contained a valuation from a prominent jeweller in Limerick that estimated its replacement value at £5,400.

The ring was an antique given to Anne Marie on her eighteenth birthday by their grandmother. Darina had been given one too, but their mother had confiscated it when she discovered that Darina had tried to sell it. Gerald had noticed that Anne Marie had stopped wearing her ring since she had taken to cycling to work. Silently apologising to his cousin once again, he pocketed the envelope and opened the door. He deliberately put the key in the lock and returned to the party.

With sixty young people hoping that tonight was going to be their lucky night, it wouldn't be long before someone discovered that the door to one of the bedrooms was open.

Brenda Clarke recognised the address at once. As soon as the duty sergeant put down the phone, she volunteered to go check it out.

'Come on, Tony,' she said to her partner, 'this one's got our name on it.'

Tony reluctantly pulled on his jacket. He had just finished his mid-shift 'lunch' and was settling down for a nap in his swivel chair. The lads in Sligo had given him a present of a back support pad when he had got his promotion to a desk job in the Big Smoke. Since being teamed up with Brenda, however, he hadn't been given much chance to rest his bad back. 'Lord preserve us from ambitious *banners*,' he muttered to the sergeant as he passed the desk on his way out.

It was hard to believe it was the same girl as before. She had altered so much since the day of the suicide, and that was a mere month ago. Brenda, who was all of twenty-four, felt ancient as she ran her keen eye over Anne Marie and took note of the differences. It was more than the new hairstyle; there was a change in her face as well. She had lost the fresh-faced, wide-eyed look that had made her appear innocent and vulnerable on that first occasion, in spite of the fact that she was over six foot tall.

She was also high on drugs.

'Hello again,' Brenda said.

Barely a month in the city and not only had Anne

Marie's looks changed, but her whole personality had as well, Brenda thought cynically. She appeared to have been arguing with the young man – her brother, or was it cousin? – the one who had taken control on the day of the suicide.

It was he who opened the door. He was obviously displeased to see the two officers – and after sniffing the air inside the flat, Brenda could see why – but Anne Marie had brushed past him and brought them into the kitchen. There, she saw that every available surface was littered with empty bottles and paper plates on which the remains of a curry and rice dish mixed with various salads made lurid patterns of yellow and pink.

'We've been robbed,' Anne Marie began. 'Someone stole my ring!'

'I'm sorry,' the young man broke in, 'she's a bit upset. There was no need for you to come out; we were going to report it in the morning after we had done a complete check to see what else was missing.'

'Someone took my ring,' Anne Marie wailed.

Another young woman came into the kitchen. Her hair was dyed a harsh shade of bronze. She was dressed as a 1970s hippie, in a cheesecloth shirt over an Indian skirt, with a leather headband in her hair and a peace sign drawn on one cheek. She stopped short when she saw the police officers.

'What's up?' she said guardedly.

'Darina, do you think you could take Anne Marie for a walk around the block,' the young man said. 'She could do with a little fresh air.'

'My ring's gone!'

The woman called Darina got the message. 'Sure thing, bro. You'll look after the . . . visitors, will you? Offer them a cup of tea, or a drop from the bottom of one of the bottles if you can find one that hasn't been sucked dry.' She smiled insolently at Tony as she passed. 'C'mon, Anne Marie, let's go walkies,' she said, leading the tall girl out of the room.

'Good party?'

Brenda cleared a chair of plates and sat down. Tony went to stand in the doorway with his arms crossed. Appearing intimidating was his speciality. He had a natural gift for it, Brenda thought admiringly as she watched the young man nervously fumble with the cord on the jug kettle.

'Yeah, good enough.' He filled the kettle from the tap and plugged it in. 'Tea? Coffee? Or something stronger?' he said, glancing quickly over at Tony.

Brenda smiled inwardly. It was just as well that no one knew what a big softie Tony was underneath. They all assumed she was the good cop in this duo. How wrong they were!

'I'll have tea, please. Tony?' Tony grunted. 'He'll have tea as well.'

'Right so. Well, what can I tell you? It was a big party – over sixty at it, I'd say. It could have been anyone.'

'Any gate-crashers?'

'Gate-crashers? It's hard to say really . . . maybe a few.'

'So when did Anne Marie – she's your cousin, by the way, isn't that right? – when did she discover that her ring was missing?'

'After the party was over. Around three o'clock, I'd say. She must have rung you straightaway.'

'I see. Eh, sorry, could you tell me your name again?'

'Gerald. Gerald Davenport.'

'OK, Gerald. So Anne Marie discovers her valuable antique ring is gone, but she doesn't tell you or your sister, she rings the Gardaí instead. Would that be right?'

'Em . . . well, yes. You see, Darina and I were tidying up in the living room. Anne Marie . . . well, she'd had a bit too much to . . . to drink, like, and . . . well, she's not used to it, so I suppose she wasn't thinking straight. I wish she had told us instead because I wouldn't have let her call you out in the middle of the night. After all, whoever took the ring is long gone by now, and with so many people coming and going, there's no way it's going to be found.'

'The ring was worth around five grand, I believe.'

'I wouldn't know, I never saw it.'

Pathetic liar, Brenda thought. She was glad she had come over; this could turn out to be a most profitable night's work. Not that there was any chance of the ring turning up. If her suspicions were correct, it was indeed long gone. But she had other fish to fry.

Gerald cleared a space on the table and set a mug down in front of Brenda. Tony took his in his hand.

'Biscuit, anyone?'

'Not for me thanks, but I'm sure Tony wouldn't say no.'

Gerald went to a press and took out a packet of chocolate biscuits. 'Sure you won't have one?'

'Positive.'

When he gave the packet to Tony, Brenda noticed that Gerald's hand was shaking. He went back to where he had been standing against the counter and put his hands in his pockets. His face had an unhealthy sheen of perspiration.

'Aren't you having a cup yourself? You look like you could do with it.'

Keep the pressure up. He was so guilt-ridden, there was no knowing what he might confess to if she stayed long enough, Brenda thought. After all, this house had concealed a murderer in one of its upstairs rooms; it would be interesting to see what was lurking in the basement.

'No thanks, I'm . . . I'm not thirsty.'

OK, time to get tough.

Brenda put down her mug. She smiled. 'So Gerry, tell me – who's your supplier?'

The poor guy blanched. 'What? I don't know what you mean.'

'Ah now Gerry, come on! If your cousin had been any higher, she'd have been floating on the ceiling. What was it you gave her?'

'I . . . I . . . nothing, I swear. I wouldn't do that! I don't know where she got . . . whatever she got! Honest to God, I don't.'

'So who supplied the party? I think I know most of them by now. Was it someone local? The guy with the short, stick-up hair who calls himself Bart Simpson, for instance? Or his sidekick Fliss? You must know Fliss – she does all the clubs in this area. Pink hair. Nose-ring. Loud. You can't miss her. Was it Fliss?'

Gerald's mouth opened, but no sound came out.

Bingo, thought Brenda. I'm on my way up!

'Did you say pink hair?'

Brenda turned. It was the sister. She had come in quietly, bypassing Tony. She leaned against the wall and stared coolly at Brenda.

'It's just there was a friend of mine from college here tonight. She's got pink hair. She's been around a few times. Had a bit of a thing for my brother, but it's over now. Isn't it Gerry?'

She left the wall and went to stand beside her brother. 'Oh and by the way, it was my fault about the ring.'

Gerald managed to look both relieved and stunned at once.

'Your fault?' Brenda tried not to let her chagrin at this turn of events show in her manner.

'Yes. You see, we had locked the bedroom doors so that nobody could get into them to make out on the beds. So there was just the one toilet in the corridor for everyone at the party. But there was a really long queue when I wanted to go, see? So I opened my bedroom to use the *en suite*, and well – I obviously forgot to lock the door again. In fact, I still have the key in my pocket.'

'I see.' Brenda knew when she was beaten. You won this round, she thought as she stood up and motioned to Tony that they were through. But there'll be another. And I'll make sure you're not around to hold his hand next time, girl.

'Jays, Darina, that was close!'

Gerald was sitting in the chair recently vacated by Brenda. The tremor had not yet left his hands. He looked at them and frowned, as though he was unsure who they belonged to.

Darina noticed, and changed her mind about the roasting she had been about to give her brother.

'Here, you're the one in need of a cup of tea,' she said instead.

Gerald gave a weak laugh. 'That's what herself said too.'

Darina boiled up the kettle again and put a fresh tea bag in Tony's mug. 'You don't mind drinking out of the same cup as a copper, do you? The dishwasher and the sink are full.' She poured the water and put two heaped spoonfuls of sugar into the mug.

Gerald took it gratefully. 'God, Darina, I don't know what I'd have done without you. It was awful – like the Spanish Inquisition, or something. I had this terrible feeling of guilt, even before she started asking me questions. I wanted to confess to all sorts of things, even things I hadn't done.'

'But you didn't tell them you took Anne Marie's ring to pay back your dealer, did you?'

Gerald's mouth dropped. 'You . . . you know?'

'Aw, c'mon Gerry, what do you think I am? As if I didn't know how expensive your habit has become! And those thugs who turned up earlier? They had "collector" written all over them! It was just too much of a coincidence that Anne Marie's ring went missing so soon after they left.'

Gerald put his head in his hands. 'Oh God, Darina, do you think Anne Marie'll figure it out too?'

'Don't worry, I covered your arse again. When I was putting her to bed, I told her about the two guys turning up. Only I didn't say they were looking for you. Instead I made up something about them being mixed up with a criminal gang that "does" parties; I let slip that your friend Fliss probably gave them the nod. She seemed to swallow it. She was even sorry for phoning the guards because she thought you were going to get into trouble. When we got back from our trot around the block I had to stop her barging into the kitchen to tell them to leave you alone.'

'You're amazing, sis, d'you know that? How can I ever make it up to you?'

'That's easy – do my share of the cleaning up! No, don't worry, that was a joke! We'll do it together in the morning. For now, a hug would be good.'

Gerald stood up and put his arms round his sister. They rocked together in silence for about a minute. Then Darina broke away. She took her brother's hands.

'Without wanting to go all Anne Marie on you, I'd just like to say that maybe you ought to cool it. You know, cut back a bit? You had a narrow escape tonight and I wouldn't like to see things go any further. So I want you to promise me that you'll stay off gear altogether, and go easy on the rest. OK? Think you can do that?'

'Sure, sis. Don't worry – after tonight, I'm not taking any more risks. I've learnt my lesson!'

Before he went to bed, Gerald took out the package he had been given earlier in the night by Deco in exchange for Anne Marie's ring. 'To show there's no hard feelings, mate,' Deco had said, patting him on the back and pushing a rolled-up plastic bag secured with an elastic band into the pocket of Gerald's jacket.

'See, we're only doing our job, like. It's The Man calls the shots, pays our wages an' all. He wasn't very happy when Fliss told him how much credit she'd given you, so he sent us down to have a word with you. But he's a reasonable man, and when I called him on the blower to ask about the ring, he said he'd accept it, even though he normally deals strictly in cash. I'm sure he'd like you to have this little token of his esteem – why don't you share it with some of your mates from college? The Man's a bit disappointed that you haven't brought him any new custom, you know. This gear's the best you'll get on the streets of Dublin; take it and enjoy. And spread the word around, would you?'

Gerald pulled off the elastic band and unrolled the

bag. Inside it were four smaller self-sealing plastic bags full of an innocuous-looking white powder. He opened up one of them.

Since the age of fifteen, Gerald had been smoking, swallowing, or snorting a variety of illegal substances, but up to now, he had never injected. He remembered his promise to Darina that he would stay away from heroin. But that was before he'd seen what was in the package. He couldn't just throw it away, could he? Pity he didn't have any syringes in the flat; he could have had a small hit tonight, to steady his nerves after the visit from the law. On the other hand, there was enough here to sell at a profit and still have plenty left for his personal use. That was a better idea. He'd wait until everything calmed down after the missing ring, then he'd review the situation. Coming up to Christmas he was going to need some cash; that would be a good time to sell. In the meantime, he had better hide this lot where Cornelius wasn't likely to stumble across it. He cast his eyes about the room.

Brenda drove slowly back to the station. 'So what do you reckon, Tony? Are we on to something here?'

'Why don't *you* tell *me*? You're the one looking to become a detective in the Special Branch.'

'Hey, pardner, don't be like that! I'm sorry if you think it was a wasted trip. I was sure our man Gerald was going to spill some goods. If my hunch is right, he knows a lot more about that missing ring than he's letting on. What if someone's putting the squeeze on him? He could be our way into the whole Rathmines scene. It would look good on your report sheet if you were involved in busting the gang that controls drugs on our patch, wouldn't it?'

'I thought we had a Drug Squad for that sort of thing.'

'Aw, Tony, where's your sense of adventure?'

'I left it back in Sligo where it can't hurt me. I'm all for the quiet life, Brenda, you know that. Why go looking for trouble? It comes to us often enough on its own.'

'Yeah, well you've got a family and all, so I can see your point of view. But I'm single and my career is my life. Superintendent before forty, that's my goal.'

'Jaysus, girl, you're on your way, that's for sure! I just hope you'll remember me when you get to the top. I'm telling you now: I'd like to retire as sergeant in Ballyshannon. Make sure and put in a good word for me!'

Darina tossed and turned for a while, envying Anne Marie her obliterating cannabis-induced slumber, but she was too restive to lie still and count sheep until she dropped off.

Gerald was in far worse straits than she had imagined. She had suspected for some time that he had been getting in over his head all right, but because Anne Marie had voiced concerns about him, Darina had perversely played down, even to herself, the extent to which her brother's habit had taken over his life. However, she had noticed immediately that the arrival of the guards had freaked him out.

That woman Brenda was no fool, Darina saw. She might well be back with a search warrant one of these days. How much had Gerald got stashed away in his room? He had left the party and gone to pay his debts with Anne Marie's ring, but even if the collectors only allowed half its value, there must have been a fair amount of credit on it. He would have been paid in kind. Darina knew her brother too well to believe that he would give any heed to her warning and cut back on his consumption. He was weak. She would have to save him from himself.

Three women, one black man and some dogs

On Monday, Anne Marie went in early to work in order to avoid her cousins' knowing smiles every time the party was mentioned. She had always prided herself on her abstemiousness; the only other time she had been under the influence was when she was four and got drunk on Crème de Cassis, which her minder had mistaken for Ribena. In fact, she had at first refused to believe the cousins when they told her that she had been stoned at the party. She had never smoked pot in her life, she told Darina indignantly, and she wasn't about to start just because she had moved to Dublin. Then Gerald told her about Brandon's totally delicious and mind-blowing hash brownies.

Dunne arrived at the office just as Anne Marie finished changing out of her cycling gear and into her smart clothes. He was whistling to himself as he came up the stairs and seemed pleasantly surprised to see his PA.

'Here already, Anne Marie? You're very keen altogether! Did you have a good weekend?'

Anne Marie flushed. 'I did . . . yes, sort of.'

'Oh? Only sort of?'

'Well, we had a party, my cousins and I, in the flat and . . . well, I did something silly.' To her surprise, Anne Marie found herself telling her boss about the episode with the brownies.

Dunne threw his head back and laughed. 'You ate a whole tray of hash brownies without knowing what was in them? You must have had a great night after that!'

'There were . . . extenuating circumstances,' Anne Marie muttered. It wasn't every day that someone informed you that you had narrowly avoided being murdered.

Dunne saw that she was embarrassed and changed the subject. 'Who are these fine-looking women?' he asked, picking up a framed black-and-white photograph of Anne Marie, Yvonne and Nano that was Anne Marie's most recent addition to her desk.

'Oh, that's me, my mother and her mother. My dad took it last year at Riverwood – that's my grandmother's place near Limerick. I like it because it's . . . you know, the three generations.'

The photograph had been taken on the steps in front of the big house. Nano was at the top, looking out towards the woods. Yvonne was one step below her, facing the other way. Anne Marie was at the bottom, smiling past the camera at the photographer.

'Your mother and grandmother are very alike,' Dunne said after examining the picture in silence for a moment. 'You must take after your father in looks.'

'Oh, I don't know about that,' murmured Anne Marie. She loved Seán dearly, but nobody who saw the two of them together could possibly maintain that she resembled him. He was of medium height, wiry, sandy-haired and freckled, whereas she was tall, fair and clear-skinned – just like Yvonne. How could anyone think she didn't look like her mother's kin? She waited until her boss had gone into his office then took up the photo again.

She saw at once what he meant. Her mother and grandmother had strong, angular features; their eyes were wide-set on either side of a long, bony nose. They both had a high forehead and a well-defined jawline. Anne Marie had the same eyes and hair, but her nose was small and her face round. It was not, as she might have thought up to now, that she was young and her features as yet unformed; it was because those genes had not been passed on to her.

The discovery was a shock to the system, as though someone had slapped her with a wet towel. Though she was unable to explain to herself why she was upset to discover that she did not look as much like her mother and grandmother as she had thought, when she put the photograph back on her desk, Anne Marie angled it away from herself so that her eyes would not fall on it while she worked.

That same evening, Anne Marie went to her first meeting with her boss. The hotel was hosting two conferences: the investment one that Dunne had asked her to attend, and an EU seminar on Human Rights. Anne Marie had arranged to meet Dunne in the foyer. She was early. There were a lot of foreigners about; while she was waiting, Anne Marie amused herself by trying to guess which of the two events they were there for. Anybody who looked Japanese, she mentally sent to the investment meeting; Africans and women in loud clothes to the Human Rights one.

At one point, the sight of a tall African man put her

in mind of Victor, the kindly stranger who'd rescued her when she'd got herself hopelessly lost in her first week in Dublin. He was something to do with Human Rights, wasn't he? Anne Marie had just begun to wonder if she mightn't bump into him again tonight when she felt a hand on her shoulder. She turned and saw her boss. Her surprise at the familiarity of the gesture must have shown on her face, because Dunne dropped his hand at once.

'Am I late? I was held up by a phone call. I hope I haven't kept you waiting,' he said.

'No, no. You're not late at all. I'm not long here myself. There's another conference taking place on the ground floor, but we're upstairs.'

'Lead the way so.'

As Anne Marie reached the stairwell, two people speaking in French were coming down. One of them was a thin, dark-haired woman dressed in black with a long, ethnic silk scarf tied at the side of her neck.

The other was Victor.

Surprised and pleased, Anne Marie stopped short. 'Hello there!'

Victor paused at the bottom step. He exchanged glances with the Frenchwoman as though to check which of them was supposed to respond.

Anne Marie blushed. He hadn't recognised her! 'It's Anne Marie. The South Circular Road? You helped me find my way, remember? It was back in early October sometime. I'd just arrived in Dublin. I was going in circles and . . . and you showed me the way. Oh! That reminds me, I still have your map-book.' She was babbling. This was awful. She wished she hadn't opened her mouth.

Victor's face cleared. 'Yes, I remember now. Anne

Marie – of course! You've . . . altered your appearance and I didn't recognise you. Forgive me. It's nice to see you again. I think you've settled down now, found your feet, haven't you?'

'Yes, yes I have, thank you.'

Behind Anne Marie, Dunne stirred impatiently. She could sense an antagonism in him towards Victor, and as Victor's eyes flicked to Dunne, she knew that the feeling was acknowledged and returned.

Anne Marie grew more flustered. She was out of her depth, but it was up to her to bring this unfortunate encounter to an end. She stuck her hand out. 'Well, I won't delay you. Enjoy your conference. Goodbye.'

'Goodbye, Anne Marie.' The startling brilliance of Victor's smile as he pressed her hand did much to repair Anne Marie's battered ego. She didn't even mind when the woman with the scarf took him possessively by the arm and resumed speaking to him in French.

As soon as they'd gone past, Dunne caught up with Anne Marie. 'Friend of yours?' he asked gruffly.

'Oh, I'm sorry! I should've introduced you, shouldn't I? But I only met him once and he didn't seem to recognise me at first. I had to remind him who I was.' Deep inside Anne Marie, a tiny stab of pain accompanied that remark.

Dunne said nothing, but he seemed to relax. In a couple of minutes, he was back to his usual expansive self. He insisted on driving her all the way home after the meeting, and even waited with the engine off to make sure that she got safely inside the door.

Desmond Dunne watched Anne Marie enter the basement flat in Rathmines and reluctantly turned the key in the ignition. He was a fool to think she might have invited him in for coffee; he was the boss and that was that. She still addressed him as Mr Dunne, even though he had told her at the start that he wouldn't mind if she called him Des.

That night, Anne Marie had a dream in which two dogs were fighting on a frozen pond over a rag-doll. The combatants were a black Labrador and Rottweiler. A French poodle looked on. She remembered the dream in the morning only because she thought it was funny.

Good Coffee

On the Saturday after the party, Anne Marie bumped into Roz again. It was not a coincidence. She had decided to spend the morning exploring the city on her bike, beginning with the street that had so con- fused her the first time she had gone looking for it. At the back of her mind was the idea that she might see Roz and thank her again for letting her have the bike for nothing.

As she approached the house, Anne Marie slowed down, hoping to be spotted by someone inside. She was not bold enough to drop in unannounced, especially since Roz hadn't got in touch with her after their first meeting. Of course, Anne Marie told herself, Roz was very busy, what with being Editor of a magazine and mother to three young children. She had her own circle of friends: high-flyers from the glamorous worlds of fashion and publishing, no doubt, so why should she be bothered with a nineteen-year-old fresh up from the country? And since the job she had mentioned obviously hadn't materialised, there was no reason for her to get in touch again. All the same, Anne Marie couldn't help glancing wistfully towards the upstairs windows, where it was possible that the children might be playing. If they looked out and saw her, she would wave to them.

Behind Anne Marie, a car pulled into the kerb. The horn blared and a shrill child's voice called her name. She braked and got off the bicycle.

'Anne Marie – it *is* you!' Roz had opened the driver's door and was getting out of the car. 'Ellie and the twins recognised you but I wasn't sure. You've changed your hair and . . . Excuse me a sec. Jake, Ruth! Out on the kerb side, if you please. And roll up that window before – oh, what's the use of talking to them.' The twins had piled out of the car, leaving the door open and spilling the contents of a sports bag on to the pavement.

'It's all right, Mammy, I'll look after it.' The eldest girl, Ellie, stooped to pick up the bag as the twins rushed over to Anne Marie.

'We were swimming. I can do the back-stroke,' shouted Jake.

'No, you can't! You're not even able to float,' scoffed his twin.

'Yes I am! Anyway, I got a certificate for swimming twenty-five metres and you didn't, so there!'

'That's 'cos I was sick. I'm way better than you at the front-stroke. Remember that time I beat you–'

'Enough! Inside, JR. Anne Marie – it's nice to see you again. I meant to get in touch, but I lost your phone number. You're getting good use out of the bike, are you?'

'Oh, it's great,' said Anne Marie. 'I was kind of hoping I'd see you to say thanks for letting me have it, but I didn't like to disturb—'

'It's our daddy's bike. He was really cross with Mammy for giving it away.'

'Ruth! Go inside at once! Sorry, Anne Marie, don't mind what she said. It's fine, really. Listen – Stephen's at home now. Why don't you come in for a cup of coffee and he can tell you himself.'

Anne Marie demurred just long enough to be considered polite.

Stephen was a shock. Anne Marie had somehow assumed that Roz's husband would be handsome, charming and full of chat – a masculine version of Roz. Instead, she was introduced to a shambling bear of a man dressed in an old cardigan and baggy jeans who was so painfully ill-at-ease in her company that he couldn't look her straight in the eye. As soon as Roz had made him say that he was very happy that Anne Marie now had his bike, he backed out of the hall and retreated to the kitchen. Minutes later, Ellie came into the sitting room carrying a tray with coffee and scones on it, but of her father who had prepared it, there was no further sign.

Roz poured the coffee and handed Anne Marie a mug. Anne Marie sniffed appreciatively. 'This smells good.'

'Mmm. I love the way Stephen makes coffee. He does it properly, with freshly ground beans, allowing it time to percolate, heating the pot and all that. I'm too impatient and you can tell by the taste. It's the same with food – Stephen's a much better cook than I am because he never rushes. My favourite day of the week is Sunday. I get to stay in bed and read the papers while the kids watch videos and Stephen does the dinner. He gets out all these cookbooks and concocts something new every week that's so yummy even the twins ask for seconds.'

The coffee may have been good, but when Roz took a sip, she frowned and put down her mug. 'That's funny, it doesn't taste right. In fact, even the smell is making me feel a bit queasy.'

'Oh, that happened to my mother,' said Anne Marie excitedly. 'She was addicted to coffee when she was a student, then all of a sudden she couldn't stand it. That's how she found out she was pregnant with me.'

Roz looked horrified. 'I'm not pregnant. No way! We've seen to that, I assure you.' She shuddered. 'God, another child – what a nightmare that would be! I'm only just recovering from the shock of having had the twins six years ago. Speaking of whom,' she added, springing up and going to the door, 'it's abnormally quiet up there. What are they at?'

As though on cue, there was a crash followed by several thumps on the ceiling above. Roz smiled wryly and sat down again. 'That's more like it! So, tell me, Anne Marie, how has Dublin been treating you? I presume you've got a job now, have you?'

'Yes, I'm a PA for a businessman called Des—'

Just then, there was another crash from upstairs. This time, however, there was silence for a moment, then a wail that started low and grew to a pain-filled crescendo.

'Excuse me,' said Roz, leaping up from her chair. 'This time, it's serious.'

While Roz was upstairs, Anne Marie looked around. This was the 'good' room, the one that was mostly kept locked, she remembered. The walls were painted eggshell-blue, and the settee that she was sitting on matched the undyed cotton curtains. There was a blue and white porcelain vase in the fireplace and a tall palm in a corner by the window.

Anne Marie guessed that she had been shown in here because Stephen had taken over the kitchen. He clearly wasn't the sociable sort. She wrinkled her nose. How could Roz could have settled for someone so . . . so *wrong* for her? With his long straggly hair, shaggy beard, thick lenses in ugly rectangular frames, he was like a throwback to the 1970s. Yvonne and Seán had photos of their student days in which all the men looked like that. Couldn't Stephen see that the world had moved on? Why didn't Roz make him change? Was it possible that she actually liked him like that?

Clasping her coffee mug with both hands, Anne Marie pondered the mechanics of falling in love. Roz and Stephen were living proof of the attraction of opposites. Did that mean it could happen to her? Was it possible that she would one day be swept off her feet by a short, balding man with crooked teeth and bad breath?

Roz came back into the sitting room with blood on her hands. Jake was beside her, holding a handkerchief to his mouth. His crying had subsided to a muffled sob. 'Sorry, Anne Marie. He's knocked out a front tooth. I'll just clean him up a bit and make sure he's all right. I won't be long.'

Anne Marie finished her coffee in a gulp and jumped up. 'Oh, the poor lad, that's awful! I am sorry. But I should go. You've got your hands full, I can see.'

'No, Please stay – it's only a milk tooth. He would

have lost it in the next year anyway. His parachuting from the top bunk just means the Tooth Fairy has to come a bit earlier – isn't that right, Jake? Actually, Anne Marie, it's great you turned up. I wanted to explain to you about that job at the magazine. But maybe you're in a hurry? Were you on your way someplace?'

'No, I've no commitments,' said Anne Marie happily. 'I just didn't want to be in the way.'

Anne Marie spent the rest of the day with Roz and her family. After lunch, while Stephen and Roz cleared up, she went out to the garden with the children and allowed them to co-opt her into their games of make-believe. She was an enthusiastic witch, a patient elephant, a convincing monster and a human swing as decreed by the twins. All this time, their sister Ellie stood on the sidelines or played by herself. Anne Marie tried several times to involve her, but Ellie shook her head and continued to watch.

Strange child, thought Anne Marie. I wonder what goes on inside her head?

By evening, Anne Marie felt she had known the family for ever. When they had come in from the garden, Ellie had unwound enough to show her bedroom and her favourite books, while the twins seemed to think that Anne Marie had been sent down from heaven to be their own giant-sized playmate.

Roz was delighted. 'You're such a hit with the three of them,' she said over tea in the kitchen while Stephen was bathing the twins. 'Where do you get the energy to play like that? I was exhausted just looking at you.'

Anne Marie flushed with pleasure. 'I don't know, I just enjoy it. Really I do! I'd no brothers and sisters at home, so maybe that's part of it.'

Roz smiled. 'Well, I'm afraid you're committed

now. The twins will be pestering me to know when you're coming over again. Let me get all your details down in my address book this minute. I felt so foolish after last time, when the phone number was rubbed off the board and I had no way of contacting you. You could have had that job as Editorial Assistant, you know. But it turns out you were already working by then, so I suppose it wouldn't have made any difference. It's a pity, though, because the girl we took on isn't going to last. She has too many airs and graces, she makes mistakes and she can't handle the pressure. If you ever decide you've had enough of being a PA, let me know. *Femme* could certainly do with someone like yourself on board.'

That night in bed, Anne Marie thought wistfully about the missed job opportunity. She knew she had a cushy number as Desmond Dunne's PA, but the idea of working on a magazine, in an office that she imagined to be full of exciting people, laughter and life was very attractive. Dunne was out more than he was in, and she had great difficulty making the work he gave her last more than a couple of hours. After that, she was reduced to watering the plants, dusting, and rearranging her drawer. Where was the challenge? What about her learning curve? I'm stagnating, Anne Marie thought gloomily. And yet, she couldn't face the thought of resigning after only a few weeks. She liked her boss, and she knew that he liked her. It was just – she couldn't help wondering at times why he employed a Personal Assistant at all. He did most of his business himself over the phone or by e-mail; she was still unclear in her own mind about what exactly his line of business was. She sighed. Dunne would be very disappointed if he thought she wanted to leave.

Besides, it would look terrible on her CV.

Maybe if I wait, something will happen, she thought. Something that will make it easier for me to hand in my notice. She tried to imagine what unforeseen event, short of death or disaster, would make her departure inevitable. Nothing occurred to her in the next two minutes, so she gave up and went to sleep. Which was just as well, because two lifetimes would not have been long enough for Anne Marie to guess how that particular dilemma was going to be resolved.

A Room of One's Own

By the end of the second week in November, Anne Marie was thoroughly dissatisfied with every aspect of her life. Dunne had gone to Hong Kong for five days, leaving her alone with nothing to do except answer the telephone when it rang, which was seldom. She had hoped to go with him; hadn't he said at the interview that the job would involve travelling? Hong Kong would have been wonderful; it was far enough away to be exotic, but it was a modern city where she would have enjoyed all the creature comforts that she, unlike her parents, required when travelling.

What made her disappointment all the more acute was the fact that for a while, Anne Marie had been certain that he was going to ask her along. Dunne had come out of his office one morning and begun to fidget at her desk, glancing at her and then away, playing with her Connemara marble paperweight while he talked about the meetings he wanted her to set up with his Asian contacts. He seemed ill at ease, which was totally out of character. He had gone on to ask her if she liked Chinese food, and to say how good the view was from the Peninsula Hotel – for all the world as though it was understood that Anne Marie would be coming too. He had even asked her if her passport was up to date!

But nothing had come of it. The next day, Dunne had acted distant, as though he was sorry for having spoken out of turn. There was no more mention of the Hong Kong trip. She was hurt to discover later that he had booked his airline ticket and hotel himself.

Anne Marie was perplexed as well as disappointed. Thinking about it as she lay awake at night, the only explanation she could come up with to fit all the facts was that Dunne's wife had vetoed her departure. She remembered how Jacqui had invented a pretext to come to the office on her second day in the job to check up on the new secretary. Even though she had been very pleasant on that occasion and the two or three other times that they had met, it was obvious that Mrs Dunne had a jealous streak. As though she had anything to worry about! The very idea of an affair with her boss was enough to make Anne Marie squirm with embarrassment.

Work was not the only thing that had turned sour. Sharing accommodation with her cousins was proving to be less congenial than Anne Marie had expected. It was tempting to blame it all on them, but that wouldn't be fair, she thought. Yes, Darina could be very aggravating at times, like when she smoked in the bedroom while Anne Marie was out, then opened the window and ineffectually waved her arms about when Anne Marie came in from work. As if that would get the smell off the clothes in the wardrobe! And Gerald was becoming more and more dreamy and detached from reality. She knew that he smoked pot, and that was his business she supposed, but recently it had got to the stage where it was almost impossible to have a proper conversation with him. Anne Marie had tried broaching her concerns with Darina, but she had brushed them off, saying that Gerald knew what was good for him and wouldn't take kindly to interference from his cousin.

In fairness, it must be just as hard for them to adapt to having me around, she told herself. My standards of cleanliness are much higher than theirs, and I can't expect them to dust and scrub and polish just to please me. Resentment crept in, however, when she thought about the collapse of the cooking arrangements. At the start, they had taken it in turn, but Anne Marie's meals were so superior to everyone else's that she now seemed to cook most nights. She knew she was a fool to allow herself be taken for granted like this, but she couldn't see a way out. Too often Darina and Gerald wasted communal money on takeaways when it was their turn, and by now Anne Marie had eaten enough of Cornelius's indigestible Irish Stew to prefer any alternative.

She sighed. Cornelius himself was another problem. He had attached himself to her right at the start and now he seemed to think that they formed a team. She found herself pushed into taking sides on the slightest issue: the two of them against Gerald and Darina. Anne Marie envied her two older cousins their close but easy relationship; it was all that she, an only child, had imagined the sibling bond to be. But Cornelius was not Gerald. In fact, thought Anne Marie sadly,

Gerald was not Gerald any more.

Maybe the time had come for her to move on. She remembered the fantasies she had entertained herself with on the train to Dublin, before she had any idea what the capital held in store for her. Now that she had a well-paid job, she could afford a place of her own. It needn't be anywhere fancy; she was realistic enough to realise that her dream pads would be totally beyond the reach of even her very generous salary, but as long as it was fairly central and met her minimum standards of hygiene and comfort, she would be happy with a bedsit. It should be fairly easy to find something suitable, shouldn't it?

A Room with a View

Desmond Dunne lay with his hands behind his head on his hotel bed. His room on the seventeenth floor of the Peninsula had huge windows with a view out over Kowloon Bay.

Why had he chickened out? What if he was wrong about her? Maybe outside of Ireland, she would have been different. He could have softened her up with a few nights on the town; champagne on ice back at the hotel, that sort of thing. He had never known it to fail before. But then he had never cared so much before. You stupid cretin, he berated himself. You want her because you know she would never fall for any of it. She's unattainable: that's the attraction.

He was lying to himself and he knew it. What had happened was that at the age of forty-nine, Desmond Dunne had for the first time in his life fallen in love.

Anne Marie! Even saying her name had become a sweet and illicit pleasure. How could he bear to see her again without declaring himself? That was the real reason he hadn't brought her with him to Hong Kong. He knew that if Anne Marie were to have the slightest inkling of what he was feeling, she would be distressed and horrified. How far he had come from the first lustful impulses that had motivated him when he had interviewed her! Now he would rather suffer the torture of self-denial than be the cause of a minute's discomfort to her. Now she filled him with entirely different longings; he wanted to impress her with great deeds, like a knight of old. He would do battle wearing her token next to his heart. Slay dragons, liberate peasants – anything to bring a smile to her face and gratitude to her heart. But in today's world, what could he do? His earlier fantasy of running for president was not really an option, but the desire remained for some sort of larger stage on which to beat his chest and make her notice him.

Maybe he would start by giving a shitload of money to charity – better still, get Anne Marie to pick the organisations herself and decide how to allocate the few million he would set aside. It would also be a good way into public life: fund a hospital ward for sick children, or a hostel for the homeless.

In the short term, there was that bit of waste ground he owned in the centre of Dublin: instead of selling it for another ten million or more, he could do something with it – turn it into a park, for instance. Yes, that would be the place to start. Get the bulldozers in and hire a landscape gardener – in a matter of weeks, the thing would be done. Who would he get to open it? Dunne mentally scrolled through the list of prominent politicians who owed him favours before settling on a certain minister who had a lot to thank him for.

Having made his decision, Dunne immediately felt energised. He'd get on his new project as soon as he returned to Dublin. Philanthrophy might even become his new hobby. Money had ceased to motivate him long ago; maybe giving some of it back would rekindle the old spark. Particularly if Anne Marie were to help him do it.

Dunne was not unaware of the irony of his situation. Having spent the greater part of his life ruthlessly amassing vast wealth, here he was imagining giving it all away for the sake of the living embodiment of everything that money could not buy: innocence, truth and goodness.

House-hunting

While her boss was in Hong Kong, Anne Marie threw herself into looking for another place to live. She had no qualms about using the telephone at work to make enquiries in the morning, which she followed up with visits in the afternoon. Hadn't Dunne himself said she could do what she liked for the five days he was away? And he was always encouraging her to ring her family in Kerry from the office. 'We don't want you getting homesick and running back down the country, now do we?' he'd say, giving her one of his trademark winks.

So on the very first afternoon, she put on her good walking shoes and set out to find a new place to live. By 5 p.m. on that same day, Anne Marie had learned all about the euphemisms employed by landlords to let rooms. She now knew that 'cosy' meant minuscule; 'spacious' meant no furniture; 'charming' meant dilapidated and 'central' meant anything up to an hour's bus-ride from the Liffey.

Still, it's only my first day, she consoled herself as she pushed open the door to the Café Firenze. It was too early to go back to the flat without questions being asked, and she was not ready to say anything to the cousins yet about her plans. Time enough to let them know when she had found a place.

The café was empty apart from a small group of Italian men sitting at the table by the window. Oscar was with them when she came in. Anne Marie couldn't help noticing how his whole demeanour changed when he spoke Italian. He had always struck her as reserved and even melancholy, but here he was chatting animatedly and laughing out loud with these men. His whole body seemed more at ease when he reverted to his mother tongue, as though learning English had somehow involved putting on a strait-jacket that prevented him from expressing his true nature.

'*Caffè latte per favore,*' Anne Marie said when he came over to take her order.

Oscar grinned. '*Certo. Anne Marie va bene?*' he asked as he tore the page off his pad and stuck it between the sugar bowl and the milk jug.

'Sorry, my Italian doesn't go beyond "please" and "thank you", but yes, I'm fine, thanks. And you?' She was too polite to ask him why he hadn't come to the Hallowe'en party when he had seemed so grateful for the invitation.

'*Molto bene, grazie,*' Oscar said, wondering why she was being so friendly today when she had completely ignored him at the party she had invited him to in the first place. He brought her the coffee and put it down beside her *Evening Herald*, which was open on the *Accommodation* page. 'Moving out, are you?'

Anne Marie clicked off her ball-point and blushed. 'Em, yes actually, I am. But I haven't told my cousins yet, so . . .'

'Don't worry, your secret's safe with me.'

One of the men from the other table had got up to go to the men's room. On his way back, however, he changed tack and came over to her table. He put his hands on Oscar's shoulders, smiled at Anne Marie, and launched into a stream of Italian, the only words of which she understood were *bella signorina*.

'He wants me to introduce you to him,' Oscar said apologetically. 'Uncle Nico, this is Anne Marie. Anne Marie – Uncle Nico.'

Uncle Nico insisted on taking her hand and kissing it, much to Anne Marie's amusement. He looks just as an Italian uncle should look, she thought: twinkling brown eyes, stocky figure, warm hands with thick, blunt fingers. After he had released her hand, Nico leaned over the table conspiratorially. 'I tell him is time he get married,' he said in a loud whisper. 'Look at him, see how pale and sad he is. Why he don't find a nice girl like you and marry her. Then he happy! What about you? You have boyfriend already?'

'Stop it, Nico!' Oscar grabbed his uncle and steered him away from Anne Marie before she could think what to reply. Back at the table with the other men, who it transpired were all Oscar's uncles, there was much laughter and teasing of poor Oscar. At one point, Nico proposed a toast and all the men solemnly raised their glasses of *grappa* and drank her health.

Anne Marie quite enjoyed the attention, though she did feel sorry for the embarrassment it was causing Oscar. It was nice to be noticed by men, and it was such a long time since anyone had kissed her that even Uncle Nico's lips on the back of her hand had made her heart beat a little bit faster.

That was the biggest disappointment about coming to Dublin. In spite of her friend Maggie's dire statistics – four women to every man in the capital city – Anne Marie had hoped that by now she would have found a boyfriend. She had pictured herself working in a big office with lots of male colleagues; even if she hadn't hit it off with any of them, there would have been outings with the other girls to clubs and pubs, office parties and all the rest of it. She had been so confident that once she left home, everything was going to fall into place. Job, flat, boyfriend – in that order. The first two had already failed to live up to her expectations; according to the law of averages, surely the third one should exceed them? But so far there was no sign of anything stirring on the horizon of her love-life. Oscar was nice, but of course he wasn't really interested. He'd probably accepted her invitation to the party out of politeness. The truth of it was that since coming to Dublin, she had met no one who remotely caught her fancy.

The Art of Letter-writing

Dear Anne Marie, wrote her grandmother. *By the time you read this letter, I will be dead. I know it will be a sad time for you*

No, no, that was all wrong. Far too maudlin. Nano scrunched up the first sheet of notepaper and began again.

My dearest Anne Marie,

It is December and in a few weeks, you will be joining me for Christmas. May I say how much I am looking forward to your visit?

I do believe the house welcomes the arrival of young people too. It is far too big for an elderly woman on her own! I am so looking forward to showing you around now that the renovations are complete. There is more to this than pride, however, because, you see, my dear, I have left Riverwood to you in my will.

I think you know that Clarissa, who you do not remember but who lived long enough to see you take your first steps here at Riverwood, stipulated that the estate should pass henceforth through the female line. Her own childhood home in England was entailed and went to a distant male cousin while she was quite young, so perhaps this was her way of righting the balance. Of course, as she also lost her husband and two sons in the world wars, and there was no one else with a claim on it, she could do what she liked with the estate.

So it was that she bequeathed it to her one-time housekeeper and later companion, Anne Davenport.

Now that I too am reaching the end of my life

Nano stopped writing. The end of her life – did she really mean that? She was sixty-five and in the whole of her health. She had made her will years ago, but since the sale of part of the estate and the renovation of the big house, she had been advised to update it. She had finished the legal side, and now she was trying to draft a letter to the main beneficiary: Anne Marie. But was it really necessary? What did she want to say in the letter? The will itself was self-explanatory; its contents would only come as a surprise to Anne Marie if her grandmother died suddenly in the next couple of years. Otherwise, she would be told when she reached her twenty-first birthday.

So really, I don't have to say anything about it at all, thought Nano happily as she tore up the second sheet and began a third time.

Dear Anne Marie,

You're coming for Christmas – how wonderful! What shall we have on the menu? I'm almost vegetarian when I'm on my own, but my farming neighbour Dermot, who bought the hundred acres north of the river, has organic turkeys – should I order one?

The hectic social life you're no doubt enjoying up in Dublin will make Riverwood *seem terribly dull, so don't think that you have to stay for more than a few days, though I would of course be delighted if you wanted to.*

Best love for now,
Nano.

She read it over. Had she struck the right tone? It didn't sound too needy, did it? Nano was looking forward to her granddaughter's visit more eagerly than she cared to admit. For although she lived an active life and had devised some rather unorthodox methods for occupying her spare hours, the truth was that Anne Marie's grandmother had begun to suffer increasingly from the most insidious of ailments to attack the old: loneliness.

Having sealed the envelope and put a stamp on it, Nano stretched and looked at the clock. It was a quarter to three; there would still be enough light to plant the daffodil bulbs that Dermot had given her. Or she could take her bike and cycle into the village to catch the last post. She could do with the exercise.

On the other hand, the forecast was for rain, and really, dusk was about to fall.

It would take her a few minutes to set everything up, by which time it would be practically dark and she would be within the rules she had set for herself.

Ten minutes later, armed with a cup of cocoa and wearing a shawl around her shoulders, Anne Davenport, aka Nano, alias La Belle Dame Sans Merci, Scarifier and Kali switched on her computer. She entered the password that allowed her to log onto her favourite games site and resumed the struggle for dominance on the planet Kyridos, which was being threatened by alien hordes controlled by the dark lord Neron, aka Stu Butterby from Portland, Oregon.

Scoop!

Sally O'Shea, junior reporter with the *Evening Echo*, was having trouble with her hat. It was a rather fetching French beret that was supposed to be worn at a jaunty angle à la Greta Garbo. Unfortunately, on this blustery day in December, it positively refused to stay on top of her bouncy red curls. 'Bloody wind', she grumbled, jamming it down for the nth time over her forehead.

Eleven o'clock on a Saturday morning – she had better things to be doing than slogging around after some fat-arsed businessman who wanted to make a name for himself. Opening a playground – phaw! It wasn't fair that she was the one got sent off to all these boring assignments when there were lots of juicy scandals going on all over the city. She was good at sniffing things out; hadn't she uncovered the Sylvester Reed story single-handedly? Of course, they'd taken it from her pretty quick, but ha ha, the senior reporter hadn't been able to dig up anything new and the story had soon died for lack of sustenance.

Sally was sure there was a book to be written about the South Circular Strangler, and she was determined that she was the one who would write it, but for the moment, her research was at a dead end. Nobody seemed to know anything about Sylvester's childhood, and those who had known him recently, like his work colleagues, proved infuriatingly tight-lipped every time she tried to interview them. Pity they couldn't be like that Vera Meaney one, who lived in the same house as the murderer and couldn't stop talking about him even though it was clear from the start that she had barely known him.

I'll have to sneak back there sometime and try to get hold of the young one that found the body, Sally thought; if he tried to kill her, then maybe they had some sort of relationship going.

It began to drizzle. Sally cast a resentful eye at the clouds and turned up the collar of her Burberry. Stupid bloody assignment; if this weather kept up, her hair would be a total frizz by the time she got home and she'd have to wash it again before she went out. She sighed. Might as well get it over with quickly.

The playground was at the corner of a small square that had until very recently been the site of a derelict factory. Sally, who had grown up not far from this area of the inner city, used to pass it on her way to school every day. Lately, it had acquired a bad reputation as being a place where druggies went to shoot heroin. Someone had ODed here last year. Now this rich git who'd made his fortune out of shady property deals had gone all goody-goody and turned it almost overnight into a pleasant little park with flowerbeds, benches, a sandpit and a well-equipped playground. 'Giving something back to the community,' he called it. Tuppence ha'penny out of the millions he'd swindled back in the 1970s and 1980s, if the rumours were true. Oh, there was a story in it, right enough, if only you could tell it the way you wanted to.

'Excuse me, Mr Dunne, but would you care to list the officials in the Corpo and the county councils to whom you passed brown envelopes in return for re-zoning and planning favours? Oh, and while you're at it, you might as well disclose the names of the government ministers you're rumoured to have in your pocket.' Fat chance of anything like that happening. These bastards were always armed to the teeth with razor-sharp lawyers; she'd be on the street if she dared to step out of line.

The rain stopped and a pale sun appeared through a break in the clouds. Thank goodness for that, thought Sally as she went through the gate and headed towards the knot of people gathered in front of the children's slide. Between it and the swings a white ribbon was hung. Dunne was there in the middle, with his PR team hovering in the background. They were waiting for the arrival of the minister who would perform the ceremony and make the usual noises about urban regeneration and the importance of green spaces and playing facilities for the city's children. Appropriately enough, a few local kids were there – invited in for authenticity, no doubt. She could hear them effing and blinding at the delay in the ceremony.

Sally reached the edge of the group at the same time as two small children who had come racing up the path after her.

'I bags first go on the slide!'

'I bags the wobbly bridge!'

Sally smiled down at them. Cute kids; a girl and a boy. Twins? Could be. From their accents, she could tell they were not from the area. So who they were with? She might ask if she could borrow them for a photo with the big man, before his own PR team spotted them. She grinned to herself: Dunne's PR people could have the gurriers from the flats. Sally looked around. That blonde beanpole carrying a couple of Pokémon backpacks – the children must be with her. Too young to be their mother; probably the au pair. Danish or German by the look of her. Sally manoeuvred herself into position near the children and got her camera ready.

'Are we allowed to go into the playground now?'

'No, but you will be in a minute. When the ribbon is cut. See, the minister's car is just arriving now.'

No, not Danish! A culchie, from Cork or someplace like that. She was waving to someone – oh, the Man Himself. Did she know him then? That was useful.

Sally got her tape recorder ready and checked the film in her camera.

'Anne Marie! It was very good of you to come!' Desmond Dunne came over and shook hands with the beanpole.

'Oh, not at all, Mr Dunne. I think it's great what you're doing. I was babysitting for a friend anyhow and I thought it would be perfect for the kids.'

Right, thought Sally; a piccie of the sweet kiddies and the nice man who made this park before the bigwig gets out of the car. Turn on the tape recorder in case he drops any gems and here we go. Smiling, Sally stepped out to take a photograph of Dunne as he hunkered down to talk to the two children.

'Hello there! Who might you be?'

'I'm Jake Hunter,' the boy said stiffly.

'And I'm Ruth McDaid Hunter,' the little girl said with a triumphalist look at her brother.

'Well, well, that's wonderful. I'm very pleased to meet you.' He offered them his hand to shake but the children refused it. The girl put her hands behind her and the boy backed away. Dunne looked surprised and a little put out, but he covered it well. He smiled broadly at them. 'And do you know who I am at all?'

There was a moment's silence. The children glanced at each other, their faces suddenly grave. They moved closer together.

'Yes.' That was the boy, but he was looking down at his shoes when he said it.

'All right then, who am I?' Dunne winked up at the beanpole called Anne Marie then turned his attention to the little girl. 'Do you know?'

Sally bent down to take a photo on the same level as the children.

The girl stuck her lower jaw out. 'You're the man that killed our granny and our auntie. Our mam saw you on the television last week and she was crying. She said you should be locked up!'

Sally gasped, but recovered herself instantly. Snap! Dunne's face registers shock and – could it be guilt? Snap, snap! The little boy, who has begun to sob, kicks Dunne on the leg. Snap, snap, snap! The beanpole has her arms around the children. She looks up in horrified bewilderment at Dunne, who is standing now. He is rigid and pale.

The PR people become aware of the commotion and move in. They are alarmed when they see Sally with her camera, but that doesn't matter any more. She doesn't need to stay for the opening of the playground – she has her story!

Crossed lines

The phone rang four times before the answering machine clicked on: *You have reached the Sackville residence. We are unable to take your call at present, but if you care to leave a message, please do so after the tone.*

Dunne smiled grimly. You usedn't to talk like that in the old days, he said inside his head. When you were slumming it with me.

To the machine, he said: 'Mary, I think you know who this is. You've seen the news, no doubt. We should talk. You know where to contact—'

He heard a click as the phone at the other end was picked up. 'Nobody calls me Mary any more.'

'So you are there. What do they call you then?'

'By my real name.'

'Oh yeah – Anastasia, to rhyme with geisha.'

'It's Anastazia – the Russian way. What do you want? Make it brief.'

'Have you been contacted by the media?'

'Not yet. I am ex-directory, you know.'

'What are you going to tell them?'

'The truth! For twenty-five years I've kept silent to protect John. Well, it's finished; the world is going to learn what really happened that evening. I shall be glad to get rid of the burden of grief that has been the cause of so many sleepless nights.'

'Spare us, Mary.'

'Hah! I can tell *you* haven't changed. You feel no remorse even now, do you? You just want to see if you can hide once again behind my family's good name as you did back then. Do you have any idea of how despicable you are? I shudder to think that I was once married to you.'

'Yeah, you were a good shudderer, I'll say that much for you.'

'Oh! How dare you . . . God, I loathe you.'

'Well, don't get yourself into a tizzy on my account then. Or have your nerves improved with age?'

'I don't have to listen to this!'

'That's right – you don't. But as long as you're going to be telling the truth, I just want to know which version of it is going out. You know as well as I do that I was not drunk when we had the accident.'

'You had been drinking all night!'

'How would you know? You dropped me like a used snot-rag as soon as we were inside your parents' front door. As for my drinking, I could have downed a bucket of that sparkling wine and still been sober.'

'How dare you! It was champagne, the very best. Daddy never serves anything else.'

'Champagne, then. Not a real drink an' anyhow. No, it wasn't the drink that went to my head on the way home in the car.'

'I don't know what you're talking about!'

'Oh, I think you do. Every time we went to visit Daddy in Dartry it was the same: you were eaten up by the thought of all you'd thrown away. Your rebellious phase didn't last long, did it? Marrying a gouger from Ballyfermot didn't seem like such a clever thing to have done when you were back with your posh friends. Remember how you used to get on my case before we ever left home? "Don't ask for a drink, wait until you're served; they're not sandwiches, they're canapés; don't use language in front of the servants, it's bad example"; on and on. The wonder is that I didn't drink myself stupid.'

'You're despicable! You crashed into that car and killed those poor, poor people because you were drunk! That's the truth of it.'

'Is it? Is it really? What about the drive home? You were always vicious after those evenings, but this time you surpassed yourself. First you told me about your affair with that poncey barrister who worked with your father, and when that didn't rattle me, you went for the jugular. I still remember the look in your eye when you informed me that John was probably not my son. You knew you'd won. But you chose your moment badly. The lights had changed, only I didn't see them. That's why you were very quick to swap places with me after the accident. You had a conscience then. Not any more, I gather.'

'I've never heard anything so outrageous. I never . . . it's just not true!'

'Save your breath. I don't care what you say to the papers. It's John I'm concerned about. Where is he? Does he know?'

'John has been in Moscow for the past year. He is in the process of setting up a programme for street children. Of course, it's only a temporary thing; he is doing his bit for the less fortunate, but very soon he'll come back and settle down to finish his law studies and join Daddy's firm. I daresay he'll learn about your disgrace in time, but I shan't be the one to break it to him.'

'Well, well. A programme for street children in Moscow? How about that! Looks like something good may have come from the two of us after all!'

Holy well

Anne Marie was babysitting again. It was the day after the incident in the park, and Stephen had gratefully accepted her offer of looking after the children for a whole day. Roz was going to need all his attention. When she learnt that the man who had ruined her life had been in contact with her children, she had shrieked and torn her hair, then she had broken down into hysterical sobbing that had frightened the twins and made Ellie turn pale.

Anne Marie felt bowed down by guilt, not just for having been the means by which the twins had come into contact with Dunne, but for having worked with him for two months and liked him. She couldn't continue to work for him now, of course; they both knew that. After her shock at the discovery that her boss was the monster who had killed Roz's mother and sister, what had upset Anne Marie the most was the expression on Dunne's face. In the look he gave her before he allowed his PR people to lead him away to greet the minister, there had been such sadness and remorse that she knew, whatever the world threw at him, the real pain and suffering would be inside. In spite of her sympathy for Roz, at that moment she couldn't help wishing him well.

The twins were still subdued when Anne Marie arrived at the house on the South Circular Road. Roz had had a bad night and was tearful and fragile. Stephen had taken charge; Anne Marie was surprised to discover how competent and self-confident he was when the need arose. Of course, he had got over his shyness with her after her second or third visit, but she had never had the opportunity to exchange more than a few words with him up to this. Now he took her aside and admitted that he was quite concerned about Roz. He wanted to take her away for the day, treat her to a couple of good meals and try to bring her out of her misery.

'I thought you might want to take the kids swimming,' he said, showing Anne Marie the sports bags he had prepared and lined up in the hall. 'It's not a very nice day for the park and they could do with some exercise. Jake and Ruth are quiet now, but once we've left, they won't be long recovering their spirits. I made pizzas this morning; you just have to put them in the oven, and there's a chocolate pudding in the fridge. For tea, I thought they could have takeaway fish and chips, or maybe if you didn't mind going out again, you could take them to a burger place. There's plenty of money in the kitty on top of the fridge; just take what you think you'll need.'

A wan-looking Roz came down the stairs and acknowledged Anne Marie with a weak smile. Stephen helped her into her overcoat and turned up the huge fake fur collar so that she almost disappeared. 'Thanks again, Anne Marie, we really appreciate this,' he whispered as he ushered his wife out the front door.

After lunch, the twins wanted to play in the garden. Anne Marie let them out until the weather turned bitterly cold and a freezing rain began to fall. Then she brought them back inside and sat them down in the playroom to watch a video. While she was clearing the kitchen, Ellie came in carrying her schoolbag. She stopped when she saw that Anne Marie was working and would have turned away, but Anne Marie smiled and pointed her to the table. 'I've wiped it already, so it's OK to put your books down. Are you doing homework?'

Ellie nodded.

'What is it? Do you need some help?'

Ellie sat in at the table and opened her satchel. 'I've two sums left for Maths, a poem to learn for Irish, and a story to write for English.'

'Ooh, I like stories. What's yours about?'

'It can be about an ancient stone circle, a hawthorn tree or a holy well. We learnt about the druids and all that last week.'

'That's great! Do you know, there's a holy well on my grandmother's land down near Limerick; it's supposed to have magical healing powers. Would you like me to tell you about it?'

Ellie sat up at once. 'Yes, please!'

'Well, it's been there for at least two thousand years, maybe a lot more. People have always known about it and used it. But when the English came, the land was given to a nobleman and he built a wall around it. However, the wall kept being broken down near the well, so eventually he realised that he wasn't going to be able to keep people away and he made a gate to let them in and out. It was still there until a few years ago when the county council widened the road. My grandmother wanted the gate put back but they said it was too dangerous because there was a bend in the road, so now she has a notice on the main gate to say that people are welcome to come in and take water if they want. Hardly anybody does any more, though.'

'Did you ever go there?'

'Oh yes. When I was a kid, I used to spend every summer at my grandmother's with my cousins. We always went down to the well to check what new wishes had been put up.'

'Wishes?'

'Yes. People would often write their wishes on a card, or hang a prayer on a branch of the holly tree beside the well. There were lots of ribbons and scraps of clothing as well. I think you were supposed to put something belonging to the sick person on the tree, say a prayer, and take the water back to them to drink.'

'Did you do that?'

Anne Marie gave an embarrassed laugh. 'Well, it wasn't exactly a sickness that I was trying to cure, but I did make a wish, once.'

'Did it work?'

'I suppose you could say it did. You see, when I was nine, my best friend Maggie and I had a falling-out just before the summer holidays. She wouldn't talk to me for two weeks and I was miserable. I couldn't bear to think that she wouldn't be my friend in September, so

I managed to steal the scrunchie she wore in her hair before the end of school. Down at Nano's, I put it on the tree and said a prayer every day.'

'How did you make her drink the water?'

'Well, I couldn't, because she wasn't there. So I drank it myself instead. And it must have worked, because she came right up to me on the first day of school, put her arm through mine and said she wanted to make sure that we were put sitting together again for the year.'

Ellie digested the story in silence and then smiled. 'Cool!' She hesitated and peered intently at the pattern on the oil-cloth, then asked: 'Could I use that for my homework? Not the exact same story, but one like it?'

'Sure, I'd be honoured. Will you let me read it when you've finished?'

Ellie nodded and set to work.

Shark with wings

Desmond Dunne put his hands behind his head, leaned back in his hand-tooled leather chair and whistled softly through his teeth. It was three days since the tempest had broken over him and there was no sign of it abating. Outside his office, the media dogs were salivating. They would joyfully tear him to pieces as soon as he stepped out onto the street.

Safe in the eye of the storm for the moment, Dunne went over in his mind the events that had brought him to this pass. The worst moment by far was the first, when two small children in the company of the woman he wanted to impress above all others had looked at him and seen, not a genial businessman with his pockets full of lollipops, but the demon who had robbed them of their granny and their aunt.

They had their mother's eyes.

She had been sitting in the front passenger seat with her safety belt on. The older child in the back had shot straight through the windscreen, killing her mother on the way.

Strangely, after the shock of being recognised by the children in the park, and the stab of pain caused by Anne Marie's horror-stricken expression, the overwhelming feeling Dunne had experienced was one of relief. Now that the darkest secret of his past was out, there was nothing more to fear. For more than two decades he had suppressed his conscience, refusing to acknowledge the need to face up to his actions and in some way, make reparation. He had let ambition take the vacant place, and set out to prove himself in the cut-throat world of business.

Inside his breast pocket, Dunne's cellphone vibrated.

Jacqui.

He ignored it.

On the wall at the far end of his office hung an enormous framed photograph of a mako shark. The mouth was open, revealing a row of curved bottom teeth set like knives into the jaw. Almost as fearsome as the teeth were the wild eyes on either side of its blunt snout. Because of the way the shark filled the entire frame, looking at the picture was a bit like standing under a jumbo jet at take-off. People glanced at it and shuddered, just as Dunne intended. In the early days, when he had yet to establish himself, it used to hang over his desk.

What most impressed people was the fact that Dunne had taken the photograph himself. It was on one of his first diving expeditions off the Great Barrier Reef. He had been about to take a picture of an innocent parrot fish, but it had streaked out of range at the same time as Dunne had sensed the approach of something big behind him. Turning, he had pressed the button on the camera before he had properly registered what was there. The shark, startled by the flash, had disappeared. It was only when Dunne had got the photos back that he realised what a lucky escape he had had. The picture, quite by fluke, was outstanding; his divemaster had offered him two thousand Australian dollars for it on the spot.

Dunne regarded the shark incident as a metaphor for his life. Grab and run was a lesson he had learnt before he was out of nappies. He was the runt of the litter, appearing eighteen years after the last of his three brothers. At home, he had been the recipient of little kindness, except on occasion from his mother, when she remembered that he existed. His brothers had been hard men, better acquainted with the inside of Mountjoy Prison than the four walls of their own homes. The drink and the fags had got them all before fifty, just as they had his old man.

Left to his own devices from the age of ten, Desmond Dunne had learned to seize opportunities when they presented themselves, often without knowing what exactly they entailed. Marriage to the aristocratic Mary/Anastazia had been like that.

They had met at the Glastonbury festival, where she was handing out anti-nuclear leaflets and smoking pot. Dunne had taken the ferry to Holyhead a week earlier with a spare shirt and underpants in a nylon sports bag, and had ended up in Glastonbury only because it was where everyone else seemed to be going. She had introduced him to pot, to her hippie friends and, back in Dublin the following week, to Mummy and Daddy. Mummy was descended from a Russian princess and Daddy was the senior partner in one of the country's most successful law firms. She thought she hated them. Dunne was paraded before them like a trophy horse. It was the force of parental disapproval that had clinched the relationship; they were married within six months.

We were doomed from the start, thought Dunne, but I did my best; I tried to fit in with her crowd. At first, this had consisted of arty student types on the fringes of society, where Dunne's working-class accent and lack of formal education were welcomed as signs of rebellion against the prevailing bourgeois morality. But the students had graduated and either capitulated or emigrated, leaving Mary bitter, disappointed, and a mother.

In his wildest dreams, Dunne could not have predicted the effect the birth of his first son would have on him. It was so unlike anything he had ever felt before that he had no name to give it. But as he'd held the infant in his arms and felt tears begin to flow, he had known that nothing in his future would ever come close.

Life's a contrary old bitch, mused Dunne. John, whom he could not be sure was his child, had absorbed all his stock of parental affection. For Jacqui's progeny, who had the Dunne genes stamped all over them, he rarely felt anything other than indifference.

It was almost ten years since he had seen John. After the divorce, Mary had poisoned the child's mind against him, so that the weekly visits gradually became an ordeal for both of them. Dunne had stopped insisting, though he always hoped that one day, John would return to him of his own accord. After all, he had been a devoted father for the child's first eight years; surely that counted in his favour? But John appeared to have assimilated the values of his upper-class grandparents who had taken him and his mother to live with them in their Dartry home after the split. When he was sixteen, he had changed his name from Dunne to Sackville.

Dunne sighed. There was no chance of reconciliation now. Even if Mary meant it when she said that John wouldn't hear about his disgrace from her, the Sackville grandparents would feel bound by no such delicacy. It wouldn't surprise him to learn that they'd already sent the relevant copy of the *Evening Echo* to Moscow by registered post.

The trouble about reaching the top, thought Dunne ruefully, was that the only direction left was down. He had a sudden vision of himself standing at the pinnacle of a tall tower, looking down on the little people at the bottom who were doing their best to topple it.

He had made plenty of enemies on the way up; now that the fatal crack in the edifice had appeared, they would all be there with their picks and their shovels. What were his options? He could cling on for dear life while they hacked and hammered. Let them have their way, then start again from the rubble. He might not reach his former heights, but he could stand a little downsizing.

Or he could jump – literally. Dunne snorted. Forget that; he was neither a coward nor an eejit. Besides, he fully intended to be the first male in his family to reach ripe old age.

No, there had to be another way. Staring at the shark on the wall opposite him, Dunne waited for it to come to him. After a few moments of intense thought, a slow smile began at the corners of his mouth. It grew, spreading to his eyes, which lit up with a long-dimmed fire. He knew what he was going to do.

Standing on the top of his tower, he would grow wings and fly.

First day at *Femme*

The porter on duty inside the entrance to the Phoenix building lowered his copy of the *Evening Echo* as Anne Marie came through the swing doors. He waited until she was at the desk, but before she had time to say anything, he held up his hand.

'I know, I know – you're a model. Here for a fashion shoot, right? Jaysus, but you're a long one! What's the weather like up there?'

Anne Marie smiled dutifully. 'Actually, I'm not a model. I'm starting work today on *Femme* magazine as assistant to Roz McDaid.'

'Is that so? Oh yeah, I heard the last one got the boot from Herself all right. She's a hard taskmaster, she is. Will you be up to it, do you think? Up to it – that's a good one, inn't it! Ha, ha.'

Anne Marie's smile was beginning to crack. 'Could you tell me how to get to the *Femme* office, please?'

'All right, if you insist. Third floor, turn left – hold on, here's someone'll take you up. Hey Dave, this young lady needs escorting. She's going your way.'

Dave turned out to be a darkly handsome man in his

late twenties or thereabouts. He had humorous grey eyes, a white smile and a diamond stud in his left earlobe. His hair was as expertly cut as his clothes. He smelt pleasantly of aftershave.

'You must be Anne Marie! Roz told me about you. Welcome aboard! I'm Dave, Art Director and General Dogsbody.' They shook hands. Anne Marie noted approvingly that his nails were clean and his handshake firm.

'Lift or stairs?' he enquired.

'Lift, I think. For today anyway!'

'Oh goodee! I was afraid you might be a fitness freak. We had one of those once. She wore ankle weights and spent her lunch hour running up and down four flights of stairs. Sad really, what happened to her.'

'What was that?'

'She'd taken to carrying weights in her hands as well. She dropped one on her foot, broke three bones and was in plaster for months. End of story – we never saw her again. Here we are. *Après vous, Mademoiselle.*'

As the lift doors closed, Dave drew close to Anne Marie. 'So tell me, has the boss warned you against me yet?' he whispered.

Anne Marie giggled nervously. 'I don't know what you mean. Roz never mentioned your name.'

Dave put his hand theatrically over his chest. 'I'm cut to the quick. She never mentioned me? Office Lothario, ladykiller extraordinaire – and handsome devil to boot. What an oversight!'

The lift pinged its arrival on the third floor before Anne Marie had time to respond. She had taken an instant liking to Dave and though she told herself that he was probably married with a whole clatter of kids, she couldn't stop a small part of her from wondering whether he might not be The One.

'This way.' Dave smiled into her eyes as he held open the glass doors to a corridor lined with poster-sized framed front covers of the magazine. 'Welcome to the wonderful world of *Femme*.'

Anne Marie was too excited to respond. She was about to start her new job, the job she had known was perfect for her ever since Roz had first mentioned it. She could hardly believe that only a few short weeks ago she had despaired of ever finding a way to leave her position as PA to Desmond Dunne. She remembered distinctly how she had wished for some unforeseen event to take care of it for her. Well, she had got her wish.

All the same, when it had come to handing in her resignation to Dunne, Anne Marie had felt sheepish and a little sad, but he had been extraordinarily nice to her. Of course he understood that she had to leave and he didn't blame her; he hoped that she would be happy in her work and in her personal life, and that . . . well, that she wouldn't think too badly of him. Anne Marie had blushed and mumbled that she couldn't. Dunne had looked relieved and pleased; for a moment, she had the impression that he was about to give her a hug, but he restrained himself and shook her hand instead. Then he presented her with a large padded envelope with what he referred to as her 'severance pay'. When she opened it back at the flat, she found that it contained five thousand pounds in cash.

The corridor curved into a large open-plan office with four workstations set well apart from each other. In the centre was a huge container holding a miniature oasis of real palm trees and ferns. It all looked terribly civilised and very far removed from Anne Marie's image of a cluttered, frenetic office with telephones ringing non-stop and lots of people shouting at each other over the din.

Roz was at the far desk with her back to them. She was talking on the telephone. There was no one else in the office as far as Anne Marie could see, but one of the workstations had a tall screen around it.

'As the boss is busy, I'll do the guided tour,' said Dave. He took her over to the desk nearest the corridor. 'This is where you will be, when you're not working with Roz. I'm over there by the window, and you can see where Roz is.'

'Who's behind the screen?'

'Nobody – at least nobody you're ever likely to meet. Isolde Phoenix, who owns *Femme*, drops in once in a blue moon, and that's where she sits. She sometimes leaves little typed notes for Roz, but otherwise we have no contact with her. She's extremely odd; I've only seen her once, and as soon as she saw me, she scurried off like a frightened rabbit. My animal magnetism was obviously too overpowering for her!'

'Running away from you – that doesn't sound odd to me!' Anne Marie risked teasing him. 'But you said her name was Phoenix – does that have anything to do with this being the Phoenix building?'

'She owns it. And *Femme* is her baby; she pays to make it the best women's glossy on the stands. Which is lucky for us; we don't have to worry about advertising to cover our costs. You'll notice there are more quality articles and fewer ads for hygienic femininity and orgasmic shampoos than in the other mags. But uh-oh, looks like I'm a naughty boy for keeping you from The Boss, who is desperately trying to attract your attention.'

Anne Marie turned. Roz, still talking on the phone, was waving frantically to her to come sit at the other side of her desk and take pencil and paper.

'Sibyl, I told you – it is *not* in with the gardening article! Yes, I've checked thoroughly; I am at this moment shaking the pages of the gardening article and nothing is falling out. No, of course I can't send a courier to Donegal! All right, all right, there's no need to get so upset, I understand . . . you have to follow the phases of the moon . . . you can't force your spirit guide to follow deadlines. It's just that I have a magazine to get out and . . . oh, hold on, Dave is signalling – I have another call. Listen, my new assistant Anne Marie has just arrived. Have you got a copy of the horoscopes there in front of you? OK, you can read them out to her. I'm handing you over now. Oh, and Sibyl . . . next time you make contact, please ask your spirit guide how soon you can get a computer!'

Roz covered the mouthpiece and spoke to Anne Marie. 'It's Sibyl – she does horoscopes and gardening, but we seem to be missing the horoscopes so could you take down what she says longhand? I'll show you how to set it up for the page after. Next month's issue has got to go to the repro house the day after tomorrow and we're way behind schedule. Oh, by the way – welcome to your new job!'

It was 9.15 when Anne Marie began working; the next time she looked at her watch it was 4.25. The magazine seemed to have lurched from one crisis to another throughout the day. After the horoscope, there was panic over a missing 'tranny', a transparency from a modelling agency that had to be returned by noon or be replaced at a cost of several hundred pounds. Roz, Dave and Anne Marie began a hunt that ended when Roz found it hidden at the back of the desk that had belonged to the last Editorial Assistant. Cursing the girl for her vindictiveness, Roz thrust the envelope into Anne Marie's hands and told her to take a taxi over to the agency in Grafton Street with it.

By the time she got back, Anne Marie's desk was piled high with work marked *urgent*. A lot of it involved undoing damage caused by the girl who had been fired; apparently, she had considered anything other than writing feature articles to be beneath her, so all the less glamorous but vitally important jobs had been left undone.

Lunch was a sandwich that Dave brought back from the nearest shop. Anne Marie was too busy even to notice what was in it. As soon as she finished eating, she began to ring the regular contributors to make sure they knew what they were supposed to be doing, and to remind them about forthcoming deadlines. It gave Anne Marie quite a thrill to introduce herself on the phone as the new Editorial Assistant, especially when the contributor was someone well known, or a freelance journalist whose work she admired.

By the time the phones finally stopped ringing and the last e-mail had gone out, it was well after 5 p.m.

Dave came over to check up on Anne Marie. 'Well, well, what do you know?' he said with a grin. 'Hey, Roz, you picked a good 'un this time. Guess what she's doing? Cleaning her mouse's insides!'

Anne Marie flushed. 'It was a bit sticky. On my computer course, we were taught to keep the equipment in good order so that it would perform well all the time, so I . . .'

She stopped when she realised that Dave was laughing at her. Roz came over and stood beside him.

'Whatever you're paying her, double it,' Dave advised.

Roz and Anne Marie looked at each other in surprise. 'Do you know,' Roz said, 'we never got round to discussing terms and conditions, did we, Anne Marie?'

Anne Marie agreed that they hadn't.

'Terms? For Roz – Boss, Your Highness, and any other obsequious form of address you care to use,' began Dave. 'For me – Darling, Gorgeous or . . . well, you get the idea. As for the conditions, you just have to remember the golden rule: Roz is always right!'

Roz gave him a slap. 'Shut up, Dave. Sorry, Anne Marie. We'll sit down and discuss your contract first thing in the morning – assuming you want to stay, that is.'

Anne Marie's face lit up. 'Oh, I do!'

Fishy business

Jacqui Dunne was worried. Something very strange was happening to her husband: he was being nice to her. He hadn't been home much since the revelations in the *Evening Echo*, but when he did turn up, he was full of concern for her and the kids. He apologised to her for the unwelcome media attention and suggested that the three of them go down to her mother's in Cork until this whole thing blew over.

Though she had never heard about the drunk-driving incident, it didn't surprise Jacqui to learn that her husband had been the cause of a fatal accident way back in his youth. It explained why he never drank when they went out and why, even at home, he was unusually abstemious for a man of his background and tastes.

It was bizarre the way the newspaper revelations had affected Des. By rights he should have gone into fighting mode, which is what he always did when he was attacked. He was merciless, hitting back twice as hard as his adversary, who was quickly beaten into submission and forced to crawl away to lick his wounds.

But Des appeared not to mind about the articles in the paper, which had now moved on from the original accusation to more broad-ranging attacks on his character and business affairs. He was suspiciously upbeat for a man whose reputation lay in tatters. He cracked jokes with the kids. He hummed as he went into his gym to work out. He thanked Jacqui for the dinner she put in front of him. He even made love to her at night. For old times' sake, he said.

Yes, there was something very fishy in all of this, thought Jacqui. She guessed that Des was planning something. He was so pleased with himself, as though he had it all worked out. He had hinted that he might be going away for a long time.

He's bought himself a bolt-hole in the South of France or Florida, she concluded, and he's going to retire there with his latest floozie. How could she have let her guard slip so far that she had no idea who it could be? Anne Marie must have been the distraction; he'd taken her on to set his wife's mind at rest and all the while his real mistress was elsewhere, tucked out of sight. She thought of her contingency plan and wished she had stashed away more loot against the day she had always known would come. A few hundred thousand pounds was not much when you suddenly found yourself out in the cold.

The post arrived. There was a letter for her from their solicitor. As she read it, Jacqui frowned, then gasped, then reached for the edge of the table and collapsed on to the nearest chair.

Now she knew why her husband was behaving so oddly. This letter proved beyond any doubt that he had lost his reason.

A million pounds each for Jason and Tiffany when they reached the age of twenty-five. Two million for herself. She got the house. He asked – asked! – only that she keep his gym equipment, in storage if necessary, for when he returned. Returned from where? If he was doing a runner, why would he want to come back?

She couldn't understand it; the solicitor's letter seemed to assume that she was the one who would be looking for a divorce. If the above conditions were agreeable to her, the solicitor wrote, an amicable separation could be arranged. Her signature on the enclosed document was required.

Jacqui ran to her desk and scrabbled among her unpaid Visa bills for the Mont Blanc pen she had been given by Des, along with the BMW, for her fortieth birthday. She rarely used it because she didn't like having to go to the bother of filling the thing with ink, but this was one signature she wanted to last! Des might be mad, but a legal document was a legal document, and if their solicitor was prepared to stand over it, then that was good enough for her.

As she scrawled her name across the bottom, Jacqui excitedly began mapping out the rest of her life. She would sell up and move down to Cork; buy a house in

Montenotte and send the kids to boarding school. She had never really made it on the social scene in Dublin, though she had once had a very pleasant conversation with Norma Smurfit, but in Cork it would be different. Soon she would be hosting elegant soirées that would be the talk of the town, and making a regular appearance in the social columns of the *Irish Examiner*, ensuring that in no time at all, anyone who was anyone in Ireland's second city would be clamouring for an introduction to its brightest socialite: Jacqui Marchant-Dunne.

Giving it all away

Desmond Dunne was on a high. It was the best feeling he'd had in a very long time, better even than cocaine, which he had taken, once only, as part of his philosophy of leaving no experience untried in his life.

The feeling he had now was better because it lasted longer, it required no chemical stimulus, and it left his mental faculties intact.

But it cost a fortune. Dunne chuckled to himself at the thought that what he had paid so far to maintain his high was enough to keep the entire population of Ireland supplied with recreational drugs for a very long time.

Set out neatly on the low table in the living room of the Baggot Street apartment were eight chequebooks, a stack of files, and a ledger with a list of names. Each name had a sum of money entered across from it, and as Dunne wrote his cheques, he ticked off the names in the ledger.

By rights, he mused as he took a break from writing cheques and flicked back through the pages he'd completed, the first name should have been his mother's. When he was four he had begun stealing money out of her purse to buy sweets or, if she'd forgotten to feed him again, a loaf of bread and some ham. He'd stolen from his brothers as well, but he'd had the shite kicked out of him for that. Even if they had been alive, he wouldn't have wanted to make it up to them. It was a pity about his ma, though; she hadn't been the best of mothers, but he had been fond of her and he'd have liked to have provided for her in her old age. Unfortunately, she had died suddenly when he was just getting started. She had met her posh daughter-in-law all right, but she hadn't lived long enough to hold her only grandchild.

The first name on the list was therefore that of the old couple who had owned the corner shop from which Dessie Dunne had lifted sweets, crisps and packets of Woodbine on a regular basis throughout his childhood. The sweets and crisps he kept for himself, but he opened the packets of Woodbine and sold the cigarettes singly to the winos outside the off-licence. There was no chance that the old couple were still alive, but Dunne had traced a grandchild and written a cheque that made good the losses the family had incurred as a result of his light fingers. Naturally, he couldn't be sure of the amount involved, so to be on the safe side he thought of a figure, doubled it, then added a couple of noughts. That would allow for inflation over a period of forty years at an annual rate well above the average.

In this way, Dunne had already completed three pages in his ledger and emptied two chequebooks. He had reached the period in his life after his divorce from Mary-who-was-now-Anastazia and before his marriage to Jacqui Marchant, the foxy fortune-hunter from Cork. By then, he was already a millionaire several times over but, as he paused to look back over his life, Dunne realised that he was at his hungriest during the years between his two marriages. He was also at his most ruthless, which is why most of the rest of the names in the ledger dated from that period.

Dunne put down his pen and stretched. It amused him to imagine the reactions of shock, incredulity and suspicion that would be aroused by the arrival of his cheques. He had already been rung up by a hysterical woman in Tipperary who had berated him for his swindling of her father and other misdeeds, both real and imagined. No amount of money could wipe out the memory, she had said. But she had cashed the cheque first. So had most of the other recipients, the quickest off the mark being those who had received amounts of six or seven figures, he noted. No one had returned his money, though he had had one stiff little note from a nun telling him that she would prefer him to make out his cheque to the Society of St Vincent de Paul.

Dunne's original idea had been to get rid of all of it, down to the last penny. He wanted to feel cleansed, naked, pared down to the resources of sinew, bone and brain. But after careful thought, he had regretfully compromised. It would not do to find himself dependent on anyone, and as his immediate-to-mid-term future held many uncertainties, he needed something to fall back on. He would keep the Baggot Street apartment. It would be let if he was forced out of circulation for any length of time, so there would be a small income for him to live off when he returned.

And the fact that he still had at least one asset should reassure those closest to him that he had not gone completely bonkers.

Suddenly, Dunne's face clouded. Those closest to him: that should mean John, but it didn't. Of all the people that he wanted to donate his money to, the one who meant most to him was the very one who would throw it back in his face. Dunne wondered if there wasn't some way in which he could finance his son's charity work in Russia without him finding out.

He thought for a few minutes, but no satisfactory plan came to mind. It was something to mull over however, and he would make sure to hold back a sum in reserve for the time when the solution would come to him.

Home again, home again

Darina was heading homewards. She didn't seriously expect the change of scene to improve her spirits, but there were certain advantages to spending the weekend in the bosom of her family. She'd save money, for a start. Knowing that they'd never see her otherwise, her parents paid for two return train tickets each term, so the journey itself was costing her nothing. She wouldn't have to buy food or drink; if they went out, her father would take care of the restaurant bill and the pub. Going home also meant that she had an excuse for not working on her latest French assignment; if she was in Limerick, she couldn't access the books she needed, could she? Finally, there was no lover to keep her in the capital. Despite her best efforts at the party, the guy from her Russian class hadn't responded to her over-tures. She didn't care about him enough to be cut up about it, but a bit of casual sex would have been nice.

Anne Marie was going home too. She was probably so excited about her new job on the magazine that she couldn't wait to run home and tell her parents about it, thought Darina as they queued for the train. She wasn't exactly jealous, because she had no interest in the type of work that Anne Marie was doing, but she did envy her cousin the way her life was moving forward. After only a short period in the capital, Anne Marie was no longer a country bumpkin but a con-fident, sophisticated city girl with a glamorous job and interesting, grown-up friends.

The cousins boarded the train and, for Anne Marie's sake, found two free seats in a non-smoking com-partment.

Gazing out the window at nothing as she waited for the train to leave, Darina wondered morosely if anything interesting would happen in her own life, and if so, when? Not while she was still a student anyway. For the next year-and-a-half she would have to put up with the French course she hated. Once she sat the first part of her finals and was free of that yoke from around her neck, she would be able in her Senior Sophister year to concentrate on her preferred subject: Russian. She sighed. Where was the fun in all of this? Student days were supposed to be a time for being irresponsible, doing wild things and not caring about the consequences, travelling the world on a shoestring and meeting new people.

At the idea of travel, Darina perked up. She would have to start organising her holidays soon. She had worked all of last summer and had no intention of doing the same this year.

On the table between her and Anne Marie lay several magazines that her cousin had bought at Heuston Station, 'for research', she had told Darina. Her eye was drawn to a page that contained a competition for a week's holiday at a Club Med resort in the Caribbean. It wasn't the sort of travel that Darina had in mind, but the picture-postcard setting appealed and she asked Anne Marie if she could have a look at it.

The resort was called Corsairs' Cove. It looked nice all right, but the blurb for Club Med didn't sound terribly attractive to Darina, who had an aversion to organised events designed to Bring Girls and Boys Together in a Range of Healthy Outdoor Activities, as the circular for the parish youth club used to put it. Another time, she would have read the caption, looked at the pictures, then turned to the next page without a second thought. But Anne Marie was engrossed in her research of the magazines that competed for readership with *Femme*, leaving Darina with nobody to talk to and nothing to occupy her mind. As she had no desire to take out the prescribed Zola novel she had brought with her for just such an eventuality, she read the competition requirements again, then idly filled in her details on the entry form and answered the three blatantly obvious questions.

Home alone

With Darina and Anne Marie gone home for the weekend, and Cornelius in college finishing a paper on statistics, the flat seemed strangely quiet.

Just what I was waiting for, thought Gerald on the

Saturday afternoon. This was his big chance; he might not get an opportunity like it again.

He had already got in everything he needed: syringes, an old metal spoon that wouldn't be missed, a candle, and the packet he had received from Deco in return for Anne Marie's ring. For a moment, Gerald wavered; he still felt bad about the theft, but he consoled himself with the thought that, had Anne Marie known that her ring had saved him from a severe beating, if not worse, then she would gladly have sacrificed it. Besides, what could he do? Give her the package and say, 'Sorry, Anne Marie, I had to borrow your ring to pay off my debts but here's some heroin to compensate you for your loss'? Yeah, right!

Gerald opened the package, took out one of the little plastic bags and poured some powder on to the spoon. He was not sure how it was supposed to look or taste, but Deco had said it was pure, and it would be bad for business to send out a dud sample. Gerald had already made contact with a student in the Classics Department who was interested in acquiring some. I don't blame her, he thought with a grin. In her shoes, I'd want something to liven up my Seneca too!

He lit the candle and held the spoon over the flame.

At that same moment, down the road in Rathmines Garda station, the long-suffering Tony was fighting a losing battle with his ambitious young colleague. 'But Brenda,' he groaned, 'what reason have we got for going back? None! We'll be done for harassment at this rate. Give them – and me – a break, won't you?'

'You've had a break while I was at my sister's wedding in St Lucia. Nearly a week, which is longer than is good for you, judging by the strain on the buttons of your uniform! Too many pastries and not enough walking the beat, I'm thinking. Come on, a brisk trot round to our friends in Belvedere Square will do you a power of good. You'll thank me for it later. And if you don't, your wife will.'

'But what are we going to say to them when we get there?'

'We're looking for the girl – Anne Marie, remember? We have a ring that we think might be the one that was stolen. That'll get us into the house. Then we'll see.'

'And where are we going to get the ring?'

'Here,' said Brenda, twisting a diamond engagement ring off the third finger on her right hand. 'My sister said she'll have my guts for garters if anything happens to it, so I'm giving it to you for safekeeping.'

'Thanks for nothing.' Tony heaved a gusty sigh and hauled himself regretfully from his armchair.

Fifteen minutes later, they turned the corner into Belvedere Square. Brenda quickened her pace and arrived at the gate of the house they were visiting ahead of Tony, who was wishing he could turn back in more ways than one. Was it too late for a career change? How about landscape gardening? Plenty of money in it, and a lot less grief.

He heard an ambulance siren on Leinster Road and hoped as he always did that it wasn't on its way to another road traffic accident. His first week on the job, he had been called to the scene of an horrific smash-up outside Sligo; the memory had never left him.

As he reached the gate where Brenda was tapping her foot impatiently, the ambulance swung round the corner and into the square. Tony saw Brenda stiffen and her eyes narrow to slits as the driver stuck his head out of the window to check the numbers on the doors.

The ambulance man spotted the two guards. He accelerated for the last few yards, then pulled smartly into the kerb beside them. At the same time, the door to the downstairs flat opened and a young man with dark hair and a florid complexion came rushing out. 'In here! Quick! I think . . . Oh God, I think he might be dead!'

The honeymoon is over

Anne Marie loved her new job. It was brilliant, she had told Yvonne and Seán; everything she could have wished for and more. Just think: in her first fortnight, she had been sent to try out different coffee bars in the city centre and rate them for their *Eating Out* page – and this counted as work, so she got overtime for it! She had also written two of the book and film reviews; when next month's issue came out, they would see her initials AME at the bottom of the column. Best of all, Roz had promised her that if things went well, she might ask her to write a features article herself in the next few months.

That wasn't to say that the other aspects of her job weren't fulfilling, she had hastened to add; unlike her predecessor, Anne Marie actually enjoyed filing, calling in copy from freelancers, making up job bags of fashion trannies, and generally lightening everyone else's load. She was the vital cog that made the machine run smoothly; without her, she had told them proudly, everything would quickly fall apart.

Yes, thought Anne Marie as she lay in her old bed on Saturday morning, Editorial Assistant of *Femme* magazine was the very best job she could have wished for herself.

And yet . . .

In one respect, *Femme* had turned out to be a great disappointment. Anne Marie had imagined that working with Roz would be wonderful. They had got on so well beforehand, and Roz had several times said how happy she was that Anne Marie had come into her life. But all that had changed after the Dunne incident.

Or rather, amended Anne Marie with a slight frown as she stared at the ceiling, *shortly* after the Dunne incident.

Thinking back carefully, she concluded that her first week or so at the magazine had been fine. She and Roz and Dave had clicked at once. They worked well as a team and shared a lot of laughs. It was true that Anne Marie had noticed that by five-thirty each evening, Roz had looked increasingly washed-out, but she had put this down to the stresses of the last few days before going to print. And anyway, Roz's attitude had not changed until later, when the magazine had already gone to the repro house and the pressure had eased off.

It was the day of the planning meeting, Anne Marie remembered, the Tuesday of her second week. At nine o'clock Dave had arrived in the office with a red rose clenched between his teeth. He went down on bended knee beside her and began to croon:

> '*Oh, sweet Anne Marie,*
> *Come run away with me.*
> *Together we will be*
> *Forever in harmony.*'

'Unlike your singing, then!' laughed Anne Marie. 'Get up out of that, you gombeen! And where did you get that rose, might I ask?'

'I plucked it with my own fair hands – out of the bouquet that arrived from an admiring fan of our excellent feature on *The Underbelly of the Celtic Tiger* last month.'

Anne Marie put on a mock pout. 'How could I run off with a man who's so stingy he won't even buy me a rose?'

Dave rose to his feet and grabbed one of her hands. 'You mean there's hope? All I have to do is spend lots of lolly and you'll say yes? *Oh frabjous day! Callooh! Callay!*'

Neither of them had noticed Roz arrive. At the sound of her voice, they both jumped.

'When the two of you have quite finished, we have a planning meeting in twenty minutes for the February issue. Anne Marie, where is the subbing I asked you to finish yesterday? Dave, what happened to those changes to the picture for the Bowie profile? I thought I told you to lose the cigarette. And check those colours again – they look all wrong to me.'

Like guilty children, Anne Marie and Dave hung their heads and set to work. Anne Marie, who had been in since twenty past eight and had already cleared her in-tray, felt particularly aggrieved by Roz's tone. She gathered up the subbed articles and brought them over to Roz, who accepted them without a word.

As the morning wore on, Roz's mood worsened. She was short with people on the phone and flew off the handle at Dave twice more. But Anne Marie felt strongly that the person Roz really had it in for was her.

Things came to a head during the planning meeting, when they were discussing feature articles for the months ahead. Dave said they ought to do something about the refugee issue. Roz agreed that they hadn't looked at that yet, and wondered who they could contact about it. Anne Marie thought at once of Victor; he worked with refugees, or rather, asylum seekers, she corrected herself. He spoke perfect English, and he was a lawyer so he would know a lot about the legal end of things. She was secretly pleased to think that here might be an opportunity to meet him again; since the evening she had bumped into him with her former boss, she had had a sense of something left unfinished. And she needed to give him back his map.

But when she proposed to contact the organisation he worked with, Roz turned on her. 'I don't need you to tell me how to do my job,' she snapped. 'I'm perfectly capable of making my own contacts, thank you very much.'

Anne Marie had swallowed the lump in her throat and fought hard to hold back the tears. What had she done to deserve this?

Behind the Editor's back, Dave had rolled his eyes and shaken his head in sympathy. 'PMS,' he mouthed silently.

Blaming Anne Marie

While Anne Marie was lying in her bed in Killorglin, trying unsuccessfully to make sense of her new boss's change in attitude towards her, in the house on the South Circular Road, Roz had just locked herself into her bathroom to get away from the twins' early-morning demands. She sat on the toilet and, putting her head in her hands, wished with all her might that she had never set eyes on Anne Marie Elliot.

Bloody Anne Marie. Bloody bloody Anne Marie and her bloody bloody bike.

The fatal encounter came back to her in painful clarity. She remembered how Ellie had called her to the door and how surprised she had been by the height of the young woman who was standing there asking about the bike. She remembered thinking that she had a sweet face which, when she heard that the bike was gone, looked as though it was about to dissolve into tears.

Roz groaned. Why did Anne Marie have to look so forlorn? she thought. Why did I have to feel sorry for her? And why on earth did I have to call her back?

In her mind, Roz played out a different version of events, one in which she kept her big mouth closed and let Anne Marie walk on down the path, through the gate, and out of her life for ever.

In this version, Stephen did not come home and get upset when he discovered that his bike was gone. He did not sulk for a week and make Roz miserable. She did not reach out to him in bed one night and he did not initiate a passionate reconciliation.

In this version of events, she was not now pregnant with their fourth child.

Darina decides to act

In the back of her mother's car, Darina sat biting her nails to the quick. Barbara Davenport was driving at over one hundred miles an hour, but it was not the speed that was bothering Darina. She was sick with fear that before they could reach St James's Hospital in Dublin, her brother would be dead of an overdose.

She blamed herself for not having followed up on her intention to sneak into Gerald's room and hunt for his stash, which she had been planning to take into her own room 'for safekeeping'. Of course, she hadn't known that he had got his hands on heroin; if she had, she would have read him the riot act after the party and made him give it back at once. But he had promised her that he would stay off gear and, like a fool, she had believed him.

Now it might be too late. Her stomach twisted itself into another knot as she imagined Gerald lying still and pale on a hospital bed with tubes coming out of him and medical staff with long faces shaking their heads when the family finally made it to his bedside.

It was Darina who had taken the call. She had thought it was some prankster on the phone and she had been about to hang up when somehow, out of the unintelligible whimpers and choking noises coming out of the receiver, she had made out the word 'overdose'. The rest she had guessed. She had managed to calm Cornelius down long enough to get the name of the hospital, then she had hung up.

Five minutes later, she and her parents were on the road to Dublin.

Don't let him die, begged Darina. Please, please, don't let him die. I'll do anything! I'll . . .

She stopped. What could she do? If there was a god, what would He, She or It want from Darina? It had to be something specific and achievable, and not a vague promise to be good for ever, which of course she would never commit herself to. She could try to give up drinking and maybe even smoking, but what would happen if she failed? She couldn't risk it.

Darina shifted agitatedly in her seat. She didn't believe in any sort of a god, so it was useless to think that she could bargain for her brother's life. She could only will him to stay alive until they got to the hospital; if she succeeded in that, somehow everything would come right. Catching a glimpse of her mother's grim profile as she swung the Mercedes past a cement lorry that was hogging the fast lane on the Naas road, Darina began to take heart. She knew that Barbara Davenport was not about to let her eldest son go without a struggle.

The outermost suburbs of Dublin came into view. Darina tried to calculate how long it would take to get to the hospital. No more than twenty minutes as long as they didn't become snarled in traffic at the M50 roundabout, she decided. Then they would know, for better or for worse.

To take her mind off the possibility that it might be 'for worse', Darina began to think about the people responsible for putting her brother's life in the balance. Whose poison had put him in hospital? Who were the faceless men behind the puppets who did the deals in the clubs? Who was making money out of her brother's weak nature?

She would like to know so that she could do something about it. Nobody put her brother's life in danger and got away with it.

Darina stopped biting her nails and began to formulate a plan.

Jesus freak

Looking at his reflection in the mirror, Daniel Davenport saw not an overweight middle-aged man with a receding hairline and gentle eyes, but a miserable loser who had failed at all the roles that life had thrust upon him: son, husband, provider, and now father.

As soon as they reached the hospital, he had begun to feel a tightness in his chest. The sensation had worsened as they approached the Intensive Care Unit, where the gowned and masked medical staff had made him deeply uneasy. And when finally he had been confronted with the sight that he had been dreading all along – his son stretched pale and immobile on the narrow hospital bed – he had fainted on the spot. A nurse had brought him a cup of sweet tea, but he could barely hold it steady on the saucer because of the tremor in his hands. In the end, Barbara had sent Darina outside with him to get a taxi that would bring him to the flat in Rathmines. 'You need to rest,' she had said. 'Take my mobile; if there's any change in his condition, I'll ring you straight away.'

Now he was alone in his children's flat, standing in front of the mirror in the corridor, filled with self-loathing. They would be far better off without me, he thought, turning away from his reflection in disgust. He wandered down the corridor to the living room at the back where there was a divan that opened out into a double bed. He and Barbara had slept there on their return from a sun holiday in Tenerife last winter.

Daniel sat on the edge of the divan and hung his head. The tight feeling was still there, like a steel band around his chest, along with a tingling sensation in his right arm.

Maybe I'm going to have a heart attack, he thought with something akin to relief. He imagined his family coming across his body when they returned to the flat later in the day. Of course there would be shock, followed by a brief period of mourning, then their lives would go on as before, only better. He was useless and he knew it.

A severe case of arrested development, he imagined the pathologist telling his students when they opened him up and found inside his chest cavity the heart of a nine-year-old boy.

Suddenly, Daniel Davenport was crying. He hadn't felt the build-up of tears, but there they were, welling from the corners of his eyes and spilling on to his hands. He knew that once they started to flow, he wouldn't be able to stop them. There was almost forty years' worth to be shed, and he had neither the strength nor the will to force them back.

And so he cried. He cried for his son in hospital and for his two other children who had a child for a father, and he cried for his wife who had never had a husband. But most of all he cried for the nine-year-old boy who had been robbed of his childhood by a still, sheet-covered figure laid out on the kitchen table of his childhood home.

The tears flowed unchecked through his fingers and onto his wrists; they trickled under his watch strap and into the sleeves of his jumper. His chest heaved as it divested itself of the weight of grief that had burdened it for most of his life until he was so racked with sobs that he was barely able to draw breath.

How long he continued in this state, Daniel could not say, but at length the painful shuddering eased and the flow of tears became almost pleasurable.

It was at this point that he became aware that he was not alone in the room.

What he saw first was the sandalled feet. Then a flowing white robe. He lifted his eyes and through a blur of tears he was able to make out long dark hair. He caught his breath. Though the figure was beardless and seemed to have light, piercing eyes, Daniel Davenport had no trouble recognising Jesus of Nazareth.

Joy flooded his heart, filling the space so recently occupied by grief. When his saviour held out his hand and said, 'Come,' Daniel Davenport unhesitatingly rose and followed him.

Bin day

Anne Marie came out of the basement flat dragging two plastic sacks of rubbish after her. She had her head down so she didn't notice Vera Meaney standing at the bottom of the steps.

'Good morning, Anne Marie,' trilled Vera. 'Tell me this and tell me no more – how is poor Gerald doing? A terrible business, wasn't it? I nearly died when I saw the ambulance arrive the other day, along with the guards and all. I have to say, Anne Marie, I feared the worst! And such a nice boy, I kept thinking to myself; he always used to say hello when we met in the hall. I was fierce upset. Then I just happened to bump into your younger cousin when he came back from the hospital and he told me that Gerald wasn't going to die of his heroin overdose, which is a lucky escape when you think about it, Anne Marie. He's still in Intensive

Care, is he? What's the latest news?'

Anne Marie looked dully at her upstairs neighbour. She hadn't slept very well since hearing about Gerald's hospitalisation and it was too early in the morning for her to be able to deal with people in loud orange jumpers. 'Morning, Vera,' she said wearily. 'Yes, he's still in Intensive Care, but he's out of danger. I haven't seen him yet, but I'll be going over to St James's later this afternoon.'

'He's out of danger? Oh, thanks be to God and thank God again! Well, make sure you give him my best regards when you see him, won't you now? Are you throwing out those magazines? You are? Well, if you don't mind, I'll take them off your hands instead. It must be wonderful to be a secretary and have plenty of money to splash out on the glossies – six of them, my, my! – but I'm just a Simple Servant, you understand, and I can't afford those little luxuries when my poor mother down in Borris is dependent on what I send her every month for all her creature comforts.'

Vera took the magazines and waved cheerily to Anne Marie on her way up the steps. Back in her room, she put the pile on the table and flicked quickly through them one after the other. It was great that they were all this month's issues; the closing dates for the competitions were ages away. Vera glanced proudly at her three-piece canary yellow suite, first prize in a competition in the Christmas issue of *Woman's Way* that she had 'borrowed' from a Peter Marks salon last year. In the kitchenette, her Le Creuset pots and her designer salt and pepper shakers were the fruits of other successful entries. Her mother had once won a car in a raffle, it was true; but if you didn't count that, Vera had

217

the edge on her in the competition stakes. Which was amazing, considering that her mother ran a newsagents and had access to all the magazines for free.

Anne Marie had gone for the most expensive publications, Vera noted with pleasure. *U*, *Image*, *IT*, as well as the foreign ones, *Marie Claire*, *Cosmopolitan* and another one she had never heard of that seemed to be aimed at a young, wild sort of person. It was called *U Yours!* with a star betweeen the 'U' and the 'Y', probably short for 'and' thought Vera. The picture on the front showed someone dressed all in black for a Christmas party, with black lipstick and a rather ferocious snarl to go with it. She put that one to the end.

Unfortunately, after leafing through this month's prizes in the Irish magazines, she found nothing that would justify the cost of a stamp. Make-up kits – she had no need of them; a foot spa – hmm, that could possibly do for her mother for Christmas, or rather her birthday in March, since Christmas would be long over by the time the competitions were judged; a collection of CDs which didn't interest her since she had no CD player, and . . . what else? Tickets to a Westlife concert – no, thanks; a weekend at the Powerscourt health farm – that was for fatties; and now she was down to the last one, *U*Yours!* which had a competition for . . . she turned to the contents page . . . a Club Med holiday!

Vera clapped her hands with pleasure. That would certainly be worth winning! The magazine was published in London, which was a pity; Vera had never won anything in any of the British magazines. Still, there was always a first time. She moistened her forefinger and turned to the page. But when she found it, what a disappointment – the competition entry form had already been cut out!

So Anne Marie was also keen to holiday at Club Med? Hmph! That hard up for a man, was she? But why did she have to enter a competition when she was obviously extremely well off? Those ankle boots she wore – Vera knew that they cost £95 in the Italian shop at the top of Grafton Street, and that was the sale price. Anne Marie had at least three designer suits as well, which she often wore into work when she wasn't on her bike. It was true that she hadn't been wearing them lately, but that just meant that they were sitting unused in her wardrobe, didn't it? Oh, she was in the money all right, that one; there was no need for the likes of her to enter competitions for foreign holidays!

The more she thought about it, the more upset Vera became at the idea that Anne Marie might end up on a Club Med holiday that by rights should be hers. She deserved it far more than Anne Marie, who had everything going for her – apart, of course, from her height. But there were plenty of tall men out there. Besides, Anne Marie was far too young for the Club Med scene. If she was after a good time, why couldn't she go to Ibiza? Club Med was for the more mature single person, like – well, like herself. Vera looked longingly at the pictures of the tropical paradise, and read the tantalising description of activities on offer at this resort and thought of how she had been robbed.

Suddenly, it came to her that she didn't need to rely on a competition to go to Club Med – she could jet off on a week's holiday there tomorrow if she wanted to. Vera would never admit to anyone how much she had saved in the twelve years she had been living in Dublin. She had been promoted three years ago to an executive grade in the Civil Service, and that had involved a big increase in salary, but she hadn't mentioned it at home in case her mother started hinting about the house needing new curtains or something. Her mother had the shop, hadn't she, and no one to look after except herself? And she was old, so she didn't need much spending money, whereas Vera was a young woman in her prime.

She took up the magazine again. Corsairs' Cove – even the name was exciting!

She wasn't going to book the holiday tomorrow; she was going to book it today!

Roz makes an announcement

For Anne Marie, the last fortnight before Christmas passed in a blur. Work was very busy as she, Roz and Dave tried to get everything sorted before the holiday season started. The January issue had already hit the shelves, but there were still a lot of holes in February's flat plan.

Anne Marie had a list as long as her arm of people to contact about forthcoming articles. Could Dave take photos of the salsa lessons they were sending one of their freelancers to as part of their Fit 'n' Fun series? The article on winter gardens – how many colour plates were there to go with it? Permission to print a recipe from a cookery book sent in for review – it went on and on.

She also had to contact the story agencies in London for pictures and stories on celebrities for the months ahead, but the holiday spirit seemed to have got into the staff there early, and she spent hours on the phone each day trying to track people down.

Roz was still out of sorts, but at least she didn't appear to be picking specifically on Anne Marie any more. Dave was just as likely to be on the receiving end of a sharp word, which made him wary of saying anything that might upset the Editor. The result was that he and Anne Marie began to work more closely together; instead of a companionable trio, there was now a pair of workers and the boss. If Anne Marie had a question, she no longer took it automatically to Roz. If Dave didn't know the answer, more often than not, she let it go. When Roz arrived in the morning, like conspirators, they made eye signals to each other to indicate what sort of a mood she was in.

It disturbed Anne Marie that her relationship with Roz had deteriorated to such an extent that they barely spoke to one another any more, but she had at least accepted that whatever was bothering Roz, it had nothing to do with her or the magazine. Dave gave as his opinion that Roz and Stephen were going through a bad patch but Anne Marie, who was still babysitting for them twice a week, could see that Stephen was as baffled as they were by the change in his wife.

At last, the mystery was solved by Roz herself. She arrived at the office late one morning and stood significantly in the centre of the room. Anne Marie, who was on the phone, hurriedly terminated her conversation and sent frantic thought-messages to Dave's back. He was absorbed in checking the layout of the fashion pages for the February issue and had not heard Roz come in. Something of Anne Marie's agitation must have communicated itself to him however, because after a minute he looked up with a puzzled expression on his face, which changed to one of understanding as he took in the scene before him. He put down his magnifying lens and went to stand beside Anne Marie.

Roz was more than usually pale. She looked like someone who had seen something awful and could not get the memory out of her mind. Shell-shocked, thought Anne Marie. She stared at them both for what seemed an age. Then she took a deep breath. 'I've been to the hospital,' she said. There was a pause, during which Anne Marie tried not to think of the terrible announcements that could follow from such a beginning.

'I'm pregnant.'

Anne Marie and Dave looked nervously at one another. For Roz, the news was obviously not a cause for celebration, but all that Anne Marie could think to say was, 'Congratulations.' It was certainly more appropriate than, 'Sorry for your trouble,' which was the only other formulaic expression that sprang to her mind.

'It's twins again,' said Roz. Then she burst into tears.

In XS

The nightclub was packed. Darina pushed her way through the crowd at the bar and out onto the dance floor. The music was so loud that she could feel it reverberating off her breastbone. It thudded and thrummed in waves she could almost see. All around her, bodies gyrated to the kanga-hammer beat, while overhead, epilepsy-inducing lights flickered on and off at split-second intervals.

It didn't take long to locate the person she was looking for; even in a place like this, pink hair stood out. Fliss was in the middle of a tight knot of girls, all of whom were dancing with their eyes closed, or wide open but vacant.

You definitely have to be stoned to enjoy this, thought Darina, marvelling at how little the club appealed to her when she wasn't. She shuddered as a heavily-perspiring girl wearing a handkerchief top fell against her. Darina shoved her off, then broke into the circle and grabbed Fliss by the arm. 'I want to talk to you,' she shouted into her ear. Fliss shook her head to show she hadn't heard. Darina tried again, but Fliss wouldn't stop dancing. Losing patience, Darina began pulling her off the dance floor.

'Here, whacha think yeh're doin'?' protested Fliss.

'I need to talk to you,' said Darina when they had reached the relative calm of a snug near the exit.

'Yeah? Well, I'm not doin' business tonight, so piss off.'

'I want to know who you get your supplies from.'

'Get stuffed! What d'yeh think I am? Stupeh?'

'My brother's in hospital. Someone must have sold him some bad gear. You'd better pray he recovers fast because if he doesn't, you're in big trouble. Now, I want the name of the person you work for, and a contact number. That's all. Then I'll leave you alone.'

Fliss rubbed her arm where Darina had hurt her. She calculated her chances of being able to out-intimidate the student and decided they weren't good. She'd heard that there was some bad stuff going round all right, but this was the first she had heard about a

223

punter being hospitalised. He was a student at Trinity College too, wasn't he? She vaguely remembered having spent a night with him; his sister had come after her on that occasion as well.

Suddenly Fliss got worried. Students had parents who had friends who were politicians and the like; when one of their own took an overdose, there were repercussions. The law would be down on her like a ton of bricks; that cow from the cop-shop in Rathmines had already hassled her more than once. Luckily Fliss had been clean on those occasions, but maybe it was time to let someone else take the heat.

'A'righ'. I'll tell yeh and then yeh bugger off, righ'?'

'Go on.'

'It's Deco and Nailer that brings the stuff to me. I've got Deco's mobile and I ring him when I'm running low on tabs and poppers and stuff. I don't deal much in gear, honest to God. It's them does most of it.'

'And where do they get it?'

'From The Man. But it's no use you asking me who he is or where he is 'cos I don't know. I never seen him. Hardly anybody has, 'cept for Deco.'

'Oh yeah? Well, in that case I'd like you to give Deco a ring and tell him that I want to meet The Man.'

Fliss's eyes opened wide in genuine amazement. 'Are yeh mad? Nobody meets The Man like that!'

'I'm not nobody. Now do it.'

Reluctantly, Fliss took out her cellphone. Turning her back on Darina, she keyed in her password and the automatic dialling code for her supplier. Deco answered at once.

'Yeah?'

'It's Fliss. I'm at XS.'

'What are you short of?'

'Nothing, it's not—'

'Then what the fuck are you ringing me for? This is a business line, not bleedin' Chat Central.'

'But—'

'No buts. Get off yer arse and start working or The Man'll have something to say about it.'

'The Man – that's what I'm ringing about. There's someone here wants to meet him.'

'What the fuck . . .? Who have you been talking to?'

'Her name's Darina. Her brother's in hospital . . . she says you gave him some bad gear. She knows your name an' all. She won't go away.'

'Is that a fact? Tell her to wait outside. I'm on me way.'

The Man

It was cold outside the club. Darina stamped her feet and stuck her hands up the sleeves of her jacket. She had no gloves and the tips of her fingers had already gone numb. She wondered if Deco would try to intimidate her, and instinctively moved closer to the bouncers standing outside the doors of the club. With them around, he wouldn't dare to try anything physical tonight, but he knew where she lived and he could make life unpleasant for her if he chose to. Darina rehearsed the part she had devised for herself and prayed that when the moment arrived, she wouldn't fluff her lines.

When they came, however, it all happened so quickly that she had no time to react. One moment, the laneway leading down to the entrance to the club was deserted; the next, she was being frog-marched by two men towards the main road. The gorilla had her by the elbow; he was so big that Darina was almost pedalling in mid-air to keep up with him. The other guy she recognised as the greasy little rat who had crashed the Hallowe'en party looking for Gerald.

The two men had taken her by surprise and therefore had the upper hand, but Darina had no intention of going meekly to whatever they had planned for her. She turned to Deco and, in as normal a tone of voice as she could manage said: 'Hey Deco, would you mind asking your pet ape here to let go of my arm. I'm perfectly well able to walk on my own.'

'Not for long if you don't shut up,' snarled Deco.

Darina wrenched her arm free and stopped in the middle of the lane. 'Would you like to hear how loud I can scream? I can give you a demonstration, right here.'

Nailer automatically backed away, but Deco came right up close and leaned towards her. Darina managed to stand her ground, although the mingled smells of Paco Rabane aftershave and curried chips made her want to gag.

'I'm a nice guy, I am,' he said softly. 'I'd never hit a bird meself, like. But Nailer here, he doesn't have those finer feelings, see? Especially not after what you're after saying about him. So—'

'Oh, cut the crap, would you?' said Darina crossly. 'It worked on my brother, but it's not going to work on me. I know and you know that you are not going to hurt me; not now and not any other time. The Man would hardly thank you when the cops come swarming all over your little operation which, believe me, they would if you laid a finger on me.'

Deco looked as though he was trying to think of a good comeback, but couldn't. 'What d'you want to see The Man for?' he asked gruffly instead.

'That's for him to know.'

'Jaysus, but you've got some lip. I've sliced people for less.'

'I thought you didn't hurt women.'

'I'm thinking I might make an exception for you.'

'Look, I've had enough of this. Are you going to take me to him or not? If you are, then let's get going; if not, then I've better things to be doing with my time.'

Deco scowled at her, then grunted to Nailer, who swung into place on her left side. This time however, he didn't take hold of her arm.

Darina tried not to let them see how nervous she was. She hadn't expected events to move quite so fast; The Man was a figure of such mythical proportions in the Dublin underworld that she had taken for granted that he would refuse to meet her tonight. What she had expected were threats, then negotiations through a middleman, then a testing period, and finally, if she was lucky, a cautious acceptance of her proposals. But here she was, being escorted – if that was the right word – by two notorious thugs who were doing exactly as she had asked and taking her to meet Dublin's most mysterious drug baron.

Or not.

XS nightclub was located at the end of a laneway near the Portobello Bridge. Turn left at the top and a path led past some apartments to the bridge and the friendly lights of the city; turn right, it ran along the canal in a deserted, tree-lined residential area.

They turned right.

'So where are you taking me, boys?' Darina made it sound jocular, though jocular was far from what she was feeling. 'I suppose you have a white Ford Transit van parked round here somewhere?'

Nailer stopped in his tracks and turned to Deco. 'How'd she know?'

Darina stifled a nervous giggle. Teach me to keep my big trap shut, she thought as Deco led them into a side-street and there, large as life, was the white Transit.

Nailer unlocked the back door and opened it. Deco motioned her inside. 'Lie down and don't move or I'll break your face,' he growled, giving her a shove. Darina half-fell into the back of the van, grazing her ankle on a toolbox just inside the door. She wondered to what use the tools in it were put; neither Deco nor Nailer appeared to her to be the DIY sort.

Oh well, it was a nice life while it lasted, she thought as Deco reached for the handle to slam the door closed.

She caught a sudden whiff of dank water and weeds. Funny that, she thought inconsequentially; I never noticed the smell of the canal before.

'Hit the floor, face down,' said Deco from the front passenger seat a moment later.

Darina willingly complied. If they didn't want her to see where they were going, it probably meant that they weren't planning to bump her off and dispose of her body. Not tonight at any rate.

She tried nevertheless to follow the course they were taking. Nailer did a U-turn in the side-street, then turned right and left. So we're heading towards town, she thought. But very quickly, they made another left and then a right, and after that Darina was completely lost.

The drive lasted almost half an hour, but Darina suspected a lot of that time was spent deliberately travelling in circles to disorient her. When they finally stopped, Deco turned to her and warned her to shut her eyes and keep them shut while Nailer opened the door.

Darina had a brief impression that there was something familiar about the location, but before she could decide what it was, a duvet jacket landed on her head. 'Keep it there,' ordered Deco. She heard him press a couple of buttons on his cellphone. 'Yeah. Righ',' was all he said, but then her arms were taken again and, with the jacket held firmly in place by Nailer, she was marched across a concrete floor. Their three sets of footsteps echoed emptily in the silence. They took a lift, but Darina was unable to say how many floors they ascended before the doors opened soundlessly and she was led out.

'This is the nearest anyone gets to The Man,' Deco said, pulling the jacket off her head. She barely had time to turn before the lift doors closed again and she was left alone.

She was in a sort of atrium – Darina was sure that's what the architect would have called it – with a glass dome overhead through which she could see reflected in the sky the orange glow of streetlights. A mosaic beneath it showed the points of the compass. That might be helpful in locating this place, she thought, if the sun was shining or if I knew anything at all about the night sky. Beside the lift was a fire door that Darina guessed led to an emergency staircase. Opposite the lift was a pair of solid oak doors with big, old-fashioned brass knobs. Two huge tubs on either side of the doors held a profusion of lush greenery. Darina had no interest in plants, but she recognised a *Dicksonia Antartica* tree fern because it was a giant version of one her mother had bought in a garden centre for £250 some years back.

The double doors opened. A woman stood a little way inside the room. She was dressed in a long green and gold gown that made it impossible to guess at her shape, or even her height. Underneath that robe-thing, she might be wearing six-inch stilettos, thought Darina. The theme was Egyptian: she had a black Cleopatra wig, gold and turquoise shadow on her eyes, which were outlined with black, and matching bangles on her wrists. The only false note in the ensemble was the antique ring on the middle finger of her right hand. It had a ruby in the centre and tiny diamonds set in gold around it.

It belonged to Anne Marie.

The woman looked her over in silence for a few seconds. 'You wanted to see The Man?' she said at last.

'Yes.'

She beckoned Darina inside and closed the doors behind them. 'Why?'

'I have a proposition for him.'

The woman crossed to a heavy mahogany desk by the window, which was hidden by floor-length brown velvet curtains. The whole room was dark and masculine, furnished to look like a nineteenth-century gentleman's library, guessed Darina as she took in the bookshelves filled with classical literature, the studded leather couch and the green and brass banker's lamp on the desk.

The woman made a sign for Darina to sit down in the chair at the other side of the desk. 'Nobody sees The Man without being vetted by me first.'

'Who are you?'

'Just call me Cleo.'

So she has a sense of humour, thought Darina. She tried to place the accent, but failed. It was too carefully neutral to allow any hint of where she might have come from originally.

'You said you had a proposition.'

'Yes. My brother's in hospital. He took an overdose.'

Cleo raised her eyebrows a fraction.

'It was The Man's heroin that put him there.'

Cleo leaned forward. 'So?'

Darina swallowed. Her mouth was dry, but her palms had begun to sweat. She hadn't rehearsed for this scenario; in all her visualisations of the vital interview, she had been face-to-face with a man. It was a shock to realise that the success of her plan depended on a kind of power-and-sex game in which the rules, though never stated, are perfectly understood by both parties. It was based on the premise that an older man and younger woman can do business together because each possesses something the other wants.

This was different. And far more dangerous. Darina sat up straight and steeled herself. She forced herself to look Cleo in the eyes. 'I want compensation.'

Cleo regarded her with a hint of amusement. 'Indeed?' She began to play with her bangles. 'How old is your brother?'

'Twenty-two.'

'Twenty-two. An adult, in other words. So he knew the risk, but he believed the reward was worth it.'

'Which is exactly how I felt about coming here.'

Cleo said nothing, but Darina sensed a subtle change in her attitude. She stopped playing with her bangles and looked at her attentively. 'How much compensation were you thinking of?'

'Twenty grand.'

'Twenty?'

'I know it's not much,' said Darina, emboldened by what she perceived as a rise in her standing. 'But Gerald is going to be all right, and that's the main thing.'

'And what would you do with this money? Give it to him?'

'Some of it, yes.'

'And the rest?'

'I'd use it to set myself up in business.'

'What sort of business?'

'Competition.'

Cleo laughed softly, but her eyes remained hard. 'The Man would not be pleased.'

'Then don't tell him.'

Once again, Cleo said nothing, but her expression now was inscrutable. Not Cleopatra, thought Darina suddenly; the Sphinx. Surreptitiously, she wiped her hands on her skirt and waited. She had put her head in a noose by coming here; at any moment, the cord could be pulled tight. The slightest wrong move, a word out of place would do it.

'What is it that you really want?'

The question took Darina by surprise. Fortunately, she had an answer ready. 'Your ring,' she said immediately. 'It belongs to my cousin.'

Cleo looked down at her hand. She twisted the ring once on her finger, then held it up to the light. 'I don't think so,' she said. 'Try again.'

Darina looked at her steadily. 'All right then. What I really want is your job.'

Cleo did not respond. Instead, she pressed a buzzer on the desk. Within seconds, the doors opened and Deco and Nailer came in. They approached the desk and, at a nod from Cleo, grabbed hold of Darina, one on either side. Before she had time to protest, they had lifted her out of the chair. Nailer held her arms while Deco frisked her. Darina gritted her teeth and submitted to the probing fingers. He made a thorough job of the body search, then told her to take off her shoes.

'My shoes?' Darina snorted in derision. 'You watch too much television!'

Deco took the shoes but ignored her. He checked them inside and out. 'She's clean,' he said to Cleo when he had finished.

She nodded. 'Wait outside.'

After the door closed, Cleo left Darina standing for a full minute.

'You may go,' she said eventually. 'If you want money for your brother, you will have to earn it.'

Darina walked slowly towards the door. When she was halfway there, Cleo addressed her back. 'Do you still want to meet The Man?'

Darina stopped. Her palms broke out once more. This was the supreme test. She could almost feel the noose tighten around her neck. What she was about to say might release the trapdoor and leave her dangling.

She didn't turn around. 'What man?' she asked quietly.

Angel

Just in time for Christmas, Anne Marie found someone to fancy. She had quickly given up on Dave, who had gently and with great tact let her know early on that he had a partner. Her name was Jo; she did graphic design and was a great cook. End of story as far as Anne Marie was concerned. In any case, she had already decided that it was a bad idea to fancy someone you had to work with every day, and that she far preferred the mock-flirting that went on between her and Dave to the real thing.

She found her new object of desire at the end of an intensive morning of Christmas shopping, when she was just about ready to collapse from hunger and exhaustion. The Winding Stair was close by. Remembering that its other function was to sell old books, Anne Marie thought she would pop in for soup and a sandwich and then browse for something for her grandmother. A nice book about Limerick, maybe. Or an old anthology of poems.

She had intended going straight up the stairs to the café, but she changed her mind as soon as she set eyes on the young man serving behind the counter. What a hunk! Tall – even taller than she was! Straight blonde hair so smooth it looked as if it had been ironed; Scandinavian blue eyes and perfect, honey-coloured skin. He was dressed in white from head to foot: white cotton jumper; white padded vest; white jeans that fitted him perfectly; white trainers. Outside were grimy streets, a dull grey sky, drably-dressed shoppers; inside was this vision of loveliness. An angel.

'Hi,' said Anne Marie.

'Hi,' said the angel. 'May I help you?'

'Yes. I'm looking for a present for my grandmother. A book.'

There was a moment's silence. 'Er . . . did you have a particular book in mind?'

'Oh! Yes, of course. That is . . . no. I mean, I had an idea: she lives near Limerick, so I thought maybe . . . something about the city. Something old.'

'Limerick, eh? Let's see . . . not *Angela's Ashes*, I presume?'

'No, she read that ages ago. She wasn't impressed.'

The angel grinned. 'Funny, that – my grandmother loved it. But then, she wasn't from Limerick.'

'Are you new here?' Anne Marie asked suddenly. 'It's just . . . I haven't seen you before. I come in here quite a bit. Not for books,' she added hastily, in case he thought that a frequent customer should know where the Books About Limerick For Grandmothers shelf was located. 'I usually just come to eat. In the café. Upstairs, you know?'

She was babbling. It always happened and she hated it, but whenever she was nervous, she couldn't stop talking nonsense. Knowing she was doing it just made her even more embarrassed.

Fortunately, the angel didn't seem to mind, or else he was politely ignoring her discomfiture. 'Yeah, I must try it myself one of these days. You're right; I am new. I started last week when college ended.'

'Are you a student at Trinity?'

'No, I'm at the National College of Art and Design.'

'So you're an artist?'

'Of sorts.'

Just then, two women who had been looking at postcards approached the counter. The angel looked apologetically at Anne Marie. 'Sorry, if you want to go ahead and have a look yourself . . .'

'Of course!' Cheeks aflame, Anne Marie backed away from the counter and turned towards the bookshelves. Instead of reading titles, however, she was running over the conversation in her head. She had made a complete fool of herself; he must think she was a nincompoop, and why oh why couldn't she just be her normal self in these situations instead of either chattering inanely or finding herself tongue-tied?

'Does the book have to be about Limerick?'

Anne Marie started. The customers had left and the angel was standing beside her. 'There are some really nice art books I could show you,' he said.

'Oh yes, she likes art. And architecture. Especially churches. Ruined ones, I mean. She's an atheist, so she never goes inside working ones.'

The angel smiled. 'Your grandmother sounds like an interesting lady.'

'She sure is!' exclaimed Anne Marie, forgetting to be embarrassed as she began to extol Nano's virtues. 'She drives a tractor, and tames horses – or she used to until a few years ago – she keeps geese instead of guard dogs and she's an ace fisherman. Fisherwoman. Whatever!'

'Wow! My grandmother plays Bingo.'

They smiled at each other.

Anne Marie's heart took flight. He was smiling! They had shared a joke! He liked her! This was it!

'I was just thinking—' said the angel, but Anne Marie interrupted him. 'What's your name?'

'Joe.'

'I'm Anne Marie.'

'OK, Anne Marie. Since your grandmother is such an amazing character, I'll show you a book I was thinking about saving for myself for Christmas. It's about bogs—'

'Bogs? Oh yes, she'd love that – she grew up on a bog.'

'Here it is, on this shelf over here. Right at the back where no one would find it.'

'I'll take it,' Anne Marie said as soon as he put it into her hands.

Joe looked surprised. 'Don't you want to have a look at it first?'

'I just know it'll be perfect,' said Anne Marie and she took out her purse.

'Thank you so much,' she said when he handed her the book in a bag and her change. She stood by the cash desk for longer than was strictly necessary, hoping that Joe would say something to prolong the exchange. But as luck would have it, another customer came along to claim his attention.

'Well, I'll be off. Thanks again. Happy Christmas. And see you in the New Year, I hope.'

She was halfway home before she remembered that she hadn't eaten lunch.

Mystery woman

Although the *Femme* office had officially closed for the end-of-year break the day before, Anne Marie was at her desk early on the morning of Christmas Eve. Not working, but wrapping presents. She hadn't managed to get all her shopping done and there were a few freebies in the pile that had come in during the month of December that Roz had said she could have. For

Aunt Barbara, there was a wonderful cookbook with recipes from around the world; for Darina, a leg-waxing kit – she might even stop using my Ladyshave, thought Anne Marie; for Matt and Cora Griffith, the couple who helped Nano run the estate, a cut-glass decanter and handmade chocolates.

As soon as she had finished her wrapping, tidied up her desk and carefully put the parcels into her bag, Anne Marie made ready to leave. Her parents' car was parked outside, by the canal. They had left it with her on their way to London, where they were visiting friends before flying on to the States for Christmas and New Year.

It was handy to have the car, thought Anne Marie; not only because it meant that she could transport all her presents in safety and comfort, but because she was able to give Gerald a lift as far as Limerick. He had only been let out of hospital the day before and she was looking forward to having a long chat with him during the drive. She wouldn't lecture him of course, but she would comment on how well he was looking now that he had put on weight, and tactfully let him know how worried she had been about him even before he had taken the overdose.

She turned off the lights in the office and walked down the corridor towards the lift. But before she called it up to the third floor, she had a sudden doubt: had she unplugged her computer after she had sent her Christmas e-mail to the States? She thought she had, but it was best to be sure. Leaving the bag at the lift, Anne Marie ran lightly back down the corridor to the office. Without bothering to turn on the lights, she dropped on all fours, crawled in under her desk and discovered that she had not, in fact pulled out the plug.

She was just getting to her feet again when a stern voice behind her said, 'Stay where you are!'

In her fright, Anne Marie bumped her head painfully against the corner of her desk. She had opened the doors to the building and locked them after her; how could someone else have got in?

'Who are you and what are you doing here?'

Anne Marie stood up cautiously. Near the fourth workstation, the one with the screen around it, was a woman dressed entirely in black. Like a cat burglar, was Anne Marie's first thought when she saw the black leggings, polo-necked jumper and soft-soled shoes. She had black hair too, cut in a severe Mary Quant bob. In the dim light, it was hard to make out her face, but from her voice, Anne Marie guessed that she was in her late thirties or early forties.

'I work here,' she said, rubbing the top of her head where she had bumped it. 'I just came in to pick up some last-minute stuff.'

The realisation that she had every right to be there suddenly made Anne Marie indignant. Who was this woman who had challenged her? What was her excuse for being inside a closed-up building on the day before Christmas? She opened her mouth to ask. But before she could say anything, the woman thrust her hand out imperiously, as though to ward off Anne Marie's curiosity. 'Go now,' she commanded. 'And make sure you lock up after you.'

Anne Marie did as she was told. It had just dawned on her that this must be the mysterious Isolde Phoenix that Dave had told her about. There was no one else it could be. It was just as well that Dave had warned her how weird the owner of *Femme* magazine was; otherwise she would have been quite put out by her rudeness. Isolde must have used the penthouse entrance round the back, then come downstairs to check what was going on when she heard Anne Marie in the office.

'But do you know the strangest thing of all?' Anne Marie said to Gerald when she was relating the incident to him in the car half an hour later. 'When she stuck out her hand to order me out of the place, I could have sworn she was wearing my ring.'

Beautiful flowers

Brandon O'Kane began Christmas morning the same way he did every other morning, with a dawn salutation to the sun. It did not matter that for the last seventeen mornings the sun had not been there to respond; the important thing was for him to perform the movements, which were part t'ai chi, part yoga and part Native-American dance, to acknowledge and give thanks for the star's continued power and beneficence. After the salutation Brandon sat on his prayer mat, did some breathing exercises and began his meditation. It lasted an hour, for most of which his mind was a complete blank and his body relaxed to such an extent that he might have been in a coma.

At the end of his meditation session, he remained sitting for some moments in the lotus position with his eyes closed, checking in with his body's organs to locate any potential source of trouble and decide on his diet for the day. He had felt a little sniffly yesterday, probably because he had allowed himself to become frustrated by the slowness of his Internet Service

Provider earlier in the week. It was possible that a cold virus had taken advantage of his diminished aura and the resultant weakness in his immune system to lodge in his sinuses. Some Echinacea and an infusion of thyme and honey should get rid of it. Everything else was in order, so Brandon allowed his thoughts to wander.

They came to rest as they so often did these days on the encounter Brandon had had in the basement flat a couple of weeks earlier. He had gone down to speak to his tenants because he had heard from a neighbour that the police had been round earlier in the day. There had been no mention of an ambulance however, so it was with some surprise that he found, when he let himself into the flat, a grief-stricken middle-aged man sobbing in the living room. Brandon had brought him upstairs to his own quarters and treated him with a few drops of Rescue Remedy, followed by soothing organic camomile tea. When Daniel had recovered enough to be able to speak, he had told Brandon about Gerald's misadventure and his own feelings of guilt and helplessness.

They had continued talking for a long time; rather, Daniel had talked and Brandon had listened until the brief afternoon had turned to evening. Then Brandon had lit candles and persuaded his patient to relax while he bathed his feet and massaged them. Almost immediately, Daniel had fallen into a deep, restorative sleep. When he woke up, Brandon had the medicine cards ready. He showed Daniel how to cast them and interpreted the messages for him.

The cards had shown that Daniel's life was at a crisis point. If he wanted to survive, he would have to make certain radical changes. Bear in the west indicated that

Daniel needed to develop the spiritual side of his being; retire to his cave and meditate, digesting the experience of his life to date. What lessons had he failed to learn? What dreams had he suppressed, considering himself unworthy of pursuing them? Daniel must enter the silence to know.

It was wonderful, Brandon thought, opening his eyes with a smile, how many beautiful flowers life had strewn in his path. First Anne Marie, and now her uncle, who might even turn out to be the more adept pupil. Anne Marie was young; he had not yet tried to interest her in any of his beliefs, but for Daniel, time pressed, so he had sent him home with plenty of reading material. Brandon would not be surprised if, early in the New Year, he had his first full-time acolyte.

He stretched, breathed deeply three times, then rose from his prayer mat and went to get dressed for Christmas.

The grandmother's tale

After breakfast on Christmas morning, Anne Marie and her grandmother set out to plant daffodil bulbs. It felt good to be out of doors. The day was bright and cold, the dew that had not quite frozen during the night sparkled in the sunshine.

'It was nice of you to agree to do this,' said Nano, 'when I'm sure you'd far rather be inside opening your presents.'

'There'll be plenty of time for that later. Besides, this is going to be fun!'

'I kept meaning to plant them last month when

Dermot gave them to me, but I never got round to it. I think we'll start over there.'

'By the family trees?'

'Yes. It would be nice to have big clumps of daffodils around them in spring, don't you think? There are lots in the grass, but none around the trees themselves.'

'Oh yes! Let's start with Robin, he's my favourite.'

'The boy or the tree?'

'Both. I used to cry over his photograph when I was younger. I think I was a little in love with him.'

'I never met him, of course, but by all accounts he was a very nice young man. As was his older brother.'

'Edward always seemed stiffer to me. Maybe because of the uniform. There aren't any photos of Robin in army gear, are there? Here, let me dig. You can plant.'

'All right. No, he joined up after Edward was killed. Clarissa couldn't bear to have photographs taken of her only other son in uniform.'

'Well, she was right, wasn't she? He died too. Will I just dig a circular hole and you can put all the bulbs in together?'

'Yes, let's try that. Poor Clarissa – she lost everyone in the two wars. Her father, her brother and her husband in the First, and her two sons in the Second. Can you lift the sod without breaking it up, do you think?'

'I'll do my best. It's nice that they all have trees to remember them by. I'd like to have one when I die, and for people to come and plant daffodils around me!'

'Yes, so would I. And as it's likely to be sooner rather than later, I may as well tell you which tree I've chosen.'

'Nano! You're only sixty-five – don't be talking about dying!'

'I'm going to be sixty-six early next year. That's good, I'll get about twenty in there. Don't worry, I'm not intending to pop my clogs just yet, but it's as well to be prepared. Just so as you know: when it happens, I'd like to be cremated and have my ashes buried under the sycamore at the back of the arboretum. OK, you can replace the sod now.'

'The sycamore?' Anne Marie stood up and leaned on her spade. 'Why the sycamore? They're like weeds. Why not one of the exotic trees?'

Nano swept a stray lock of hair off her forehead. A faraway look came into her eyes. 'It's to do with making peace,' she said softly.

'Oh. So it was a sycamore that killed Grandad, was it?'

'Yes, it was. I'll just tread this down a bit, then we're ready to do the other side.'

'What happened exactly?'

'He was cycling home in a storm. The tree was struck by lightning and a branch fell and killed him.'

Anne Marie lifted the sod from the other side. 'It must have been awful being left to raise two small kids on your own. Is that when you got the job here at—'

'Three.'

'Sorry?'

'Three. Children.'

Anne Marie frowned. 'Three children? But there's only Uncle Dan and Yvonne. Oh, I remember, there was a baby that died too, wasn't there?'

Nano looked away. She reached down and took a handful of bulbs from the wheelbarrow. 'He wasn't a baby,' she said quietly. 'And he didn't die. He was murdered.'

Christmas greetings

Roz hated Christmas. She hated the falseness of it; the artificial trees, the fake snow, the put-on cheer, the ho-ho-ho bonhomie – none of which disguised the fact that in the twenty-first century, Christmas was no more and no less than a festival of orgiastic commercialism, when parents fought each other in toyshops for the latest must-have toys for the children they saw only at weekends.

She hated the duty visits to her father and Debbie, and to Stephen's mother. The twins' natural exuberance had to be curtailed with threats and bribes that invariably failed, giving the two older women the opportunity to remark, with thin-lipped smiles, that it was, of course, very difficult to combine motherhood with a career.

This year, Christmas was going to be even worse than usual. Roz was not one of those women who enjoy pregnancy. The thought of the new life growing inside her did not thrill; rather, it distressed her to imagine the tiny embryos lodged in her womb, sucking life and nourishment from her body, and ballooning to hundreds of times their original size until she all but disappeared behind the bump. She was still suffering from nausea; six weeks of violent aversion to certain smells and tastes and the constant feeling that she wanted to puke but never quite managing it. It was coming to an end, but would soon be followed by heartburn, when the acid reflux after every meal would make eating a trial and she would be forced to sleep sitting up. Then came the worst time, the last trimester, when Roz's tiny frame would be distended to monstrous proportions and the only time she would feel comfortable was when her body was supported by water in a full bath or in a swimming pool.

But worse, far worse than the physical symptoms was what being pregnant did to her emotions. To Roz it seemed as if pregnancy dissolved her tough adult carapace, so vital for living in the grown-up world, making her vulnerable to the pain of every living creature on the planet. When she was pregnant, she could not bear to look at programmes on the National Geographic channel, delighted in by the twins, that showed animals being torn apart by predators. Any story of cruelty distressed her, but stories of cruelty to children almost sent her out of her mind. Abduction, rape, murder; she relived the horror of each incident a thousand times. When she was pregnant with Ellie in the early 1990s, the word 'Belgium' had been enough to send her into paroxysms of grief.

It was so unfair that, just when she had thought she was safe at last, she was being made to go through it all again. Stephen had been very supportive when she told him; full of remorse for the slip-up that had led to this unwanted pregnancy, he let her know that he would go along with whatever decision she made regarding it. Roz was grateful, though she knew that, in spite of her vociferous support down the years for a woman's right to choose, when it came down to it, abortion was not for her. That was even before she had learned that she was carrying twins.

My life was going along so nicely, thought Roz in anguish as she lay in bed on Christmas morning; why did this have to happen? She had forgotten the vague feelings of dissatisfaction that had been troubling her a few months earlier; now all her problems seemed to stem from this new pregnancy. We'll have to change the car, she thought, and I'll have to give up my study for the new babies' bedroom. We won't be able to go camping in France next summer, and I'll have to get a full-time nanny again.

Nappies, bottles, buggies: all the paraphernalia of babyhood that she had so joyfully disposed of once the twins had started school, it would all have to be acquired again.

Roz looked at the clock and heaved a last sigh. Nine o'clock. And a Merry bloody Christmas to me too, she thought as she swung her legs out of the bed and went to tell the twins that they could open their presents.

Christmas pud

'Well, that wasn't so bad, was it?'

'No. I was afraid it was going to be a lot worse.'

Christmas dinner in the Davenport household had come to an end. Now the relations were at the door, putting on coats and kissing cheeks. Cornelius was there, helping his grandmother and aunts carry their parcels out to the car. Gerald and Darina were in the conservatory having a smoke and conducting a post mortem on the dreaded annual gathering of the clan.

'You got off lightly, considering,' said Darina.

'I nearly died! Don't you think that was punishment enough?'

'I do, but I'm surprised that the parents agree. I was expecting the old dear to barbecue you. But she's been like a lamb to everyone. And the spread she put on for us today – I've never tasted anything like it!'

They agreed that Barbara, who was an excellent

cook when she had the time and the inclination, had surpassed herself this year. From the asparagus soufflé at the start to the goose provided by Nano, and the mouth-watering array of light sorbets and death-defying chocolate desserts, everything had been divinely delicious.

'I think I must have put on a stone in the last four hours,' Gerald said, patting his stomach with satisfaction.

'About bloody time. If you'd got any thinner than you were, you'd have been transparent!'

'That bad? I thought the scales in the hospital must be wrong when they weighed me last week and I was under eight stone. Still, a few more days of the old dear's home cooking and I'll be grand.'

'Has she said anything at all about . . . you know?'

'Not a word. In fact, you're right; she has been awfully nice to me. Do you think I've been forgiven?'

'Difficult to say. She could hardly come down on you when Gran and the aunts were around, could she? And you made sure not to arrive until after they got here yesterday. But on the other hand, she's been in such high good humour all day that I am tempted to say "yes". Maybe she figures you've learnt your lesson. Anyway, we're going to find out soon, because there's the aunts' car leaving. It's down to the Davenports now.'

Darina finished her cigarette and stubbed it into one of her mother's potted palms. She blew the smoke thoughtfully towards the glass roof. It was weird. Nothing had been said about Gerald's actions, but there was no tenseness in the atmosphere. She could sense no suppressed anger in either of her parents. In fact, they were both seething with something else entirely. They kept smiling at each other and touching each other's hands during dinner.

If it weren't so disgusting an idea, Darina would have suggested to her brother that the folks looked as though they had fallen in love all over again.

Just then, Cornelius stuck his head into the conservatory. 'We're wanted in the dining room. You're to come now.' He delivered his message without looking at them and left.

Darina put her arm around Gerald's shoulder and squeezed him. 'Well, bro, looks like this is it. I knew it was too good to last. Whatever happens, remember I'm on your side. When they disown you, I'll take you in.'

Gerald carefully extinguished his half-finished cigarette and put it in his pocket.

'Thanks, I'm counting on it,' he said.

In the dining room, the table had been cleared and reset with the best china tea service. The champagne flutes had been set out as well, and on the sideboard was a bucket with a bottle of vintage champagne on ice.

Daniel was sitting in the big carver at the head of the table. Cornelius was in his usual seat on his father's right-hand side. Barbara was standing behind her husband's chair.

Darina threw a quick glance at each of their faces, trying to gauge what was coming. Cornelius looked completely at sea, same as ever. Her father seemed quietly elated, but at the same time apprehensive. He kept running his tongue over his lips and playing with his table napkin.

But it was her mother's expression as she stood behind the carver with her hand resting on her husband's shoulder that made Darina's face turn pale. She suddenly knew without a doubt that something momentous was about to occur; something that would change all their lives forever. She sat down and clasped her hands tightly in her lap.

'Now that we're all here,' Barbara began, 'I'd just like to say that I hope you have all enjoyed this Christmas as much as I have.'

There followed a flow of compliments and thanks, with even Darina lavishing praise on everything from the décor to the dinner.

'Good. I did try my best to make this year extra-special.' Barbara paused and engaged each of her children's eyes in turn. 'You see,' she said slowly, 'this is the last Christmas we will be having here as a family.'

There was a strangled cry from the far side of the table. Cornelius half-rose from his chair and then collapsed back down. He put his head on to the table and moaned.

'Cornelius! Sit up straight and hear what your mother has to say!'

Cornelius was so surprised by his father's tone that he did as he was told.

Dan reached up to his shoulder and covered his wife's hand with his own. 'Go on, dear.'

'Thank you, dear. Yes, I know it probably comes as a bit of a shock. Children expect their parents to continue as they have always done, even after they themselves have upped and left. Well, for various reasons, that is neither possible nor desirable for us. Now that the three of you are reared, your father and I have been discussing what we want to do with the rest of our lives. You know that in the last year I have started up my own business; I am happy to say that it is going very well. I have more and more work coming in; I spend a lot of time travelling to Dublin and other parts of the country, and the upshot of it all is that I no longer have the time or the energy to look after this big house. Your father and I have decided to sell. I am thinking of relocating to Dublin eventually; in the meantime, I have bought a nice apartment in Limerick City where you will all be very welcome to visit me, of course.'

There was silence in the room.

Cornelius was the first to break it. He stared at Barbara with barely concealed venom. 'And what about Dad?' he spat.

'Oh, don't you worry about me, Con,' his father said. 'I'll be all right. I'll be staying on here for a bit longer, while I make up my mind what I want to do next.'

But Cornelius was beside himself. He jumped up, knocking over his chair, and pointed an accusing finger at Barbara. 'It's you . . . you . . . bloody bitch! You're doing this to him! You're nothing but a selfish, selfish . . . cow . . . and I hate you!'

He let out a great sob and ran out of the room, stumbling over the fallen chair and knocking against the table on his way.

There was silence again. Everyone listened to Cornelius's feet thumping up the stairs and heard the slam of his bedroom door. Dan squeezed his wife's hand.

'It's all right, dear. I'll speak to him in a few minutes. Go on with what you were saying.'

'Thank you, dear.' Barbara moved away from her husband and picked up Cornelius's fallen chair. She sat down.

'Now then, we come to the part that concerns you children. Your father and I have tried to be good parents to you,' she began. 'Now that you are all over eighteen, that means knowing when to let go. I think you will agree that we have not interfered in your lives much since you left school. We don't expect you to be perfect; it is only by making mistakes that you learn what's what, after all. But there are limits.'

She turned to her eldest son. 'You, Gerald, have seriously overstepped the limit. I don't know what is going to happen with your drugs charge. I understand that there are certain unusual aspects to the case, but it is possible that you will be sentenced to prison. I would hate to see that happen; prison would do you no good whatsoever.'

Gerald swallowed hard. He could hardly believe that his mother was sitting there calmly discussing the prospect of his incarceration. He had never considered that the incident in the flat could go so far. He had somehow assumed that because he had escaped with his life, the problem had gone away. Now here was his mother talking about a prison sentence!

Suddenly, Gerald began to feel very scared.

'If the case is dismissed, or if it happens that you are let off with a suspended sentence, here is what your father and I have decided. You will leave Trinity, where you have wasted the last two-and-a-half years. You will come back to Limerick and take over the management of the factory. You have no business qualifications, but that doesn't matter – you can study for the MBA at night. Besides, as soon as Cornelius has finished his degree, he will return to take care of the more prosaic aspects of the business. You will be the ideas man. You have flair and imagination; your brother has a good head for figures and an enormous capacity for hard work. Between you, we expect you to turn the factory into the number one shoe manufacturer in the country.'

Gerald was too stunned to say anything. It was Darina who asked, 'What about you, Dad? If you're handing over the reins at the factory, what will you do?'

Daniel smiled at her. 'Well now, when I've worked that one out myself, I'll be sure to let you know. For the time being, I don't plan on changing my routine. Gerald will be staying at home after ye have all left, which will be nice. I'll show him the ropes down at the factory for a few months. My mother and I are going to Italy for Easter; I daresay I'll have thought of something by then.'

'You're taking Nano to Italy for a holiday?' Darina couldn't keep the surprise from her voice.

Her father turned pink. 'As a matter of fact,' he said happily, 'she's taking me.'

Darina looked nervously at her mother and then away. She cleared her throat. 'Ah . . . and what about me?' she asked in a small voice.

'We'll decide that at the end of this academic year. You are the one with the most academic ability; I would like to see you get a degree. But if your results don't improve, we will not support you financially any more. That doesn't mean you couldn't continue, of course, but you would have to pay your own way. Do I make myself clear?'

'Very,' Darina said, chastened.

Back in the conservatory, Gerald took his half-finished cigarette out of his pocket and lit up, inhaling greedily.

'Well, how about that?' he said with a nervous laugh. 'Did you have any idea . . .?'

'Not a clue. At least, not until we were in there and I saw the way the folks were behaving with each other, all lovey-dovey. That struck me as very strange.'

'What's going on, Dar? I don't understand – are they splitting up or what? If they sell this house, the old man won't have anywhere to live. And we won't have a family home any more. They can't do that to us.'

'Oh yes they can! And I'd say they've been planning it for quite a while; that's how they were able to present it to us as a *fait accompli*. If it makes you feel any better, I don't think your misdemeanours had anything to do with their decision – except the bit about you taking over the business, which would have been something they added on at the last minute.'

'Yeah, what do you think of that – Gerald Davenport, Entrepreneur Shoemaker!'

'As a matter of fact, I think it's not a bad idea, if you could bear to work with Corny. You're very creative, which is something that place could do with, and as long as he keeps control of the money, the two of you could really make a go of it. Of course, that means I'm going to be left on my own with Anne Marie and Corny back in Dublin for the rest of this academic year. Aargh, how will I survive?!'

Jamie's Willow

'I'm not surprised you've never heard about Jamie,' said Nano to Anne Marie late on Christmas Day. They had opened their presents, eaten their frugal Christmas dinner, pulled crackers and done the washing up. Now they were relaxing in the library in front of a blazing log fire. On a low table between their two wing chairs were plates of sandwiches, mince pies and a silver tea set. Anne Marie had asked her grandmother, if she didn't mind, to tell her about the uncle she had never known existed.

'For so long, I couldn't bear to hear his name mentioned. Your mother was very young, of course, so she would have no memories of him, and poor Daniel didn't dare talk to anyone about his dead elder brother.

'Jamie was only eight when his father died, but he became the man of the family. I leaned on him – too much, probably, in view of his age. He never complained, though, and soon I got used to treating him almost as another adult. We grew very close.

'But like all people who are very close, we needed breathing space – time apart from one another. So when Jamie announced one Sunday morning shortly before his eleventh birthday that he was running away, I just said, "Fine, I'll make some sandwiches." He took the lunch I made for him and put it in his canvas backpack, along with his book, a change of clothes and a torch. I think the torch was to frighten me into thinking that he would be gone for the night. I went to the door to wave him off. We'd had a little argument the night before, so there was no kissing, just a stiff little wave from him when he reached the gate.'

Nano stopped and took up the poker. She prodded the logs in the fire so that they collapsed in a shower of sparks.

'I often think that if I had just called to him then and said, "Come on back, Jamie, we'll go on a picnic later

255

today," he would have been happy to agree. But I had decided it would be good for him to have a day all to himself; he worked very hard and I was worried that his childhood was passing him by. So I said nothing. Instead, I smiled and let him go.

'When he hadn't returned by tea-time, I began to get worried. It would still be light for another five hours or so, but I think I knew in my bones that something was wrong. I left the other two with a neighbour and went to look for him.'

She stopped poking and stared into the flames. 'I didn't find him; the police did. Two days later they brought him back to me wrapped in a blanket, so that for one wild moment of joy I believed he was alive. Then they laid him out on the table. He had been strangled and his body dumped in a ditch.'

'Oh my God,' whispered Anne Marie.

'Nowadays, there would be all sorts of forensic tests done. His last movements would be reconstructed. Back then, there was none of that. But I did my own investigating, and I have my idea about what happened. I knew that he would have gone to the river that runs through the estate. He and Daniel often played in it after school when I was working in the kitchen here and they were waiting for me to finish so we could go home together. I found the core of an apple near the pool under the bridge, so there was confirmation that I was right. I guessed that he'd have swum, climbed trees, and played until late afternoon. Then he'd have got hungry and started to think of home. He was always hungry; it was impossible to imagine him missing a meal.'

'I think he went onto the road and began to walk home. I think a car came along and stopped. I think someone offered Jamie a lift home. Someone he knew. I think he accepted.'

There was silence when Nano stopped talking, broken only by the crackle of burning wood.

For a while, Anne Marie was unable to speak. It was one thing to hear about the deaths in the war of the unfortunate young men who should have inherited Riverwood; it was quite another to discover that her own family had been touched by the tragedy of a young boy's death.

'Oh, Nano,' she said eventually. 'I don't know what to say . . . there is nothing to say . . . except, I never would have guessed. I mean, nobody could tell from you that there was this awful episode in your life.'

'There isn't a day goes by when I don't think about him. But the pain does lessen with time – if we let it. I know that I held on to mine for far too long. Clarissa saw and she tried to help, but I was too immersed in my own pain to learn from hers. I'm afraid I was a very poor mother to my other two children.'

'Nano! How can you say that? Yvonne's always told me that she had a wonderful childhood.'

'Maybe. She was too young to remember the time before. After Jamie's death, we came to live here at Riverwood. Clarissa made me her companion; soon she became very attached to your mother, which was wonderful for both of them. But poor Danny was left out in the cold. I could hardly bear to see him because he reminded me of Jamie, and Clarissa had long since decided that she would invest no more of herself in the male sex.'

Nano stared into the fire for a couple of seconds before continuing in a wistful tone: 'I just hope it's not too late to make amends. I drove over to see your uncle the other day; he's on his own a lot now that Barbara's business has taken off. We had a very long and . . . well . . . interesting talk, and the upshot of it is that we are going to take a trip together, just the two of us, next Easter.'

'A trip? Where to?'

'Italy. I've always wanted to see Florence and Rome and Venice. And now that the renovations on the house are finally complete, I think I can safely leave Riverwood for a couple of weeks.'

'Two weeks in Italy – cool! Make sure you send me a postcard.'

Anne Marie spent the week between Christmas and New Year at Riverwood. In the mornings, she and Nano went for a long walk through the estate, varying their route each time so as to take in as much of the three hundred acres as possible. Nano pointed out all the improvements she and the estate manager had had carried out over the last few years: resurfacing of the driveways; renovation of the walled garden; tree-planting on the edges of the wood; restoration of the two old stone bridges across the river.

She explained how she had decided some years back that the only way to raise the money necessary to carry out all the urgent repairs on the house and grounds was to sell off a large tract of the estate, and hoped that Anne Marie approved of her decision.

'Dermot and his father before him have leased the land for so long that I almost felt it belonged to them by rights,' she said as they strolled down towards the river on New Year's Eve. 'And of course there's no danger of the land or the river being poisoned with chemicals now that Dermot has gone organic. Did I tell you that he's given up the other kind of farming altogether and is concentrating entirely on organic produce?'

'Yes, Nano, you did. I think you must have mentioned it at least ten times this week! And it was his organic beef that we ate in last night's stir-fry, wasn't it? So just what are you trying to tell me?'

Nano grinned. 'All right, then. He's a lovely young man, he's my neighbour and he's single. There!'

'Nano, you're matchmaking!' said Anne Marie, half-amused, half-scandalised.

Nano had the grace to look sheepish. 'Well, why not?'

'Because . . . because well, for starters I'm nineteen and he's in his thirties.'

'Are you sure that's the reason? Maybe you've got a beau in Dublin that you haven't told me about.'

Anne Marie blushed. 'No, I haven't.'

'Are you sure? Go on, there must be someone.'

'Well, there is this guy I like . . .'

As Anne Marie began to tell Nano about Joe in the Winding Stair, she realised that she had dreamt about him the night before. The dream had slipped from her mind on waking, but now that the subject of Joe had been brought up, it was coming back to her. It was a pleasant dream with suitably erotic overtones, but in one respect it was rather startling: in it, Joe was black.

'Have you been on a date with him?'

'What? Oh, sorry – no, not yet.' Anne Marie left the intriguing matter of Joe's ethnic barrier-hopping and tuned back into the conversation with her grand-mother. 'I've only met him a couple of times,' she said, 'but I think he likes me too. I'm hoping he'll ask me out one of these days.'

They strolled in companionable silence as far as Jamie's Willow, the tree Nano had planted in the spot where she believed her eldest son had spent his last afternoon. When they were younger, Anne Marie and the cousins had often swung from its branches into the river without ever stopping to consider how the tree had got its name.

'You know, when I was young,' began Nano when they reached the riverbank, 'my sisters used to tell me that a woman always marries the third man in her life. Never the first or the second.'

'Really? I've never heard that.'

Nano leaned against the rough bole of the willow and absentmindedly ran a hand down one of the tree's bare twigs. 'I think it might have been something people said back then. I suppose it was to stop young girls from becoming infatuated with the first man they encountered and deciding he was the one. But in my case it didn't work: your grandad was practically the first man I laid eyes on after my father.'

Anne Marie giggled. 'You ran away with him and caused a scandal, didn't you? And you were only seventeen.'

Nano sighed. 'It was all such a long time ago. And everything has changed so much since then. Your mother keeps asking me to write it all down. I suppose she's right; I have had an eventful life, and it would be good to record some of it. Did I ever show you Clarissa's journals? They are wonderful. She lived through some terrible experiences – and some good ones, too. There's a book there for anyone who has the time and the patience to sift through almost seventy years of material.'

But Anne Marie was not interested in hearing about Clarissa. 'I can't believe that you already had a child when you were my age,' she said. 'I mean, I couldn't begin to imagine myself as a mother now. What was it like for you? I suppose having a child made you grow up very quickly.'

'Not a bit of it! I hadn't a clue. Neither had James. But it was all a great adventure. We played house and muddled along somehow.'

'But when Grandad died, that must have been a terrible awakening. Was that when you finally grew up? I mean, is that what made you feel like an adult?'

'No, sweetheart; that only made me feel like dying myself.' A distant look came into Nano's eyes, but then she visibly shook herself and turned to look kindly at Anne Marie. 'You want to know when you can expect to feel all grown-up, is that it?'

Anne Marie went pink. 'Yes. I thought . . . when I was eighteen, but that didn't happen, so now I'm wondering if it's twenty-one, or maybe twenty-five—'

'Seventy.'

'Sorry?'

'I said "seventy". That's when I've decided that I'll finally feel like a grown-up!'

Anne Marie's jaw dropped. 'You mean even you . . . don't feel . . .?'

Nano began to climb the bank to the bridge. At the top she leaned over and smiled down at her grand-daughter. 'How about a game of Pooh-sticks?'

Upstairs, downstairs

Darina was not looking forward to coming back to Dublin. Without Gerald, she would be lost. Because of her close relationship with her elder brother, she had never felt the need for making friends. At her convent school, she had always kept herself aloof from the gaggles of girls who spent hours in one another's company, whispering confidences, gossiping, or discussing the endlessly fascinating topic of boys. Darina despised all-female environments, foetid with secrets and slippery with shifting allegiances and petty jealousies. She far preferred the company of men, whose testosterone-fuelled impulses had at the very least the merit of being easy to understand.

Fuck it or kill it: nothing complicated about that.

Now she would have to adjust to life in Dublin without her only ally. Anne Marie and Cornelius had each other, but she had nobody. Hilary term stretched ahead flat and featureless, a succession of dull days spent in the library and duller evenings at home with her younger brother and her cousin.

'I'll turn into a right egg-head,' she moaned to Gerald the day before she was due to return, 'because without you around to hang out with I'll have to take refuge in studying. No more clubbing, no more parties, no more pubs. Just nineteenth-century French literature, with a little *thème* and *version* for light relief. God, I'll be such a bore!'

'Oh, I don't know,' said Gerald. 'It might work out for the best yet. I was probably a bad influence. The old dear is right: you're the one with the brains, it'd be a pity to see you waste them. And besides, I'm not sure there's room in the shoe factory for yet another failed Davenport.'

Darina squeezed her brother's arm. 'Don't talk like that, bro. You're not a failure! You're going to do great things here, I know you are. It's just – I'm going to miss you.'

'Likewise, sis. I've never spent any time alone with the old man and I'm a bit nervous about it. I think he is too. It's weird to think that we were all those years living together and we don't really know each other at all. The next few months will be . . . interesting, I should think.'

'Yeah, I'll bet they will. You're to stay in touch, you hear? I want a long phone call at least once a week, and I'll write and let you know how things are working out in the flat now that we're a threesome.'

But when Darina reached Dublin, there was a surprise in store for her. It was not going to be a threesome, because Anne Marie had moved out.

'I'd no idea that this was going to happen,' Anne Marie told her cousin as she showed her round her new flat. 'But when I got back from Nano's the other day, there was a note from Brandon saying I was to go upstairs and see him. So I did, and he asked me if I would oblige him by moving into Sylvester's old place. I didn't know what to say. I mean, I was happy downstairs with all of ye—' She stopped and coloured. Honesty demanded that she qualify that statement. 'At least, most of the time I was happy, and naturally, I wasn't too keen on moving into a room that had such bad memories. But then I saw what he'd done with it, and he kept going on about negative and positive energy and feng shui and God knows what – so, in the end, I said yes. You don't mind, do you?' finished Anne Marie, looking anxiously at her cousin.

Darina looked around. She had never seen Sylvester's room so she had no basis for comparison, but she was fairly sure that it had looked nothing like this. Brandon had spared no expense in creating a low-key, minimalist haven in which everything was both beautiful and functional. The large room had been divided to separate the living and sleeping areas. Anne Marie's bedroom was done in blond wood and shades of white: her bed was a wide futon covered with a swan-white counterpane; the windows were draped in white voile and the fitted wardrobe was solid beech the same colour as her hair.

The living room had a three-seater couch and two armchairs, a coffee table and a corner unit for a television and a music system. At the back, a new kitchen had been fitted, with sleek modern units in another light-coloured wood combined with glass and stainless steel. An arch and a breakfast bar marked it out as a separate space without divorcing it entirely from the main room.

'It must cost a fortune,' she said at last.

Anne Marie looked embarrassed. 'Well, no actually, he's giving it to me at a very reasonable rent. More or less what I was paying downstairs, in fact.'

'He must really fancy you so,' sniffed Darina. She couldn't bring herself to say what she felt, which was that this was quite simply the nicest living space that she had ever seen and how come Anne Marie had got so lucky?

'You know it's nothing like that,' said Anne Marie, blushing furiously. 'He felt bad about what had happened here with Sylvester and . . . and he considers himself responsible somehow and he wanted to . . . to make it up to me. That's all.'

Suddenly, Darina smiled. 'It's OK, coz,' she said. 'I'm green with envy, of course, but I'll get over it. It's a fabulous place and I hope you'll be really happy here.' To her own and Anne Marie's surprise, Darina gave her cousin a hug as she prepared to leave. 'I suppose we're going to have to find some new people to share the costs now that you and Gerry are gone from downstairs.' She sighed. 'I hate the thought of sharing with strangers, but there you are. Corny and I certainly won't be able to afford it on our own.'

'Oh, didn't he tell you? Cornelius, I mean; Brandon's agreed to let you have downstairs for less than what you were paying before. It was something he discussed with your dad apparently, when Gerald was taken into hospital. I don't know the ins and the outs of it, but your rent isn't going up, that's definite.'

'Oh, that is good news! Well, I'd better be getting back downstairs. Thank you for showing me round, coz, and remember to come visit us every now and then in the basement or Corny will be heartbroken.' She stopped at the door. 'Maybe . . . I was thinking . . . I'd like to do a dinner sometime next week. Do you think you'd be free?'

'Thanks, Darina. That's very nice of you. Just name the day. I'll bring a bottle of wine, and if you want me to make anything, let me know.'

'Wine'll be fine,' said Darina gruffly.

Guess who's coming to dinner?

During the month of January, Anne Marie paid numerous visits to the Winding Stair. Joe always seemed pleased to see her.

On her first visit of the New Year, Anne Marie informed the object of her fancy that the book about bogs had been a great success. Nano had spent over an hour looking at the pictures and reminiscing about her girlhood on the Bog of Allen.

'They weren't good memories,' she told him, 'because her family was very poor. The house was a shambles: the thatch leaked, the chimney smoked and they all got ill every winter. But she really liked the book – she said it gave her a new view of bogs. It showed her the beauty she had overlooked as a girl when her only thought was how to escape from a life of poverty and hardship.'

Joe was glad that the book had gone down well. He told Anne Marie that his grandmother had given him a pair of knitted socks as she did every year and that he had given her a computer-enhanced album of family photographs that he had made himself.

'She must have been really pleased with that,' said Anne Marie. 'It's lovely when you get a present that someone with artistic talent has taken time to make.'

'I don't know,' said Joe. 'She kept asking why there were so many pictures of the postman and where was her husband.'

'Oh dear!'

Joe shrugged. 'She gets a bit confused, does poor Gran. The last time I went to visit her, she thought I was the plumber and she made me take a look at what was blocking her sink. Fortunately, I was able to fix it for her. But she does have her good days too, when she tells me about old times and about my dad when he was small.'

Anne Marie interpreted the fact of their attachment to their grandmothers as yet another sign that she and Joe were meant to be together. But January marched on and there was no sign of the relationship progressing to a more intimate footing. Whenever Anne

Marie came into the shop, they chatted pleasantly to one another, but Joe never asked her about herself or her job or anything that might be construed as showing an interest in her.

He's probably got a girlfriend already, she thought glumly, so I should just stop thinking about him. But in spite of her best intentions to stay away, the handlebars on her bicycle automatically turned to lead her down to the Quays most lunchtimes during the first fortnight of the month.

Dave teased her unmercifully. She hadn't told him about Joe, but he seemed to have an uncanny knack for rooting out her secrets. 'Trouble with the BF?' he'd asked her early in the New Year, and when she had blushed and replied that there wasn't any boyfriend, he had tapped the side of his nose knowingly and said that in that case, she should leave it to him to find someone for her.

Over the next couple of weeks, Dave regularly asked for BF situation updates, and Anne Marie was obliged to admit that she had got nowhere. 'I'm probably not his type,' she sighed one evening as she was kitting up for the cycle home. 'Otherwise, I'm sure he'd have asked me out by now.'

Dave nodded sympathetically. 'It's tough out there in the singles' market,' he agreed, 'especially for beautiful but bashful Kerry maids. What you need is for a friendly matchmaker who knows you well and has your best interests at heart to set you up with one of his mates. So – are you free next Saturday?'

As soon as Dave ascertained that she had nothing planned, he invited her to dinner to make up a foursome with Jo and a male friend whom he assured her she would fall in love with as soon as she set eyes on him. 'But you'd better act fast,' he warned her. 'This is a once-off, never-to-be-repeated offer on a very desirable piece of male property. He'll be snapped up as soon as he comes on the market. Fortunately, as one of his best buddies, I am in the position to offer you this unique preview. So what do you say?'

Anne Marie was happy enough to accept. According to Roz, even if the mystery man turned out to be completely unfanciable, the evening would be worth it for the pleasure of sampling Jo's gourmet cooking.

So it was that Anne Marie arrived at Dave's Lansdowne Road apartment at precisely eight o'clock on Saturday night carrying a bunch of flowers and a box of her own home-made shortbread.

Dave opened the door and threw his arms around her. 'Anne Marie, *ma chère*! So good of you to come. And so punctual! Come in, come in. I think my other half is still in the shower. Let me take your jacket – ooh, I like it. New, from Kilkenny Design, right? Nice cut to it, and I bet it keeps out the rain. And flowers – how did you know? We both adore them, especially lilies. Make yourself at home, my dear, while I go put these in water.'

Anne Marie went into the living room and sat in one of the black leather armchairs that formed part of a three-piece suite. Black dominated the room; one of the walls was painted black and hung with silver-framed etchings; the square rug in the centre of the floor was black with a splash of vibrant red and a band of white running through it. Though it was not what she would have chosen for herself, Anne Marie rather liked the décor, with the single exception of a sculpture of a naked male warrior, which she would have preferred not to have had in the room on her first meeting with the mystery man Dave had chosen for her.

She was just wondering whether anyone would notice if she turned the offending piece discreetly towards the wall when a door opened in the corridor at the far side of the room. A young man appeared, his straight blond hair newly-washed and shining in the overhead light. He stopped short when he saw Anne Marie. 'Well, well, this is a surprise! How are you tonight, Anne Marie?'

Anne Marie was too happy to make any intelligible response. It was Joe – her Joe from the Winding Stair! Smiling and blushing prettily, she shook hands with him, marvelling that Dave could have found the one boy in Dublin that she had set her heart on. It was uncanny – how had Dave known? Had he followed her to the bookshop one lunchtime without her being aware of it? Had he gone behind her back and secretly made arrangements to bring them together? Anne Marie didn't care. This was the best, most wonderful thing that had happened to her in all of her nineteen years. She couldn't wait for the evening to be over so that she could throw her arms around Dave and give him the biggest bear hug of his life.

Dave reappeared carrying a rectangular glass vase with the lilies in it. 'Oh, you've met each other then. That's good.'

'We have met lots.' said Joe. 'Haven't we, Anne Marie?'

Anne Marie smiled and nodded. 'I go to the Winding Stair quite often,' she said, turning to Dave. 'But I've never seen you there,' she added archly. 'So you must have been very discreet.'

Dave looked bemused. 'I do go there the odd time.

It's a bit far for lunchtime, though, unless you have a bike and ride there like you do. But why would I want to see Joe during the day when I see so much of him at night?' He smiled at the blond hunk.

'You mean you two are pretty good friends?'

Dave and Joe looked at her blankly. Joe turned to Dave as though he was expecting him to respond. But Dave was staring at Anne Marie, looking more and more alarmed as the seconds ticked by.

Joe cleared his throat. 'Yes, you could say that,' he said cautiously. He began to back away from Anne Marie. 'Uh . . . I've just remembered there's something I have to see to in the kitchen,' he said, giving Dave a hard look as he passed close to him. 'Why don't you show Anne Marie the view from the bedroom while I'm gone. I'm sure she'll find it most illuminating.'

It took Dave nearly ten minutes to persuade Anne Marie to come out of the bathroom.

'Anne Marie, I swear I thought you knew,' he said through the door. 'I thought it was obvious.' He tried a joke: 'I mean, what straight guy do you know with a body like mine or Joe's?'

The sobs grew louder.

Eventually, Dave went to the kitchen and came back with a bowl of soup. He left it on the floor outside the door. 'It's Joe's latest concoction: pumpkin soup with nutmeg and . . .' He sniffed the steam rising from the bowl, 'all sorts of other wonderful ingredients that I can't begin to identify. I'll leave it outside the door here and bring you a spoon, all right?'

The bolt on the inside of the door was pulled back. The door handle turned. Anne Marie came out with her hair pulled down around her face. 'Just . . . don't say anything, OK?'

'Promise,' said Dave. 'Anything. As long as you'll stay and have dinner with us, please.'

Anne Marie stayed. The fourth person, the mystery man, didn't turn up. 'Must have gone back to his girlfriend,' said Joe when they eventually gave up waiting and sat down to eat their reheated soup. 'He's a dotcom millionaire; she's a model. They have regular bust-ups, but they always seem to get back together afterwards.'

'Well, if he didn't even have the decency to ring and let you know that he wasn't coming, then I'm glad I'm not going to meet him,' Anne Marie said stoutly.

In spite of its inauspicious start, the evening was a great success. Joe's vegetarian fare was so tasty and filling that Anne Marie found she didn't miss meat at all. Dave was an expert host who managed to make her feel at ease in spite of her almighty gaffe. Now that she knew the truth, she was forced to concede that he and Joe did make a good couple. Still, whenever she looked up and caught Joe's eye, she couldn't help blushing and looking away in confusion. He was so gorgeous!

She stayed quite late and drank more wine than she was used to.

When it was time to go, Dave and Joe accompanied her down on the lift to the entrance. 'Are you sure you'll be all right on your bike?' Dave asked anxiously. 'You could leave it here, you know; I could run you home in the car no problem.'

'Not at all, I'll be grand. Sure it's a clear night and I've got all the gear.'

She put on her jacket and reflective vest and took out her gloves and helmet. Leaving them on the pannier, she went over to the two men to say her goodbyes. 'I had a lovely evening, honestly,' she said. 'And I'm sorry for embarrassing you both earlier on.'

Dave grinned. 'That's all right. It'll make a great story down at The George.'

'You wouldn't!' gasped Anne Marie.

'That's right, I wouldn't,' said Dave. He gave her a hug. 'I didn't think they made wide-eyed innocence any more, even down in Kerry. But I'm glad there's still a little of it around. The world would be a poorer place without it!'

Joe held out his hand. 'It's been a real pleasure, Anne Marie. Please come again. And I'm sorry that, you know . . . I can't be what you want.'

'That's OK,' said Anne Marie gravely. 'I'll get over it.' Suppressing a smile, she turned back to her bike and put on her helmet. Just before she swung her leg over the crossbar, she looked over her shoulder at him. 'But if you ever change your mind – about women, I mean . . .'

'I'll burst his balls,' said Dave. 'Now go home, you Jezebel, before I scratch your eyes out!'

With Brenda in Bray

The seaside resort of Bray had nothing of the quality of a picture postcard when Darina arrived there on a bleak Sunday morning in January. She left the DART station and walked down to the promenade with her hands crossed over each other in the pockets of her jacket to provide protection for her front. It was a man's padded jacket that she had bought secondhand from Age Action and the zip had broken after a week.

As soon as she turned out of the sheltered side-street on to the promenade, Darina gasped. A south-easterly wind was raging in from the sea, tossing plumes of water high above the barrier rail and drenching the grass up to a distance of six feet. It was bitterly cold and there wasn't a soul in sight. 'Bloody hell,' she muttered under her breath, 'if she's after standing me up, I'll kill her.' She checked her watch again: a quarter to ten. Darina had deliberately timed her arrival fifteen minutes late so that she would not be forced to stand around in the cold. But it looked now as though someone else had had the same idea – or she had taken a look at the weather and decided she wasn't going to get out of bed.

Just then, Darina's eye was caught by a spot of colour far down the promenade. It was hard to say what it was, but it appeared to be moving rapidly in her direction. She squinted her eyes to get a better view and thought she could make out a running figure – but who in their right mind would be out running on a day like this?

Darina walked slowly along the road until she came level with the empty bandstand, then she crossed over and took shelter behind it. She'd give the copper five minutes; if she didn't turn up by then, the deal was off and she was going home.

The bandstand offered little more than notional protection from the biting wind, which searched out and invaded every opening in Darina's layers of clothing. She shivered and wondered if it was worth the hassle to find a cigarette in her bag and try to light up.

While she debated with herself, the running figure came closer. Darina saw that it was a woman dressed in a grey tracksuit with a red fleece vest over it, a white bandanna, red ear-muffs and gloves. She nimbly side-stepped a wave that came crashing over the barrier and sprinted across the grass to the bandstand.

'What are you doing? Training for the Iron Woman?' shouted Darina as soon as Garda Brenda Clarke came within earshot.

The other woman waved her hand and shook her head to show that she wasn't ready to talk just yet. She jogged on past Darina, swinging her arms in wide arcs, then back, lifting her knees as high as her chest. She slowed to a walk and came to a halt just in front of the bandstand.

'You were late,' she said, bending down to touch her toes, 'so I went for a quick dash to the end of the promenade and back.' She leaned over to one side, then the other, stretching her arms and exhaling hard. 'I cycled fifty miles yesterday; I'll do a proper run after you've gone and this afternoon I might try and get a five-kilometre swim in.' She stood up and jogged on the spot.

'You're planning on swimming in that?' Darina was horrified.

'Maybe. If it calms down a bit. If not I'll go to the pool. I'm training for the triathlon. During the week, the most I get in is two out of the three, so at the weekends I try to do all of them at least once.'

Darina decided that she'd manage without that cigarette after all.

'So, what have you got for me?' Brenda asked. She had checked her recovery time and finished her cooling down exercises and her stretches. Now they were walking past the closed up Amusements in the direction of Bray Head.

'Can't we go in somewhere for a coffee? I'm freezing,' moaned Darina.

'No, we can't,' said Brenda firmly. 'This won't take long; just give me what you have and then you can go.'

'OK, but at least let us go up the town where the wind can't take the skin off me.'

Brenda nodded and led the way inland.

'So, how did the meeting go?' she asked when they had reached the first street running parallel with the coast.

'All right, I think. Like I said on the phone, it's not going to be easy to penetrate this operation.'

'But you believe that the person you're dealing with is the boss?'

'Pretty sure, yeah. She's clever and she likes playing games. I think The Man is a figment of her imagination.'

'Hmmm, I'm not so sure I like the sound of that.'

'What do you mean?'

'Well, The Man is legendary. We know that all sorts of stuff goes back to him: drugs, money-laundering, brothels – the lot. For one reason or another, we've never been able to put the squeeze on him. And now you're saying he doesn't exist? I don't think anybody in the Drug Squad would buy that.'

'Why not? Makes sense: you can't find him because he isn't there.'

'Then who's responsible for the dead bodies that turn up every so often on his patch? Three of his dealers met with lethal accidents in the last couple of years. Word was The Man had ordered it.'

'Why?'

'Two of them were trying to increase their profits by mixing a little rat poison with the heroin, but they put some kids in hospital and the Drug Squad was called in. I think The Man got scared; they say one of the dealers was his nephew and he was afraid his cover would be blown.'

'He had his own nephew topped? Jesus! And the third?'

'Eh . . . he was working with us.'

'What! He was a cop?'

'No, of course not. He was a dealer with a habit, but he was trying to give up the gear and get a life. He was on a Methadone programme and sticking to it pretty well. But his nerves weren't great; the slightest pressure and he'd have crumbled. I believe The Man got suspicious and brought him in for interrogation.'

Darina shuddered. 'God, it's awful what goes on when you scratch the surface of society, look behind the curtains of everyday life or whatever.'

'You ain't seen nothing yet,' said Brenda grimly. 'That's why I didn't want you to get involved. You don't know the sort of people you're messing with.'

'Oh, I'm getting the picture all right. But you know I would have gone ahead and done this on my own anyway.'

'I hope your brother appreciates what you're doing for him.'

Darina shrugged. 'I don't plan on telling him. I just want him left alone, remember?'

'Yeah, I know. I got him off the hook for you, didn't I?'

'And in return, here I am, out at sparrowfart on the lousiest day of the year in what has to be the most unlikely of venues for a meeting with a copper. And before you ask: no, I wasn't followed and yes, I do always check.'

'Good. You'll live longer that way. Now you can hand over that packet. Was it the usual suspects that delivered it?'

'Deco and Nailer? Yeah – they asked me to meet them outside XS like before. Said Cleo had decided to give me a little gear on credit and warned me what would happen to me if I didn't show a nice profit on it.'

'Well, you don't have to worry. I've got the cash here. Ten grand in used notes so as to be untraceable, though of course I've got the serial numbers just in case.'

'Right. Here's the packet of deadly white powder. What are you going to do with it, just as a matter of interest?'

'Give it to the Drug Squad, of course.'

'So are you working with them now?'

Brenda looked uncomfortable. 'Well, not exactly. I mean, it's unofficial. I've got a . . . a contact there who's quite high up and he has agreed to go along with this.'

'But you're still attached to Rathmines. And they know nothing about it. Am I right?'

Brenda nodded. 'I am so far out on a limb here that I can't even see the tree. This had better work, or I'll be out on my ear.'

'And I'll be dead,' Darina said shortly.

She opened her daypack, took out a plastic Dunnes Stores bag and handed it to the garda. Brenda took it, then unzipped her fleece and after putting in Darina's bag, pulled out a white envelope wrapped in clingfilm. 'I'll ask you not to count it here, if that's all right.'

'Oh, I trust you. Is there more where that came from?'

'I don't know,' said Brenda. 'As it's unofficial, the

money end of things is a bit tricky. But there should be enough for another drop in a few months. I'll talk to my . . . contact about it.'

Darina looked at her shrewdly. 'He's married, isn't he?' she asked, and had the satisfaction of seeing Brenda's face drop, then turn scarlet. 'It's all right, I won't ask any more awkward questions,' she went on. 'How you get the money is your business. As long as it's there when I need it.'

'Right. OK. Well, that's it – you've got your packet, I've got mine. I'll be off, so. Unless you want to come running up Bray Head with me?'

'Not a chance!'

Darina watched Brenda as she jogged to the end of the street, crossed and began to run down towards the promenade. Then she took out her cigarettes, turned into the wall and lit up.

So the tough-as-old-boots copper had a weak spot after all, and she, Darina, had discovered it. She flicked her match onto the pavement and smiled to herself as she remembered the look on Brenda's face. An affair with a high-ranking, married colleague, no less.

She walked quickly to the centre of the town and found a café that was serving breakfast. Watching Brenda get up to all that physical activity had given her an appetite; a Danish pastry and a cappuccino would hit the spot nicely, she decided.

Secrets and lies

The bar in Buswell's was almost empty, to the relief of a certain government minister who needed a quiet moment to get over the shock of what had been waiting for him on the inside page of this morning's *Irish Times*. He ordered a double whiskey and took it to a small table in the corner. There, hunched over his glass, he opened the paper again and surreptitiously began to read once more the article that had caused him so much anxiety on first reading.

It was no less alarming second time round.

On New Year's Day, Desmond Dunne had gone into his local garda station and had himself arrested on charges of bribery and corruption.

He was about to spill the beans.

The minister wondered bitterly what sort of a deal the financier had done. Immunity from prosecution? A nominal fine? Revenue must have come after him big time to make him do something like this. Of course, his reputation was already destroyed after that report in the paper a few weeks ago. It turned out that in his young days he had killed a mother and a little girl while driving under the influence – that probably explained why he had never taken alcohol at any of their meetings. Never trust a man who won't take a drink with you, thought the minister sourly. He had read the earlier story with a certain malicious glee, but he would have taken less pleasure in Dunne's downfall had he realised that the financier was planning on bringing a whole truckload of politicians with him. How soon would his name appear on the list? What would he do about it?

Taking a handkerchief from his pocket, the minister mopped at the perspiration that had broken out on his brow. How would he survive the shame of it? Would his wife stick by him? She had turned a blind eye to his relationship with his constituency office manager, but this might be more than she could swallow. And his daughters! They were at the age where everything was either black or white, good or bad and there was no such thing as the middle ground. They would despise him! How could he explain that it would have been impossible for him to have got to where he was today if he hadn't taken advantage of the opportunities that had come his way down through the years? After all, if he hadn't, then someone else would have.

The minister's efforts to console himself with this line of reasoning were largely unsuccessful, though the thought that he was not going to be alone was some comfort. He couldn't help but wonder just how many of his colleagues were going through the same anguish that he was at this very moment.

'Ye on yer own dere, Paddy? 'Tis awful lonely you're looking. Ye don't mind if I join you?'

The minister looked up to see a Cork TD, whose tenacity in fighting his constituents' corner had earned him the nickname of 'the terrier', holding a pint of Guinness in one hand and a glass of whiskey in the other. In Dublin political circles, he was equally well-known for his lack of tact and the carrying quality of his sing-song voice, so the minister tried to close the paper and make his excuses, desperate to get out before the terrier began snapping round his ankles.

Too late. The TD had leaned over to see what was in the paper, spilling a few drops of his stout on to the page as the minister edged it away from him.

'What's dat I see you reading? De Dunne scandal, is it? Terrible business altogether!' He sat himself heavily in the chair opposite the minister. 'Dey say he's after naming all sorts of names. Will we have anudder tribunal, d'ye tink?'

The minister stood up abruptly. He drained his glass in one gulp and put it back on the table. 'You'll have to excuse me, Barra. I have . . . aah . . . to meet the Taoiseach in a few minutes.'

The Cork TD looked up, his bland moon face belied by the shrewdness of his pale blue eyes. 'Dat's all right, Paddy. Ye've tings on yer mind. Away wit ye so; I understand.'

Love among the palms

Life was going swimmingly for Anne Marie. She loved her new apartment with its clean, Scandinavian lines and airy lightness, and it suited her to be living close to her cousins without having to share with them. They had agreed to eat together once a week, taking it in turns to cook. She was pleased to see that Darina and Cornelius were getting on better now that Gerald was out of the picture; they were civil to each other at table and Darina had even taken to calling her brother Con instead of Corny.

Anne Marie missed Gerald's company, but found that she was fast acquiring a new male friend. In the days that followed the dinner at his apartment, Dave had been touchingly considerate to her, enquiring after her health and emotional well-being at least three times a day. In the end, she had had to tell him that she really had got over her disappointment and that she actually preferred it when he teased her now and again. Dave had grinned and admitted that he had missed that aspect of their relationship too.

From that moment on, they grew even closer.

Knowing he was gay and therefore not interested in her sexually meant that Anne Marie relaxed in a way that she found impossible with other men, except of course for Seán. She liked the way Dave commented on her appearance, admiring any new item of clothing she bought and passing on tips about new beauty products he thought might interest her, so that Anne Marie began to feel as though he were her best girlfriend as well.

Roz was in much better form too now that she had entered the second trimester of her pregnancy. She was not yet reconciled to having two more babies, but she did occasionally manage to sound philosophical about her predicament, and now that the three of them were once more working as a team, the atmosphere in the office was much better. Roz began to pass over more and more of the regular columns to Anne Marie, on the basis that she would have to get used to doing them before Roz went on maternity leave. She praised Anne Marie's work, saying that she had never yet had an assistant whose grammar and spelling matched her own. She also said that she looked forward to seeing Anne Marie's first feature article on refugees.

During the second half of January, this became Anne Marie's main task. Before she tried to contact Victor, she wanted to learn as much about the issue of asylum seekers as she possibly could. She read everything she could get her hands on, from back issues of the *Irish Times* to articles in the free magazines that were pushed through the letterbox of the house in Belvedere Square. She became familiar with EU regulations governing the movement of migrants and researched the causes of mass movements of population in the twenty-first century. Only when she had taken enough notes to write a small book did she feel ready to contact ARASI, the Association for Refugees and Asylum Seekers in Ireland to try and set up an interview with Victor.

On the morning that she made the phone call, it so happened that Victor wasn't there, but a woman with an East European accent took a message and said that he would get back to her later that afternoon. When Anne Marie put the phone down, she discovered that her heart was thumping unnaturally fast. She had been dreading speaking over the phone to Victor, in case nerves made her babble incoherently, but she realised now that she had also been looking forward to hearing his voice.

Unless she wanted her whole day to be dominated by anticipation of that return phone call, Anne Marie knew she had better find something to occupy her mind fully. Fortunately, that was not difficult. After she had subbed Dave's fashion and beauty articles, she helped Roz choose the month's star letter, then spent until lunchtime on the phone to PR agencies trying to line up some celebrity interviews for the months ahead.

When the phone call did come, Anne Marie was so engrossed in rewriting a particularly bad article from a freelancer ('That's it – she's history,' said Roz when she read it) that she had no time to panic. Before she knew it, she had arranged to meet Victor the following afternoon at the entrance to the Botanic Gardens.

Next morning, Anne Marie dressed carefully for the occasion. She wore one of her designer outfits from her old job as Desmond Dunne's PA into the office, occasioning wolf-whistles from Dave, who pretended that the sight of her legs was sending him crazy. After lunch, she put on make-up, something that she very rarely did.

'What d'you think?' she asked Dave when she came out of the bathroom. 'Do I look OK? I haven't over-done it with the rouge or the eye shadow, have I?'

'You look hot, babe. Or should I say cool. Yes, very cool, with your hair pinned back and your face made up. Makes you look older. Older and more sophisticated.'

'Just the effect I wanted to create,' said Anne Marie with a happy smile.

'Whoa! Steady on there, let me grab a tissue. Lipstick on the teeth – can't have that.'

Dave wiped off the offending marks, then made Anne Marie blot her lips on the folded-up tissue. 'Much better,' he said when she had done. 'You'll be able to worm all sorts of secrets out of him now!'

Anne Marie made sure to arrive in plenty of time. She took the bus across town, the fact that this was her first foray to the Northside making the trip that little bit adventurous. She stayed on the bus when it passed by the entrance to the Gardens, and allowed it to take her another two stops before she got off at the top of a hill, opposite a strange grey building with sloping sides that turned out to be the Meteorological Office. At the bottom of the hill, she came upon a church shaped like a pyramid, echoing the form of the cedar in front of it. Glasnevin was much nicer than Rathmines, she decided, so why did the cousins have this thing about the Southside being a far better place to live?

Anne Marie reached the gates of the Botanic Gardens with three minutes to spare. It was a clear, bright day, but too cold to remain standing in the one spot for long, so she went inside and had a look around. Close to the entrance there was an interpretive centre with tea rooms, where she could maybe invite Victor for coffee after the interview was over. She walked towards the porter's window next to the interpretive centre, where a middle-aged man with a pleasant face was sitting reading a book. He looked up as she passed and greeted her with a smile.

Smiling back at him, Anne Marie suddenly realised that, although she was a little nervous about the forthcoming interview, she was nevertheless extremely happy.

She walked further along the path, trying to figure out why it was that she felt this way. Sure, everything in her life was going well, but that had often been the case before and yet she had rarely been transported by joy because of it. This feeling was more like what she used to experience as a child when, playing on the beach in summer, or running through the meadows at Riverwood, she would suddenly feel so light with happiness as to be almost weightless. There had been no reason for it back then; it had come as a gift and she had accepted it as such without trying to analyse it.

Lost in contemplation of those earlier transports, Anne Marie forgot to be on the lookout for Victor. It was only when she heard someone call her name that she turned and saw him. He was standing in front of the porter's window, an *Irish Times* tucked under his arm. Victor immediately waved to the porter, who nodded and went back to his book.

'I thought it was you,' said Victor, 'but I decided to check with Willie whether anyone else had come in the last few minutes. How are you, Anne Marie?'

'I'm fine, thanks,' replied Anne Marie, taking off her glove to shake hands with him. Victor was not wearing gloves, so it was a surprise to find that his hand was warm.

'You have been moving round a lot since we first met,' Victor smiled. 'I think you must have changed jobs at least once.'

Anne Marie glanced at the paper in his hand. It had a big picture of Dunne on the front page. 'Em . . . yes, I began working at *Femme* a couple of months ago.'

Victor followed her glance. 'He was your former employer, was he not? I remember seeing you with him when we met for the second time. He appears to be in a bit of trouble these days, doesn't he?'

Anne Marie's face clouded. She didn't like talking about her former boss, whose picture had rarely been out of the papers ever since the first evening tabloid had reported on his extraordinary confession a few weeks back. (*I Dunne it! Tycoon Tells Truth At Last!*) Out of respect for Roz, the matter was never discussed at work, and at home the cousins had quickly learnt that Anne Marie was not to be drawn on the subject. In fact, Anne Marie owed Darina a debt of gratitude for getting rid of the redheaded reporter who had turned up at the basement flat one evening offering all kinds of inducements for an exclusive interview with the girl who was the key to two major stories she had uncovered. According to Cornelius, even Darina had had enormous difficulty in getting rid of her once she had got her foot in the door.

Now Anne Marie frowned and shook her head slightly. 'You shouldn't believe everything you read in the papers,' she said defensively, avoiding Victor's eyes.

'Oh, I'm sorry. You must be tired of people asking you questions.'

'No, it's not that,' began Anne Marie. 'It's just . . .' She hesitated.

'You liked him, didn't you?'

'He was very good to me. That's all I can say. I know nothing about his past history.'

Victor smiled. 'Fair enough,' he said. 'We shan't speak of it any more.'

Instead, he proposed a tour of the Gardens.

'Do you come here often?' Anne Marie asked as they set off along the path towards a tall, rather dilapidated glasshouse.

'I visit the Palm House whenever I feel homesick,' answered Victor. He was a walking a little ahead of Anne Marie, so she couldn't see his face to tell whether he was joking or not.

'Oh. And . . . is that often?' she asked timidly.

'All the time.' He turned and smiled, but his eyes were serious.

'Would you mind . . . I mean, how would it be if I started the interview in the Palm House? Or would you prefer to wait and do it in the tea rooms after our walk?'

'The Palm House will be fine.'

It was like walking into a jungle. Anne Marie caught her breath as the humid heat hit her when she followed Victor through a long glasshouse filled with poinsettias and cyclamens, then went down four steps into the Palm House itself. The high, curved dome of the glasshouse was almost entirely obstructed from view by the luxuriant growth of palm trees, most of which must have been there a very long time to have reached their present height, thought Anne Marie. There was a circular walkway about halfway up, but to her disappointment, it was not open to the public.

The Palm House was empty apart from the two of them. When they had done the tour, Victor and Anne Marie sat on the steps leading into the Orchid House, and the interview began.

Once the tape recorder was switched on, Victor immediately began to speak, as though he wanted it to be clear that he was taking the lead in the interview. 'What you have to realise,' he began, 'is that, contrary to what the popular press seems to believe, the vast majority of asylum seekers have no desire to be here in Ireland whatsoever.'

He looked at her challengingly, but Anne Marie said nothing. It hurt her to think that he might be speaking for himself too when he said this, but she merely nodded for him to continue. 'Asylum seekers are people forced to leave their homeland by circumstances beyond their control. War, persecution, genocide, religious fanaticism; these are some of the factors which lead people to uproot themselves and seek a better life elsewhere.'

'What about economic migrants?' Anne Marie interjected.

Victor gave a short laugh. 'Ah yes. The question always is: did you really have to leave? Have you got the scars to prove it? Tell us how you were tortured, show us your broken fingers, the burn marks on your genitals.'

Anne Marie was sitting at the top of the steps, Victor below her. He looked up at her mockingly. 'And yet, you Irish should know all about economic migrants. How many Americans came originally from these shores? Millions, wasn't it?'

'Oh, you mean during the Famine? Yes, I suppose—'

'Ah, the Famine! The last great hunger in Europe, which shocked because it shouldn't have happened in this part of the world in the middle of the nineteenth century. Hundreds of thousands of Irish people crossed the ocean to a strange land rather than stay at home and starve to death. And they were the lucky ones; there were ships to take them, and a country willing to receive them. It is not so easy nowadays. The famines are no longer in Europe, of course, and there are no boats to take the starving Africans to a new land. Can you imagine it? Instead of seeing the pot-bellied children with flies crawling in and out of their mouths, and their stick-like parents with the hollow eyes staring at you dully from your TV screens, just imagine if you saw them arrive on boats at Dún Laoghaire, Cork, Rosslare. What would the Irish people, so generous in their donations to charity, do then?'

Anne Marie had her notepad out and was busy writing. Victor was being deliberately provocative, but that didn't matter. What he said was true and it was important to record exactly what he felt about these issues. Now she lifted her head and looked down at him in some surprise. He had been in full spate; she was sure there was plenty more where that came from.

'You are recording all of this?' he asked her softly. 'Does that mean you intend to publish it? Or will my rantings be edited out as usual?'

Anne Marie became alarmed. 'You've been interviewed before? But I didn't come across any articles.'

'Oh, I've been interviewed all right. Not here, but in Germany, France, England, the USA.'

'Oh,' said Anne Marie, taken aback. She hadn't realised that he was so well-travelled. 'Well, in that case, I should warn you: This is my first feature article and I'm not too sure how to go about it. But I had intended showing it to you anyway, to make sure that you agreed with everything I wrote, so if you think I haven't reflected your views, there'll be a chance to change the text before it goes into print.'

Victor smiled, and the sudden shock of white in his dark face almost took her breath away. 'Then I have nothing to fear. Now, I am sure you have plenty of questions of your own to put to me, so please – go ahead.'

Anne Marie sat up straight and took out her neatly-typed list. Although the tape was on, she took notes as well to remind herself of how Victor looked and behaved when he made certain points.

As the minutes ticked by, he seemed to grow more relaxed. Occasionally, she made a comment herself, or gently drew him back to the question when he wandered off the point, but in the main, she was content to let him speak unprompted.

After about half an hour, she stopped taking notes altogether. They had covered most of the points she had wanted to raise, and now it was more of a discussion than a question-and-answer session. 'You are very well-informed,' Victor commented after they had been talking for some minutes about the legal aspects of the granting and refusing of asylum. 'I have to say that I'm impressed.'

Anne Marie flushed at the compliment. She began to imagine how she would describe Victor in her article. Handsome? Oh yes! But could she put that in? Maybe she could say it in other words. Talk about his manly profile. His straight nose and flared nostrils; his full lips and dazzlingly white smile. His athletic body. The casual grace with which he carried himself.

The way his eyes flashed when he was carried away by passion.

Passion.

Anne Marie swallowed. Something very strange was happening. A hot flush originating deep inside her was spreading throughout her body, making her knees tremble and her cheeks glow. Victor was still talking but she could no longer hear what he was saying. She was mesmerised by his hands, the long fingers slender and beautiful, the much lighter palms criss-crossed by dark lines that she had a sudden urge to trace.

His hair was short and crinkly; it came to a neat end above the collar of his shirt. She wished she could feel what it was like to the touch.

Those lips – they must be wonderful for kissing.

Suddenly, she realised that Victor had stopped talking and was looking at her strangely. 'I said, would you like to finish up over coffee? Or would you prefer to walk around the Gardens?'

Anne Marie forced herself to focus on his words. Walk? Drink coffee? No, that was not what she wanted to do. Tentatively, as though in a dream, she reached out to stroke the hand that was resting on his knee, just inches away from her. At the last instant, however, she pulled back. She had suddenly woken up and become conscious of what was on her mind. She flushed scarlet.

Victor looked at her in silence for a long moment, a variety of emotions flitting across his proud, handsome face. There was understanding, then doubt, a spasm of something like pain and finally, acceptance.

Anne Marie watched him intently, unable to breathe for the tightness in her chest. She thought she'd die if he touched her; she knew she would if he didn't.

Very slowly, Victor lifted his hand from his knee. He reached across the vast gulf that separated him from Anne Marie and with infinite gentleness, he touched the tips of his fingers to her flaming cheeks.

'I live nearby,' he said softly.

Woman in love

It was like nothing she had ever experienced or believed possible to experience. It was like dying. It was like being reborn. It was so gigantic that body and mind were not enough to encompass it. Riding back across town on the top of the number 19 bus in the evening, Anne Marie felt as though her boundaries had dissolved and she had become one with the universe. Her heartbeat was the heartbeat of all the passengers; her smile was on every face. She got off the bus and she was the air she breathed; she was the frosty darkness and the bare trees on Leinster Road.

When she arrived home, Anne Marie wasted no time. Without bothering to switch on lights, she tore off the clothes she had put on less than an hour earlier, dropped them on the floor and got into bed, the better to relive what had happened to her. She closed her eyes and touched her cheek the way Victor had done in the Palm House, and she replayed in her head everything from then until the moment two hours later when he had raised himself above the tangle of sheets and whispered: 'Are you sure you want me to do this?'

So this is love, she said over and over as waves of heat and pleasure beat over her that were but echoes of the tidal waves that had rocked her to the core earlier in the afternoon. She felt exalted and yet humbled, and amazed that someone as ordinary as she could feel this way.

Nobody told me it was going to be like this, she thought, burying her head in the crook of her arm to sniff at the lingering smell of her lover. She had completed a rite of passage, but nothing she had heard or read could have prepared her for it. She thought of her parents and her grandmother, and marvelled that they had been through it too and yet they continued to behave like normal people. Anne Marie was certain that she would never be the same again. She was changed, utterly and forever.

Next morning, Dave, who was waiting to tease Anne Marie about sleeping it out, changed his mind when he saw her. She was forty minutes late for work, but one look was enough to inform him that innuendoes about overtime and continuing the interview with her refugee in more comfortable surroundings were unworkable because that was exactly what had happened. Besides, when Anne Marie came in, he no longer felt inclined to tease. There was something about her, an aura that made him suddenly chary of showing her disrespect.

'She was like a goddess,' he said to Joe in bed that night. 'It was the way she moved: proud and erect, and yet with this fluid grace that she didn't have before.'

'Which goddess?' asked Joe sleepily. 'Artemis?'

'No, not any more,' said Dave with a hint of regret in his voice. 'That was before. When she was virginal. Now she's Aphrodite.'

'You mean, Audrey Hepburn becomes Isabella Rosselini?'

'That's just it!' said Dave happily. 'Isn't it lucky that I've always adored them both?'

Over the next couple of weeks, other people noticed the change in Anne Marie. Roz saw that she was living in a world of her own, going through the motions as far as work was concerned, but emotionally detached from it. If she guessed the reason, she said nothing; not even to Dave. Anne Marie was such an asset to the magazine that Roz was happy to cut her a little slack for a while, so she returned phone calls and generally covered for her assistant when necessary without saying anything about it.

Darina and Cornelius saw very little of their cousin, but when they did, they were both aware that she was not her usual self. Darina, who had a fair idea as to the cause, was impressed and not a little envious; although she had had several sexual partners to date, she had yet to experience what it was like to be madly in love. It bothered her that Anne Marie had got there before her and she was very curious to know who it was that had captured her cousin's heart. Cornelius disapproved of the change in his cousin's behaviour. He saw her riding her bike like a Valkyrie, helmet forgotten and hair flying, and hoped that whatever had got into her, it wouldn't last.

Brandon saw and smiled. Another milestone passed; she had to experience the physical before she could renounce it in favour of the spiritual side of her nature. The universe was taking care of his godchild as he had requested.

Vera Meaney was of the opinion that Anne Marie had got above herself since she had moved upstairs. She used to be very nice when she was sharing with her cousins in the basement; now she strode past her new neighbour as though she didn't see her. Vera had left a note on the door asking Anne Marie to come over for tea some evening and not only had she received no reply but she had found the note trampled underfoot on the landing the next morning. Vera was most put out; she desperately wanted to see what Brandon had done with the new apartment, which by rights he should have offered to her, and in order to wangle an invitation from Anne Marie, she would have to entice her to tea in her own place first. But Anne Marie had spurned her invitation. And after I had gone to the expense of getting in a cake from the Tea Time Express, thought Vera resentfully.

As for Anne Marie, she lived for the moment each evening when she reached Victor's tiny bedsit in Glasnevin. She knew she was wanton; for the first week she was so driven by lust that he barely had time to close the door behind her before she started pulling off his clothes. Each time she lay with him, Anne Marie was stirred anew by the glorious contrast in their skin colour: black-white, white-black. 'Like Irish coffee,' she had said to him after the first time. 'Or Guinness,' he had smiled back.

They made love repeatedly, then fell into an exhausted sleep in each other's arms. Sometimes Anne Marie woke up in the morning in time to cycle back to Rathmines for a shower; more often she had to make do with freshening up in the bathroom at *Femme*, hoping that liberal spraying of perfume would be enough to disguise the musky animal scent that she and Victor created between them.

But the truth of it was that she no longer cared what

people thought of her. At the chemist's, she stared the assistant boldly in the eye when she asked him for three packets of condoms, extra-large and extra-strong. If the lovers got out of bed at the weekend to go for a walk in the Botanics, under her winter coat she wore an African *mumu* of Victor's without any underwear.

Of course, things could not continue indefinitely this way. Towards the end of the second week, Victor asked if they could meet in town instead of at his flat, because he had to spend the afternoon talking with a Nigerian woman who had been sexually assaulted by her landlord. Anne Marie was happy to agree; she saw it as an indication that they had reached a new stage in their relationship.

Being out and about with Victor was wonderful in itself. We make a stunning couple, thought Anne Marie as she caught sight of their reflection in the window of a bank in Westmoreland Street. He was the taller of the two by a few inches, and as far as she was concerned, there was no better-looking man on earth. With her arm linked proudly through his, she met the stares, some of them admiring, others curious, a few frankly hostile, of people coming towards them and felt herself to be the luckiest woman alive.

As they strolled through Temple Bar, Anne Marie began to imagine what it would be like to be officially accepted as Victor's girlfriend. She would meet an entirely new set of people, most of them foreign; she would have the chance to improve her spoken French; she would gain enough material for a whole series of articles on immigrants in Dublin. She was already looking forward to introducing Victor to her family; Seán and Yvonne would take to him at once, she was sure; Nano maybe not so readily. Not because he was

African, Anne Marie hastened to explain to herself, but because moodiness was something Nano couldn't abide.

Victor was moody. It was his only fault, as far as Anne Marie could see, and she well understood how his experiences in Africa could have made him that way. Not that he spoke about them to her; she knew only the barest outline of his personal history. That he had been adopted as a baby by Scottish missionaries, for example; that he had grown up in Botswana and Kenya, that he had studied law at Oxford; that he had returned to Africa and worked as an advocate for Human Rights in different countries, including Rwanda and Zaïre. That he had been through horrors she knew because at night when he began shouting in a strange language and fighting an invisible foe, she it was who soothed him and reassured him that it was only a dream.

Once, when he was in a playful mood, she asked the questions lovers ask: What did you think of me when you saw me for the first time? Did you feel about me the way I felt about you? How soon did you know that we were going to end up together?

The answers were not all to her liking. 'The first time I saw you,' Victor said, 'I thought you were as tall as an African woman.' He was staring at the ceiling when he said it, and by the needle-prick of pain in her heart, she knew that he was not talking about African women in general, but about a particular African woman. 'My next thought,' he went on, 'when you were looking so lost and distressed was that you were very young and should not be allowed out on your own!'

She laughed and tickled him for revenge, but the memory stayed with her and became the first intimation that there were thorns in the rose garden of love.

Tough competition

On a dirty grey morning in the middle of January, while Darina, who had taken her mother's warning to heart, was slaving away in the Lecky Library, in an office in a nondescript part of East London, two ageing punkettes and their young Editorial Assistant were deciding on the winner of the *U*Yours!* Club Med holiday competition.

'Where wuz the last one from, then?' asked Ziggy, the Editor, picking at the scab that had formed around the spike she had recently had inserted beneath her bottom lip.

''Ere in London, remember?' Jade, the peroxide blonde Arts Director replied. 'Turned out she knew your flatmate's brother or somefink.'

'Oh yeah. We wuz afraid of being accused of whachacallit?'

'Nepotism?' suggested Imelda, the eighteen-year-old Editorial Assistant. Although she was the only one to have been born within hearing of the Bow bells, she spoke the kind of English that the other two had long abandoned in favour of what they believed to be Cockney.

Ziggy looked at her with dislike. 'Nah, favouritism. Anyway, we got lots of readers in London; wot we need is a winner from somewhere where we don't got so many.'

'Wot about Scotland? Oh 'ang on, the one before

wuz from there,' said Jade. 'I remember cuz I 'ad to ring 'er an' I couldn't understand a word she wuz saying.'

'Here's one from a man in Bradford,' said Imelda, who was the only one reading the entries they had received.

'Don't be stupid,' Ziggy said. 'We're not giving it to a bloke. It's strictly chicks only wiv us, innit Jade?'

'That's righ'. Here, pass us over a few of those envelopes. Might as well 'ave a bit of a larf meself. Let's see . . . first one up's from Llan . . . Llan – oh, somewhere in Wales.'

'Anyone wot lives in a place wif a name like that don't deserve to go to Club Med,' declared Ziggy. 'Next?'

'What about Ireland? I've seen three or four of them so far,' said Imelda, whose mother came from County Wexford.

'I dunno – they probably got awful Mick names like Shove-on or Shin-aid.'

'And Shame-us Oh Shockin-zee,' screeched Jade. 'Remember 'im? Bright red 'air and freckles – you wuz mad about 'im until the time 'e he barfed all over you at the Sex Pistols concert!'

Ziggy scowled at her.

'Actually,' said Imelda, 'this last one's name is Darina Davenport. She's from Limerick.'

'Limerick? Y'mean like the poem? Is there really a place called that, then?' Ziggy looked incredulous.

'Yes, and it's a long way from Dublin. I'm surprised anybody down there has ever heard of this magazine,' said Imelda, having just decided that two weeks at *U*Yours!* was quite enough and she would rather continue her work experience at the local sausage plant.

'Fancy that!' exclaimed Ziggy, who had entirely failed to pick up on her assistant's sarcasm. 'Well, we'll 'ave to give it to this Darina-person so. You can ring 'er today, or write to 'er or whatever. Just don't forget to check she got the answers right first.'

What the postman brought

Darina was in limbo when she got the letter informing her that she was the winner of a Club Med holiday. She had gone up the back stairs to pick up post from the main hall, but she had forgotten to put the snib on the lock at the bottom and the door had slammed itself closed before she could reach it on the way down again. Now she would have to go back up the connecting stairs and out through the hall door, then around to the basement flat at the bottom of the steps. She didn't have her keys, but she was hoping that the draught responsible for slamming the connecting door had been caused by Cornelius's return home. Before she left the confines of the enclosed stairway, however, Darina switched on the low-energy light that Brandon had recently had fitted and sat down on a step to look at her post.

The first one she picked up was a funny postcard with a picture of The Old Woman Who Lived In A Shoe. It was from Gerald, who had scrawled a few lines on the back to say that he was getting on fine in Limerick and that he hoped she wasn't studying too hard (ha, ha!). Next, there was a note from her tutor in the Russian Department asking her to call in and see her, which immediately made Darina feel guilty. She had been neglecting her second subject for months now, and knew that if she wasn't careful, there would be an NS sent to her home in Limerick to show that her attendance at lectures and seminars was Not Satisfactory. The irony of it was, thought Darina regretfully, she liked Russian far better than French and wished that she could spend more time on it.

The last envelope had a London postmark and a weird logo showing the screaming head of a punk rock chick. Even after she had opened it and read the short letter informing her that she was the lucky winner of a week's holiday in Corsairs' Cove on the lovely Caribbean island of Martinique, Darina had no idea what it was about. It took her the best part of two minutes to remember that she had filled in a competition entry form in a magazine she had been reading on the train down to Limerick before Christmas.

And Anne Marie must have cut it out and put it in the post for me, thought Darina in amazement. Good ol' Anne Marie! A week in the Caribbean – well, well! That should be worth a few quid. She checked the dates and discovered that the holiday fell in the spring break, so in theory she could go. But that sort of package deal held no appeal for her; she would far rather have the money to spend as she pleased. She wondered if Anne Marie would be interested in buying it, at a slight discount seeing as she did have something to do with the winning of it. On the other hand, her cousin was probably too caught up with her mystery lover to want to go anywhere further than his bed.

Darina sighed. How long was it since she had had sex? Too long. She stared down at the letter in her hand. Maybe a Club Med holiday was just what she needed.

All in the stars

Spring was in the air. The breezes that blew Anne Marie's hair as she cycled north to Glasnevin began to lose their cutting edge. When she arrived at Victor's place, she no longer had to wait for her face to defrost before she could feel his kisses. Daylight lingered a little longer each evening, so that by the end of the month of February, she was arriving before darkness.

Spring was in Anne Marie too. It coursed through her veins, bringing a bloom to her cheeks and a sparkle to her eyes. She was heady with love, life and happiness.

Dave, who knew a good thing when he saw it, captured her at the height of her splendour. It was on a Saturday towards the end of February when Victor was attending a conference and Anne Marie was at a loose end. Dave suggested a trip to the Wicklow Mountains and asked if she would mind if he took some photos of her as he had 'a few ends of rolls to use up'. Anne Marie didn't mind, but she was a little surprised when they arrived at the car park behind the pub at the foot of Lugnaquilla and she discovered that Dave had brought along several coats, jackets, hats and accessories, as well as a full make-up kit for the shots.

'But I'm not a fashion model!' she protested as he began to select items from the boot of the car for her to try on.

'No, you're the real thing and that's even better,' said Dave. 'Besides, this is just for fun. I'm out of practice since leaving *Vogue*, and I like to keep the hand in when I can.'

They spent the rest of the morning on the hills. Dave shot five full rolls as well as the ends he claimed to have left in his different cameras. It was warm work; after each session, they had to come back to the car park for Anne Marie to change, then set off again carrying Dave's photographic paraphernalia between them.

At one o'clock, they broke for lunch. Dave had brought a flask and a picnic basket filled with goodies. 'You have to try some of Joe's vegetarian pâté,' he said, 'it's simply divine. There's a selection of filled rolls as well. And I think he has put in a few of his yummy chocolate brownies for after.'

Anne Marie winced at the mention of brownies, but she didn't tell Dave about her experience at the Hallowe'en party in the flat. That all seemed like such a long time ago now; almost another life. BV: Before Victor. She smiled to think how young and innocent she had been back then.

'Good, aren't they?' Dave said as she took another roll from the basket.

'Mmm. Joe looks after you well!'

'Yes, he does, doesn't he? I'm a lucky man and I know it.'

After they had finished eating, Dave shook the crumbs off the newspaper he had spread out on the seat of the car. 'Oh look, horoscopes!' he exclaimed as he was starting to fold it again. 'I wonder what the stars have in store for us. Let's see . . . Capricorn: *You've been taking the bull by the horns recently.* Well, really! How dare they write about my sex life like that! *It is time to sit back and relax while others cater to your needs.* Oooh, lovely; I simply must bring this home to Joe! What does it say for him? Gemini . . . Gemini . . . here we are: *Spring is here; time to take the finger out and get down to all those jobs you've been leaving to others.* How *did* they know? I am definitely saving this. What are you, Anne Marie? Virgo, isn't it?'

Anne Marie nodded. 'It's got to be something good,' she declared. 'I feel as though I could conquer the world these days!'

Dave smiled affectionately at her. 'I'm sure you could too,' he said. 'Let's see if your horoscope agrees.' He ran his finger across the signs of the zodiac until he came to the right one, then began to read aloud. 'Virgo . . .'

He frowned. 'Uh oh, better put off those plans for world domination; this is not the time. Listen to this: *March winds blow bad tidings your way; lie low and don't try to fight what's coming.* Poor Anne Marie! That's not very encouraging, is it?'

'It's all right, Dave,' smiled Anne Marie, 'there's no need to look so tragic. I don't mind what it says. Anyway, you know as well as I do that it's all a load of rubbish.'

Dave slapped his cheeks in mock-horror. 'Bless us, what heresy is this? Just wait until I tell Sibyl what you said – she'll put a hex on you!'

Anne Marie tossed her hair and grinned. 'Try it and I'll set Brandon on you. And I'll bet his magic is stronger than hers!'

Dunne's joy

It had all changed. The warders' cottages were gone, demolished to make way for the new women's prison. Dunne missed the view along the avenue that had led from the North Circular Road up to the imposing prison gates through which his father and brothers had passed more times than he could remember.

Now he was going through the gates himself.

Even though he had imagined this eventuality, the sentence had come as a surprise. In his speech, Mr Justice Hart, known to the guards as Bleedin' Hart for his leniency towards the young drug addicts who regularly appeared before him on charges of petty larceny, had spoken passionately about the decline in morals among the country's leaders. He had deplored the widespread view that corruption was not only permissible, but was an inevitable fact of life in the new Ireland. He had noted that although Desmond Dunne had taken the unusual step of initiating procedures against himself, at no stage had he expressed, by word or demeanour, any remorse for his wrongdoing down through the years. Therefore, argued the judge, his recent actions could be construed as yet another cynical manipulation of the system to suit his own devious purposes. Mr Justice Hart wished it to be made clear that the country's criminal justice system was not open to abuse in this fashion.

Desmond Dunne would be remanded in custody for a period of five years.

As all hell broke loose in the Circuit Court, Dunne's counsel leapt to his feet, ready to protest vociferously at the severity of the sentence. But Dunne shook his head even before the judge refused leave to appeal.

True, he hadn't seen it coming. A hefty fine, community service, yes; prison, no. But that was all right. It was good that life continued to hold some surprises.

Still in handcuffs, Dunne was helped out of the van by the prison officer on duty at the Circuit Court who had taken charge of him after sentence had been passed. At the General Office inside the main gate of Mountjoy, details of his committal were noted, after which he was taken to the prison proper, where his handcuffs were removed and he was accompanied down to Reception in the basement.

There, after more form-filling, he was photographed, told to strip and sent to the shower. His personal belongings were bagged and put in a locker. The medics examined him. He was issued with prison clothes: cheap denim trousers, a T-shirt, denim jacket and white runners.

For a man who had just received a five-year sentence, Dunne was unusually ebullient. He wisecracked throughout the admission procedure, in spite of the fact that the young officer accompanying him was clearly not impressed. 'Mr Daly to you, sir,' he said stiffly when Dunne addressed him as 'son'.

It was while he was being transferred to his cell that Dunne finally made his entrance. As he was being led through the Circle, the hub of the prison from where every landing was visible, he stopped and took a deep breath.

'Ah yes, just when I was beginning to think that everything had changed, there it is: that old familiar Mountjoy smell. Piss pots, boiled cabbage and dried spunk. Unmistakable!'

A tall prison officer with grey hair and a neat beard stopped what he was doing and looked keenly at the new prisoner. 'Mr Daly – just a minute, if you please,' he said.

'Yes, Chief Officer,' said the warder, motioning to Dunne to stay where he was.

'Would that be Desmond Dunne you have there?'

'Yes, Mr Cleary.'

'Taking him up to A Division, are you?'

'Yes, sir.'

'He wanted to put me in D, but I asked for A. I'm bound to know a few of the heads up there,' interposed Dunne.

The Chief Officer came over to him. 'Dessie Dunne. Well, well.' He called to another, older officer. 'Come here, Mr Byrne, and tell me what you think of our latest arrival. Did you ever think you'd live to see the day?'

The old prison officer looked Dunne slowly up and down. 'Not another one of Wacko Dunne's lads, is it? I thought they were all dead.'

'It certainly is. The youngest. Do you remember him as a nipper coming in on visits? A terror even then, he was. I caught him going out of the Detail Office one day with a pair of handcuffs and my wallet. But I might have known I only had to bide my time.'

He turned to Dunne. 'Well Dessie, I can retire happy now. You're where you belong.'

Dunne grinned back. 'It's nice to see a familiar face. I was beginning to think I'd have to reinvent the legend all on me own.'

'No, no – we want none of that. The Dunnes were a right pack of gougers,' he explained to the young warder, who was looking perplexed. 'Any time there was a riot, they were sure to be in the thick of it. Up on the roof with the Republicans and all. You know, Dessie, your brother Razor nearly took my head off with a slate back in seventy-two; I still have the scar.'

Dunne laughed. 'Yeah, you didn't want to mess with Razor. But don't worry, I won't be giving you grief. Head down, do me whack, that'll be me.'

'Too right! Any trouble from this man, Mr Daly, let

me know. It'll be a great pleasure to clap him in leg irons and apply the thumbscrews if he so much as sneezes out of turn!'

The young prison officer looked from one man to the other in consternation. They were grinning at each other like the best of mates. 'Yes, Mr Cleary,' he said dubiously before leading his prisoner away.

The cell was a double one. Its other occupant wasn't around, but the lower bunk was made up. Dunne accordingly began to make up the top one, having first taken down the mattress and banged it against the wall a few times.

Lying on his bed some minutes later, he wondered how long his present elation was going to last. It wasn't natural, he reflected, to feel good about going to prison. The reaction would have to set in, sooner or later. Five years: with remission, three-and-a-half. He'd be fifty-three by the time he got out.

The prospect didn't faze him in the least.

Reaching under his pillow, Dunne took out an orange-covered booklet entitled *Information for Persons in Custody* and began reading.

The End of the Affair

After Anne Marie had been with Victor for six weeks, she arranged a dinner to introduce him to the cousins. She would have got round to it in time, she told herself, but Darina had forced her hand by asking her straight out when she was going to bring her boyfriend downstairs to meet them.

The truth was, Victor rarely came to Rathmines. Their affair was conducted for the most part in his little room near the Botanic Gardens and on neutral territory in Temple Bar. Twice only had Victor returned to her place, and on both those occasions he had arrived late and left early in the morning before anyone was up. Anne Marie was happy with this arrangement for the time being; deep down, she sensed that her relationship with Victor was precarious; he was allowing her to love him, but his own emotions were far less engaged. If she pushed things, he was likely to recoil.

But when Darina asked how come she hadn't introduced her boyfriend to the cousins, Anne Marie had no good answer. If she made an excuse, it would sound as though she didn't want them to meet. Then her cousins would assume that she was ashamed of the relationship, which was so far from being the case that it upset Anne Marie even to imagine it. So she overcame her misgivings and proposed to host a dinner for Victor and the cousins on the night before St Patrick's Day.

Victor was less than enthusiastic. After checking his diary, he admitted he had no other engagements that Friday night, but to Anne Marie it was obvious that he wished he had. She wanted to explain to him that it hadn't been her idea, but she was afraid of making matters worse. In the end, she said nothing, but from that moment on she began to have a bad feeling about the evening.

To compound matters, early in the week, she had an unexpected phone call at work:

'How's my best girl?'

'Seán! I'm grand, thanks. And yourselves?'

'Not a bother. How are you fixed for St Patrick's

Day? Were you planning on going to see the parade with anybody?'

'Well, no. I—'

'That's great, because I've a surprise for you: your mother and I are coming up for the weekend.'

The pencil Anne Marie was twiddling between her fingers snapped in two. 'You're coming to Dublin? This weekend?' She tried to keep the dismay out of her voice.

'It's been years, decades even, since I last saw the parade in Dublin. I can't wait to join the crowds in O'Connell Street and ogle those high-stepping American cheerleaders strutting their stuff in the lashing rain. Did I ever tell you about the time I had one shelter under my umbrella—'

'Where are you going to stay?'

'Where are we going to stay?' Seán sounded taken aback. 'Well, I was hoping – I should say *we* were hoping – that our daughter, who I've heard tell lives in a very fancy apartment in Dublin, might put us up.'

'Oh, but I can't!' protested Anne Marie. 'I mean, I'd love to and all . . . but my new place is just for one person. There's only one bed and . . . and . . . sorry, there just isn't any room!'

There was a moment's silence, then Seán gave a little laugh. 'Sure, isn't one bed enough? We'll all squeeze in together and be grand and cosy.'

'You could stay in the basement, maybe,' said Anne Marie unhappily. 'I'd have to ask Darina and Cornelius, of course, but I'm sure it would be fine.'

'Don't worry, I was only joking,' said Seán. 'We're not planning to leave Killorglin before six on Friday, so it'll be very late before we get in. I'd say we'll stop along the way – in Kildare maybe, or Naas. But we were hoping to see you on Saturday, if you could spare us a few hours. Yvonne suggested lunch in the Dome at the top of the Stephen's Green Centre. Half past twelve – think you can make it?'

'Lunch on St Patrick's Day? Yes, of course I'll be there. Look Seán, I didn't mean to make it sound as though you weren't welcome or anything. I mean, I'm really looking forward to seeing you and everything. It's just—'

'Don't be apologising! We only decided yesterday that we were coming up; you have your own life to lead and can't be expected to change your plans at the drop of a hat. And there's no cause to go asking Darina and Cornelius about the basement. When we get to Dublin on Saturday, we'll just book into a B&B somewhere nearby.'

'Are you sure? I feel bad now—'

'Don't. Yvonne sends her love. Bye, kiddo, see you on Saturday.'

After Seán hung up, Anne Marie slowly replaced the receiver at her end and put her head in her hands. Now she would have to tell Victor that her parents were coming up for the weekend. He would at once suspect a set-up. She was dying to introduce him to her family, but he had told her that he wasn't ready for it yet. She respected his wishes and was happy to take things slowly. The cousins were to have been the first test; if the evening went well, then she thought he might in time be persuaded to meet the rest of her extended family.

Secretly, Anne Marie dreamt of bringing Victor to Riverwood. She saw the two of them walking arm-in-arm by the river, admiring the trees in the arboretum and visiting the holy well to make a wish. She knew what hers would be: to return to the same spot at the same time every year, accompanied by a steadily-growing number of lithe, long-limbed children with brown eyes and skin tones ranging from beech to mahogany.

Now, just to complicate matters, her parents were coming to Dublin this very weekend. She wanted to see them, but she wanted to spend as much time as possible with Victor, too. But they weren't to meet. Oh, what a mess!

'Something wrong, Anne Marie?'

Anne Marie started. Roz was standing over her, looking concerned. In her hand she had a list of feature articles that the magazine was running in the months ahead. The April issue of *Femme*, which contained Anne Marie's piece on refugees, had already gone to the repro house and was due to appear on the shelves in a few days, but Anne Marie was supposed to have contacted the regular contributors about future articles. Guiltily, she took the list from Roz. 'No, I'm OK. Sorry, I forgot all about this. I'll write the briefs for the articles now and get them out to our regulars before this evening.'

'There's no real hurry,' said Roz. 'I mean, if you're not feeling well or something . . .'

'No, I'm fine. Honestly.'

Once again, Anne Marie took refuge in work. By concentrating very hard on what she was supposed to be doing to the exclusion of all else, she managed to stave off the feeling of impending doom that had become associated with the end of the week.

On Friday evening, Victor came early as Anne Marie

had requested, but he was in the worst possible form. The Nigerian woman who had been attacked by her landlord had taken an overdose of sleeping tablets on Thursday and then phoned Victor to tell him what she'd done. Once he'd got her to hospital to have her stomach pumped, Victor had had to take care of her children. With the help of the social services, the situation was resolved now, but Anne Marie could see that her lover was both physically and mentally exhausted. While she set the table and kept an eye on the cooker, he kicked off his shoes and lay down on the couch.

Darina and Cornelius arrived fifteen minutes later. Victor had fallen asleep where he lay, so Anne Marie was obliged to leave the cooker and dash to the door, wooden spoon in hand, to let them in on the second knock.

'Hi coz,' said Darina, who was first in. 'I didn't know whether the meal called for red or white wine, so I got lager instead. Here you go. Is Victor here yet – oh!' She had turned and seen the body on the couch.

'Who's that?' Cornelius, following on his sister's heels, was looking aghast at Victor.

Anne Marie had that sinking feeling again. Was it possible that she hadn't told her cousins anything at all about her lover? Not even that he was black?

Apparently, yes.

'Victor – Darina and Cornelius are here,' she said, shaking him by the shoulder while glancing apologetically at her cousins. She wished that he could at least have been vertical when they arrived. It would have made a better impression.

'Sorry about this; he's had a hard couple of days and he's very tired.'

As Victor yawned and reluctantly opened his eyes, Darina sidled up to Anne Marie. 'You never told us your boyfriend was . . . A Person of Colour,' she whispered delightedly. 'I think it's wonderful, but Con's not a great one for surprises. It might have been kinder to inform him in advance.'

Anne Marie turned to her youngest cousin, who looked as though he had been hit over the head with a mallet. 'Victor is from Africa,' she said quickly. 'He's a Human Rights lawyer. He studied at Oxford and he has a British passport because he was adopted by Scottish missionaries when he was a baby.'

As soon as she had spoken, she hated herself for it. She wasn't ashamed of Victor, but by trying to make Cornelius feel that her lover was less alien than he looked, she realised that she had in a sense betrayed him. Miserably, she finished the introductions and then stood back as her cousins shook hands with Victor. There was an awkward moment of silence as they stood looking at one another, unsure what to do next.

It was Darina who broke the ice. 'Well, mine's a beer,' she said, heading towards the kitchen with her sixpack.

'Oh, yes – sorry! What's everybody else having?' Flustered, Anne Marie followed her and poured orange juice for Cornelius. Darina opened two bottles of beer and gave one to Victor. The two of them wandered back into the living room and sat down on the couch. Cornelius took his glass, hesitated for a moment, then slowly returned to the living area. He took a chair from the head of the table and placed it next to the couch. He sat down and contemplated his glass.

From her perch by the cooker, Anne Marie threw

anxious glances into the room every now and then. Darina was quizzing Victor about his work in Human Rights and Victor, to her relief, was responding positively. Soon they were deep in conversation. Cornelius was looking left out, but Anne Marie felt that there was not much she could do about that. If he couldn't handle the fact that she had a black boyfriend, then it was his problem.

So she told herself, but when it came down to it, Anne Marie couldn't bear to have anyone feel uncomfortable in her home without trying to do something about it.

'Cornelius, could you give me a hand here, please?' she called, taking four plates out of an overhead press. After her cousin had set them on the table, she found some other little jobs for him to do until it was time to summon the others to the table.

Dinner was a disaster. Anne Marie had wanted to try something African, and had scoured the city to find the right ingredients. The bean stew was spiced with authentic *piri piri* sauce. *Abale samalani: Friends take care* warned the label. Victor and Darina had no problem with the fieriness, but no sooner had Cornelius taken a mouthful than he leapt up from his place, slopping the contents of his bowl on to the cloth, ran to the kitchen and stuck his mouth under the tap. To make matters worse, the cornmeal that accompanied the bean sauce was stodgy and indigestible. And there was not enough bread to go round. The mangoes that Anne Marie had bought for dessert were fibrous and stuck in the teeth. Her white linen tablecloth was ruined by the sauce spilled by Cornelius on his hasty removal from the table.

None of this would have mattered if everyone had

been relaxed and good-humoured about it. But Darina was the only one who behaved as she normally did. Anne Marie herself was tense; Victor, tired and out of sorts; Cornelius, silent and brooding. Conversation was strained, except when Darina was doing the talking. But eventually she seemed to get tired of holding it all together; shortly before ten o'clock she stood up abruptly and said she had an essay to finish before she went down to Limerick the next day. Thanking Anne Marie for the evening, she shook hands again with Victor and hustled Cornelius out of the room in front of her.

As soon as the cousins had left, Anne Marie threw herself at Victor. Her need to reaffirm their closeness was so great that she led him over to the couch and they made love there and then.

Afterwards, as they washed the dishes together, Victor appeared more relaxed than at any time during the evening. When they had finished putting away the last of the cutlery, he smiled and, looping the tea-towel behind her neck, pulled her towards him for a kiss. Anne Marie's heart sang and she allowed herself to hope for the future.

Next morning after making love they lay together, her head tucked into his neck. She was contemplating as she so often did, the exquisite contrast of her milk-white arm on his ebony chest. She knew that he was awake, but she didn't want to disturb the perfect tranquillity of the moment by talking. To savour it all the more, she closed her eyes and snuggled into the crook of his arm.

'Anne Marie?'

Her eyes snapped open. Her heart stopped. This was

it: the moment she had been dreading since Victor had first touched her cheek in the Palm House of the Botanic Gardens.

She could predict the words he would use. She remained perfectly still, willing him not to say how much he valued their time together, how he wished there was some way to do this that would not hurt her. She could feel him draw into his lungs the breath that would give voice to the end of their love.

'Anne Marie, I—'

'No!' She raised herself on one elbow and put a finger on his lips. 'Shhh!' She lifted her finger gently then, satisfied that he was not going to speak, she began to trace the curve of his jaw. 'It's all right. I know,' she whispered.

Her tears splashed onto his cheeks. Ignoring them, she continued to trace the lines of his face.

'Once more,' she said softly.

Victor took her hand and began to kiss her fingers one by one.

When the door closed behind her lover for the last time, Anne Marie didn't look up. Before he reached the landing, the loss of him had manifested itself as a searing pain in her solar plexus that hurt more than she could have believed possible. Doubled up under the duvet, she buried her face in the pillow and howled her grief.

The Dome

It was after midday when Anne Marie remembered her lunch date with her parents. Her first thought was that she couldn't possibly see them; she would ring them on their cellphone and say she wasn't well. But she realised at once that that would merely postpone the inevitable, because they would want to come straight to her flat to look after her. So she crawled out of bed and dragged herself to the bathroom. Standing in front of the mirror, she stared at her tear-streaked cheeks and red puffy eyes and knew there was nothing she could do to make herself presentable in time. She showered and dressed, put on her rain gear and lifted her bike down the steps to the road.

St Patrick's Day and it was raining on the parade.

On the Rathmines Road, she cycled past three African men. None of them looked remotely like Victor, but seeing them was a painful reminder of the one that she would never see again. The rain beat down, mingling with her tears.

It had to end, sooner or later. She knew that, had known it from the start. But why now, when there was so much still to learn about each other? They had only just begun to explore beyond the physical and for Anne Marie it was almost as thrilling to uncover little windows into her lover's mind as it was to uncover his body.

But in the end, that was what had driven him away. Victor did not want to be known. Part of the conversation at dinner came back to her. Darina, barging in where Anne Marie feared to tread, had asked him about his experiences in the war zones of Africa. Had he lost anyone close to him? she had asked, and Anne Marie had waited with bated breath for the answer.

Yes, he had.

Family?

'My woman,' Victor had replied.

His woman. Not his wife or his girlfriend. To Anne Marie's ears, My Woman sounded far sweeter and far more intimate. He had lost her, to death perhaps, and yet she still held the greater part of his heart. Anne Marie knew that she could never be My Woman. To cover her hurt, she had begun to clear the table and when she had returned with coffee, the conversation had moved back to Victor's work with asylum seekers in Ireland.

How long could we have gone on if last night hadn't happened? Anne Marie asked herself as she crossed the canal. She was tempted to think: indefinitely, but she knew it was not true. A few weeks? Maybe. Now that he was gone, she believed that she would have settled for days.

When she reached the Dome, Anne Marie was wet and bedraggled enough that the effects of her crying bout were not so obvious. Yvonne was sitting alone at a table by the window; catching sight of Anne Marie, she raised her arm in greeting.

'You poor thing, you're drenched!' she said when Anne Marie reached the table. 'Here, let me help you with that.'

While Anne Marie took off her pull-ups, Yvonne shook out her jacket and hung it on the back of the chair. Then they embraced. 'Good to see you, darling,' said Yvonne as they sat down. 'How are things?'

'Er . . . fine,' mumbled Anne Marie. 'Where's Seán?'

'He's coming. I think he wanted to see a bit of the parade. He'll join us in a while. Would you like a coffee or something while we're waiting?' Yvonne spoke in a rush, then pushed back her chair, ready to stand up and go to the counter to order something for Anne Marie.

'Wait! It's OK, I don't need anything now. This water will be fine.' Anne Marie took one of the glasses on the table and filled it with water from an earthenware jug.

'Oh. Right. Well, this is nice.' Yvonne smiled brightly at her daughter.

Anne Marie had a vague feeling that things were not quite right. Her mother seemed unsure of herself, which was very unusual. And where was Seán? He wouldn't have been fooled by the rain, she thought; he would have seen at once that something was wrong with her. Although the last thing she wanted was to be probed on what was making her miserable, Anne Marie couldn't help feeling aggrieved that her mother hadn't even noticed that she was out of sorts.

After they had exchanged news about the relations, there came a moment when neither of them seemed to know what to say next. Yvonne opened her mouth, and then shut it again. She stared at Anne Marie with a glazed look in her eye. She poured herself a glass of water, which she then left untouched on the table.

Just when Anne Marie had decided that her mother had guessed that something was wrong but was too discreet to mention it, Yvonne reached across the table and put her hand on top of her daughter's. 'Anne Marie, there's something I need to tell you,' she announced.

Anne Marie looked up in surprise. Yvonne was visibly nervous, which in itself was so unprecedented as to alarm her. What on earth was coming next?

Remembering Roz's surprise announcement, Anne Marie straightened. Maybe her mother was pregnant! That would certainly be a shock, though not necessarily an unpleasant one; in fact, Anne Marie would be thrilled to learn that she was going to have a little sister or brother. I could be godmother, she thought, and spoil him or her rotten!

But that was not what Yvonne had to say. Having captured her daughter's attention, she withdrew her hand and started to fiddle with the spoon beside her coffee cup. 'Since you left home,' she began, 'your . . . Seán and I have been thinking and . . . well, we've made a decision. We're going to go away for a while.'

'Go away? Where?' Anne Marie was puzzled. Her parents were always going away; what was so unusual about that?

'Where? Well, Tanzania, most likely. Papua New Guinea is another possibility. You see, we want to work in the developing world and we've applied to VSO to go away as volunteers. In Tanzania, there's a good chance that we'd be appointed to the same region.'

'What's VSO?'

'Voluntary Service Overseas. They send people away for . . . a few years.'

'How few?'

'Two or three. Five, maybe.'

'Five years?'

'Just maybe. Two or three is more usual.'

'What about your jobs in Killorglin? And the house?'

'We're going to let the house, to the substitute teachers, in fact. And we've got leave of absence for the initial contract. After that, we'll see.'

'So it's all settled, is it?'

'More or less. Anne Marie, do you mind terribly? We've talked about it for a long time, Seán and I; ever since we began travelling, really. We've visited some of the poorest countries in the world and our lives have been enriched by our experiences there. We feel it's

321

time to give something back. I know that it'll be hard for you, and we wouldn't have considered it except that Nano was so positive. She will be delighted to have you stay at Riverwood any weekend you feel like getting out of Dublin; in fact, she says you're to make it your home.'

Shaken, Anne Marie sat back in her chair. So that was it – her parents were going away. Leaving her. Just like Victor. She felt a lump in her throat and swallowed it back. If she started to cry now, she'd never stop.

'Well,' she said in a small voice, 'that's news all right. I don't know what to say. It sounds great, and I think it's a good idea and all . . .'

'You'll be able to come and visit us. We could go on holiday to Zanzibar.'

Zanzibar. It sounded exotic and wonderful. She wondered if Victor had ever been there. If she went, was there any chance that she might bump into him?

'There's something else.'

Anne Marie looked up. Yvonne's face was drawn tight, her eyes were wide with something that to Anne Marie looked very like fear.

'What?'

Yvonne looked away, then back. She bit her lip. 'It concerns your . . . Seán.'

'What about him?'

'He's not your father.'

Anne Marie had the strangest sensation. She felt as though she were falling off the edge of the world. Everything in her life that had seemed fixed and certain was coming undone. She too was unravelling, faster and faster, losing herself as she plummeted into the void.

'Anne Marie! Oh God, I'm sorry . . . Are you all

right? Here, take a drink of water. *Anne Marie?* Hold on, let me pull out your chair . . . put your head between your legs.' Yvonne held her daughter's shoulders for a minute, then raised her again. 'Let me see. That's better, you're not so pale any more. You're going to be all right.'

Yvonne made her drink, then sprinkled water on her face. She took a paper napkin and reached over to dry it off. Anne Marie caught her wrist. 'Stop!' She wiped her face with her hand and stared hard at her mother. 'What did you just say?'

Yvonne looked down at the paper napkin. She crumpled it in her fist. 'You heard me,' she said quietly.

'Then – who – is – my – father?' Anne Marie forced the words out one by one.

Yvonne looked at her in surprise. 'But can't you guess? I mean, isn't it obvious?'

Anne Marie glared at her. In that moment, she hated her mother more than she had thought it was possible to hate anyone. 'No,' she spat, 'it is not.'

'Your father is – was – Elliot. That's why we gave you his name. I—'

'Leave me.'

'What?'

'I said leave me. Go away. I want to be on my own.'

Yvonne seemed undecided, but when Anne Marie looked stonily at her again, she slowly picked up her bag and lifted her jacket from the back of the chair. 'He'll be here soon,' she said to Anne Marie's back.

After her mother had gone, Anne Marie sat with her hands in her lap, staring at nothing. A waiter came to clear away Yvonne's empty coffee cup. He wiped the table, and asked Anne Marie if she wanted anything, but she neither saw nor heard him.

Seán was not her father. The man who meant more to her than any other turned out to be completely unrelated to her. She thought bitterly of her other male relations; blood linked her forever to the likes of Cornelius and Uncle Dan, but with four fatal little words, Seán had become the man who had married her mother.

Suddenly, Anne Marie felt sick. It just couldn't be true! She thought back over the nineteen years of her life. For as much of that time as she could remember, Seán had been the one who mattered. Yvonne was the practical parent; she had organised their lives, taken care of the finances, made sure Anne Marie had her vaccinations, new shoes, her lunch for school each day. But Seán had played with her, read her stories, blown raspberries on her stomach at bedtime. Seán had carried her on his shoulders and shown her birds' nests; Seán had kissed her bruises and made them better. Seán was the one she had turned to in times of trouble.

Outside, the rain was getting heavier. At the corner of Grafton Street, two young people, heedless of the downpour, were locked in an embrace. A group of tourists in brightly-coloured rain capes crossed the road and went into the Green. Anne Marie's gaze travelled upwards to the arch above the entrance. She read the inscription. *Fortissimus suis militibus hoc monumentum eblana dedicavit MCMVII.* If Seán were there, he'd help her translate it. Anne Marie clenched her hands into fists and bit the inside of her lip. Her vision blurred as tears sprang to her eyes.

Suddenly, she felt a tap on her shoulder. She turned around. Seán was standing behind her chair. He'd been out in the rain; his wirebrush hair was plastered to his head. Beneath the freckles, his cheeks were pale and drawn. His eyes were full of misery. Anne Marie took one look at his dear, ugly face and jumped up. She flung her arms around his neck.

'Daddy! Oh, Daddy!' she cried.

Father's Day

Anne Marie clung to Seán for an age, oblivious to the wet seeping from his sodden jacket into her cotton jumper. She held him tight, as though his nearness could give the lie to what her mother had revealed.

Eventually, Seán took her hands and gently removed them from his neck. 'My precious girl, allow me to dry your tears.' He took a handkerchief out of his pocket. 'It's damp but clean,' he said with a sad smile as he wiped her eyes. 'Let's get out of here,' he added, when a family carrying their trays to the next table stared curiously at them. 'It looks like the rain has eased off a bit. We could walk to Rathmines. Or get the bus if they're running with the parade on.'

Anne Marie agreed to walk home. She hadn't eaten since the night before, but food was far from being a concern at this point in time.

They went out to South King Street, where she had locked her bike. 'What about Yvonne?' she said reluctantly as Seán took the bike from her and began to wheel it along the path to the pedestrian lights.

'She'll follow later.' He paused, and then gave Anne Marie a pleading look. 'Don't be too hard on her, love. It was a joint decision not to tell you until we felt that you were old enough to handle it. We wanted to wait until you were well settled in Dublin. From your phone calls and visits we know that you've got a job that you're happy with now, and a nice place to live, and friends of your own. We had to be sure that you were doing well before we could think about going away, and we decided that when we knew about our posting abroad, we'd also tell you about your true parentage. Did we do wrong?'

'You mean, to give me all the shocks at once? "We're going away for five years and by the way your father isn't your father." Did you think the one would lessen the other?' Anne Marie asked bitterly.

Seán wheeled the bike into St Stephen's Green and stopped under a tree. He turned to face Anne Marie. 'I've been dreading this moment for almost twenty years,' he said. 'When you were little, it nearly broke my heart to imagine it. I would have given anything not to have you go through it. Truth hurts, and I didn't want you hurt. But I believe it's your right and your duty to know who you are. Just let me say that if I could have fathered children, I couldn't have loved any of my offspring more than I love you.'

Anne Marie hung her head. 'I'm sorry,' she said. 'I wasn't thinking how difficult this must be for you too.' She gave an embarrassed laugh. 'You know, when Yvonne said she had some news this morning, I thought she was pregnant!'

Seán shook his head. 'Impossible. With me anyway. Sperm count in the minus numbers, same as the brother.'

'Oh! It's a family thing? So that's why Uncle Éamonn and Aunt Gloria adopted those Russian babies?' Lights were beginning to come on for Anne Marie. She started to walk on. 'And that's why,' she went on in a hard voice, 'Granny Hughes never seemed pleased to see me. I used to wonder what I'd done wrong. I never got a card for my birthday, and she was always cold to me when we went to visit. It all makes sense now.'

'Yeah, well she was a stubborn old countrywoman,' said Seán, wheeling the bike beside her. 'She gave Yvonne hell. And she got worse as she grew older. That's why I started to visit her on my own. She was quite likely to take you aside and tell you that you were illegitimate.'

'So, what was my biological father like? You were friends, weren't you?'

'The best!' exclaimed Seán. 'I'm so sorry you couldn't know him, Anne Marie. He was a very special person. We'll be telling you about him over the next few months. There are photographs, and letters that you've never seen. We kept everything.'

'What about his family? Do I have relatives in the States that I don't know about?'

'Hard to say. Elliot's mother was an alcoholic; she died just after he was born. He never knew who his father was. He grew up in different institutions and foster families, none of which seemed to be very good to him. But he overcame his background and worked hard to make something of himself. When we met, he was working in the canteen and doing bartending at night to pay his college fees. He was very special, Anne Marie, believe me.' There were tears in Seán's eyes as he continued. 'You have so many of his qualities. His gentleness, his generosity and kindness, his consideration for others. He was especially drawn to those who had no one, which is in fact how he met his end.'

'What do you mean?'

Seán sighed. 'He used to visit the down-and-outs

who lived near the river. He'd bring them food, or cigarettes, and just sit with them and listen. One night, a woman fell into the river. Or she jumped – who knows? He tried to save her, but he couldn't. They both drowned.'

Anne Marie was silent. She thought of the photograph that Desmond Dunne had made her see properly for the first time by pointing out that she did not look as much like her mother and grandmother as she had believed. At the time, she had felt disturbed, but without knowing why. Now she knew. Unconsciously, she put her hand to her face and felt its contour. That roundness was something she had inherited from her biological father, the unknowable Elliot.

And in spite of the stories that Seán and Yvonne would tell her, Elliot would remain forever unknowable. He had died nearly twenty years ago, when he was not much older than she was now. Anne Marie pictured a boy with blond hair and good teeth, mild blue eyes and a snub nose. In her mind, he was more like a brother than anything else, and in time, she thought she could come to love his memory as such. But he could never be her father.

Her father was right here, pushing her bicycle through St Stephen's Green on St Patrick's Day in the rain.

Of Shoes and Trips and Healing Acts

Darina couldn't wait to get back to Limerick. She had so much to tell Gerald! Imagine Anne Marie having a black boyfriend! Wasn't that just amazing? Darina was dying to tell her brother about last night's dinner. How poor Anne Marie was nervous as hell and kept dropping things and how Cornelius had sat with such a sourpuss on him that they thought it was because he was horrified by Anne Marie's African lover when in reality it was toothache. Then there was Victor, who had refused to be drawn on most topics but had revealed that he had lost his Significant Other in the civil war in Burundi.

That was unnecessarily cruel, reflected Darina, remembering her cousin's pained expression, for she was sure that Victor knew what he was doing. Anne Marie was crazy about him, but Victor's feelings for her cousin were hard to guess. She suspected that his heart was still his own. He could walk away at any time.

I pity Anne Marie when he does, thought Darina as she took her seat in the train.

At Limerick Junction, she was met by Gerald himself.

'My God, what's this? You're jangling car keys!' she said after they had hugged each other.

'Yeah, I thought it was about time I learnt to drive. My test is next week, so you can tell me if you see me making any mistakes on the way home.'

'Will you teach me?' asked Darina as she flung her bag into the back of the station wagon. 'I've got nearly a week before my Club Med holiday; we could get up early and go out for an hour or so. It'd be good practice for you too.'

'How early is early? You're talking to a working man now, remember.'

'That's right, I'd forgotten. How is the shoe business coming along?'

'Actually, things are looking up. I've got a few ideas for new lines—'

'Like fetish footwear?' interrupted Darina with a laugh. 'Black thigh boots with fuck-me heels and red size eleven stilettos?'

'Nah, there's a crowd in England does them already. And Dan wasn't too keen.'

'Jesus, I was joking! And who's Dan?'

'Daniel, Dad, the old man – whatever.'

'So you're on first-name terms? I see. How's he getting on without the old dear – or should I say *Barbara*?'

'We're managing fine. She drops in the odd time, and she'll be over tomorrow to see you, but the bachelor life seems to suit Dad. Did you know that he always wanted to be a priest when he was young?'

'You're joking!'

'Not a bit of it. He used to sneak into Glenstal on his way home from school and listen to the monks singing. It was the only time he was happy as a teenager, he said. And here's something else I bet you didn't know: he had an older brother who was murdered.'

'What!'

'It's true. His name was Jamie. He was eleven when it happened. Dad adored him. He says he was too young to be terribly affected when his father was killed, but he never got over Jamie's death.'

'He told you all this?'

'Oh, we've had a good few heart-to-heart talks – and d'you know what? I've got really fond of the old man. I always thought he was a bit stuffy and boring, but now that I'm getting to know him, he's really very interesting.'

'What happened to the poor brother?'

'Some pervert got him when he was coming home from Riverwood; Nano found the place by the bridge where he had been playing. She thinks it was someone he knew; Dad even said she suspected the parish priest.'

'Jesus!'

'Well, she was always anti-clerical, so it's probably just her imagination. Though Dad did mention that after his father's death, the PP was round at once trying to offer the consolation of Mother Church and all that crap. Later, he was against her working at Riverwood because Clarissa was such an influential Protestant. He was afraid that she was going to be a bad influence and kept calling to the house, trying to lay down the law. But when Jamie was murdered, there wasn't a dicky bird from him. In fact, he never came near Nano. Then a few months later, he got sent off to the Missions. Strange, don't you think?'

Darina shuddered. 'Creepy. Just imagine, we should have had an Uncle Jamie.' She sat up suddenly. 'Jamie's Willow! Is that . . .? I often wondered where the name came from, but I never thought of asking.'

'Nano wouldn't have told you. She couldn't bear to talk about him; that's why we never even heard of his existence. Poor Dad – he was always second fiddle as far as his mother was concerned. Funnily enough, they seem to be getting closer lately, probably because of the trip to Italy. Dad's been over at Riverwood nearly every day this week, planning the holiday like it was an expedition to Everest or something. He's pleased as Punch about it, so be sure to ask plenty of questions about where and what and get him to speak some Italian for you – it'll make his day!'

Darina did as her brother suggested. That evening after dinner, she asked Daniel to tell her what sight-seeing he and Nano had planned for their fortnight away. Her father didn't need to be asked twice. Within minutes, the table was covered with maps and tourist brochures and Darina was treated to a full account of the itinerary, which appeared to take in every major church and monument in Northern Italy.

'Are you sure you'll have the stamina for all that sightseeing?' she asked. 'And what about Nano? She's not too keen on churches, I thought.'

Daniel coloured. 'Well, it's true that she wouldn't have as much interest in them as I would,' he admitted. 'But she did say that I was to choose what I wanted to do. And besides, we're going up into the mountains for a few days as well, which will suit her.'

'Well, I think it's great that you're starting to travel at your age,' said Darina. 'And I hope you do lots more of it.'

'To broaden my mind, is it?' Daniel asked with a smile. 'You never know; I just might get a taste for travelling on this trip. Maybe I'll be bitten by the bug as much as Yvonne. This year, Italy – next year, Patagonia!'

When Darina looked faintly alarmed, he gave a soft laugh. 'Don't worry, I'm not that adventurous. But who knows what hidden desires may be stimulated by this trip? It might be the first of many changes in your old man. Once the path to the rainbow is glimpsed, is it not incumbent upon us to set our feet on it and follow it to the end of our dreams?' He cleared up the brochures and put them on the sideboard. 'And now, my dears, I am tired. I shall away to bed. Be sure to put the guard in front of the fire and set the alarm before you retire.' He raised his hand. 'Good night.'

Darina and Gerald waited until he had left the room before they exploded into laughter. 'What on earth was all that about?' spluttered Darina.

'I dunno, but he has been going around with all these New Age books tucked under his arm. They must be giving him ideas.'

'Or was it the Chianti at dinner? He's certainly acting strangely. The way he said good night to us there with his hand out as though he was blessing us reminded me of Brandon!'

'I think he's discovering his inner child, healing the hurt within and all that,' said Gerald. 'Transforming himself. And why not? It must have been awful growing up knowing that you could never compensate for the one that was dead.'

'Speaking of transformation,' said Darina, who was growing bored with this talk of their father, 'I was thinking of doing a bit myself. I had this idea that I might get all my hair cut off when I'm in Paris. What d'you think?' She pulled her hair back from her face. 'The colour is growing out, so I have to do something with it. But I've never had it short before. Would it suit me?'

'Well, I'm not a great judge of that sort of thing,' said Gerald diplomatically, 'but I suppose you could give it a try. It would be handy for the tropical climate in the Caribbean anyhow.'

'Yeah, I think I will, so. I want to buy some new clothes as well. I've spent hardly anything this term, and the week at Club Med is absolutely free, so I'll have loads of dosh to spend in Paris before I go.' She yawned and stretched. 'I think I can understand how the old man feels. I'm fed up with myself as I am. I want a change; a radical change.'

Hacked-off hackette

Sally O'Shea was standing outside the Four Courts feeling hard done by. Twice in the past six months she had uncovered major stories for the *Evening Echo*, and twice she had been taken off them as soon as it had become apparent that they were big news. The Editor had patted her on the back, then assigned her to some piddling story like the lifts not working again in the Ballymun Flats. She was particularly aggrieved over the Dunne affair, which never would have come to light if it hadn't been for her. And unlike the Sylvester Reed story, which had sunk without trace after three days, Dunne's was set to go on for a very long time.

On her mornings off, Sally came to the Circuit Court to listen to Dunne give evidence. It was unprecedented for a crooked property developer to stand up in court and incriminate himself, and both the press and the public gallery were thronged to capacity every day.

She hadn't been in court the day before, but she knew that Dunne had spent the morning accounting for the disposal of his ill-gotten gains. An incredulous public had heard how he had made a list of all the people he had cheated in the past and sent each of them a cheque to make good what he had stolen. The papers had gone wild at the revelations, and the radio chat shows had had several phone calls from people confirming that they had received some of this conscience money.

Now the hangers-on were having their fun.

'Hey Dessie, give us some lolly. You Dunne us wrong too!'

Sally pressed to the front, eager to get a good look

at the billionaire she had helped to bring down. Dunne appeared unabashed by the jeers of the crowd; if anything, he seemed to be enjoying the heckling.

'Me granny says you cheated her back in 1964. She wants her money now,' cried one young man with a skinhead haircut.

'Get up the yard; she was giving it away even then!' he shouted back.

Sally desperately wanted to talk to Dunne. There was bound to be an unofficial biography within the next few months; the opportunity to make a fast buck out of the story while it was still fresh was not going to be overlooked by her rivals. But if she could get his permission, then she could tell the story as he wanted it told. It could be her way of making up for exposing him in the first place. Well, that was the way she would put it to him.

Sally was close enough now to Dunne to pluck him by the sleeve and tell him in an undertone that she would like to write about his life. Dunne turned to her and grinned. It was a bit late to be offering him the ride of his life, he said loudly, but if she was around in a few years' time, he'd gladly take her up on the offer.

Sally turned away from the ribald laughter that greeted this reply. Dunne had not only recognised her; he had sussed her motives at once. And he was having none of it. She elbowed her way out of the crowd and crossed the road to the Liffey. Staring down at the bog-brown water, she stamped her foot in frustration. Why did nothing ever work out for her? She knew she was good; all she wanted was the chance to make her name. But so far, everything she started had either been taken from her or had led to a dead end.

The Sylvester story, for instance; she had tried so

hard to unearth basic facts about the innocuous-looking little man who had turned out to be the South Circular Strangler, such as where he was born and educated, but even that information had proved impossible to find. He didn't seem to have existed until he was twenty and had started the job as an archivist that he had continued to hold until his suicide.

The only lead she had got was the snippet, gleaned from one of his colleagues, that Sylvester had been a regular visitor to a nursing home in Dalkey for retired nuns. He had been overheard on the telephone one day calling the home to let Sr Annunciata know that he would be late arriving for his visit the following Sunday.

Some lead.

Sally sighed. She was hungry for success; the fire in her belly gnawed and gnawed, but she had nothing to feed it.

Except Sr Annunciata.

Sally squinted down the Liffey towards O'Connell Bridge. The number 8 bus to Dalkey left from Eden Quay on the other side. She had the afternoon off. If Sr Annunciata turned out to be another dead end, she could always go down to Bullock Harbour and watch the boats.

What the hell, thought Sally. It's not as though I've anything to lose.

Welcome to the Club

The first bus of the week had arrived at the Club Méditerranée resort of Corsairs' Cove. François Poireau, head of scuba diving, pulled his rainbow-patterned pareo lower to reveal more washboard stomach and adjusted the knot so that it sat suggestively at the point where the curved V of his muscles disappeared into his swimming trunks.

The first guests alighted, a group of eight women from New York with big hair and nail extensions. François switched on a smile and welcomed them to the paradisiacal resort of Corsairs' Cove.

'Everything is here for you to have a good time,' he said in his best French accent as he ushered the group towards the amphitheatre where they would shortly be addressed by the *chef de village*.

'I can see that!' laughed the woman at the front. She cupped her hands in the air to demonstrate to her friends the firm curve of his buttocks as they followed him along a narrow path lined with hibiscus bushes in gaudy bloom. Egged on by their cheers, the woman quickened her step until she caught up with him.

'My name's Ginny and I hope you're going to help me have a good time, Handsome,' she said, patting him on the bum. 'Because believe me – I intend to!'

François removed her hand and held it up by the wrist. He smiled. 'I am François. Of course we all do whatever we can to make your stay agreeable. I think you will enjoy the picnic on Wednesday. Why don't you sign up for it tonight?' He dropped her hand and stood back to allow the women to enter the amphitheatre. They smiled flirtatiously as they passed him.

'Picnic – yeah!' said one of the women at the back. 'I heard about them – they're a blast. You know, Ginny, they do this great game with lemons . . .'

The woman called Ginny wasn't listening. She was rubbing her wrist and trying to persuade herself that she had imagined the look of intense dislike she'd seen in the eyes of the hunk called François.

The second bus was already disgorging passengers by the time François got back.

'*Merde*,' he swore under his breath. He liked to be there from the start to be sure he made the right choice. Twice it had happened that halfway through the week he had realised he'd made a mistake when he had suddenly come across the woman he should have been with in some out-of-the-way place like the silkscreen-painting class. That was the problem: his kind of woman didn't want to be seen. Although she came to Club Med hoping against hope that someone would find her, she perversely made it almost impossible by hiding in her room during the day and going for long, solitary walks on the beach at night. She ate at odd hours and never came to the shows. The only time he was sure to catch her was when she stepped off the bus on arrival.

'Eh, Poireau!' Benito, the Sicilian in charge of the snorkelling team, which also organised the famous picnics, came running from the direction of the bar. He put his hand on François's shoulder. 'I miss the first arrival – was Charlot there?'

Charlot, the *chef de village*, had called a meeting of the GO staff the previous day to bawl them out for not being present in force to welcome the busloads of guests that arrived in waves each Saturday. The snorkelling team had borne the brunt of his wrath.

'No, he went straight onstage. There's another bus due in half an hour and he wants this lot out of the way before they get here.' As he spoke, François kept an eye on the stream of holidaymakers wending their way towards the amphitheatre in the wake of the head of the hostess team. Mostly men this time, and a few couples. Nothing for him. But wait – there! One of the last to get out of the bus. 'Benito! Benito! Look – one for you!'

'What? Oh, oh, *oh*! Is she real? I close my eyes and I open again.'

Mostly, Benito spoke in heavily-accented French or English, but now he lapsed into his own incomprehensible brand of Italian as he kissed his fingers and praised the skies for sending him such a magnificent creature.

'What do you think?' he said, reverting to French. 'One hundred and twenty kilos? It's possible, no?'

The African-American woman who had just stepped off the bus put down her bags and took out a handkerchief to wipe her face. She was wearing a tight ribbed tank top in shocking pink, and purple lycra cycling shorts. Her arms were the size of a man's thighs. Her legs were like tree trunks.

'It's not a woman, it's a force of nature,' murmured François.

Benito did not see the good-humoured intelligence in the woman's eyes, nor did he care that she had an attractive face. 'One hundred and twenty kilos! Fucking shit – I can win! That will make nine thousand nine hundred kilograms – only just one more hundred to go. I can do it by Wednesday – yes! That *figlio di putta* Steve – I make him suck my cock! I know he cheated last season in Cancun – he was counting in American pounds instead of kilograms. Now I win! Ten thousand kilos of flesh in one season: I am the champion fucker of Club Med!'

The Sicilian was too jubilant to pay attention to the woman who was last to get off the bus. François noticed that she was younger than the normal Club Med crowd and too ungroomed to be American. Thin and pale, her short spiky hair was dyed white blonde, so that she looked rather like the young Annie Lennox. She stared hard at Benito as he crowed about his imminent victory, then watched in silence as he approached the black woman and offered to carry her purse to her room.

François guessed that she had understood every word.

Twenty minutes later, the third and last bus of this arrival turned into the Club Med compound.

Vera Meaney clapped her hands with delight when she saw the colonial-style bungalows in their lush-but-tamed tropical setting and the beach of pearly-white sand that was private Club Med property. The brochure hadn't lied – it was Paradise! There was no sign of the welcome party, however. The brochure had also promised that the staff, the *Gentils Organisateurs* – or GOs, as she must remember to call them – would be present for the arrival of the guests, the *Gentils Membres*, dressed in local costume and singing the Club Med anthem. Oh well, not to worry, it was only a teensy disappointment and it certainly wouldn't stop her enjoying the first moments of her holiday.

Vera was the last to alight. As she reached the door of the bus, she adjusted her sundress so that it covered the straps of her bra, set her bag on her shoulder and carefully lowered her foot to the first step. She was glad she had bought the white sandals even if the heels were rather high. They had dainty narrow straps that showed off her neat ankles better than the canvas wedges that had been her first choice.

The bus driver, not bothering to check that the last passenger was safely off, pushed a button and the door began to slide shut. With a cry, Vera pitched forward. Expecting to hit the gravel with disastrous consequences, she closed her eyes and put out her hands to break her fall.

But it was the manly arms of a near-naked GO that received her. He clasped her firmly by the shoulders, righted her and settled the bag back into place. Vera's eyes travelled upwards from the knot of the cotton wrap that was pressing into her belly, past the hairless whorl of his navel to a wide, muscular chest and shoulders that could hold up the world, until they finally came to rest on his face, a face of such surpassing male beauty that it ought to be stamped on coins.

François's green eyes looked tenderly into hers. 'Welcome to Corsairs' Cove,' he said softly.

Alternative holiday

It took Darina all of ten minutes to decide that Club Med was not for her. In the amphitheatre she listened to the *chef de village* give his welcome spiel and watched the lithe, bronzed GOs perform Crazy Signs, a dance that was like a cross between the Hokey Cokey and the Lambada. To her consternation, the *chef de village* made it clear that everyone was expected to join in; at a sign from him, half of the GOs leapt from the stage and came running up the steps to show the uninitiated GMs how it was done. Amid screams of laughter and cries of, 'Over here, Gorgeous!' Darina made her escape.

Her information pack informed her that it was a four-kilometre walk from Club Med to the nearest village, a fishing port beyond the headland that marked the northern limit of the resort beach. Darina dumped her bags in her room and set off. There was a path at the end of the beach that wound up a wooded slope to a barred gate by a road. A sign in French on the other side of the gate informed people that the beach below was strictly for the use of Club Mediterranée members.

It took Darina just under an hour to arrive at the port. There wasn't much activity; the only people on the tiny pier were four fishermen mending lobster pots. She tried to engage them in conversation, but they weren't disposed to be friendly and replied in monosyllables. It was only when it emerged that she was Irish, not French or American, that they relaxed and began to talk to her freely.

She learned that the locals resented the presence of the luxurious resort, which had become the biggest employer in the area without bringing about any increase in their standard of living. Wages were low; the vast profits made by the company out of this most popular of Caribbean resorts were made in New York and Paris. Once they arrived, the holidaymakers were discouraged from venturing outside the Club Med compound, and the locals were forbidden from hawking their souvenirs on the private beach.

Coco, the youngest of the fishermen, offered Darina a hand-rolled cigarette. When she drew on it, Darina discovered it was pure cannabis. She nodded her appreciation and leant back against the pier wall to enjoy the reefer with the afternoon sun on her face.

After the other men had left, Coco invited her onto his boat where they could make waves together. He jerked his hips to make his meaning clear. Darina smiled and shook her head. Right now, she was feeling far too mellow for sex.

Coco shrugged and came to sit beside her on the pier. He was about twenty-five and fairly attractive, she thought, though not as much as he believed himself to be. He was long and lean, and she loved the caramel colour of his skin, but his teeth were uneven and his hair was in dreadlocks that reached halfway down his back. Still, he was a darn sight better than the overweight, loud-shirted Americans she had seen getting off the buses at the Club.

Passing the reefer back, Darina asked Coco about himself. He told her he had three sisters and a wife, all of whom worked as cleaners in Club Med. He also made money there, he added with a wicked grin; for example, there was a French teacher who came over every year for a week in February and paid him as much as he made in half a year of fishing to fuck her all night long.

Darina quickly decided that Coco, with his dreadlocks and laid-back attitude to life, was more interesting than anyone she was likely to meet at Club Med. Even if they didn't make waves together, it would be good to see him again. When it was time to go, she asked him if he was free tomorrow. It took her a while to persuade him that she really wasn't looking for a black stud, but eventually he agreed to meet her the next day and for a reasonable sum show her around the southern part of the island.

Annunciation

It was Sunday and Sally O'Shea was once more on her way to Dalkey to meet with Sr Annunciata. The first visit had been a bit of a teaser on both sides. Sally had gone out without any expectations, so she hadn't been too disappointed when the matron, a rather ferocious middle-aged nun, had informed her gruffly that she could not possibly allow her to visit one of her patients unannounced and off the street, so to speak. Sally had put on her best crestfallen face and turned to go. The matron had called her back. It was against the regulations, but if Sr Annunciata agreed, she was prepared to allow Sally to visit for a short time. Sr Annunciata had been a bit down lately and the matron thought a new face might cheer her up. Sally was to be sure not to upset her, however, or the visit would be terminated immediately and Sally would not be allowed back.

Sr Annunciata was neither as old nor as feeble as Sally had expected. A dry, thin woman, she was sitting in an invalid chair in the large bay window of the Common Room looking out to sea when Sally was brought to her. Sally had introduced herself and sat on the window seat facing the nun. The nun had ignored her. Sally had admired the view. The nun had sniffed. So Sally had told her that she was an investigative journalist and that she wanted to write a book about Sylvester Reed. She knew he had been a regular visitor during his lifetime and she was hoping that Sr Annunciata would help her with it. Sr Annunciata had said nothing for a while, then she had told Sally to come back on Sunday, at 2 p.m. sharp. She was to bring chocolates.

I hope she likes Quality Street, thought Sally as she

got off the DART in Dalkey Station and began the walk up the hill to the nursing home where the last remnants of a once-great teaching Order were put out to pasture. In the few days since her first visit, she had taken out her notes on Sylvester and read over everything she had found out at the time of his suicide. It didn't amount to much. Maybe today she would be able to add to it. Her Walkman had a discreet microphone that she would clip under her lapel so that she could record the conversation if it began to get interesting.

Walking up the short driveway to the solid, redbrick Victorian building that had 'institution' written all over it, Sally speculated about the relationship between Sylvester and Sr Annunciata. Aunt? Distant cousin? Or maybe they were not related at all and he had been some sort of twisted holy Joe who visited nuns when he wasn't strangling virgins.

Sr Annunciata was expecting her, the Filipina nurse told Sally as she led her to the shabby, overheated Common Room. It was wonderful what the prospect of a visit did for them, she confided. Sr Annunciata had had a bath and put on her best clothes for the first time in months. Sally was pleased. On her first visit, she had thought about concealing the true nature of her interest, but she had quickly changed her mind once she had met the nun. Sr Annunciata was not in the least bit doddery and Sally had instinctively known that she would clam up at once if she suspected that her visitor was being in any way evasive or condescending.

The nun certainly had gone to some trouble with her appearance today. On the first occasion, she had been wearing a nightdress with an ancient cardigan over it, thick man's socks and slippers. Now she was dressed in a long brown tweed skirt, a high-necked blouse and a fern-green Aran sweater. She was wearing tights and brown Scholl shoes with laces. When she stood up, she was a head taller than Sally and ramrod straight.

'Come to my room,' she commanded as soon as the nurse had left. Without waiting to see if Sally was following, she went striding down a series of corridors and up a flight of stairs to the floor above. Sally trotted after her trying not to feel like a pupil summoned to the head nun's office for some terrible breach of school rules.

Sr Annunciata's bedroom also overlooked the sea. It would be a beautiful room, thought Sally, if this place were renovated as a luxury hotel. The ceiling was high and wood panelled; there were two huge windows and the floor was solid oak. But instead of a four-poster bed, rich William Morris-style wallpaper and *en suite* facilities, Sr Annunciata's room boasted an old hospital bed, layers of gloss paint in a colour somewhere between avocado and mustard, and sanitary ware consisting of a cracked porcelain hand basin in the corner.

'Sit,' said the nun, indicating one of two plastic chairs set on either side of an antique table with spindly legs that looked totally out of place in the room.

Sally sat down and surreptitiously reached her hand into her bag to find the controls on the Walkman. She hoped she would be able to tell by feel which one was the 'record' button.

'I asked you to bring me some chocolates,' the nun said, taking her place opposite Sally.

'Oh, yes – here they are. I hope you like them,' said Sally, wondering if she shouldn't have brought a bag of Thornton's handmade instead.

Sr Annunciata clicked her tongue reprovingly. 'They're not for me, I never eat sweet things. They are for the old nuns. I dole them out as treats after meals.'

Sally looked at her and shuddered inwardly. Imagine being in your seventies and calling other people old!

She took out her notepad, located the buttons on her Walkman, checked that the microphone lead was still concealed under her jacket and opened her mouth to ask the first of a series of questions she had prepared about Sylvester Reed.

'Not so fast!'

Sr Annunciata reached over and put her hand on the notepad. She turned it round so that she could read the questions for herself. She looked severely at Sally as she pushed the pad back to her.

'What I am going to tell you is the story of my own life. You will take it down or record it, as you please. You will come back here every Sunday and show me what you have written. If I am happy with it, I will continue my story. When it is finished, then and only then will I consider telling you about the life of my son Sylvester.'

Picnic time

If Darina shunned the whole Club Med scene, appearing in the resort only at mealtimes and at night, the same was not true of Vera. From the moment of her miraculous rescue at the hands of the most beautiful man she had ever seen, her holiday became like a dream that she never wanted to end.

The miraculous rescue was only the beginning of it.

After he had saved her, François had shown her to her bungalow, a twin room she was to share with a woman due to arrive from Canada later in the evening.

That left them plenty of time, François assured Vera as he led her to the bed. There, he swiftly but gently relieved her of the cumbersome weight of her virginity. For that alone, Vera would have worshipped him, but when he had made it clear that it was not a once-off, welcome-to-the-club performance and that he wanted to see her again, she knew that God had answered her prayers after all.

François was full of little attentions, like walking her into dinner on his arm each night, pulling out her chair, smiling at her from onstage when he was in a show. He invited her to accompany him every morning on the diving boat, even though he was too busy to do more than blow her the odd kiss. Vera was happy just being able to watch him, and she used the time that he was underwater to lie out on the deck and deepen her tan.

All the other women who had come to Club Med looking for a good time were envious. She could see them staring at her with resentful eyes when François leant over and kissed her, or put his arm protectively around her. There was one girl in particular who had nearly choked on her soup when she had seen them together on the first night. A skinny blonde; French, most likely, as Vera had heard her converse with the black barmen earlier that evening. It was gratifying to remember how she had goggled at Vera and François when they had sat down at her table. She had been taken by such a bad fit of coughing that she had had to leave the table, and Vera hadn't seen her since.

Today was Wednesday, the day of the picnic. It

dawned bright and blue, just like every other day in Club Med. Vera had her shower and joined François at breakfast. She had spent most of the night in his room, but he got up early in the morning, so she always returned to her own bungalow around sunrise.

In the restaurant, they were joined at the table by a small, stocky GO whom Vera had seen giving out equipment at the snorkelling shack. He grinned at Vera then turned to speak to François in French. Vera, who couldn't understand a word, addressed herself to her plate of tropical fruits instead.

'So, Poireau,' said Benito, 'is your girlfriend going to do our games on the beach?'

'She'll do anything I ask her,' said François. 'But I'm not going to be at your picnic, so I can't show you.'

'Too bad. She looks . . . how do they say it – tight?'

'Uptight. She's not, believe me.'

'So prove it.'

'OK. What would you like her to do?'

'Doubles. Me with her roommate. After, we swap.'

'No problem. I'll get two bottles of champagne on credit from the bar. If she does it, you pay. If not, I pay.'

Pleasures of the mind

While the sybaritic GMs rushed down to the pier to board the boats that would take them to Picnic Island, Darina stayed in the Club Med compound. This was the one day in the week that it was safe to wander around without having to smile or talk to people. She had watched Vera being handed onto the first boat, so there was no fear of bumping into her in the grounds.

Once she had got over the shock of seeing her neighbour at dinner the first night, Darina had done her best to see without being seen. She was fascinated by the odd coupling of Vera and the god-like GO who was constantly at her side. What was his angle? If the horrible little Italian she'd overheard on the first day went after big women because of some competition about weight, was this guy involved in a dogfight to see who could come up with the ugliest woman, like in that film with River Phoenix? It had to be something like that.

Whatever his motivation, he was good at what he did. Vera might have been royalty, the way he looked after her. What's more, he seemed to enjoy doing it.

As for Vera, she truly was transformed by his attentions. She now walked erect, head up and shoulders back. Her prominent bust, which she had always seemed at pains to disguise, was suddenly thrust in the face of the world. The stoop was gone. She had even developed a provocative swing to her hips, which Darina found most out of character.

Before, Vera had behaved like a woman who knew she'd been shortchanged in the looks department. Now she appeared to believe the opposite. Was it an Ugly Duckling syndrome? Had Vera looked in the mirror and decided she'd turned into a beauty overnight?

Granted, other things helped. Vera's normally sallow skin had quickly turned mahogany in the tropical sun, but it was more than that. She really had become if not beautiful, then striking. What the

French called *jolie-laide*. Could sex do that for you?

Darina sighed. First Anne Marie, and now Vera. What was wrong with her? Maybe she should have said 'yes' to Coco. Would she have been transformed? She sighed again. Hardly. She couldn't imagine any man having that effect on her. Maybe I'm not meant for love, thought Darina glumly as she wandered through the deserted complex. I'll probably have a road-to-Damascus experience and end up a nun. Mother Darina of Calcutta. God, what a prospect!

Darina shook her head to get rid of the nightmare vision of herself in a nun's habit doing good among the downtrodden. She had passed through the bar and was near the hostess desk, an area normally swamped by male GMs buying bar-beads and trying it on with the hostess on duty.

Now that the place was empty, she noticed for the first time that there was a bookcase in an alcove behind the desk. Darina went to investigate. Among the run-of-the-mill thrillers, blockbusters and self-improvement manuals she found some unexpected titles. *The Sacred Pipe: Black Elk's Account of the Seven Rites of the Oglala Sioux*, about a Native-American shaman; *None To Accompany Me*, a Nadine Gordimer novel that she'd already read, and a couple of thick Dickens paperbacks.

She'd taken down *Martin Chuzzlewit* and was wondering if she could bear to start on something so wordy when she heard someone coming up behind her. Glancing round, she saw a shortish man dressed in a floral shirt and baggy shorts who was obviously on his way to the library. He had brown hair and a sandy beard, round, gold-rimmed glasses and a sunburnt nose. He was carrying four hardback books. He seemed startled to see her.

'Excuse me, I do beg your pardon,' he began. 'I should like to put in some books.'

'Fire ahead,' said Darina. 'I'm going anyway – there's nothing here for me.'

The man hesitated as though he wasn't sure it was safe to proceed. Darina stood back to let him at the bookcase. He was obviously the shy, retiring, intellectual type. Once he'd left, she would have a decko to see what he had been reading.

The man blinked at her and looked away. 'It's unusual to find a young person interested in reading on this type of vacation,' he said to the bookcase. 'Are you a guest here?'

'Yeah, but only because I won this trip. I'd never have come to Club Med otherwise. All this organised fun – not my scene at all. Oh, sorry! I didn't mean . . .'

'That's quite all right. Against my better judgement I was persuaded that a week at a resort such as this was exactly what I needed to cure my insomnia. Luckily, I brought plenty of reading material.' He held up the books that he had cleared space for on the bottom shelf. 'Well, that's my contribution to the library. I do hope you find something to suit you. Goodbye.' He nodded to Darina and scurried off.

Darina immediately turned to examine the books left by the little man. 'Yes!' she exclaimed as her eyes greedily took in the titles, which were almost all in Russian. Gogol's *The Inspector General*; *The Bronze Horseman* and *Evgenii Onegin* by Pushkin, with an English translation by Vladimir Nabokov; poems by Anna Akhmatova, and Bulgakov's *The Master and Margerita*. Some of them were prescribed texts for Darina's third-year Russian literature course, and the only one she had read so far was the last one, which was her all-time favourite book and one of the reasons she had decided to study Russian in the first place. She stuffed the lot of them into her bag and left without a backward glance.

Which is why she didn't see the man who had left the books step out from behind a pillar and smile to himself in satisfaction.

That evening, curiosity brought Darina down to the water sports pier in time to meet the returning revellers. She watched as the two boats docked, packed with the swinging singles who had given this resort its racy reputation. They looked rather subdued after their day of fun and games on a deserted island. Too much sun, she concluded. Many of the men had TV-screen red patches on their backs that they hadn't been able to cover with sun block. And nobody to do it for them, Darina silently mocked. There were far more men than women, she noticed, which might account for the sullen atmosphere. The male GOs appeared to have done well; most of them had a woman under their arm as they sauntered up the pier towards the guest bungalows.

Just then, Vera appeared at the top of the gangway. She was wearing a fluorescent lime bikini that made the most of her considerable assets, and had tied a pareo around her hips the way the GOs did. Watching her assume a film-star pose as she put on her dark glasses and scanned the faces below, Darina had to admit that Vera was imposing, to say the least. Her GO arrived and stood in front of Darina; Vera fluttered her fingers and sashayed down the gangplank to meet him. He kissed her hand and from behind his back produced a hibiscus blossom, which he fastened behind her ear.

Cheap, thought Darina, watching Vera blush with pleasure; cheap, but effective. Vera passed so close, Darina could almost have reached out and touched her, but the god-like GO absorbed so much of her neighbour's attention that she seemed barely to notice there were other people around.

Suddenly, there was a commotion on the boat. Darina turned. The big African-American woman who had sat in front of her on the bus was rounding on the obnoxious little Italian. Her voice was loud enough to be heard all the way to the bar at the end of the pier.

'For the last time, you little jerk, I will not fuck with you. You been pestering me for five days and I have just about had it. You got the hots for this black lady? Then maybe this will cool you down!'

There was a high-pitched scream as the big woman reached down and grabbed Benito by the crotch. Her other hand closed around his throat. With as little effort as if he'd been a baby, the woman lifted him up over her head in a weightlifter's hold, walked over to the other side of the boat and, to roars of approval from the sidelines, flung him into the sea. Darina put two fingers in her mouth and added her ear-splitting whistle to the general cheers.

Writer's cramp

Sally O'Shea was coming down with the 'flu. Her head was throbbing, her bones ached and her sinuses felt as though they'd been filled with glue. Under normal circumstances, she would have called in sick and taken herself over to Rialto to be fussed back to health by her mother. Even now, the thought of lying on the couch of her parents' front room, wrapped in a duvet and woozy from the hot whiskies in whose medicinal properties Mrs O'Shea had absolute faith was very tempting.

But Sally couldn't afford to give in to illness. Not now, when so much depended on being able to make it back to Dalkey on Sunday for the second instalment of the extraordinary tale of Bernadatte Reed aka Sr Regina Maria Annunciata.

Sally knew that this was her big break. The story had everything: sex, betrayal, death, and even murder. Last week she had heard about the nun's emotionally deprived childhood on a small farm somewhere in the South (*possible intimations of incest*, Sally had privately recorded) and the escape route provided by education with the nuns. Next came her own vows and apparently blissful years of contemplative life in a cloister in France, ended only by the need for her to return home to care for her dying parents.

And that was where the narrative had stopped. Like a true professional, Sr Annunciata had broken off just at the exciting bit. This Sunday she was to take up the story again and tell Sally about the betrayal of trust that had led to her pregnancy and disgrace. But before she did that, Sally had to get her approval for what she had written so far.

And that was why Sally couldn't afford to be sick. For the past two nights she had sat up in her dingy Inchicore bedsit after her return from work and written until her hand ached so much that she could barely hold the pen. She had forgotten the need for sleep, nourishing food and warm surroundings in her determination to get it all down. Black coffee and a single-bar electric fire were what had kept her going so far. Today it seemed that her body was crying, 'Enough!' and demanding that she look after it.

But it would have to wait. If she gave in to the symptoms now, she knew she would be laid up for at least a week. If she fought the virus on her feet, she might be able to keep the worst of it at bay until after Sunday.

A few days' grace is all I ask, Sally begged her body as she dragged herself over to the kettle and tore open a sachet of Lemsip. Today to finish, tomorrow to get it all onto a diskette, Saturday to edit and print it out for Her Nibs, then it's Sunday. 'Just let me have until Sunday,' she whispered, warming her hands on the mug, 'and next week, I promise I'll take you over to Mam's and pamper you something rotten.'

On Sunday, Sylvester would enter the story.

Bibliophile

It was Sports Day at Club Med. On her return from a day-long excursion with Coco, Darina asked to be dropped off at the port so that she could walk back to the compound on her own. It was her favourite time of the afternoon, when the heat had lost its fierceness and the light breeze felt like a caress on her skin. If she timed it well, she would reach the top of the hill in time to see the sun set over the water, then a short dash would bring her inside the compound before darkness fell. With any luck, the other holidaymakers would still be in the shower, and Darina would get to the bar in the lull between the end of the sports events and the beginning of dinner.

Leaving the port, the beaten-earth road climbed steeply. It was lined on both sides with trees, but not the jungly kind that she'd seen on a trip with Coco to the interior. It was a lot drier on this part of the island, she realised; that was why there was so little undergrowth along here. The forest was more open; you could walk through it easily, along one of the many paths that she could see from the road. She was wondering which one she would take if she wanted to find a short cut back to the compound when the snap of a stick made her whirl round. Someone was coming out of the trees on her left, but Darina was dazzled by the rays of the setting sun and couldn't make out who it was.

'Hello?' She shaded her eyes and tried to focus on the approaching figure.

'Good evening. I'm sorry if I startled you. I heard someone coming along the road, and as I didn't wish to make small talk with any of my fellow holiday-makers, I went a little way into the trees.'

Darina recognised the voice of the man who had left the Russian books in the library. She frowned, rather annoyed to discover that she was not the only one shunning the enforced jollity of a Club Med holiday.

'But instead of passing by, you stopped, and of course I had not been thinking of you when I was dismissing the Club Med crowd.'

'What makes you think I'm any better than them?' Darina challenged him.

'You are here, not there. And you read Gogol. Besides, I didn't mean to imply that I consider myself superior to the hedonists below, merely that I have little in common with them. And from the rarity of your appearance at the organised events, I must conclude that you feel the same way. Would you mind my walking with you?'

Darina shrugged. 'Sure, why not?' She was embarrassed both by the fact that he seemed to have guessed what she was thinking, and that he knew she had taken all four of his books from the library. She might have to put them back now. Or maybe she could put them back, then sneak them out again on the last day. They were good hardback editions; infinitely nicer than the cheap secondhand paperbacks she would have bought for herself.

'Are you enjoying your reading? How did you find *The Inspector General*? Did you like the Akhmatova poems?'

'Well, actually, I em . . . I haven't had time to look at them yet. I was starting with *The Master and Margerita* because I really like it, and I've read bits of *Evgenii Onegin*, but I was saving the others for . . . for the end of the week.'

'Oh please, don't be shy about taking them home with you. I am delighted that they have found someone to appreciate them.'

Darina grinned shamefacedly. 'Oh. Right. Thanks a lot – they're lovely. In fact, I don't know how you can buy books like that and then just let them go.'

'Well, the truth is I'm an addict. My apartment in New York is bursting at the seams with books – there's positively no room for any more. But I cannot stop myself from visiting bookshops and acquiring new ones. I tried it for a while and I was utterly miserable. So I made a bargain with myself; I could continue to buy books only if I was prepared to give them away afterwards. By leaving them on park benches or in the dentist's waiting-room, I like to imagine that some of the world's great literature is passed on to people who might not otherwise have encountered it. This is the first time I have actually witnessed a pick-up, so to speak. I must confess that I hid and watched you take my books the other day. I was rather pleased that you recognised their worth.'

'Well, as long as you don't mind – I'm very glad to have them,' she said.

The book-lover's name was Donald Garvey. He was a thirty-nine-year-old Professor of Russian Studies, specialising in Church Slavonic. He lived alone in an apartment in Manhattan. His mother had died six months earlier and he had been suffering from bouts of insomnia ever since. After the failure of the usual remedies, his physician had finally advised him to go for a complete change of scene; a holiday somewhere like Club Med where he would be forced to interact with other people.

So much Darina learnt as they continued down the hill together. He was kind of cute, she decided, though not at all the type of man she'd expected to meet at Club Med.

'So you're here under doctor's orders,' she said.

'Yes. And you because you won a competition. Is that right?'

'Yeah. I don't even know why I went in for it – it's not as though I thought I'd enjoy a Club Med holiday or anything.'

'But you seem to have found some distractions outside of the club.'

Darina looked at him sharply. Had he been following her or what?

'I was in the village the other day and I noticed you

coming back in a boat with one of the locals. I thought it was rather enterprising of you to have found a guide to take you round the island.'

'That was Coco. He offered to show me a lot more too, if I was interested.' Would the Prof pick up on the double entendre? He seemed a bit square.

'I see. And er, did you avail yourself of the offer?'

'Actually, no. I wasn't in the humour at the time. I might though, before I leave.'

'Indeed. In that case, I don't suppose you would be interested in having dinner with me tonight.'

Darina smiled to herself. So he wasn't as green as he was cabbage-looking! She shrugged. 'Sure, why not? I've been eating by myself for the last few nights; a bit of company would make a change.'

'In that case, I'll reserve a table for two misfits at the beach restaurant. Eight o'clock?'

'Sounds good to me.'

Standing under the shower, Darina wondered if the Prof would make a move on her after dinner, and if he did, how far she would let him go. She got the impression that he didn't often ask women out. When she had agreed to have dinner with him, he'd looked ridiculously pleased, as though she'd been the Queen of Sheba or something.

So would she, or wouldn't she? She had come to Club Med with the intention of screwing herself silly, but this was the second time that the opportunity had arisen, and she was hesitating.

What would Don be like naked? He was not the sort she usually went for – all that hair might be off-putting. Then again, there was something warm and animal about it . . . like fur. It might be nice to run her fingers through it, or to rub her face in it. To her surprise and delight, Darina discovered that the prospect gave her a pleasant shivery feeling that augured well for the evening's end.

He was waiting for her at the bar, looking spruce in a short-sleeved white shirt and black trousers. The beach restaurant had waiter service, so as soon as she arrived, they were led to their table for two over-looking the sea. Don suggested champagne, but Darina opted for white wine instead. The waiter left with their order.

'So tell me, has Club Med cured your insomnia?' Darina, wearing a little black dress that she had bought in Paris, spoke aggressively to cover her nervousness. The other restaurant was brightly lit and loud; this one had candles and soulful jazz playing softly in the background. She was afraid that romance was *de rigueur*.

'No, but I seem to suffer less from headaches here than in New York.'

'Have you had grief counselling or anything like that?'

Don smiled self-deprecatingly. 'Oh, I doubt that would do any good. You see, it is not the fact of my mother's death that disturbs me. She was almost eighty and she had been ailing for a long time. It is the discovery after she died that I was adopted that I seem unable to come to terms with on an emotional level. So my physician tells me, at any rate.'

'You were adopted and you didn't know until after your mother died? Amazing! How did you find out?'

'It was all there, along with her will. No letter, nothing addressed to me personally; just the legal documents. And a religious medal that may have been mine.'

'Do you know the circumstances of your adoption? Could you trace your birth family if you wanted to?'

Don opened his hands. 'Is this what I must do? I thought it should make little difference to my life to know that the people who raised me were not my natural parents, but perhaps I was wrong. I should like to move on, but that appears to be impossible. I am being driven to increasingly outlandish remedies, the latest of which is this Club Med vacation, which until this evening was looking to be as wasteful of my time and money as all the rest.'

He smiled at Darina, then looked down at his glass, as though afraid that she might take offence at the compliment.

Darina hardly noticed it; she was far too interested in his story. 'Oh, but you should!' she exclaimed. 'I mean, what have you got to lose? If they turn out to be losers or crack merchants, you'll know you got the better deal. If they're nice, you might just acquire a whole new family.'

Don looked slightly bemused. 'Well, that's one way of looking at it. Unfortunately, I have no idea where to begin looking. Apart from the medal, there are no clues as to my background.'

'Well, it's Catholic, isn't it? Garvey is an Irish name, so I'm assuming your adoptive parents were Irish-American Catholics. Maybe you were adopted in Ireland! Lots of babies were in the fifties and sixties, you know. The Church had some sort of a racket going with Irish Catholics in the States; it was on TV a few years ago, and I think there's a book about it. I could send it to you, if you like.'

Don pushed his spectacles on to the bridge of his nose. 'Oh! I . . . Thank you. It's rather sudden, though. Pardon me; I am grateful for your interest, but . . .'

The waiter appeared and showed the bottle of wine to Don, who nodded at once.

'You're not sure you want to take it any further. That's OK.' Darina sat back while the waiter poured her wine. 'But if I were you,' she continued when he'd left, 'I'd die if I didn't find out everything there was to be known about my birth family. Don't you find it exciting? A mystery to be solved? Think of it: you could be anybody!'

Suddenly Don smiled. 'You have a refreshing way of looking at the world, Darina. And you know, maybe you're right. For the past six months, I've been feeling that there's something missing in my life; a part of me I didn't know existed. When I tried to ignore it, the headaches started. Maybe it's time to stop fighting and . . . go with the flow.'

'Great! You can come to Ireland, so. I'll put you up in Dublin while you do research into your background.'

Darina stopped, surprised by what she had just said. Did she mean it? How would she feel if Donald Garvey were to turn up on her doorstep? She looked at him. He was staring at her as though he couldn't believe his ears. She grinned. She would feel just fine.

After dinner, Darina invited Don to come skinny-dipping with her. She was not one hundred per cent sure that she wanted to go to bed with him, but a full moon suspended like a Chinese lantern over the tropical waters of the Caribbean was not something to be wasted.

They returned to their separate rooms to get ready. Darina put on the two-piece swimsuit she had bought in Paris and not yet worn and threw a towel around her shoulders. They met at the scuba shack and began to walk along the beach, side by side but without touching. Darina was more nervous about this escapade than she cared to admit. After a minute of embarrassed silence, she began to talk in a rush about the last time she had gone swimming in the nude with some wild friends and had almost been arrested.

Don stopped and turned to face her. 'It doesn't have to be like this,' he said quietly. 'If you're not comfortable, I can leave. It won't be a problem. We can still be friends in the morning.'

Darina looked out at the moonlit sea. She longed to feel the warm water caressing her skin, to wave her arms and see the blue-green phosphorescence that made her feel as though she were surrounded by fluid stars. The question was: did she want to share all this with Don? She looked at him, undecided. He had given her an honourable way out. She knew that he meant it when he said that they could meet in the morning and there would be no awkwardness. She was grateful to him for that.

Don waited for her decision. The moonlight glinted on the rim of his glasses.

He's used to rejection, thought Darina. He expects me to send him packing. She considered a moment longer.

'Can I say stop?'

'Of course,' said Don gravely.

'At any time?'

'At any time.'

Darina grinned. Taking her towel from around her neck, she threw it to him. 'OK, then, here's the deal: you stay if you can catch me!'

Without waiting for his response, she began to run down the beach, pulling the top of her swimsuit off as she went.

Pin-up

It was after three in the morning when they parted company. Don had been as good as his word; she had said 'stop' and he had stopped.

It was good doing it this way, mused Darina as she padded barefoot back to her bungalow; it made her feel safe. Being naked with Don in the water had been very nice, but he was different to other men she had been with: older, more mature and . . . more male. Darina had begun to feel overwhelmed, and she had called a halt to their cavorting. There was always tomorrow night to finish what they had started, if that was what she wanted.

She passed by the photographer's shack. Light was spilling out from the open doorway and Terri, the photographer, was sitting outside smoking a cigarette. Darina stopped. She had spoken to Terri on the first day and found her interesting, but their paths hadn't crossed since.

'Hi,' said Darina. 'Working late?'

'Yeah. Tonight's my busiest. Picnic and Sports Day. I'll sell a bunch tomorrow, rest Saturday, then it all starts over.'

'Can I see some of the picnic ones?' Darina asked, curious to learn what exactly went on when the swinging singles were spirited off to their deserted island.

'Sure.' Terri led the way inside.

She showed Darina the photos she had blown up to 6 × 8 format for the glass display case at the entrance to the restaurant the next day. They were not as bad as Darina had expected. Nobody was entirely naked, and if the saucy beach games had included the infamous blow-job competition, there was no photographic record of it.

She looked out for pictures of Vera, but there were none, though Darina thought she might have caught a glimpse of her in the background of a photo showing a couple eating a banana from both ends.

She was about to leave when Terri spread out another batch. 'Wet T-shirt contest,' she said. 'They always sell well on weeks like this when there are too many guys.'

Darina's eyes almost popped out of their sockets. There, on the very top, was Vera Meaney in all her splendour.

It could have been a picture for a soft-porn magazine. Vera's head was thrown back and her centrefold breasts thrust outwards. A skimpy white T-shirt clung to her, outlining prominent nipples and dark aureolas.

'She's something else, right?' That was Terri. 'She won, natch. I got a load of shots of her; the guys'll love them.'

'I'll take four!'

Terri gave her a startled look.

'Don't worry, they're for my brother,' said Darina, who was barely able to contain her excitement. 'I'll choose them now, and you put them aside for me, OK? I'll be back tomorrow with the money.'

She chose the three sexiest poses, then picked up one of Vera being caressed from behind by the good-looking GO. 'What's the deal with this guy?' she asked. 'He doesn't look her type, if you know what I mean.'

Terri made a wry face. 'François? He's beautiful, right? But he always chooses ugly women. It's like he does it on purpose to rub people's noses in it. You should see how mad it makes the female GMs. Not to mention certain GOs on the hostess team.'

'What's in it for him?'

'Good question,' said Terri. 'He told me once. He's got a racehorse in California, a Ferrari and two motor-bikes, more gold jewellery than he knows what to do with and an open invitation to visit these women in every major city in the world.'

'Presents?'

'You bet. He's picky, too. He looks for the ugly ones, he says, because they are so grateful to him that they will do anything. But he has standards. They have to have good bodies – I mean, look at this one: if you forget the face, she could be a Pirelli pin-up. He doesn't do fat. Fat disgusts him.'

Darina sensed bitterness beneath the offhand tone. Terri was pretty, but fat. She obviously had a thing for him, and François made her pay for it.

'Well, guys like that usually get their come uppance in the end,' said Darina. 'Remember Dorian Grey?'

Terri looked at her blankly, so she soon made her excuses and went on to her bed.

Bibi

Next night, while Darina was taking her clothes off in front of Don, on the other side of the Atlantic, her mother was putting hers back on. Across the room, which was in a new waterfront apartment overlooking the River Shannon, in a bed strategically placed to allow its occupants a view of the river, a man lay asleep.

Glancing over at him while she slipped on her shoes, Barbara smiled to see how oblivious he was to the world. The duvet covered him only to the waist, and he lay on his back with one arm flung across the pillow, the other across his naked chest.

Sleeping like a baby, bless him! Mind you, he deserves it, she thought, shivering deliciously as memories of his night's exertions came back to her.

Sex was wonderful, not just for the pleasure it generated while it was happening, but for the way it made you feel in between times, thought Barbara. Going into the bathroom to put her make-up on, she marvelled yet again that it was only now, with her fiftieth birthday looming, that she was discovering just how good it could be.

Throughout her married life, sex had meant a quick fumble in the darkness, a brief, shameful coupling and palpable relief when it was all over. Poor Dan! He had suffered as much as she had from his lack of sex drive. Self-esteem had never been his strong point to begin with. Anne Davenport had a lot to answer for on that score, she thought.

Once they were married and his failings in the bedroom had been uncovered, however, Barbara had been unable to hide her disappointment and frustration. She was twenty-three! The thought of all the joyless years ahead of her was too much; on their honeymoon, she had broken down and wept bitter tears. It was then that Dan, from the depths of his mortification and unhappiness, had proposed a solution that had probably saved their marriage. She could have relationships with other men, he said; the only thing he asked was that if there were any children, they should be his, and consequently, that they would stay together until the children were reared.

Strange, Barbara mused, how having the option of looking elsewhere for sex had been enough. She had only exercised her prerogative twice. The first time was in the first year of her marriage, to prove that she could; the second time was five years ago at a weekend Reiki workshop, where she had fallen in lust with one of the other students after he had given her a neck massage.

Apart from those two incidents, she had remained faithful to Dan. Her frustrated sexual energy had been channelled elsewhere: into night classes on everything from Art History to Woodwork. She had collected diplomas instead of lovers and now she was reaping the benefits of those sexually barren years.

Bibi Bracken, Image Consultant. It was a job title she had invented for herself, but in the nine months that she had been practising, her name had become well known in the places that counted. Barbara loved her work, and it constantly amazed her how everything in her life seemed to have been leading to this point. Anyone could see how Interior Design and Colour-me-beautiful sessions might come in useful, but who could have predicted that those night classes in Psychology, Gourmet Cookery and Archaeology would come in so handy?

Barbara carefully applied eyeliner to her lower lids.

It turned out that the breadth of her knowledge and skills were deeply impressive to prospective clients; after talking to her for a while, they took it for granted that she could do just about anything. They recommended her to their friends for jobs as varied as making a shop-front more attractive to choosing the car that best reflected their personality or the menu for a grand dinner party.

What gave Barbara the greatest buzz, however, was working on her clients themselves. She was proud of the radical transformations she achieved in their physical appearance, without making them resort to draconian diets or surgery.

Take the man in the bed, for example. When Barbara first met him, he was George Arthur McLoughlin, a weedy, thirty-six-year-old jeweller with chipped front teeth and poor eyesight, who wore moth-eaten jumpers and lived alone in a set of dingy over-the-shop rooms in the city centre. He made some unusual brooches in his spare time, but his living was the jewellery shop that had been in the family for five generations.

Barbara changed all that the day she went into his shop to have a watch fixed. She liked his brooches. They got talking. She itched right away to take him in hand and make his name. He was doubtful, she was persuasive. She won.

She got him to sell the rooms he was living in and buy into the same waterfront development in which she had purchased an apartment. She persuaded him to grow his hair long enough to wear in a ponytail. She introduced him to contact lenses and a dentist.

A year on, he was *art mac lochlainn*, master silversmith, with a workshop in the trendy new craft centre and e-mail orders for his highly-prized pieces coming in from all over the world. He wore bright shirts, sported an earring and worked out in a gym twice a week.

He was also her lover. Barbara had been coming

here at least three nights a week for the past four months, and it was still as good as ever. They were both making up for lost time.

Barbara smiled at her reflection. She looked better at forty-nine than she had at twenty-nine. Her hair, skin and eyes glowed with health, and her new-found fulfilment showed itself in the way she moved. For the first time in her life, Barbara knew what it was to feel sexy.

And it's all thanks to you, she thought, opening the door of the bathroom so she could gaze fondly at her lover's muscular torso.

Of course it couldn't last; she knew that. She hoped she would have the sense to pull out in time, before the first signs of wear began to show. Would she recognise them? Right now, they were at the peak of their relationship; in mixed gatherings where there were lots of attractive younger women, Art only had eyes for her. How much longer would that be the case?

Suddenly, Barbara began to doubt herself. What if she didn't recognise the signs? Worse – what if, recognising them, she chose to deny them and clung to her lover like a drowning woman? Would it not be better to end it all now, when it was so good that they would be left with only beautiful memories?

No! cried her body.

Yes, said her mind; it could be your supreme accomplishment.

It was a hard moment for Barbara. She wished she had not started the train of thought that had led to this, but there was no going back from it now. She sighed and leaned her head against the doorjamb while she made her choice.

She crossed to the bed. Leaning over her lover, she

closed her eyes. She breathed deeply through her nose, memorising the smell of him. She gazed at the handsome features she had uncovered for the world to admire. She planted a full-lipped red kiss on his cheek. He let out a long breath, but he did not move.

Barbara went back to the bathroom. She took out her lipstick again and unscrewed it. Hardly believing what she was doing, she began to write on the mirror.

She made it short and affectionate. She made it final.

Weekend blues

It was like coming out of anaesthetic to find that the pain was just as bad as before.

For a whole week Anne Marie had been numbed by the shock of learning the truth about her parentage. Before she went to sleep at night, it was Seán's face that haunted her. When she woke in the morning, it was the thought that he was abandoning her by going to Africa for five years that brought tears to her eyes.

But when Saturday came, her first waking thought was of Victor.

At this moment one week ago I was still happy, she told herself sadly, after she had glanced at the clock and found that it was not yet eight o'clock.

She remembered how peaceful she had felt lying beside her lover, his arm around her shoulder, hers across his chest. The disastrous dinner of the night before had already receded in her mind; it was of no importance now, except perhaps as an incident to make them smile when they looked back on it in years to come.

Then Victor had said her name.

How did I know? thought Anne Marie as pain flooded her once again. How did I know just by the way he said my name?

She turned onto her stomach and hugged the pillow fiercely.

Never to see him again? Never to hold him? The prospect was unthinkable!

Surely he didn't mean it? It was all a misunderstanding: if she were to go over to Glasnevin today, he would probably welcome her with open arms. He had been out of sorts last week because of what had happened to the Nigerian woman, that was all.

Energised by this new line of thought, Anne Marie threw back the duvet and swung her legs out of the bed. She would get up and cycle over there this minute! They would make mad, passionate love in his room and by this evening it would be as though the whole nightmare week hadn't happened.

She managed to sustain the illusion until she was under the shower and the first rush of cold water brought her back to her senses.

It was over. Victor had ended it because she had become a burden to him.

Anne Marie turned the water up as hot as she could bear.

Scald away the memories. Mortify the flesh. Hide the tears.

For the next week, Anne Marie lived in the *Femme* office. She threw herself into her job with demonic energy. As soon as she finished her own work, she began to pester Roz and Dave for more. She arrived early and stayed so late that one morning Roz showed her a note from the elusive Isolde Phoenix informing staff that under no circumstances were they to remain in the building after 8 p.m. She grew thin because she forgot to eat. Her hair became dull, her face wan. She told no one of her pain.

By the time the second Saturday came round, Anne Marie looked as wretched as she felt. Once again, she thought of going to Victor, of begging him to take her back, just for a little while. She would propose a phased withdrawal, or come to an agreement that they would meet twice a month, for instance. No strings attached.

Once again, she thought better of it. But knowing that her resistance was at its lowest point, she cast about for someone to spend the day with. Someone who would take her mind off Victor, or at least prevent her from jumping on her bike and cycling over to the Northside. Unfortunately, her cousins were unavailable; Darina was not due back from her Club Med holiday until late on Sunday night, and Cornelius had gone home for the weekend. Dave and Joe would be happy to see her, but an afternoon with a cosy couple was not what she needed just now.

That left Roz. Anne Marie very much wished to spend time with the *Femme* Editor and her family but she was feeling guilty for the way she had shamefully abandoned them as soon as Victor had appeared on the scene. In the past two months she had gone from being a constant visitor and babysitter in the house on the South Circular Road to a virtual stranger. Whatever about Roz and Stephen, she feared that the children would find it hard to forgive her desertion.

By the beginning of the afternoon, Anne Marie could bear it no longer. She took out her bike and kitted up for the dirty weather. She was going to one of two places; if there was no one in at Roz's, or if they didn't want to see her, she would turn her bicycle round and head across the city. Fate would decide.

When she reached the South Circular Road, the family car was parked outside the house so Anne Marie knew that someone was in. She locked her bike to the railings and rang the doorbell, more nervous than she would have believed possible. She heard feet thundering down the stairs and pulled back her hood so that the children would recognise her.

The door was thrown open.

This was it; she would either be invited in and everything would be as it used to be, or they would slam the door in her face and she would know that she had lost their affection for ever.

'It *is* Anne Marie! See, I was right!'

Ruth jumped up and down in excitement. 'I saw you from the window upstairs,' she shouted, grabbing Anne Marie by the hand and pulling her into the hall.

Not to be outdone, her brother Jake, who had slid down the banisters and was standing on the narrow outside ledge of the fourth step, launched himself into Anne Marie's arms. She caught him and staggered backwards, lost her footing and ended up on the floor with the twins on top of her.

There was a moment of stunned silence, then Jake jumped up.

'I didn't mean to hurt her, I didn't, I didn't!' The child looked up in anguish at Roz and Stephen, who had appeared in the hall. 'It was an accident,' he wailed. 'We just fell.'

Anne Marie was lying on the floor, sobbing uncontrollably.

Au revoir and *Merci*

Once more, the buses were lined up and the GOs, dressed in their colourful pareos, were smiling and waving to the GMs. This time, however, the movement was in the other direction; the guests were departing for the airport and their homes in New York, Boston, Newfoundland and the rest of cold North America.

Standing beside Charlot at the door of the first bus, François smiled and waved with the rest of them.

'Goodbye, have a nice trip.'

'Come again to Club Med.'

'Safe home. I hope we see you again.'

The women simpered and blew kisses from the top step of the bus; the men glowered and hunched their shoulders.

'Thank God we're seeing the last of that lot,' muttered the *chef de village* through his Club Med smile as a group of six men who had been singularly unsuccessful in pulling women hulked past them. 'The jacuzzi is closed for two days to clear the broken beer bottles out and two of the hostesses have complained about assault. I'll have to send them to the club in St Lucia for a few days to get over it.'

'Maybe next week will be better,' said François. 'What does it look like so far?'

'Fifty male to forty female and the last ten per cent unknown.'

'Well, that's not so bad. It was more than two to one this time.'

'Yeah. But in among the next lot we've got thirty-five miners from Alaska.'

'Oh shit! Better tell the kitchens: no red meat and lots of chocolate desserts.'

'And a trip midweek to Fort-de-France? What do you think?'

'Clients for *Mama Lou*? Make sure she gives group discount; she was way over the top last time. I'll go in and organise it this afternoon if you like; I have to buy some supplies for the scuba shack anyway.'

'Would you? That would be great. And by the way, your latest ladyfriend gave you a glowing report. I'm sure you'll make top GO again this year. I—'

Charlot stopped abruptly as a pretty, blue-eyed blonde with spiked hair and earrings caught François by the neck and pulled him down to her. She kissed him full on the lips and released him.

'I just couldn't resist that,' she said in perfect French, 'you are too beautiful!'

Before either of the men had a chance to respond, she went on, 'And I must thank you, François, for the splendid job you did on Vera. She is truly transformed – I hardly recognised her when she left this morning.' She patted him on the chest. '*Châpeau, mon vieux!*'

François and Charlot exchanged bemused glances. Who on earth was she? François had noticed her once or twice and assumed she was a GO from another resort having a short break. She certainly wasn't like any GM he had ever seen.

Charlot hadn't seen her at all. But now she was approaching him, her hand extended and a smile that he didn't quite trust on her lips.

'For a free holiday, this was brilliant! If ever I see another competition for a week at Club Med, I'll be sure to enter it!'

'*Bordel de merde!*' Charlot burst out. 'You are the winner? Each evening from the stage I asked to know who had won the holiday and nobody came forward.

You were supposed to take part in the promotion of Club Med. What about the photographs? I must send them to New York and Paris. I told them that they made a mistake; that it was not this week.'

The young woman grinned. 'Sorry, chief. Promotion is not my scene at all. But thanks again for the wonderful time I had.'

She pinched his cheek and climbed onto the first step of the bus, then turned and blew kisses the way Vera had done. '*Au revoir! Merci encore! Bonne continuation!*' she called as the doors closed, while François and Charlot stood with their mouths open and uncustomary looks of stupefaction on their faces.

The nun's knickers

The woman was mad. Absolutely bonkers. A raving lunatic.

Or else she's completely sane and I'm the one that's barking.

Sally O'Shea put her hand on her forehead and stared at her flushed reflection in the mirror of the visitors' bathroom. She had just spent the most extraordinary afternoon with Sr Annunciata and she was not the better of it yet.

I've definitely got a temperature, she thought, so maybe I was hallucinating.

Had she or had she not seen the nun partially undress in front of her? Had Sr Annunciata really pulled down the top of her interlocking knickers and made Sally look at the scars that covered her belly?

It was at the end of her story. She had told Sally

about the funeral of her parents, who had died within two days of one another, and about the priest who had come every day during the following weeks to offer her consolation.

That was when things had started to get strange.

Sr Annunciata's eyes took on a fixed look, and she began to rock her upper body back and forth as she talked. Sally grew alarmed: the nun was obviously reliving some traumatic event and unaware that she had an audience. Fragments of prayers mixed with profanation came out of her mouth in a rush. She began to wring her hands, something that Sally had until that moment believed to be merely a figure of speech.

Then she stood up and unbuttoned her blouse.

She showed Sally a number of welts, burn-marks, knife-slashes, and a particularly nasty-looking seam that ran from her navel down to her pubic bone. Strangely enough, that was the only scar that had a reasonable explanation: it was the result of the emergency Caesarean that had brought Sylvester Reed into the world.

'I wouldn't push,' the nun crowed with fierce pride. 'I didn't want to give birth to any child of sin.'

'But surely,' Sally protested, 'you couldn't blame the baby; it wasn't his fault that he came to be there!'

'Satan's spawn! I was deceived! The devil used me! He dressed as a man of God and made me lie with him.'

'You mean it was the priest? He raped you, and you got pregnant. Oh my God!'

The story emerged piece by piece. The priest had impregnated her without the nun understanding what was happening. When her condition became obvious and his part in it discovered, he was sent posthaste out to the Missions. The church had paid her a small allowance and found her a position in a Catholic school in England, which had allowed her to rear her son in obscurity for fifteen years. The allowance had stopped when the priest died in Africa. Sr Annunciata had returned to Ireland and as soon as Sylvester finished school, she had re-entered the convent.

Sally splashed water on her face and dried it on the roller towel. She was shivering, but whether it was from the aftermath of what she had just heard or a sign that she was about to be hit by full-blown 'flu, she couldn't tell.

She would get a taxi over to her mother's, she decided, and surrender herself to a couple of days of maternal cosseting, then she would go home and make a transcript of today's tape. There was a lot of juicy meat in it, and at least one utterance that Sally had found puzzling at the time. She would go back over the tape carefully to check what exactly Sr Annunciata had said at the end of the story.

To Sally it had sounded like: *I should have kept the other one.*

Goosebumps

Vera Meaney paid off the taxi driver and trundled her suitcase along the path to the bottom of the steps leading to her hall door. Although there was a vicious March wind blowing, she refused to put her coat on over her lemon sundress. What was the point of a tan if you couldn't show it off? No doubt there were faces at windows all along this side of the square, wondering who the glamorous woman that had alighted from the taxi was. Conscious of these unknown eyes on her, Vera tried to carry the case up the steps in a ladylike fashion. But it was no good; she needed both hands to lift it and as soon as it was off the ground, she tottered on her high heels and almost fell against the railings.

I'll have to get a man to help me, thought Vera, not without a certain amount of anticipatory pleasure.

The house whose door was beside hers at the top of the steps was home to a large number of lads. But they were students in Kevin Street and they played rock music very loud. She often heard them using bad language too.

On the whole, she thought not.

The younger boy from downstairs on the other hand, was polite and a little old-fashioned in his formality. He was at Trinity studying Business, she knew, and when he finished, he was going to take over the family firm. She couldn't remember what exactly they did, but the business was obviously doing very well if the parents could afford to send three children to university at the same time.

Vera left her case and walked around to the side of the house. If Cornelius was at home, he would help her carry it upstairs and then she would invite him in for a cup of tea and a chat. She could tell him about her Caribbean holiday, maybe without mentioning that it was in Club Med, as that might shock him. Certainly, if he knew some of the things she had got up to while she was there, he would be shocked!

Now that she had landed back into her old life in Dublin, Vera herself was more than a little shocked when she thought about her week of sun and sex.

What François did to her and got her to do to him when they were alone was one thing, but when he had proposed doing the same things with the Italian GO and her roommate, that was another. Of course, Vera had agreed, but if she was being honest, she would have to admit that she hadn't enjoyed that experiment. It had come as a relief when her roommate had freaked out and screamed at Benito that he was a pervert and threatened to castrate him with her nail file. How she and François had laughed about that afterwards!

Now that she was adept in the art of love, Vera had no intention of lying alone in her king-size bed any more. Before leaving Club Med, her GO mentor had given her a crash course in seduction, which she intended to put into practice. Up to this, marriage had been the be-all and end-all of her ambition; thanks to François, she knew now that it was merely a passport to respectability. It was far easier to have affairs once you were safely married, he had assured her; the best thing she could do would be to find a rich, dull husband as soon as possible and then begin to enjoy herself.

Before she rang the doorbell, Vera went back for her coat. She was beginning to get goosebumps on her arms. And besides, it wouldn't do to scare the boy off with her cleavage at this early stage.

The summons

Darina's new look was high maintenance. As soon as she got back from her holiday, she had to dye her hair with peroxide to cover the dark roots that had begun to show, and every morning, she had to treat it with gel to keep the spikes in place. Her tanned skin demanded oils and unctions to keep it smooth, and the stubble on her legs had to be kept at bay with the waxing kit Anne Marie had given her for Christmas.

To her own surprise, Darina took to the new beauty régime without difficulty. Reaction to her transformation had been so positive that she felt she had to make the effort. Her family had been completely bowled over; even Cornelius had said that she looked smashing, like a film star or that singer from Eurythmics.

Darina herself was ambivalent about her new status as a blonde babe. Turning heads in the street was a novelty, but she suspected that she would get tired of it in time, and she was not altogether happy about the preferential treatment she got now that she was a pretty young thing. In the library, she no longer had trouble finding a place to sit; there was always a guy who was willing to time-share with her or even give up his table entirely. It was unfair that the world was kinder to beautiful people, but she was prepared to go along with it at least until the exams were over.

Having worked so hard at French since Christmas, Darina had no real fears on that score, but she had a lot of catching up to do for Russian. Fortunately, her encounter with Don at Club Med had reawakened her interest in the subject and she found that she enjoyed reading not only the prescribed texts, but other works by Dostoevsky, Pushkin and Tolstoy that were not on the course. She sought out the Russian language assistants and went drinking with them in O'Neill's in the evening; after a couple of pints of Guinness, she found that her fluency improved dramatically and she could hold her own no matter how heavy the ideological discussions became.

One evening about two weeks after her return from holidays, Darina arrived home somewhat the worse for wear following a particularly intense session with Grigorii Borisovich and Olga Petrovna to find that Anne Marie was waiting for her in the basement flat. It was past ten o'clock and Cornelius, who had been keeping Anne Marie company in the kitchen, jumped up as soon as his sister came in.

'Well, there's Darina for you now,' he said, 'so if you don't mind, Anne Marie, I'm rather tired and I'll be off to bed.'

Darina briefly thought that it was unlike her brother to make it so blatantly obvious that he had merely stayed with their cousin out of politeness, especially when only a few months earlier he had been dogging her every step, but she didn't dwell on it.

'How are things, coz?' she said as Cornelius darted out of the room. Her head was beginning to ache so she filled a pint glass from the tap and took it to the table.

'All right,' said Anne Marie, looking down at the table.

No they're not, thought Darina, but she didn't say anything. She had been up to see her cousin briefly the day after she got back from her holiday, and had learnt that Victor was no longer on the scene. She knew that there was little or nothing she could do to make the pain go away.

'Darina, I've got something I need to talk to you about,' began Anne Marie. She lifted up her head, and Darina noticed for the first time how pasty-faced and unwell she looked. 'I need your advice.'

Darina sat up. This was something new. Anne Marie, whose life had always been as perfectly ordered as her room, needed advice from the most disreputable of her cousins? Well, that was a turn-up for the books!

'Sure, coz. I'd be glad to help. What would you—'

At that moment, they were interrupted by a thunderous knocking on the door. Anne Marie gave a cry and Darina jumped in her seat.

'Who on earth could that be?' she muttered as she pushed her chair back and stood up.

'Don't . . . I mean . . . be careful, Darina,' said Anne Marie anxiously. 'It's very late for someone to be calling. Maybe I should get Cornelius, just in case.'

When she opened the door, Darina was still smiling at the thought of her younger brother playing the hero.

The smile faded at once.

'What do you two want?' she said roughly, closing the door over so that Anne Marie wouldn't be able to see.

'Darina. She there?'

It was Deco and Nailer, dressed as usual like extras from a gangster movie.

Darina grinned. 'Maybe she is, and maybe she isn't. Why don't you take off the shades and have a look.'

'Fuck it, it *is* her!' Deco hit Nailer with the back of his fist, as though Nailer had disagreed with him on the identity of the woman at the door. 'She's after disguising herself!'

'So what's the meaning of this, boys? It's not a social call, is it?'

'Ye're wanted. We've come to get you.'

'Who wants me? The Man himself?'

'I told you before, the likes of you don't get near

The Man. Now cut the crap and let's get moving.'

'Sorry boys, but I've got company tonight. Besides, I'm not in the humour for going out.'

Deco gave an evil grin. 'Hear that, Nailer? She's not in the humour. She might need a bit of persuasion. I know you've been dying for a go at her; maybe tonight's your lucky night.'

'Aw, shut up!' Darina went back inside the flat. 'I'll be out in five minutes,' she said and slammed the door in their faces.

'Darina, is everything OK?' Anne Marie appeared in the corridor looking scared. 'I tried to call Cornelius, but he doesn't seem to be in his room. Who were those men? They didn't sound very nice.'

'No, they're not. But there's nothing to worry about. Listen, I'm afraid I'm going to have to go out for a while. Would you mind if we left our discussion until tomorrow evening?'

Anne Marie looked crestfallen. 'All right, if that's what suits you. Oh wait – I can't tomorrow; I'm babysitting for Roz.'

'What time?'

'Half past six. I was going to cycle over straight from work.'

'Tell you what: I'll pick you up from your office and we can go somewhere for a coffee – how about that?'

'Yes, yes, that would be fine. Are you sure you don't mind?'

'Not a bit. I've got to rush now, sorry.'

Darina disappeared for a minute or so. When she came back into the kitchen, she was doing up the buttons on her coat. Anne Marie was sitting at the table again, looking forlorn. Another time, Darina might have felt bad about deserting someone who clearly needed to talk, but now she was impatient for her cousin to be gone.

'Em . . . you came down the back stairs, did you?'

'No. I thought it might be rude, so I came round and knocked.'

'Well, I'd rather you went back up that way, if it's OK. And in future, please do use the stairs. You're family, for heaven's sake.'

With a last look in her bag to check that she had everything she needed, Darina nodded to her cousin and left.

'I hope you brought the limo this time,' she said as she followed Deco out to the road. 'I'm getting a bit tired of lying on the floor of your bloody van. I've got all this new clobber too and I don't want it destroyed.'

Neither man answered, but when the back of the Ford Transit was opened and she was stepping in, she felt that Nailer took malicious pleasure in shoving her hard before he slammed the doors.

Darina had been expecting this summons. It was quite some time since she had had any dealings with Cleo, and she knew that her failure to contact Deco for more supplies would not have gone unnoticed. Crouched in the back of the van, she rooted in her bag for some chewing gum – she needed something to help her concentrate her mind on the forthcoming interview. She located her packet of Wrigley's, opened it, folded a piece of gum in half and popped it in her mouth.

The drill with Deco and Nailer was the same as on the other occasion: before she got out of the van, they made her put on a blindfold and led her across an echoing hallway, into a lift and up an unguessable number of floors to the top of a building.

By surreptitiously checking her watch, Darina found that the trip had taken only twenty minutes this time, so she figured that the building they were in was a lot closer to Rathmines and Portobello than the two men wanted her to know. How long would it be before Cleo trusted her enough to allow her to come openly?

No sooner had the question posed itself than Darina had the answer in a flash: never. In a moment of illumination, she realised that if ever she made this journey without a blindfold, it would mean only one thing: that she would not be returning to tell of it. She shivered.

'Cold?' Deco grinned nastily as he stepped out of the lift with Darina. 'Or is it nerves?'

'Don't be ridiculous,' said Darina. She blew a bubble, then popped it loudly.

Outside the lift, Deco took her bag and went through the contents carefully. 'What's this?' he said, taking out a box of Black Magic chocolates. 'You got the munchies or something?'

'It's a present, and it's not for you.'

'She doesn't like chocolate.'

'Who says it's chocolate?'

Deco scowled and made to open the box, but a voice behind him made him stop.

'That will do. I'll call when I need you.'

It was Cleo. Behind her, the door into the study was open, allowing Darina to catch sight of a blazing coal fire. Tonight, Cleo was wearing a long black dress slashed to the thigh on one side. Her eyelids were painted dark mauve and her lips plum. The wig was still black, but it was longer and the hair was smoother.

Mata Hari? thought Darina. Then: I wonder who she's expecting after me.

It occurred to her that she might be wrong; maybe Cleo was no more than the handmaiden of some sinister and immensely powerful drugs baron called simply The Man.

Having dismissed Deco, Cleo ushered Darina into the study and closed the door. She sat in the big chair behind the desk.

'You have been away? I see that you're tanned. And you've changed your hairstyle.'

'Yeah,' said Darina, heading for the fire. 'I treated myself to a holiday in the Caribbean.'

Cleo smiled, but the smile went nowhere near her eyes. 'Well, it appears to have done you a world of good. One thing, however: I don't like it when my people leave the country without letting me know beforehand.'

Darina stretched out her hands to the flames, which turned out to be gas. She would have to tread very carefully for the rest of the evening. She daren't play the innocent because Cleo would sniff her out at once, but at the same time she didn't want to antagonise her by being bolshie and difficult. She turned and reached for her bag.

'I brought you back a present.'

'Oh?'

'Yeah.' Uninvited, Darina sat on the big leather couch and fumbled in her bag for the Black Magic box. She took it out and handed it to Cleo.

'Chocolates?'

'Special chocolates. Try one.'

Cleo opened the box and chose a sweet. She unwrapped it slowly.

'A bit of Bob Marley.'

Cleo raised an eyebrow.

'Cannabis resin. Very good, believe me. I could put you in touch with the supplier if you like.'

Cleo sat back. 'So are you telling me that this jaunt of yours was by way of being a business trip?' Her voice was silken, but Darina was not fooled.

'Of course not! I thought I deserved a break. I've been studying very hard, you know, and thanks to our little deal, I was able to afford a sun holiday. While I was there, I just happened to sample some of the local weed and thought it was worth investigating. What's the problem?'

She glared at Cleo as though she meant it. Had she overdone the indignation? She hoped not.

'Well, thank you for thinking of us,' said Cleo in a placatory voice. 'But next time, make sure you inform us before you go away. We like to know what's going on.'

Darina shrugged. 'Yeah, all right. If that's what you want.' She wondered again if she had got it all wrong and there really was a Man or if Cleo was merely using the royal 'we'.

'You did well last time. Ten thousand, and so quickly too. What's your secret? Have the student grants gone up again?'

Darina opened her eyes wide. 'Students? I don't sell to students!'

'Who then?' Cleo leaned forward.

'South County Dublin dinkies. That's where the money is.'

'What's a dinky?'

'Dual Income, No Kids Yet.'

Cleo smiled, and this time Darina knew it was for real. The atmosphere became less charged. She dared to relax her buttocks, which had been clenched in anxiety ever since she had come into the room.

'I see. So you'll be ready to start selling again soon?'

Darina's face clouded. 'Next term's going to be difficult. It's very short, and I've a lot of catching up to do before the exams.' She made herself look thoughtful. 'I might be able to do something in college coming up to Trinity Ball, but it would be mostly tabs and poppers and stuff like that. Small beer, really.'

Cleo said nothing. She opened a drawer in the desk and took out something made of black plastic. 'This is for you,' she said, sliding it across the desk. 'Keep it with you always and whenever it bleeps, you ring Deco at once. Got that?'

Darina got up and took the bleeper. 'Yeah, I got that.'

'You may take your chocolates back too.'

'You don't like them?'

'I like money.'

Cleo summoned Deco on her cellphone and stood up. 'And another thing,' she said as Darina reached the door. 'In future, please do not chew gum in my presence. I find it most unladylike.'

Anne Marie's dilemma

Anne Marie was glad when Darina showed up at the *Femme* office a little before five o'clock. It was a beautiful spring day, the first in a long time, and she wanted to be out of doors. As soon as Darina appeared, she grabbed her coat.

'Bye, Dave, Roz,' she shouted. 'See you in the morning.'

Darina, however, appeared to be in no hurry to leave.

'Wow, nice office,' she said, looking round her in awe. 'Loads of room and those plants – God, it's like a jungle.' She went over to the giant trough in the centre of the room and stood in front of it. She seemed lost in admiration of the greenery for a few seconds, then Dave called on Anne Marie to introduce him, and when she had finished talking on the phone, Roz came over to say hello as well. To Anne Marie's consternation, it looked as though they were going to be caught up in useless chit-chat.

At last, she managed to hustle her cousin down the corridor to the lift. Darina was still wearing the thoughtful frown she had assumed when she was standing in front of the oasis.

'Who else is in this building?' she asked Anne Marie once they were in the lift. 'It's huge, but there doesn't seem to be a lot of life in it.'

'Well, there's an insurance company on the ground floor, and there used to be a literary agency on the first floor, but they left. I think those offices are still vacant. On the second—'

'Who's on the top floor?' Darina interrupted her.

'The top? Nobody. At least, not a business firm. It's a penthouse as far as I know. There's a lift to it round the back, by the canal. The woman who owns the building might use it occasionally, but she doesn't live there.'

'A woman owns this place?' For some reason, this information seemed to interest Darina. She looked up eagerly at Anne Marie. 'What's her name?'

'Isolde Phoenix. The building is called after her. She's a bit of a recluse, apparently.'

Anne Marie was about to add that she had seen the mystery woman once, just before Christmas, and that she could have sworn Isolde was wearing her stolen ring. But she thought better of it. Darina was sure to ridicule the idea, and Anne Marie didn't want to start off their meeting feeling at a disadvantage.

Darina remained lost in thought while they crossed the foyer and went outside. Anne Marie's bike was locked to a stand at the side of the building; while she was unlocking it, Darina walked a bit further and stood looking up and down the canal.

'OK, I'm ready,' called Anne Marie.

Darina slowly turned her back on the canal and rejoined her cousin.

'Let's go to the Old Schoolhouse,' said Anne Marie. 'It's not so far and it's grand and quiet. You can get something to eat and coffee, or a drink if you prefer.'

'No drink, thanks. I'd only want a smoke.'

'Have you given up?' asked Anne Marie in surprise.

'You mean you hadn't noticed? I stopped when I was away. It didn't seem so hard then, but since coming home I think I must have chewed my way through enough gum to coat the soles of every shoe in Dublin. It gets harder, not easier as the days go by.'

'Well, I think it's great that you're trying,' said Anne Marie. 'Gerald's given up too; he told me when he rang the other week.'

'Yeah, and have you seen the size of him? He was all skin and bone before, but now he's beginning to look positively porcine. I don't want to put on weight the way he did; that's why I'm on the gum instead.'

Some twenty minutes later, the cousins were sitting in

a nook in the converted schoolhouse with toasted sandwiches and coffees in front of them.

Darina stirred sugar into her espresso and licked the spoon. Then she put it down and turned to Anne Marie. 'So, what was it you wanted to ask my advice about?'

Anne Marie had been waiting for her cue. 'It's this,' she said, taking an envelope out of her satchel and putting it on the table. 'Read it.'

The handwriting on the outside of the envelope was big and bold. Darina opened it. The letter inside was brief. She scanned it quickly and put it down.

'He wants you to visit him in prison? Why?'

'Well, I spoke to his solicitor like he asked in the letter, and it seems his family have moved to Cork, and besides, he's giving his wife a divorce, so they probably won't be visiting him at all. His eldest son is in Moscow and there's no one else he wants to see.'

'But why you?'

Anne Marie coloured. 'That's the point: I don't know. We got on well when I worked for him, but I don't know why he'd want me to see him in . . . his new circumstances.'

'Do you want to see him?'

'I . . . I don't know.' Anne Marie put her head in her hands. 'I was very fond of him, and he was always good to me, but . . . to go inside a prison? I'm not sure I could do that.'

'Well, if that's all that's bothering you, then I don't know why you wanted my advice,' said Darina brusquely. 'It's simple: you either like the guy enough to overcome your squeamishness or you don't. And if you really want to know what I think, then here it is: I think you should visit him. Not just because your man asked, but because it's an opportunity being presented to you. Why refuse what life throws your way? You know, I nearly didn't go on that Club Med holiday, and you wouldn't believe how glad I am not to have missed out on that.' Darina's face lit up and she smiled to herself for a moment. Then she became brisk again. 'If it was me, I'd go, flying,' she said. 'But if you're nervous and want some moral support, we could go together. Provided he agrees, of course.'

'Would you?' Anne Marie brightened at once. 'Oh, that would be brilliant. Thank you, thank you so much!'

'No problem,' said Darina. She stood up. 'Thanks for the sandwiches and coffee. I'd better be getting back to the library now. *The Inspector General* is waiting for me!'

Leaving Anne Marie nonplussed, she swung her bag onto her shoulder and left.

Before she went into the library for another night of studying, Darina made a phone call.

'Can I see you? . . . Tonight . . . Yes, it's urgent . . . I'm in Trinity . . . No way! This is your big break, so you can come to me . . . Top floor of the Arts Block, outside the Russian Department . . . Half nine's fine. OK, see you then. Bye.'

Mountjoy Hotel

It was Anne Marie's first sortie north of the Liffey since the end of her affair with Victor and she was expecting to be hit by painful memories at every turn.

But nothing of the sort happened. When she used to cycle to Glasnevin, Anne Marie had taken the scenic route: along Clonliffe Road then right onto a leafy section of the Drumcondra Road, past the Archbishop's Palace and onto Botanic Avenue, at the end of which Victor had his lodgings. Darina, who wanted to explore the north inner city, led the way on foot from Parnell Street to Summerhill and along the North Circular Road.

It was a different world. Just a stone's throw from the leafy middle-class streets were cheerless blocks of flats in a concrete wasteland, where it was hard to imagine anything of beauty coming to flower.

'I wonder how many of the people round here end up in Mountjoy,' said Darina as they passed a gang of small boys jumping up and down on the bonnet of a burnt-out car on Rutland Street. 'I'll bet the percentage is a lot higher than from Rathgar. 'Course, the biggest criminals never end up behind bars, do they? Except for this guy we're going to see, and him only because he put himself there. Why do you think that was?'

'I don't know,' said Anne Marie shortly. She didn't like the area they were in and kept throwing nervous glances about her as she clasped her bag tightly to her chest.

'The papers haven't given him any credit for it anyhow,' Darina went on. 'I went and read up on the trial the other day. They seem to be saying that it was all a publicity stunt or something. They even questioned his motives for paying back money to the people he stole from. But you know him better than the reporters who wrote the articles; do you believe he's sincere?'

'I really couldn't say.' Anne Marie moved closer to Darina as a group of gum-chewing adolescent girls taking up the entire pavement came towards them. 'Why don't you ask him yourself?'

'OK, I will. Hey, cool it, will you? You nearly knocked me into the gutter.'

The girls divided into two waves.

'Got any smokes?' asked the one nearest to Darina as she drew level with her.

'Sorry, I've given up.'

Her friend gazed up at Anne Marie in amazement as she passed. 'Jaysus, d'yeh see the size of yer one?'

'She goes on and on, like a bleedin' tapeworm,' her companion agreed as they linked arms behind the cousins once more.

It was a shock to Anne Marie to see how the months in prison had changed Desmond Dunne. She knew of course that he would no longer be wearing his tailored suits, but beyond that, she had expected him to look the same as always. However, the man who was led from the prison into the visiting room was nothing like the urbane Mr Dunne who used to wear bespoke tailored suits and drive a top-of-the-range Mercedes.

This man looked like a convict. His steel-grey hair was cropped close to his skull. He was dressed in a plain white T-shirt and prison-issue jeans.

For Anne Marie, it was like seeing him naked. The T-shirt stretched tightly across his torso, and his arms bulged out from the sleeves like a prizefighter's. His eyes, which she had never really noticed before, were a clear, piercing blue.

Strangely, he seemed perfectly at ease in his new surroundings.

'Thank you for coming,' he said gravely when they came to stand opposite him at the long table.

'You're welcome,' mumbled Anne Marie, hardly daring to look at him.

'You must be Darina,' Dunne went on. He indicated the glass barrier that rose several feet above the table. 'The screws will only get twitchy if I try to shake hands over that. But it's nice to meet you anyway.'

'The pleasure is mine,' said Darina with a grin that showed she meant it.

They all sat down, Dunne on one side of the barrier and the cousins on the other. If Anne Marie couldn't think of a thing to say, Darina was in her element. Her eyes gleamed, she lowered her voice and leant forward. 'What's it like, being in the nick?' she asked. 'Are you surrounded by murderers and rapists and all sorts of unsavoury characters?'

Dunne grinned back. 'Well, there's a fella in the next cell who did his wife in with a monkey wrench. And a nicer man you couldn't hope to meet.'

Horrified, Anne Marie looked up sharply.

Dunne winked at her. 'I'm only having you on, Anne Marie,' he said. 'Actually, they're mostly a bunch of sad saps.' He grew serious. 'Everything against them from the start. Some of them as young as ten when they get onto drugs. Heroin: devil's dandruff, they call it. After that, it's in and out of Mountjoy Hotel; revolving door, you know the story.'

'What about you?' asked Darina boldly. 'You had it all and you threw it away. Why?'

Dunne stretched and clasped his hands at the back of his head. His eyes flicked to Anne Marie, then turned back to Darina. 'Let's just say that I saw the error of my ways. I wanted to pay my debt to society, clean the slate, start over. Restitution and all that malarkey.'

'Bullshit!'

Anne Marie gave a little gasp. She couldn't help feeling shy in Dunne's presence. He wasn't her boss any more, but somehow, she found him even more daunting now than when she had been working for him.

Apparently Darina had no such problem. Anne Marie could see that her cousin and Dunne had hit it off at once. She wasn't exactly jealous, but she did wish that she could be a little more like Darina, just for the next half-hour. It would be terrible if Dunne thought she was ashamed to talk to him, when really it was just that she was feeling awkward and out of place. She risked a quick look at him. He seemed delighted with the turn the conversation was taking.

'Here's what I think,' Darina smiled. 'I think you're giving them all the two fingers. Confound the bastards by doing exactly what they least expect. You've got a master plan, haven't you? As soon as you're out of here, you'll climb back up to where you were before and this time, they won't be able to touch you!'

'You know what? You're good,' said Dunne. He leant forward now and brought his elbows to rest on the counter. 'And apart from the master plan bit, you're not far off the mark. I don't know about afterwards; one of the good things about being in here is that you learn to take each day as it comes. For me, that's enough at the moment.'

'I hear you've got a son in Moscow,' said Darina, changing the subject. 'I'm going there this summer. I could say hello from you if you like.'

Dunne dropped his hands onto the counter. He

appeared stunned. 'You're going to Moscow? Is that the truth?'

'Yeah, 'course it is. I study Russian, don't I? I have to go for two months to practise my spoken language.'

'Well, well,' said Dunne with a slow smile. 'How would you like to have your ticket paid and a bit of pocket money on top?'

Darina's expression said that she would like that very much.

Dunne told her about John's work with street children and how he had been racking his brains to think of a way to support it without his son finding out.

'What does he look like?' Darina brazenly asked. 'Is he anything like you?'

Anne Marie, the silent observer, saw a flicker of pain cross her former boss's face. 'I wouldn't know about that,' he said with a forced smile. 'Tell you what: why don't you tell me when you get back.'

'He's amazing! I'd love to work for someone like that,' said Darina as they left the prison. She looked accusingly at her cousin. 'Except for when he asked you directly about your new job, you were very quiet in there – what was the matter?'

'I . . . it felt awkward,' said Anne Marie. 'He was different. More . . . physical or something, I don't know. I just didn't know how to relate to him.'

Darina smiled. 'Yeah, talk about animal magnetism. He's in fine shape for a man his age.' She licked her lips. 'God, if his son is anything like him, I'm going to have a whale of a time in Moscow!'

Back in his cell, Dunne climbed onto his bunk and lay in his favourite thinking position, flat on his back with his hands behind his head. He was trying to remember a conversation he had had a long time ago with a priest in Ballyfermot. He was sixteen or seventeen at the time and the priest, who was not very much older, had taken him aside after a youth club function for a talk.

You have great talents, the priest had told him, and you'll go far whatever you choose to do.

In spite of his inborn mistrust of the clergy, Dunne had been impressed enough by the young priest's sincerity, and something else – which he now decided was goodness – to hold his tongue and listen.

The priest had talked a lot about choices and paths and decisions and how important it was to take the right one.

'And how are you supposed to know that you are doing the right thing?' Dunne had challenged him.

'Things start to happen,' the priest had said. 'Strange things; wonderful things. They may seem like miracles, but they're not. They happen because you are living your life as you are meant to. You are at one with God's plan.'

Was that what was happening now? Forgetting the God bit, was he living the way he was meant to?

Dunne thought back over his adult life. There had been low points, such as losing John, and the fatal accident in which a mother and daughter had died, but on the whole, he would have said that it was a life most people would have envied. A good life.

Yet it was only now, after he had turned his back on it entirely, that the magic was beginning to happen. Anne Marie's cousin was going to see John! He hardly dared to formulate his hope, but undefined, shapeless, it was very much there: reconciliation with his beloved son.

Resurrection

By Easter, Anne Marie was ready for rebirth. The cherry trees were in blossom, birds were twittering joyously in the ivy outside her bedroom window and the April sunshine had worked its way into her heart.

She woke one Saturday morning knowing that she was cured.

It was cause for celebration. Dressing quickly, Anne Marie left the house in Belvedere Square and headed along the Rathmines Road to the Café Firenze.

Oscar smiled broadly as he came over with the coffee menu.

'Anne Marie – what a surprise! How good of you to come back and visit us. How is your new home?'

Anne Marie looked puzzled, then abashed. Of course! The last time she had been in here, she had been looking for a new place to live. That was ages ago, back in the new year. Oscar clearly assumed that she had moved miles away.

'Em . . . it's very nice,' she said, then added guiltily: 'Actually, I didn't move far . . . just upstairs in fact, but I've been very busy these past few months.'

'Yes, you look as though you've been working very hard. What can I get you? Cappuccino?'

'Please. And an almond croissant.'

Oscar went away and came back a couple of minutes later with her order.

Watching him deftly set out knife, paper napkin, plate and cup on the table, Anne Marie was sorry that she had not been to the café in so long. It was here that she had first felt that Dublin might in time come to feel like home, and that was because Oscar had smiled at her. She remembered how his smile had warmed her, and how the simple fact of being recognised and made to feel welcome had brightened up her day.

'How about you, Oscar?' she asked now, nodding to him to pull out the chair opposite her. 'What have you been up to these past few months?'

Oscar glanced round to make sure the café was empty, then sat down on the edge of the seat. 'Nothing much. Work, mostly. My parents are here at the moment.'

'Oh, that is nice! Are they on holiday?'

'Not exactly. Uncle Giorgio needed a break, so he's gone back to Italy; my parents have come to cover for him in the restaurant.'

'Oh!' exclaimed Anne Marie. 'My uncle and grand-mother are in Italy at the moment. They're doing the sights in Florence and Siena, then they're heading into the mountains.'

'Really? That's where my family is from: the mountains of Tuscany. It's a beautiful region.'

'But you grew up in England, right?'

'Sadly, yes.' Oscar spread his hands. 'First Bradford, then London. But England has never felt like home.'

'That is hard,' said Anne Marie. 'I can sympathise because I'm in a somewhat similar situation.'

She told Oscar about her parents' decision to work in Africa, and how she was going to have to go home soon to move her stuff to her grandmother's house. 'I'm lucky, I suppose,' she conceded. 'I mean, Nano's wonderful, and I love going to Riverwood. But it's her home, not mine. I know it's silly, but I feel sort of . . . rootless. I like to know where I belong.'

'Ah, Anne Marie, we are alike, you and I!'

The café door opened and Oscar jumped up. Leaning over the table, he continued in an undertone:

'Lost souls wandering in the wilderness – where will we finally come to rest?'

Anne Marie laughed and took out her purse. He waved it away. 'No, this is on the house. To say "welcome back" and "please come again."'

Sisterly love

By Eastertime, Darina had been back at lectures for a week. Cornelius was going down to Limerick for the Bank Holiday weekend, and Darina debated with herself whether she should accompany him. She would get lots of work done if she stayed in Dublin, but there were several good reasons for going home. If Barbara was around, there would be great food and a family get-together. Darina knew she could do with a few good meals; she had already shed the pounds she had put on at Club Med and was beginning to look like a stick insect again.

But it was more than that. Since the shock announcement at Christmas that her parents were, if not splitting up, then moving apart, Darina found that she needed to go back to Limerick more often. Of course she was dying to see Gerald, but that wasn't it. She hated to admit it to herself, but the changes in the Davenport household had made her feel insecure, and any excuse for a family gathering was good enough to send her rushing home.

She had just made up her mind to go, when a summons from her tutor after class on the Thursday morning made her change her mind.

Wondering what she had done wrong now, Darina

followed the tutor into her office and sat down apprehensively. To her enormous surprise, instead of finding fault with her, the tutor began to congratulate her on her work and say that she had never before seen such a dramatic improvement in a student's performance over such a short period of time.

'I knew you had it in you,' the tutor went on, 'which is why I felt entirely justified in taking you to task last term. But it gives me far more pleasure to be able to tell you that your latest essay was outstanding, and that if you keep up the good work, you should have no trouble getting a First in the exams.'

Reeling from this unexpected praise, Darina went straight to the library. A First in the exams! My God, she thought. That is worth working for!

When she got home late that evening, Darina went to tell Cornelius that she wouldn't be going down to Limerick with him. In the light of what her tutor had said, she couldn't afford to slacken off now.

The light was on in her brother's room, but when she knocked, there was no answer. She tried the door and found it locked. Had he fallen asleep over his books? She checked the living room again, then stood outside his room and called his name a few times, to no effect.

Darina went into the kitchen to make herself a cup of tea. There was almost certainly no need to worry. Cornelius was not Gerald and it was impossible to imagine him having any kind of an accident. All the same, she was relieved when she turned around a couple of minutes later to find him coming into the kitchen.

'Corny – Con – There you are! I was looking for you

everywhere. Did you doze off in your room or something?'

Cornelius looked fearful, then shifty. 'Ah, em . . . I just went out for a minute and . . . yeah, that was it.'

Darina's kettle had just boiled, so she missed most of what he said. After he had declined the offer of a cup of tea, she told him that she was staying up in Dublin to do some more studying for the exams and asked him to give her love to the folks when he went down the following day. A few minutes later, Darina heard her brother in the shower.

Having the flat to herself for the weekend, Darina decided not to go into college to study. The weather was so fine that she brought her books and a rug out to the back garden and read lying on the grass in the dappled shade of an apple tree. She couldn't be bothered cooking for herself, but when the hunger pangs became unbearable, she made herself a sandwich with whatever leftovers she could find and brought it outside to eat.

Halfway through the afternoon, Darina was distracted from her studies by the feeling that she was being observed. She twisted onto her side and squinted towards the house. As soon as her eyes had readjusted their focus, she saw that there was indeed someone watching her from a window on the second floor. She recognised her landlord by his long white robe and dark hair. When Brandon saw that she was aware of him, he raised his hand in greeting. Darina wasn't sure how to respond. If she nodded and turned back to her books, he might think she was rude, but they could hardly carry on a conversation in sign language. At least the rent was paid, so whatever was on his mind, it wasn't money they owed him. Brandon solved the communication problem by making it clear that he wished to join Darina in the garden. She replied to his request with a nod and set about tidying up her books and papers in order to make room for him on the rug.

'I trust that you are enjoying the favourable weather,' said Brandon when he reached her spot under the apple tree. Darina, who had been unsuccessfully racking her brains to figure out what had caused her landlord to seek her out, replied with a formulaic observation on the spell of good weather.

'Em . . . why don't you sit down?' she said, tucking her legs under her and gesturing to the large vacant space on the rug.

'Thank you, that is most kind,' said the landlord, lowering himself until his heels and buttocks were in contact with each other and the rug, whereupon he slid into the lotus position and settled his robe over his crossed legs.

Darina waited.

'It's about your brother,' began Brandon.

'Oh?' Darina sat up.

'He's been going upstairs a lot recently.'

Darina looked at her landlord in puzzlement. 'Upstairs? But Gerald is down in Limerick.'

'I mean your other brother.'

'Cornelius?'

'Cornelius. Yes.'

Darina wondered what Brandon was getting at. It was true that Cornelius had been going upstairs a lot of late – but so what?

'He's very fond of Anne Marie,' she said. 'He probably misses her from the basement.'

Brandon shook his head.

Darina's smile faded. 'No? Not Anne Marie?' She stared at the landlord as the meaning of his silence sunk in. 'Then . . . you mean . . . Vera? Vera Meaney? Vera and . . . Oh my God!'

Brandon said nothing but she could see from his face that she was on the right track.

'Your brother is an innocent. As is your father. It is an admirable quality; however, like children, such people need to be protected.'

To Darina's surprise, her landlord then stood up, joined his palms together and bowed to her, turned and left.

Darina swallowed. Her mind flew from the strangeness of the conversation to its implications for her brother and her family. She had witnessed the change in Vera brought about by the hunk François and she could well believe that with her new-found confidence, Vera was ready to add to her list of conquests. Then an even worse thought occurred to her. What if Vera didn't intend simply to play with her brother? What if her intentions were of another nature altogether?

'She'll hook him,' Darina said to herself in an undertone. 'She'll pretend to be pregnant or something. Before I know it, I could have Vera Meaney for a sister-in-law! God, I'm going to have to act fast!'

She sprang up from the rug. To act – yes, but how? Vera was away for the weekend, so she couldn't march up the stairs and confront her. Besides, that would do no good. Technically, her brother was an adult and wouldn't take kindly to his sister's interference. No, there had to be another way.

By the time Darina reached the door of the basement flat, she knew exactly what she was going to do.

*

The photos were still in the stiffened envelope that Terri, the photographer, had sold them in. She took them out and spread them over the kitchen table. The one with François feeling Vera from behind: definitely. And another one – the one with the banner saying *Winner: Wet T-shirt Contest* in the background? Yes, that should do it.

Pity I haven't got copies, thought Darina. But if this works, nobody else need see any of them. It meant she wouldn't be able to take the pictures down to Limerick to gloat over with Gerald, but that was a small price to pay for saving her younger brother from the clutches of Vera Meaney.

She took a blank sheet of paper and a felt pen and wrote in big block letters: *LEAVE MY BROTHER ALONE*. She didn't bother to sign it before she slipped it into the envelope with the photos she had selected.

There was no need for stealth as both Anne Marie and Vera were away for the Easter weekend. Darina slipped the envelope under Vera's door, then stood up and shook her fist at the room. 'I've said it before, and I say it again,' she whispered fiercely. 'Nobody messes with my brother and gets away with it!'

Flashbacks

Roz was glad that Anne Marie was back to her usual self. While the affair with Victor was going on she had watched over her with anxiety, knowing that the higher you fly, the harder you fall. When Anne Marie did come crashing down to earth, she remained in the background ready to offer consolation, meals, a sympathetic ear or whatever it was that her young assistant might need.

But Anne Marie had seemed to want to do it on her own. She had lost herself in work and kept her grief private. Roz had let her get on with it.

And in the end, Anne Marie had come back, just as Roz had hoped she would. After her tearful reunion with the twins and Ellie, she had sat in the kitchen and unburdened herself.

Roz had listened and refrained from coming out with the usual platitudes. Instead, she had squeezed Anne Marie's hand and, to distract her from her troubles, told her about how she had come to marry Stephen.

When they met, Roz said, she had been working for *Vogue* in London and going out with a very bright, handsome, rich and ambitious advertising executive. Lowering her voice, she had added that Mark was great in bed; in fact, he was great at everything he did.

At this point, Roz could see that she had caught Anne Marie's attention. It was easy to guess what she was thinking: why on earth had Roz settled for someone like Stephen when she could have had Mark?

'I wasn't even in love with Stephen at the time,' Roz admitted. 'I'd known him for ages and thought he was terribly nice, but I didn't fancy him at all.'

'So what happened?'

'Mark asked me to marry him.'

'And you said no?'

'I said I'd think about it. I was only twenty-three, after all. But I did think, a lot. I thought about the qualities I would look for in the man I wanted to be father to my children. The man I would have to spend the rest of my life with. Suddenly, Mark didn't seem like such a great catch.'

'So you dropped him?'

'First I asked Stephen if he was available and if he thought he would be a good husband and father. He said yes to both. So I married him instead, had Ellie and came back to Ireland.'

'What happened to Mark?'

'He became even richer and more successful. He's onto his third wife, I believe, and he's not even forty.'

Anne Marie had thought about the story and then smiled. She was glad that things had worked out for Roz, she said, and she hoped she'd be as lucky some day.

Roz smiled to herself, thinking how it hadn't been quite that simple. She had taken a long time to make up her mind, and several times she had almost succumbed to the attractions of life with Mark. She hadn't told Anne Marie about the sleepless nights of indecision; the two-timing while she dithered, and the fact that after she had in the end followed her head rather than her heart, she had spent more than a year wondering if she had made the right choice.

The main thing was that her story seemed to have done some good. Roz had followed it up by saying that Anne Marie was lucky to have experienced passion on such a grand scale once in her life. It might happen again, of course, but it was more likely that from now on, Anne Marie's affairs of the heart would be slower to kindle, their flames would burn less brightly but more steadily and it would take a lot to put them out.

A couple of weeks had gone by since their little tête-à-tête, and it gave Roz pleasure to see how much Anne Marie had improved. She was beginning to put on the weight she had lost; her face had filled back out to its natural roundness and her hair, which she was letting grow, was sleek and shiny once more. At work, she was no longer driven; she did what she had to do and was ready to help out where necessary, but she didn't hang around the office after hours trying to fill the emptiness inside her with unnecessary tasks.

Mind you, thought Roz, it wasn't a bad thing that Anne Marie's workaholic period came when it did: it meant that they were ahead of themselves for once in the planning of the magazine. There were lots of feature articles to choose from for June and July, and at a push, they might even have enough to get them through until September, when Roz hoped to be back at work. She was going to promote Anne Marie to Deputy Editor, a change in title that was merely an excuse to raise her salary, and the magazine would take on a temporary Editorial Assistant for the period of Roz's maternity leave.

The babies were due in June; although she was not looking forward to the increase in her family size, Roz couldn't wait for the pregnancy to be over. For the last few weeks she had been feeling permanently tired and out of sorts. Every part of her, from her neck to her ankles, was swollen to unnatural proportions and her breasts were excruciatingly sore.

After the birth, Roz was planning to take the bare three months' leave and then escape back to the haven of normality that was *Femme*. Of course, she would need to find a really good nanny; preferably someone in her fifties whose children were reared but still had the energy to look after five of someone else's. Roz didn't care how much it cost. If I found the right person, I'd willingly hand over my pay packet just to get out of that madhouse, she thought guiltily.

Five children! She, Roz McDaid, who had intended remaining childless at least until her fortieth birthday, was at thirty-six about to be mother to a horde, a tribe, a swarming, pullulating mass of five human beings. She shuddered at the thought of the dark subconscious promptings that must have led her to this pass.

Lately, her dreams had involved disturbing flash-backs to the accident in which she had lost her mother and her sister. She saw the car come speeding at them from the right; she saw her mother change gear and move off from the lights; she felt the warning scream that wouldn't leave her throat and then, just before the impact, she woke up, trembling and tearful. Was it the pregnancy that made her more susceptible to these nightmares? Or was it the fact that the monster responsible for the deaths was so much in the news lately?

At least now he was safely behind bars where he belonged. Roz only wished that they would throw away the key and let him rot forever.

The Vanishing

'But how did she get all her stuff out without anybody seeing? That's what I don't understand.'

Shoulders slumped, Cornelius stood in the doorway of the kitchen and brought up once again the topic that had kept the house in Belvedere Square humming for almost a week.

'Look, Corny,' said Darina, leaning back on her chair, 'I told you – the house was empty on the Bank Holiday Monday. I took a day off and went to Bray. What does it matter anyway? She's gone and that's that.'

'Yes, but it's so strange. Brandon is quite upset, you know. He doesn't like it when tenants up and leave without any notice like that.'

'Especially when they strip the room of everything that's not nailed down. She even took the lightbulbs, for crying out loud!'

Cornelius scowled. 'We don't know that. I think Brandon was exaggerating.' His face darkened. 'You don't think . . . she wasn't trying to get away from him, was she? Maybe he was pestering her.'

Darina gave a snort of laughter. 'Brandon and Vera Meaney? Oh please! Besides,' she went on brutally, 'the idea of Vera being pestered by a man is untenable. She'd love every second of it. The way she is, at her age any attention is welcome attention.'

'What do you mean? Twenty-five is not old.'

'Hah! The last time she saw twenty-five was on the bus to Lucan! Thirty-five, more like. Anyway,' goaded Darina, 'what are you so concerned about Vera Meaney for? Anyone would think you fancied her, the way you've been going on about her all week. Personally, I say it's good riddance.'

Cornelius flushed, but said nothing.

'And not to turn the tables or anything, but shouldn't you be studying?' his sister continued. 'The exams are in a few weeks and you don't seem to have done much work this term. Forgive me if I'm wrong, but I believe you need to knuckle down to some revision. Dad and Gerald are counting on you to do well, remember. Just forget about Vera and think about the things that matter, like getting a good degree.'

Cornelius looked sharply at his sister. She was smiling innocently at him, a highlighter pen in her mouth and her books open on the kitchen table. He glanced down at the pages of notes she had made in the last few hours and nodded. 'Yes, I have to admit you have a point,' he agreed. 'I have been a little lackadaisical this term. Thank you for your advice. I will act on it immediately.'

Darina waited until Cornelius had left the kitchen then let out a sigh of exasperation. She hadn't expected her action against Vera to be so successful. Her intention had been merely to make Vera drop her brother like a hot brick and turn her attentions elsewhere. Cornelius would have moped a bit and then got over it. But Vera had done a vanishing act instead, and the mystery of her sudden departure was preoccupying Cornelius more than was good for him. Darina hoped that her little peptalk would do the trick, the arguments of duty and familial expectations being sure-fire winners where her brother was concerned.

In other respects, Vera's departure was most welcome and timely. Brandon had declared that he wasn't taking another tenant to replace her; the house had exactly the right energy balance, he'd told Anne Marie, and he wanted to keep it that way. The latest news was that Vera's room was going to be fitted out as a guest suite for visiting friends, which made Darina think immediately of Donald Garvey. The Professor had written to say that he was making arrangements – for better or for worse – to come to Ireland in order to research his roots at the end of the semester. It would suit Darina perfectly to have him staying in the house without being dependent on her. She made a mental note to go up and discuss it with Brandon at the weekend.

Later that morning Darina went up the back stairs to the hall to check the post. There was nothing for her or Cornelius, but Anne Marie had got a postcard from Italy. Darina turned it over and read it.

Dear Anne Marie,

Having a splendid time. Weather, food and company glorious. Met some wonderful Italian brothers at the airport – they've invited us to stay with them! This week for visiting churches (yawn!), next week to the mountains and our new friends. One brother has a restaurant in Dublin – must try it together some day.

XXX Nano

P.S. Love to Darina and Cornelius – Dan promises he'll start his cards tomorrow!

They're well home by now, thought Darina. I must give Dad a ring tonight, find out how the holiday with his old dear went.

Knave of Hearts

Nano pushed the firing button of her joystick and blasted the tarantula that was about to drop onto her heroine's neck. She swivelled the joystick and her heroine sprang to the left, crouching behind a rock while she reloaded. Nano checked her statistics: not much left on her lifeline, and no medicines in the inventory. If she could get Vanda out of the cave and into the woods, there were certain to be some healing herbs that would restore her to full vigour and allow her to proceed to her next test, the Castle of Doom.

Slowly, Nano brought Vanda out of hiding. She gave her the last flare from the knapsack and sent her running lightly towards the exit of the cave. A rustling on the ground warned that more tarantulas were in hot pursuit; Vanda turned and shrivelled them to nothing with her fire blaster. Good, thought Nano, you're in the clear. On to the woods and some healing. She made Vanda put her weapon back in her pack so that her hands would be free to help her climb over the boulders that blocked the way out.

The boulders were slippery; twice Vanda fell back to the floor of the cave, using up a little more of her lifeline each time. On the third attempt, Nano sent her by a different route, closer to the walls. Here, the boulders were dry and Vanda made good progress. She had just reached the top and was preparing to jump down the other side when from the walls of the cave came a tremendous roar and a horde of dark creatures issued from hidden passages on either side. Too late, Nano remembered the evil War Hogs, troll-like creatures with pig snouts and boar tusks that guarded the entrance. Before she had time to react, their spears and arrows had pierced Vanda and she fell for the last time to the floor of the cave, where she lay unmoving as her lifeline drained away.

Game over.

The screen flashed its invitation to play again. Nano

417

stretched and consulted the clock by the computer. It was only 2:37. She wouldn't sleep if she went back to bed now, so she might as well continue. But did she want to? The game, lent to her by the Griffiths' eldest boy, Michael, was exciting enough, but Nano wasn't really in the mood. She debated with herself for a few more moments, then reluctantly took the CD out and shut down her computer.

The trouble was, she couldn't settle to anything since her return from Italy. She would start something, then become distracted and find that she was daydreaming about the holiday.

It had been magical from start to finish. Before they left, Daniel had forgiven her for what she perceived as her neglect of him down the years, and she had embraced him and called him her dearly beloved son. While they were away, they talked and talked, sharing their dreams, memories, joys and sorrows. After visiting the sights together, they went into the mountains.

And then!

Then the impossible, the unthinkable, the unimaginable had happened.

Nano pushed back her chair and stood up. She left the little study, formerly Clarissa's dressing room, and returned to the bedroom. She turned on the main light. By the window was a long, oval cheval mirror. Nano went and stood before it.

'Look at you,' she said severely to her reflection. 'What are you like? Sixty-six years of age and a grandmother. Far too old for this sort of lark!'

She pulled her hair back off her face. It looked exactly as she remembered it: all sharp angles and shadows. Nothing to admire, apart perhaps from her eyes, which were still a clear blue-grey, and her teeth, which were all her own. 'But then, you never were a beauty,' she said, 'and I can't understand how it happened first time round either.'

She glanced up at the wall to the studio portrait of her husband taken in the year before his death. 'Why you went for me and not one of my pretty sisters, I'll never know,' she said softly, before quickly looking away.

It wouldn't do to dwell for long on memories of James Davenport, killed at twenty-nine by a bolt of lightning. Her laughing, dancing-eyed James, with his soft northern *ayes* and *surelys*; not only a university student and a Protestant by birth but a committed atheist!

She would have followed him to the ends of the earth and beyond. When he proposed that they flit to London and get married in a registry office, she thought her seventeen-year-old heart would burst with happiness. He had taught her everything, laughing at how quickly her unschooled mind soaked up knowledge and new ideas. She too had embraced atheism and thumbed her nose at the old, Catholic God whose lowering countenance had cast a shadow over her girlhood.

Seven years of bliss. Then God had taken His revenge.

Killing her husband had required split-second timing; any sooner, and James would have braked before the branch was sundered from the tree; any later and he would have pedalled fast to be beyond reach when it fell.

An Act of God, the parish priest had called it. She remembered his pug face as he offered empty words of consolation and urged acceptance of divine will. He had disapproved of what he perceived to be a mixed marriage, and made sure that the children were brought up in the one true faith. The lightning bolt confirmed his view that God too had been displeased by the union.

Outwardly, Nano had capitulated. She went to Mass on Sundays for the first year of her widowhood, baptised the baby and sent the older children to the local national school. But inside, she remained true to her husband's teachings. It took the death of Jamie two years later to break her. Although she would never afterwards enter a church to worship, when her firstborn's body was laid out on the kitchen table, she had bowed her head and acknowledged the awful majesty of God.

The years had done nothing to alter Nano's secret but implacable hatred of the Creator who had taken from her what she most cherished in this or any other life. But strangely, as soon as Nano had in her heart acknowledged Him, her life had begun to change for the better. It appeared that God was not interested in her adoration, only in her recognition of His existence. As soon as that was achieved, He changed his tune and began to shower her with good things.

On the day after Jamie was buried, Clarissa promoted Nano from housekeeper to companion and brought her to live at Riverwood. There, she watched her remaining children grow up surrounded by all that was best in man and nature. In time, her children married, had children of their own. Clarissa died peacefully in her sleep, and Nano, who had been born in a hovel on a bog, suddenly became the owner of a magnificent five-hundred acre estate that boasted an ancient wood, two rivers and some of the best agricultural land in the country.

And to crown it all, at sixty-six, when her thoughts should be turned towards the grave, God went and played His trump card.

The Knave of Hearts.

Nano smiled wryly at her reflection. What a grotesque joke, to have her fall in love in the autumn of her days.

She glanced up again at James. 'He's nothing like you,' she said apologetically. 'I don't understand it, because you were and still are my ideal of a man. He's had a lot of sadness in his life too. He lost his fiancée just before they were due to be married and he has remained single ever since. He's quiet and deep and very gentle – how do you think it's possible that we should have hit it off? He loves books, and nature, so I suppose we do have that in common, but is it enough? Are we not just two pathetic, lonely old creatures clutching at a last chance of happiness?'

To Nano, it seemed that James's laughing eyes said it didn't matter. She knew that he would have urged her to go for it; it had been one of his dictums that you should never say no to what life throws in your path.

Giorgio was the only man since James to have made an impression on her. Not that she had lacked suitors in the past; after Clarissa's death, her status as a landowner had brought a procession of men of all ages and stations in life to her door, intent on offering manly protection to the poor defenceless widow and her fatherless children. She had sent every one of them away with a flea in his ear.

Giorgio was different. He had seemed as surprised by the obvious attraction between them as she was. A tall, somewhat stooped man, with snow-white hair and large, melancholy brown eyes, he looked more like a musician or an artist than a restaurateur. Of course, he was past retiring age; the only reason he had not retired so far, he told Nano, was that he had no reason not to work.

At the end of their holiday, she had invited her new *amore* and his extended family to Riverwood for a week, as a way of repaying the hospitality shown to her and Daniel in Tuscany.

That would be in the summer. Meanwhile, Nano was sure that there were several good reasons why she needed to go to Dublin for a weekend.

The Big 'C'

In the middle of May there was a heatwave. Temperatures leapt without warning to twenty-five degrees and the country threw itself into summer with such reckless abandon that after the first weekend, half the population was suffering from heat stroke or sunburn.

Roz, who had spent much of the Bank Holiday weekend lying on the tiles in the bathroom with a damp towel over her face, was not sorry to be back at work. At least there was air-conditioning in the office. She was wondering if she could turn it on full blast without protests from the others when Anne Marie bounced in looking the picture of health and vitality.

'Morning all! Isn't the weather glorious?' she chirruped. 'I spent the whole weekend in shorts – it was wonderful to feel the sun on my skin after the long winter.'

Roz ignored her.

Dave tut-tutted. 'What about the bye-law you were infringing.'

'Bye-law? What are you talking about?'

'There has to be a height restriction on the amount of leg that can be bared like that.'

Anne Marie stuck out her tongue at him. 'I was in the back garden. Nobody saw me.' She came over to the other side of Roz's desk and sat down. Roz nodded to her and went on proofreading the article she'd been working on.

'You OK?' said Anne Marie when Roz finally laid down her pencil. 'You look tired.'

Roz stretched and began to massage her lower back with her fists.

'I'm shattered. I'd a terrible weekend – the heat nearly killed me, it was so sudden. The system didn't have time to get used to it.' She patted her belly. 'This pair didn't like it either – they never stopped kicking me. And my boobs are really sore, especially the left one. Every time I turned in the bed, the pain woke me up.' She looked down at her chest and frowned. 'It's still rock-hard. Funny, I don't remember that from my other pregnancies. My boobs got bigger all right, but they were never this painful.'

Anne Marie clucked sympathetically. 'You poor thing! There's us saying how wonderful the hot weather is, but of course it's not for you, is it? Have you seen your doctor recently? Maybe she could, you know, check them for you.'

Roz's head jerked up. She glared at Anne Marie from across the desk. 'What for? Are you an expert on pregnancy all of a sudden? For your information, it's perfectly normal to have sore breasts in the third trimester. There's absolutely nothing wrong with them!' Pushing her chair back, she levered herself to her feet and reached for her bag. 'Excuse me, I have to go to the toilet,' she said haughtily as she swept past Anne Marie.

Dave came over and sat on the edge of Anne Marie's desk. 'Well, well – what was all that about? Have you had a quarrel? I do love a good catfight. Tell me, what did you say to her? I'll write it down and use it myself.'

'It's not funny,' said Anne Marie. She told him what had happened.

'Hormones,' said Dave. 'And the heat. Just wait and see, she'll be all apologies when she comes back in.'

Dave was right. When Roz returned after ten minutes, she looked refreshed and contrite.

'Sorry,' she said to Anne Marie. 'I've been narky all weekend. Lack of sleep, I suppose. And this trip to London – I wish I didn't have to go. London's so unbearable when it's hot.'

'Can't you postpone it?'

'No, the courier brought my ticket first thing. Besides, I've been trying for ages to set up an interview with this woman for our first *She Made It!* feature about successful Irishwomen abroad. Can you believe that seven o'clock tomorrow morning was the only window in this one's schedule?'

'What time is your flight?'

'Just after two. I'll go home first and have a quiet coffee with Stephen. He'll drive me to the airport before picking the kids up from school.'

'When are you coming back?'

'I've left it open, but probably tomorrow evening. I thought I'd do a bit of shopping while I'm over. I threw out all the twins' baby stuff years ago and I've nothing bought for these poor chisellers yet.'

Just before she left the office, Roz, having checked the coast was clear, picked up her phone and dialled a number in London.

'Jane, it's Roz.'

'Roz! How are you? How's the bump?'

'Large and lively. Can't wait to be rid of it. Listen, this is just a quickie. I'm coming over to do an interview and I was wondering: are you still seeing that Harley Street breast man you mentioned last time we talked?'

'Yes, I am. Oh Roz, I know I shouldn't, but he's very hard to give up. You're not going to lecture me again about married men, are you?'

'What? Oh, no! No, it's just . . . would you be able to arrange for me to see him at short notice – like tomorrow, around mid-morning?'

'You want an appointment? Why, what's wrong?'

'Nothing – there's nothing wrong! It's just me being paranoid. I'm a bit sore and I'd rather not see my own doctor because she wants me on maternity leave already. I'm trying to stay on at *Femme* until the last minute so that I'll have more time at home after the twins are born. I thought if I could pop in to see your man, he could do a quick check, maybe prescribe some pain-killers or something.'

'Tomorrow morning? I'm sure I can arrange something. I'll ring you back in half an hour to let you know. Do I get to see you too?'

'Of course! How about lunch? You could take me to that little Greek place you're always on about.'

'I'd love to. Call by the gallery when Alastair has finished with you.'

'Perfect. You have my mobile number to ring me back on, don't you?'

'Sure do! Talk to you in a while. Bye.'

Roz hung up, checked her watch, then conscientiously put a pound coin in a box on her desk marked *private calls.*

Dr Alastair Goodman was a handsome man in his fifties. On the principle that opposites attract, Roz could see why her scatty artist friend Jane was attracted to him. He was well-groomed and reassuringly successful-looking; just the sort of person you would want to entrust with your life. He was also Englishly formal and reserved; he greeted Roz with distant politeness and made no reference to their mutual friend as he examined her.

It was impossible for Roz to tell from his manner whether she should feel concerned when he began to talk about doing a needle biopsy, followed by a mammogram and an ultrasound. Jane had said he was very thorough and left nothing to chance – surely that was all it was? Roz sighed. There goes my afternoon shopping, she thought as his secretary handed her a list of appointments.

The mammogram was excruciating. The machine operator, a mere slip of a girl, manipulated Roz's breasts into place on the machine as though they weren't attached to a body. 'Just hold still now,' she said.

Roz screamed as the metal clamped on to her flesh.

The operator looked at her askance. 'I have to do this, you know,' she said sullenly.

It took a stream of foul language from Roz to make her marginally release the pressure.

After a hasty lunch with her friend, Roz spent the rest of the afternoon dressing and undressing, answering questions, filling in forms. By the time she got back to her hotel, she was exhausted and tearful. It took a long, hot bath to wash away the memory of the humiliations her body had suffered during the day.

After her soak, Roz was too tired to eat, but before she could think about resting, she had to ring Stephen to let him know that she wouldn't be home. There was no way she could face the return journey that night. Fortunately, she'd warned him she might be away an extra day, telling him she might have to conduct the interview in two sessions if she didn't get what she wanted in one.

'So it was a tough one?' he commiserated.

'Oh yes, a real bitch,' said Roz, deliberately ambiguous. She had disliked the woman intensely and curtailed the interview as a result. She was going to scratch her altogether; there were plenty more names on the list of succesful Irish *entrepreneuses*.

'The children will miss you,' said Stephen. 'I told them you might be back in time to tuck them in.'

'Oh dear, tell them I'm sorry. Kiss them for me and say I'll bring them back something nice from London tomorrow.'

'I hope you're resting – you sound tired. I know you've haven't seen Jane for a while, but it probably isn't a good idea to go out painting the town red tonight.'

Roz didn't tell him that she'd already seen Jane at lunchtime. Instead, she made her voice sound light and teasing. 'Oh, I don't know. A meal, a show and a couple of clubs are probably just what I need right now. I could introduce the twins to techno music. I'm sure they'd go for it!'

'Hmm. Well, take care. Ring me from Heathrow so I can be at the airport in time to pick you up.'

As soon as Stephen had rung off, Roz crawled under the duvet and fell into an obliterating sleep.

Next morning, she woke feeling more refreshed than she'd done in weeks. Amazing what just one day away from the kids can do, she thought guiltily. Not to mention the luxury of having a big bed all to myself for a change.

As she was shown into Dr Goodman's waiting room for the results of her tests, Roz planned how best to apologise to Jane's boyfriend for needlessly imposing on him. Should she make a joke of it? Or take her cue from him and remain polite but distant. That was probably best; he wasn't the jokey type.

She'd got no further than that when the secretary told her the doctor would see her now. Roz was pleased. In and out before ten o'clock. With a bit of luck she'd get to Heathrow by twelve and be home when the children got back from school. She knocked on the solid mahogany door and waited for Dr Goodman's, 'Come in,' before she turned the handle. She hadn't quite entered the room when the telephone on the desk rang. Dr Goodman reached for it immediately. As he did so, Roz imagined that she saw a look of relief cross his features. Motioning for her to sit, he listened to his caller and took notes.

Roz looked around. It was a man's room, furnished in dark wood and leather. Glass-fronted bookcases housed rows of weighty medical volumes. A portrait in oils of a stern-faced ancestor hung on the wall directly behind the desk. On the desk itself was a studio portrait of a pretty young woman with long blonde hair in graduate's cap and gown. His daughter?

Probably. She looked like the sort of daughter an eminent surgeon would have. Clever and beautiful.

The only other splash of colour and life in the room came from a child's painting stuck to the back of the examination-room door with Blue-Tack. It was a stick figure with wild grey hair and jug ears. Underneath, in crooked lettering, was written: *Poppa. By Jack.*

Roz was disappointed. A second marriage? And Jane? Although she knew that his personal life had no bearing on his talents as a surgeon, Roz couldn't help the fact that this indication of multiple relationships lowered Dr Goodman in her esteem.

The one-sided telephone call was coming to an end. Dr Goodman drew a line beneath his scribbled notes and tore the page off his pad. As he rang off, Roz decided to take the lead in the conversational gambits. She would comment on the child's painting – say what a good likeness it was. Would he smile, she wondered.

Dr Goodman was too quick for her. He put down the phone and pulled his chair into the desk. He formed a tent with his fingers and looked at her gravely.

'You have breast cancer,' he said quietly. 'It is spreading rapidly. It needs urgent treatment.'

Roz sat still.

Behind her, she heard the tick of a clock. Oh yes, the grandfather clock, just inside the door. She'd noticed it on her first visit. It was preparing to strike; she could hear the wheels and cogs gearing up. There was a whirr and a click and then finally: boing, boing, boing. Ten times.

'I'm sorry,' the doctor said. 'You're very young for this sort of cancer.'

Roz jerked as one of the twins kicked her beneath the ribs.

'You will need surgery. I . . . er . . . spoke to a colleague in Dublin. If you want, I could make the arrangements.'

'For surgery?'

Dr Goodman nodded.

'What exactly . . .?

'Radical bi-lateral mastectomy.'

'Bilateral?'

'The cancer has already spread to the right breast. It is too late to save it.'

Roz opened her mouth, but no words came out.

When she left the doctor's room, Jane was waiting. She looked worried. 'Roz, Alastair rang me this morning and asked me to meet you here. Does that mean . . .? Is it . . .? What did he say?'

Roz looked mutely at her friend.

Jane paled. 'Oh my God! It's yes, isn't it? You do have cancer.' Letting out a wail, she ran to Roz and put her arms around her.

They clung to each other, Jane's tears trickling through Roz's hair down on to the back of her neck.

Anne Marie in charge

Anne Marie was not expecting bad news when her cellphone went off shortly after seven o'clock on that Thursday evening. She had the notion that bad news always came in the middle of the night, making you sick with dread as you fumbled in the dark for the light switch before you picked up the phone.

It took her several seconds to recognise Stephen's voice, and a lot longer to take on board that Roz was in hospital in London undergoing an emergency Caesarean after going into labour at her friend's flat.

Once she had got the message however, Stephen didn't need to say any more. Grabbing her bag, she threw a few overnight things into it and raced downstairs to the hall and her bike. She arrived at the house on the South Circular Road just as Stephen's taxi to the airport was pulling up.

'Go on,' she shouted as he came out the door, travel bag in hand and a jacket over his arm. 'I'll look after everything, don't worry.'

'My . . . my mother's not well. Leopardstown too far . . . c-c-c-can't come,' Stephen stammered, clutching her sleeve as she lifted the bike up the porch steps.

'It's OK, honestly. Roz needs you and I'll be glad to hold the fort. It's a bit early – thirty-three weeks, isn't it? There are no complications, I hope?'

Stephen stared at her, his eyes huge behind the ugly brown frames of his glasses. Then without answering, he turned away and with bowed head scuttled down the p   o the waiting taxi.

The children were at the table in the kitchen, unfinished plates of fish fingers, beans and rice in front of them. They turned as one when Anne Marie came into the kitchen.

'Is our mammy going to die?' Jake asked, his fierce expression belied by the quaver in his voice.

'No, of course she's not,' said Anne Marie, horrified. 'Where did you get such an idea?'

'Ellie said it. She heard Daddy talking on the phone.'

Anne Marie came over to the table, pulled out a

chair and sat down between the twins and their older sister. 'Listen to me, all of you. Your mammy went into hospital to have the babies. I know she wasn't expecting them to be born so soon, or else she wouldn't have gone away to London, but there's no need to worry. They'll look after her there just as well as here.' She smiled and put her arms around Jake and Ellie. 'Isn't it funny to think that your little sisters or brothers will be able to have British passports?'

'Daddy's afraid,' burst out Ruth. 'He sat down on the stairs and started to cry. Ellie saw him.' She put her thumb in her mouth and began to suck.

Anne Marie turned to the older child. 'It was the shock,' she said gently. 'He wanted to be there at the birth, and bring you in to see the new babies, with flowers and chocolates for your mammy.'

'Daddies don't cry,' Jake said belligerently. 'Our daddy never cried before.'

'Well, my daddy does. He even cries if there's a sad film on TV!' she told him.

Ruth took her thumb out. 'Ellie said that Mammy's going to die because she's ten and that's the age Mammy was when *her* mammy died.'

Anne Marie gulped. 'Ellie! You can't believe things like that. Roz is having babies – she's not going to die!'

Ellie stood up. She said nothing but Anne Marie could see her body quivering. She stayed poised for a second, a wild look in her eye, then ran from the room.

'What's cancer?' asked Jake.

It was a long time before the children settled for the night. Anne Marie hadn't been able to disguise her shock at hearing the 'C' word; though she had reassured the twins that there was nothing for them to be concerned about, they seemed to put more store by Ellie's stark prediction.

Eventually, she succeeded in bathing Ruth and Jake and getting them ready for bed. They clung to her after their bedtime story, so she remained in the room until they drifted off to sleep together in the bottom bunk.

Ellie wasn't asleep, but she wouldn't answer when Anne Marie went into her room to say good night. After smoothing the covers and kissing the top of the unresponsive head, Anne Marie reluctantly left her alone, reflecting that she far preferred the twins' tantrums and high jinks to their sister's unfathomable silences.

Stephen rang at midnight. The babies were fine, but Roz had gone directly from one theatre to another and she was at this minute undergoing surgery for breast cancer.

So it was true! Anne Marie was speechless while Stephen told her in a flat voice how he had arrived just in time to hold Roz's hand before she was wheeled away. She heard that at Roz's request the operation was being performed by a Dr Goodman, who was a friend of her friend Jane. It was too early to tell if the cancer had spread to other parts of the body, but it was clear that Roz would need chemotherapy and radiotherapy when she came home. Stephen was staying in the hospital for the next few days, but as soon as Roz was stable he would come back to be with the children.

There was little comfort to be offered on either side. Anne Marie didn't hide from Stephen that she was worried about Ellie, who had got it into her head that history was destined to repeat itself. Stephen said he would ring again and speak to her before school.

At three o'clock, Jake woke up screaming. When she went in to comfort him, Anne Marie found that he had wet the bed. She bathed the twins again, changed them and took them into the spare room with her, where they dropped off again quickly, snuggled up against her. Anne Marie herself lay awake until morning, wondering how she was going to cope.

Aftercare

Roz was woken from the anaesthetic by the need to throw up. In her half-drugged state, she couldn't understand why she wasn't able to brace herself on her arms, but could only turn her head to the side to puke. Someone held a kidney bowl and spoke to her in words that refused to form coherent messages in her brain. In between bouts of vomiting, she tried to sink back into the peaceful dark, but then the voice became sharp and on her cheeks she felt the sting of slaps.

As soon as the nausea had passed, she was wheeled by unseen hands along corridors bright with artificial light, into a lift and out again, down another corridor and into a room with light blue curtains on rails. A man with a beard and glasses bent over her, his eyes full of loving concern. She sort of recognised him, but she couldn't quite remember where she had seen him before.

Her eyes closed once more, but she wasn't allowed to rest. Without warning, she was manhandled on to a bed, the pain as she was seized under the arms making her cry out. Someone covered her with a sheet and blanket, tucking the edges under the mattress the way she liked it.

Mammy!

Roz smiled. She was beginning to remember now. She was in hospital to have her adenoids taken out. Mammy was there, waiting for her to wake up, and soon Ellie would come in with Daddy and eat the grapes they'd brought for Roz.

It's nice that I know what's going to happen, thought Roz, even though it hasn't happened yet.

Before the strangeness of this could penetrate her addled brain, Roz heard her name called. She opened her eyes reluctantly and saw the man with the beard again.

'Roz? Are you awake?' He put his hand on her forehead and smoothed her hair. 'It's me, love. I'm here, right beside you.'

'Stephen?' She wasn't sure where the name came from, but it belonged to him, of that she was certain. He was in the hospital with her, but why? Because there was bad news, that's why.

It was all coming back to her now. They had been on their way home from a Christmas party. Something awful had happened. She was in hospital and when she woke up they were going to tell her about the awful thing.

'Oh!' Roz tried to sit up, but the pain in her upper body was too great. 'Where are they?' she said agitatedly. 'I can't see them. Oh no! They're dead, aren't they?'

Stephen took her hand and squeezed it. 'No, darling, of course not! The twins are fine! A girl and a boy, just like last time. They'll be brought in as soon as you're ready to see them.'

Twins.

Roz felt the tears build up behind her closed eyelids. She was back in the present. She knew where she was and why.

If only she could have stayed in the past a little longer; it was so nice being back in the time before the first awful thing.

Rescue Remedy

Lying awake between the twins, Anne Marie made a mental list of things she had to do in the next twenty-four hours.

Seven o'clock: get up, start breakfast. Ten past seven: call kids, help twins dress for school. All downstairs by half seven. Half an hour for breakfast and brushing teeth, so they should be ready at eight o'clock. That left half an hour for playtime or a video – under the circumstances, surely no one would object – while she put on a wash and cleared up.

Half eight: bring kids to neighbours for lift to school, cycle on to *Femme*. Dash home at lunchtime to pick up a few changes of clothes, back to work for an hour or two, then here for the rest of the evening.

Dinner? Ask Ellie what they all like to eat; this not the time for innovation. After dinner, out to the park for a couple of hours? Make them good and tired so they'll sleep. Once they're safely in bed, hang out washing, clean up kitchen and, hopefully, relax in front of the TV for an hour or so before hitting the sack.

That was the plan. What happened was this: Jake

woke Anne Marie at a quarter to eight by sitting up abruptly and shouting that he needed to pee – now! They stumbled together to the bathroom, where he almost managed to make it to the bowl. Anne Marie cleaned him up and wiped the bathroom floor, then rushed into Ellie's room to open the curtains and tell her to hurry or she'd be late for school. Ellie didn't respond. When Anne Marie pulled back the duvet, she found the eldest girl lying awake and fully clothed in the same clothes she had on yesterday. She refused to make eye-contact, turning her head to the wall when Anne Marie pleaded with her to say something.

Throughout breakfast, Ruth whinged that if Ellie wasn't going to school, then she wasn't, and Jake played savage games with his food.

Stephen rang to say that the surgeon had been in to talk to him and seemed happy with the way the operation had gone. Anne Marie explained about Ellie. Stephen spoke to her and she reluctantly got ready for school.

They were on their way out the door when Jake asked what was in his lunchbox.

Back inside while Anne Marie made lunches for the three of them. At nine o'clock, she decided that she would have to drive them to school. No car keys; Stephen must have taken them with him by mistake. They took a taxi. Anne Marie kept it running while she accompanied the children to their classrooms and spoke with the school principal. She finally got to the *Femme* office after ten, to the great relief of Dave, who was finding it impossible to cover for two absent colleagues.

At half past eleven, the school principal rang. Ruth had thrown up in class and Jake was running amok in the yard. Eleanor was catatonic and refused to communicate with anyone.

Anne Marie took another taxi to the school and brought the children home. She cleaned Ruth and changed her, then sat the children in front of the television. What video would they like to watch? Nobody answered, so Anne Marie riffled through the collection. *Toy Story*? No, too loud and frenetic. Something animated from Disney would be best, she thought, something sweet and fluffy. Her eye fell on a cover showing a tiny fawn surrounded by darling woodland creatures. Of course: *Bambi*!

She covered the children with a duvet for comfort, switched on the TV and left them to it. Now to clear up the kitchen and tackle that load of washing, which had doubled in size since this morning.

Before she even got to the kitchen, however, Anne Marie skidded in a pool of water and almost lost her footing. The light under the stairs was on. She opened the door with a sinking feeling, knowing already what she would find. Last evening, she had taken a ready meal out of the freezer for herself. She had turned off the light, or so she thought. But the light was still on, so she must have flipped the switch underneath – the one for the freezer.

Anne Marie spent the next fifteen minutes emptying the freezer and mopping up the spillage. She had just finished squeezing out the floor-cloth when there was a loud wail from the living room. What now? Surely Jake wasn't up to his usual tricks already? He'd seemed so subdued when she'd brought him home from school.

They were huddled in a tight little knot, with Ellie in the centre. Their eyes, wide and fearful, were fixed on the screen.

Anne Marie turned around just in time to see Bambi's mother get shot.

By mid-afternoon, Anne Marie was ready to lie down on the floor and give up. After her appalling blunder with the video, she felt that she had lost all credibility with the children. Ellie had locked herself into her bedroom and refused to open the door; Jake was rude and violent, and Ruth clung to her like a limpet. Nothing helped, not even the Rescue Remedy that she found in a press in the kitchen and administered first to herself and then to the twins.

Her phone rang. Oh no, thought Anne Marie, prising her arm free from Ruth's clutches to reach the pocket with her cellphone in it. What would she tell Stephen? He couldn't leave Roz now, but if he heard how bad things were at home, he would be torn both ways. She could try to put a brave voice on things, but if he spoke to the children, he would know at once that she just was not coping.

It wasn't Stephen.

After she had finished her short conversation, Anne Marie put away the phone and with a whoop, picked Ruth up and swung her in the air. 'We're saved – Nano's coming!' she cried.

The child, startled out of her misery by the sudden change in Anne Marie, giggled along with her.

By the time the taxi pulled up and Nano got out, the twins had forgotten their troubles entirely. Anne Marie's grandmother had long taken on mythical proportions for them; the stories they heard about her on the nights that Anne Marie babysat were the stuff of legend. Jake in particular couldn't wait to meet the granny who could tame wild horses and knew how to shoot a gun. He stood beside Ruth, nose pressed against the window of the front room, determined to be the first to announce her arrival.

Although she had never met the twins before, Nano seemed instinctively to know what to do when they bounded towards her. After the greetings were over, she turned to Jake, squatting on her hunkers so that she was at his eye-level.

'I know you must be very excited about having a new baby brother,' she said to him, 'and since you didn't have time to get him a present yet, I brought along a catalogue for you to choose something out of.'

'A gun! No, wait – Polar Mission Action Man! Or a WWF wrestler. The Undertaker, he's really cool!'

'I don't think you'll find anything like that in there,' smiled Nano, handing him a Mothercare catalogue. 'He is only a teensy baby, after all. But in a few years, he'll be terribly happy to have a big brother who'll show him all those great things.'

Ruth's lower lip began to tremble. 'What about me? Why can't I choose a present too,' she began.

'Oh, you'll get your turn, don't worry,' said Nano. 'But first I have something important to ask you.' She lowered her voice conspiratorially. 'Do you think you could take me upstairs and introduce me to your sister? I hear she's not well and I'd like to see if I can help. And then maybe you could show me your room. I'll bet you've got some really nice books and toys.'

It was like magic. Or Mary Poppins, thought Anne Marie when, after a very few minutes upstairs, Nano reappeared holding Ellie by the hand.

'Eleanor and I are going for a little walk,' she

announced, 'and while we're gone, Ruth and Jake are going to help you, Anne Marie. Jake knows how to work the dishwasher, he told me, so he'll look after the washing up, and Ruth would like to help with the laundry. We're going to be baking this afternoon too, so they should find some aprons or change into old clothes to get ready.'

If it was magic, it was very ordinary magic, Anne Marie decided later. Involving the children in simple but worthwhile tasks seemed to be important. It hadn't occurred to her that they could help with the jobs she had been putting off until after they were in bed, nor that they could have a say in decisions such as what to do with the food from the freezer. She marvelled at how easy Nano made it all seem.

'Sausages?' her grandmother asked, holding up a bag with a kilo of semi-frozen pork sausages in it.

'Give away,' the children replied. 'There are too many, and anyway, we're fed up with sausages.'

'OK. This goes on the Giving Away pile. What about this mince? Does anyone like spaghetti bolognese?'

'Yes!'

'Good. That's what we'll have this evening then, and the rest we'll cook and put back in the freezer for Shepherd's Pie next week. Now what's next? Ooh, look – soggy fish fingers! Who'd like them?'

'Ugh! Bin, bin!' they shouted.

Everyone helped with the cooking. Ellie chopped, Ruth stirred, and Jake did whatever Nano asked him, hovering behind her like an eager pageboy waiting on a queen.

By evening, they had prepared enough meals to last the weekend, and filled the oven with scones, muffins and apple tart. The children were proud and happy; when Stephen rang and put them on to Roz, they all began shouting their achievements down the phone at once. Anne Marie had to calm them down and send them out of the kitchen one at a time to talk.

When the children were in bed, Nano opened a bottle of Italian wine she had brought back from her holiday. Anne Marie put out cheese and crackers. They opened the French doors to the garden and sat side by side on the step, where the delicate perfume of night-scented stock was borne to them in gentle wafts.

'I can't begin to tell you how wonderful it is to have you here,' Anne Marie said with a heartfelt sigh.

'Likewise,' said her grandmother, giving her a hug.

After a while Nano, on Anne Marie's insistence, took out her holiday photos. As well as pictures of Daniel in front of various cathedrals, and Nano sitting at the tables of cafés on a piazza, there were several that featured a tall man with a mane of white hair standing on the tops of mountains. 'Who is this?' asked Anne Marie. 'His face is familiar, but I can't imagine where I could have seen him before.'

'Can't you?' Nano smiled. 'Darina picked it up at once. Do you remember I told you that one of the brothers we met owned a restaurant in Dublin?'

Anne Marie's eyes opened wide. 'Of course – the Café Firenze! This is Oscar's Uncle Giorgio, isn't it? Oscar told me he was going back to Italy for a break, and I knew that you and Uncle Dan were going to the same area, but I never thought . . . well, what a coincidence! We love that restaurant, you know. We'll have to go there together before you leave.'

Nano smiled. 'I was thinking we could take the children there for lunch tomorrow.'

'Yes, yes! That would be perfect. We can meet here and – oh!' Anne Marie stopped. 'Nano, where are you staying? Not in a hotel, I hope. You could sleep here, if you like, in the spare room. I'll make up a bed for myself on the sofa.'

'That's all right, dear,' said Nano gently. 'I have made other arrangements. But perhaps in a few minutes you would be so kind as to ring for a taxi?'

Darina's big mistake

The exams were over. Darina should have been relieved, but instead she was more apprehensive than ever. Relations with Cleo had taken a turn for the worse since the morning Darina had ignored her bleeper, which had gone off on her way into an exam. She had rung Deco later on, and he had been so polite and understanding that Darina knew at once something was up. For the past few days, she had been waiting for a summons to appear once more before the mysterious woman who might or might not be the mastermind behind a vast criminal enterprise involving drugs, prostitution and racketeering.

Before the start of the exams she had met with Brenda, but far from reassuring Darina, the meeting with the garda had left her feeling more vulnerable than ever. Brenda had been evasive and ill-at-ease; when pressed by Darina, she had admitted that she wasn't sure whether her lover would follow through on the plan that they had worked out for bringing in Cleo. He had bigger fish to fry, she intimated; the Drug Squad had been following a shipment of heroin for the last few months and Customs were expected to make a major seizure any week now. Until that was safely out of the way, she couldn't guarantee that there would be the manpower necessary to follow Darina's operation.

Darina had put a brave face on it. 'I'll just have to stay clear of Deco and company until then,' she said. 'Lock the doors at night and not go out after sundown.' Though it wasn't dark until eleven, she somehow expected that Deco and Nailer wouldn't dare to operate openly any earlier in the day.

She was wrong. They picked her up in broad daylight in Dame Street. She was walking in the direction of Trinity, trying to avoid the pedestrians rushing to cross at the lights in front of the Central Bank. Next thing she knew, she was seized by the arm and pushed into the back of a black Lexus, which took off from the lights as soon as they changed. Like the first time, it happened so quickly that she barely had time to be surprised.

'Nice to see you too, Deco,' said Darina when she had recovered herself. She was squashed in the middle of the back seat, between Deco and a dark-skinned stranger wearing a black suit and wraparound shades.

Nailer was driving. Darina leaned forward to speak to him. 'Glad you left the van behind. I like travelling in style, so I do.'

Nailer did not give any sign that he had heard her.

Darina turned to the stranger. 'Hello, I'm Darina,' she said, holding out her hand. 'And you are . . .? No? Oh well, suit yourself.' She withdrew her hand and reached into her bag. At once, a dark hand shot out and fastened onto her wrist.

'Whacha think ye're doin'?' That was Deco; the stranger said nothing at all.

'I'm getting a chewing gum, if you don't mind,' said Darina. 'God, you're a jumpy lot, aren't you? What did you think I was going to do? Spray you with homemade Mace?'

Her wrist was released. Darina resisted the urge to cradle it until the pain eased. Whatever you do, don't let them get to you, she warned herself. She put a piece of gum in her mouth and began to chew.

At Trinity, Nailer made an illegal right turn onto Lower Grafton Street. As the car followed the college railings round to Nassau Street, Darina hoped against hope that she might see someone she recognised. She was not sure what good it would do, since the windows at the side and back were tinted, but at the very least she would take it as a sign that all was not lost.

When they reached Greene's bookshop and she had seen no one, she gave up. Instead, she began to wonder what was going to happen to her. She stole a look at the man beside her. He was exactly the sort of person she would hire as a killer if she were Cleo. Was that what he was? Had he been brought in to dispose of the thorn in Cleo's side named Darina? Her palms began to sweat. Was this her last journey? She had told herself that if ever she was allowed to see where they were taking her, it could only mean one thing. Now she wanted to undo that conviction.

It was no use. As they continued along Merrion Square in the direction of the canal, Darina's heart began to thump painfully fast. She knew where they were heading. As the Phoenix building came into view, it gave her little comfort to see that she had been right about everything. Cleo's hidey-hole was the penthouse of the building in which Anne Marie worked. Cleo was in reality Isolde Phoenix, a supposedly reclusive and eccentric millionaire who owned her own women's magazine.

Maybe Anne Marie will appear on her bike and rescue me at the last moment, thought Darina desperately as the car swung in through electronically controlled gates and into an underground car park.

The canal smell hit her full force when she stepped out of the car, reminding her of her first trip, when she had been tantalised by the impression of something familiar before Deco had put the jacket over her head.

As before, they took the lift. Darina chewed her gum loudly in order to persuade herself if not her captors that she wasn't afraid.

In the atrium, the men surrounded her.

'Hand over yer bag,' ordered Deco.

Darina slipped her tote bag off her shoulder and gave it to him. 'And there was me thinking I was trusted now,' she said mock-sorrowfully. 'I suppose you'll be turning out my pockets as well. Here, I'll do it for you, will I?' She reached into the pockets of her baggy grey hipsters and pulled them inside out. 'See? This is all there is.'

In her left hand was a set of keys and a crumpled tissue; in her right, some change and a couple of tampons. She jangled the keys in Deco's face. 'Look: no 007 exploding keyring, no secret cameras. Satisfied? Or would you like me to open these up for you?' She thrust her right hand with the tampons under Deco's nose.

'Fuck off!'

The dark-skinned man nodded to Deco and went to the door. He knocked twice then stepped back. Darina took a deep breath. The door opened and Cleo stood before them. She offered no word of greeting, but turned and strode back towards the desk. Deco went in first, followed by the dark stranger, then Darina. Behind her, as though to cut off any means of escape, loomed the intimidating bulk of Nailer.

Darina made to cross the threshold, then stopped short. 'Oh! I forgot,' she said, opening her mouth to Nailer. 'Chewing gum – herself doesn't like it. I'll just get rid of it out here, will I?'

Without waiting for an answer, she slipped past him to the oasis of palms and ferns by the door. 'Don't worry, I'll pick it up on the way out,' she said, pulling the gum out in a long string.

Nailer turned away in distaste. Quickly, Darina took from her pocket a small black object the size of a button. When she had opened her hand to Deco, it had lain concealed on her palm beneath the tampons. Predictably, Deco had proved squeamish when she had thrust these items of feminine hygiene in his face and had consequently been far more lax about searching her than on previous occasions.

The object was a tracking device, given to her by Brenda at their last-but-one meeting. If Darina's instincts turned out to be correct, her life might well depend on this marvel of acoustic miniaturisation. She just hoped that whatever difficulties Brenda had been experiencing with her lover in the Drug Squad, they had been ironed out by now. This was not the time for him to have decided to go back to his wife.

Today's meeting with Cleo was clearly intended to intimidate Darina. Instead of dismissing her heavies, Cleo had them line up at her back as she took her seat in the big armchair behind the desk.

But Darina had no intention of playing ball.

'Hey, cool view!' She walked past the desk and over to the windows that ran the length of two walls. On her previous visits they had been obscured by tightly drawn curtains.

'That's the Grand Canal Dock, isn't it?' she said, pointing to the expanse of water visible beyond Charlotte Quay. 'I heard Bono has an apartment somewhere round here. Or was it The Edge? Imagine seeing U2 jamming on a balcony just across from your window!' She knocked on the glass. 'Howya, Bono? How's it going?'

Shit. Triple-glazing. The cavalry wouldn't be coming in this way, then.

'Shut up and sit down.'

Cleo was not in a friendly mood. Darina did as she was told.

'When you came to me,' Cleo began slowly, 'you wanted to do business. I accommodated you. Six months have gone by and we have had one trans-action.' She leaned across the table. 'Frankly, I am not impressed. When I try to contact you, you are unavailable. This is not good. I begin to wonder about your commitment. I ask myself if I made a mistake.'

Darina made herself slouch in the hard upright chair that had been provided for her. 'God, you're a nervous nellie, aren't you?' she said scathingly. 'I had exams; I was studying. In case we ever fell out, I thought it might be a good idea to have an alternative career plan, you understand.'

Cleo said nothing but her face tightened and her eyes turned hard.

Uh oh, thought Darina; she's one of those people who consider sarcasm to be the lowest form of wit.

'Perhaps you would care to explain something to

me,' said Cleo softly. 'In the past few weeks, I have been getting reports from my source in the Drug Squad that there is shortly going to be a major drugs haul in Dublin. Naturally, I am concerned. The operation that is being planned is so top secret that my source could provide no details as to time or place. All he knows is that they have someone working from the inside, not a regular tout but someone new, someone they've never used before.'

Darina sat up. 'And you think that someone is me?' she said, doing her best to sound both incredulous and offended. 'Oh, for heaven's sake! I'm like you: I'm in this for the money. I know I haven't done much business lately, but I've already explained that I was taken up with study. I'm going to Russia a couple of weeks from now, but when I get back, I'll be needing some cash and you can count on me to sell a whole heap then. If you like, I'll check out the scene in Moscow; they say trade is flourishing there since the free market took over from Communism.'

'Enough with the games already!' Cleo slapped the table angrily. 'We know you've been into the Drug Squad HQ several times in the past three months. You may as well tell me now what you know, because one way or another, I'm going to get it out of you.'

'What are you talking about? I've never been near any Drugs HQ! I don't even know where it is!' This time, Darina's indignation was real.

Cleo smirked and twisted the ring that had once been Anne Marie's. 'But we picked you up two minutes after you left Dublin Castle today.'

It took a moment for the significance of what Cleo was saying to sink in. Then Darina almost laughed aloud. It was too ludicrous. She thought of the pains she and Brenda had taken over their rendezvous, Darina always using public phones and arranging to meet in places where there was not the slightest chance of them being seen by the wrong eyes. And all the while, Darina had blithely entered Dublin Castle several times a week, never suspecting that she was attracting Cleo's attention. Would it do her any good to explain that she went to Dublin Castle to have lunch in the Chester Beatty library café or, when it was fine, to sit in the little park and eat her sandwiches?

Somehow, she doubted it.

The stranger with the look of a killer stepped forward.

Cleo held up her hand as though to restrain him. 'So what's it to be? Do we do this the easy way? Or do I hand you over to Carlos and let him do it the hard way?'

In recovery

Roz was amazed by how kind people could be. From the moment she was brought from the theatre to her room in the hospital, she never had to ring for a nurse to come and raise her pillows or bring a bedpan. Word seemed to have gone out that she was a special patient, and the nurses knew what she needed before she knew it herself.

Dr Goodman was a regular visitor, even when Jane wasn't there. He hovered awkwardly at the bottom of the bed, examined her notes, and told her that he was very pleased with her progress.

A fortnight after their birth, the babies were

thriving, thanks to unlimited donations of breast milk from sympathetic mothers. Some of them had written touchingly-worded cards, which joined the many others from friends at home on the ledge above her bed.

Anna and Ben. Stephen had chosen the names and Roz had agreed. The twins were beautiful: tiny but perfect. As long as they weren't separated, they never cried; nestled together under the warm lamp of their incubator, they sucked each other's thumbs and were content.

As soon as all three of them were ready to go home, the owner of the gallery where Jane worked had promised he would send them under medical supervision in his private jet. Roz had nothing to do but get better, and her body was taking care of that by itself. Every day marked a new milestone. Sit up; hold a cup and drink from a straw. Feed herself. Stretch her arms over her head. Walk the length of the room.

Hospital staff commented on her amazing powers of recovery. How nicely her scars were knitting, how elastic were her muscles.

Roz was unimpressed. Part of her mind was stuck in a time warp, making her feel remote and detached from her physical self. She was a child in hospital for a minor operation. She had a mother and a sister. At the sound of visitors' footsteps in the corridor, she would look eagerly towards the door, impatient for them to arrive. She had no interest in what was happening here and now; once Stephen had left for Dublin, she forgot about the babies for long periods.

Jane was a constant presence. It was restful to have her near, relating the latest in her soap-opera affair with Dr Goodman. Soon, Roz felt as though she knew the main players as intimately as those on *The Street*.

Alastair, the brilliant surgeon, is passive and allows things to happen to him. His daughter Tess, single mother to Jack, is clever but wild. Eva, a well-known figure in the theatre world, is the wicked stepmother who snared Alastair after his first wife died. Jane and Tess and Jack are devoted to each other. Jack calls Jane 'Auntie,' and Eva 'Witchy' or 'Poo-face'. The plot centres round Jane's, Tess's and Jack's schemes to get rid of Poo-face so that Jane can marry Alastair and they can all live happily ever after.

It was entertaining and it kept Roz's mind occupied so that for hours at a time she forgot that her mother and sister were dead.

She started chemotherapy. The drug was lurid yellow and viscous, reminding her of engine oil. She watched, fascinated, the first time the nurse pumped it through the needle in the vein on the back of her hand. She could feel its cold progress up her arm, round her shoulder to the back of her throat. She gagged on the metallic taste it left in its wake. They're poisoning me, she thought helplessly. She imagined the yellow toxin circulating round her body, killing off billions of cells, among them the ones that had inexplicably gone berserk and caused her to have breast cancer. Talk about overkill! She would lose her hair, her nails would go brittle, her skin would deteriorate and she would be prone to infection as her immune system reeled under the assault. But what was the alternative? A cure at Lourdes? Chinese herbs? Seaweed baths and yoga?

Someone gave her a book of short stories by Lorrie Moore. Roz found herself in one of them. *In her other life*, she read, *she had been a believer in alternative medicine. Now, suddenly, alternative medicine seems the*

*wacko maiden aunt to the Nice Big Daddy of
Conventional Treatment. How quickly the old girl faints
and gives way, leaves one just standing there. Chemo? Of
course: chemo! Why, by all means: chemo! Absolutely!
Chemo!*

It was drastic, but it worked.

Didn't it?

The Sting

It was Brenda's finest hour. She had been on patrol in
Portobello when the call from Central Control had
come. Special Branch were following a black Lexus
they'd had under surveillance for some time. They had
just witnessed the abduction of a young woman on
Dame Street and were calling for back-up. The car was
currently travelling east on Mount Street.

While Tony drove where she told him, Brenda got on
her cellphone and called her lover in the Drug Squad.
'We're in business,' she said tersely, and rang off.

Because she knew where they were going, they
arrived before the Lexus. They remained out of sight
until it had disappeared into the underground car park.

The car following it came slowly to a halt by the
canal. In the passenger seat Brenda recognised DI
Martin, the inspector who had discovered that the
suicide in the house in Belvedere Square was the South
Circular Strangler. He was Special Branch now, having
earned a lot of kudos over the Sylvester Reed affair.

He was also one of those macho gits who believed
that a woman's place was face down underneath a man.
She knew she would have to forestall him or he'd have

her out of here before the fun started. She strode over to the car with Tony following in her wake.

'DI Martin, isn't it?' she said, extending her hand as soon as the detective was out of the car. 'I'm Brenda Clarke, this is Tony Kelly. We were at that suicide in Belvedere Square last year. I'm glad you're here. The Lexus went round the back – there's an underground car park with an electronic steel shutter and a lift that goes straight to the penthouse. That's where they've taken the girl.'

Martin looked completely bemused, just as she had hoped. Before he had time to recover himself, she pressed on: 'There's going to be a raid on the penthouse – drugs have been watching it for weeks now. It wasn't supposed to happen until there was clear evidence that the shipment had landed, but if they picked up the girl in broad daylight, then it would be dangerous to wait any longer.'

Martin scowled and puffed out his chest, preparing to take control. Just then, another unmarked car pulled up and four men from the Drug Squad got out. Martin turned away from Brenda and strode towards them. 'What's the story?' he said peevishly. 'We've been tailing an international contract killer who flew in yesterday from Amsterdam. Why was I not informed that Drugs are involved?'

One of the newcomers, a handsome man of about fifty, glanced over at Brenda and nodded briefly. Then he turned to Martin. 'Superintendent Tom Brady,' he said, holding out his hand. 'I'll be leading this operation. Declan Martin, right? I spoke to your Chief on the way over. Sorry there was no time to brief you earlier; this latest development has caught us all on the hop. But it's good to have you on board. The

Emergency Response Unit is on its way – oh! Here they are now.'

A large van had pulled up close to the building. Brenda's heart thrilled as the doors at the back opened and an army of black clad police officers was silently disgorged. This was living!

Within minutes, everything was set up. Brenda had been quizzed about the layout of the Phoenix building from Darina's perspective, and her information compared with that provided by an architect's drawing of the place which her lover had unfurled over the bonnet of the car. Once she had told all she knew however, her usefulness was at an end. It was clear that Superintendent Tom Brady wanted her there as little as Martin did. Their special relationship meant that he didn't dare suggest that she and Tony return to their station in Rathmines, but he wasn't about to give them any active role in the operation. At best, they would be unwelcome observers. That was not acceptable.

'Come on Tony,' she whispered as the teams spread out around the building. 'We've got work to do.'

Tony's shoulders drooped. 'Why do I get the feeling that you don't mean checking the tax discs on cars along the canal?' he said resignedly as he followed her down the ramp that led to the underground car park.

It worked even better than she could have hoped. The ERU disabled the electronic surveillance system and all security gates. They used the emergency stairs to reach the roof, securing it and all the floors in between. With the building surrounded on the outside as well, there was little chance of their quarry getting away.

Brenda took the lift.

As the doors opened at the penthouse floor, she

gave a quick glance left and right before she signalled the all clear to Tony, who was wearing the glazed look of a condemned man being led to the gallows. 'We need to create a distraction,' she had explained to him on the way up. 'While the lads are getting ready to abseil through the bathroom window or whatever, we have to make sure those inside are kept busy. For Darina's sake.'

On the other side of the fire door, she could sense the consternation of the men in black, who had not been expecting this development. There would be urgent radio messages passing between them and the chiefs on the roof.

At a sign from Brenda, Tony raised his fist to bang on the door.

'Wait!' Brenda pointed to the door handles. She mimed turning them. One each, at the same time. Of course, the doors were more than likely locked, but it would do no harm to try.

They crept to the doors and each placed a hand on the handles. 'One, two, three – now!' mouthed Brenda.

The handles turned. As though to cover the sound of their entry, as the doors swung open, from inside the room there came a cry of pain.

Brenda had a couple of seconds to take in the scene before her. In a chair with her back to the door, Darina was slumped forward, pressing a hand against her jaw. On one side of her stood a dark man in a black suit. He was holding a length of rubber, passing it restlessly from one hand to the other. On either side of him, also with their backs to the door, were Deco and Nailer, figures familiar to Brenda from Darina's descriptions of them.

The one person facing the door was a woman sitting

across a desk from Darina. She had a cold smile on her face, as though she was just beginning to enjoy herself. She hadn't noticed the door opening, but as Brenda advanced, she raised her head sharply.

'We would have knocked, only the door was open,' Brenda said pleasantly. 'We heard a cry. Looks like we just got here in time, doesn't it? Hmm, I wonder what we can do you lot for?'

There was an instant's shocked silence, then pandemonium. The dark man reached inside his jacket, but before he could pull out a weapon, a door at the back of the room burst open and the combined forces of the ERU, the Special Branch and the Drug Squad rushed in. Behind Brenda, the men who had been lurking in the stairwell took up sniper positions on the floor. Within seconds, Deco, Nailer and the hired killer had been disarmed and arrested for possession of firearms under Section 30 of the Offences Against the State Act.

The woman Brenda recognised as Cleo screeched at the detective who came to handcuff her, spitting bad language and clawing at him with long red nails. In his efforts to defend himself, he caught her head with his arm. A black wig went sailing onto the desk. Underneath it, the woman was bald except for a few wisps of mousy hair over her ears.

The detective wiped his bloody lip and grinned. 'Looks like someone's having a bad hair day,' he jeered as he snapped the handcuffs onto her wrists and pushed her into line with the three men.

'Who's this? Do we cuff her too?' One of the Drug Squad officers was standing over Darina.

Brenda quickly stepped forward and addressed Tom Brady. 'Sir, she's a dealer on our patch. We've had her under surveillance for the last few months. Her brother was caught in possession last year but somebody got him off. I think we should get a search warrant for her place too.'

Tom Brady gave her a look that said 'I'll deal with you later,' but then he nodded. 'Take them all in,' he ordered. He took out a warrant and waved it in front of the captives. 'And the rest of you make sure you give this place a thorough going-over.'

Brenda was walking on air. She grabbed Tony by the arm as they returned to their car. 'Did you see their faces when we walked in? Talk about the element of surprise! Wasn't it brilliant? Didn't it give you a rush? God, this is better than sex! I'm definitely getting into the Drug Squad. Or Special Branch; that's got to be exciting too. No more domestics, no more drunk drivers, no more walking the beat for me! From now on, I'm going to be where the action's at!'

Tony leaned on the bonnet of the car and took some deep breaths. Then he handed Brenda the keys. 'I think you'd better drive,' he said weakly.

On suffering

Arriving early for work one bright Monday morning in June, Anne Marie found the doors of the Phoenix building locked against her. She tried rattling them a few times in case the porter had made a mistake and turned the key after letting someone in, but when that produced no result, she stood back and looked up at the silent building with a puzzled frown. She had often come in at this time before; unless there was a Bank Holiday Monday that she had forgotten about, she could think of no reason why the place should be so dead.

While she was debating what to do next, a young garda appeared from around the canal side of the building. He stopped to examine Anne Marie's bicycle, which she had locked to the rack near the corner, then looked around to find out who it belonged to.

'Good morning,' called Anne Marie. 'I wonder if you could tell me what's going on. Why are the doors locked? I need to get up to my office.'

The garda ignored her questions. 'And who might you be?' he asked, taking notebook and pen out from under his fluorescent yellow jacket as he approached.

'I'm Deputy Editor of *Femme* magazine on the third floor,' said Anne Marie impatiently. 'Anne Marie Elliot, spelt with two "l"s and one "t". What's all this about anyway?'

The garda puffed his chest out pompously. 'I'm going to have to ask you for your address and a contact telephone number.'

'Please tell me what's going on first.'

'This building is closed until further notice. I am not at liberty to disclose further details.'

'In that case,' said Anne Marie in exasperation, 'I'll just have to find out for myself.'

Taking out her cellphone, she turned her back on the garda and began to walk the other way as she waited for Dave to pick up.

'Hi, it's Anne Marie,' she began.

'Anne Marie! Where are you? I've been trying to reach you all weekend. Naughty girl – you had your mobile switched off. Now why was that? Hmm? Hmm?'

'Stop it, Dave! Just tell me what's going on.'

'You mean you haven't heard? You didn't listen to the news – not even once? My, my, he must have been good!'

'Dave!'

'OK, OK. It's Isolde Phoenix. She's been arrested and had all her assets seized. Drugs, apparently.'

'Really? Oh Lord!'

'That's not all. Get this: her real name is Martina Duggan. Back in the eighties she was a small-time prostitute with a couple of convictions for soliciting. She only avoided being sentenced by skipping bail. She disappeared, then reappeared ten years later as our mysterious Lady of the Night, wandering the corridors of the empty *Femme* magazine, dreaming no doubt of the handsome Art Director who—'

'Does this mean we're out of a job?'

'Well, I should think so! July is about ready to go out, but I doubt if there'll be an August. Or any month after that. Pity, really. I was going to try to persuade the new Deputy Editor to let me do a *Pooftah* column.'

'Dave, this is serious! How can you be so flippant? What does Roz say? Have you spoken to her?'

'Eh, no,' said Dave, suddenly subdued. 'I rang on Saturday, but Roz wouldn't come to the phone. I spoke to Stephen instead. He said she's going through a bad patch, very down about everything.'

'Oh no! She seemed fine when I saw her after her chemotherapy last week. I'd better get over there and check on her. How about you? What are you going to do now?'

'Well, Joe is about to fix us breakfast, then I thought

I might persuade him to come back to bed for the morning and, well, I hadn't thought beyond that, really.'

'Dave, you're impossible! Look, I'll give you a ring later on to let you know how Roz is, then I think we should sit down and discuss what we're going to do.'

'Come for dinner tonight. We'll talk then. And don't forget to tell Roz that her favourite fags send her their love. Bye for now, petal.'

Anne Marie rang off, put away her phone and went to unlock her bicycle. The young policeman followed her, but he seemed less sure of himself when he asked her for her address this time. Up close, she was a whole head taller than him.

The door to the house on the South Circular Road was opened by a bald man wearing gold-rimmed Roddy Doyle glasses. Anne Marie took a step back. 'I'm sorry,' she stammered. 'I wanted to see Roz, but if this is a bad time, I can come back later.'

Maybe Roz was hosting a cancer support group, she thought, or this might be one of those volunteers she had heard about, fellow-sufferers who visited people in their homes.

'Anne Marie, come on in. I tried to get hold of you yesterday, but your phone was off.'

'Stephen?' Anne Marie's mouth dropped open. 'My God, it *is* you!' Dazed, she went inside and allowed herself to be kissed on the cheek.

'We had a shaving party on Friday. Roz's hair had been falling out in dribs and drabs for ten days, so I suggested that it might be better to do it properly. I offered to go first. It seemed silly to keep the beard then, so it went too. And the twins insisted that I get new glasses, so here I am, cleanshaven and "with it" for the first time in almost twenty years.'

Anne Marie couldn't take her eyes off the bald pate. 'It's . . . it really suits you! But you look completely different. I'm sorry – I just can't seem to get used to it.'

'That's OK, you're not alone. The baby twins haven't quite accepted the new look yet.'

'How are they doing? May I see them? And Roz – how is she?'

Stephen shrugged and looked away. 'You tell me,' he said softly. 'She's in the garden. I'll put the kettle on for coffee. Ask Roz if she'll have herbal tea.'

The reclining chair was set in the far corner of the garden, the first spot to be lit by the morning sun as it rose above the rooftops. Wrapped in a sleeping bag, Roz was lying with her legs drawn up to her chest and her head facing the neighbours' wall. A soft woollen bonnet hid her head.

Anne Marie carried a folding chair from the patio dining set and placed it on the grass beside the recliner.

'Hello,' she said tentatively.

Roz didn't acknowledge her.

'I've just come from the office. Everything was locked up and there was a garda on duty outside. I suppose you know about Isolde Phoenix being arrested? Does that mean the end of the road for *Femme*?'

She waited, but there was no response. Before the silence could become awkward, Anne Marie tried again: 'Do you think there's a chance that someone might buy the magazine and keep us on as staff? I'd hate to think that this is the end of our working together. I've learnt so much from you, and it's been a great experience, not just from the job point of view either. Dave feels the same. He sends his and Joe's love, by the way.'

Roz remained lying with her face averted. She gave no sign of having heard a word Anne Marie had said.

'Oh, Stephen asked if you'd like a herbal tea. The kettle should have boiled by now. What'll it be?'

There was silence again, and Anne Marie was about to get up and go back into the kitchen under the pretext of checking on the kettle when suddenly, Roz spoke.

'How come some people are so good at life?' she burst out. 'They sail through from birth to ripe old age without ever encountering pain along the way. Take the Keoghs next door.' Without turning her head, Roz lifted her chin to indicate the neighbouring wall. 'Last year, they celebrated their golden wedding anniversary. Their four children were there, with their eight grandchildren. Two daughters, two sons; four granddaughters, four grandsons. Such perfect symmetry! All the grown-ups are successful; all the children are talented. How did the Keoghs do it? What's their secret? How do you reach the age of seventy without coming a cropper at least once? Apart from when their dog died, they've never known the pain of loss. Their own parents are still alive, for crying out loud!'

Anne Marie sat on the edge of her seat and wondered what to do. She had never seen Roz like this before. Should she try to cheer her up with inane chatter, or should she go in to Stephen and say that she didn't think her presence was doing Roz any good?

'If suffering is supposed to be good for the soul,' continued Roz in the same tone, 'why don't we all get an equal dose of it? Why do some people get away scot-free and others get more than their fair share? Am I a better person than Mrs Keogh because I've suffered more? Am I? *Am I?*' Her voice grew plaintive. 'No, I'm not. I want it to stop! I want the suffering to stop now!'

Stephen came out with a tray. To Anne Marie's relief, after he had poured the coffee and offered her a biscuit, he stayed in the garden with them.

Roz took no notice of the cup of camomile tea that her husband had put on the grass beside her, but she lifted her head to allow him to replace the pillow that had slipped down behind her back. She said no more, but lay with her hands beneath her cheek and stared at the Keoghs' garden wall. Anne Marie and Stephen drank coffee and talked about the children.

Back inside the house some minutes later, Anne Marie agreed that Roz was behaving strangely. Stephen confessed to being at a loss as to how to respond to his wife's altered state of mind. 'This is so unlike her,' he said unhappily. 'She's always been a fighter, but something's happened to change that. I just don't understand. She seems to have shrivelled up inside. After doing so well at the beginning – she bounced back very quickly after the surgery and the first chemo sessions. But these last few days . . . I don't know. Sometimes I think she's not with us at all. She seems to be living in some different reality, back in her childhood. Before the accident that killed her mother and sister.'

'Oh dear. This latest trauma must have brought back the other one. I suppose she's never got over losing them like that – I mean, it's not something you can ever get over, is it?' Anne Marie bit her lower lip and hesitated before continuing, 'This probably isn't the right time to mention it, but . . . speaking of the accident, there is something I should tell you. It's about the man who was responsible for their deaths.'

'Desmond Dunne – you used to work for him, right? He's in Mountjoy now, isn't he? Good riddance, I say.'

'Yes . . . that's sort of connected to what I have to say. He asked me to visit him in prison. I know that sounds weird, but . . . he was very good to me when he was my boss and . . . and if I didn't go, he'd have no one, so I went with my cousin about a month ago and then again on my own last week. We talked about the accident and . . . he seems very remorseful. The thing is . . . he wants to meet Roz.'

'What!'

'Yes, I know. I told him I thought it was a bad idea, especially now that she's ill, but when I mentioned about the cancer, he was even more insistent that I ask.'

'In case I die without forgiving him?'

Stephen and Anne Marie jumped. They hadn't heard Roz come in from the garden, but when they turned, there was her tiny figure framed in the doorway.

Anne Marie flushed. 'Oh God, Roz, I'm sorry!' she stammered. 'I shouldn't have said anything . . . I'll tell him to forget it. I didn't mean to upset you, honest!'

Roz came into the kitchen and leaned against the French doors. She crossed her arms tightly over her chest. 'Upset? Yes, I'm upset. But you don't understand. You don't understand at all. None of you!' She glared at Anne Marie and then at Stephen, who made a move towards her. She put out a hand to stop him. When she began to speak again, there was a haunted look in her eyes, and her voice had an edge of hysteria to it.

'You see, you weren't there. I was! I *know* what happened. So does he. He guessed. That's why he wants to see me.'

'Roz, sweetheart, you'll never have to face him, I promise you,' began Stephen.

'Stop! It's not the way you think!' Roz was beside herself, but she wouldn't allow Stephen to come near her. With her arms wrapped about her shoulders, she began to rock back and forth against the doorframe. 'It's not true what I said after the accident,' she continued in a shrill voice. 'It wasn't his fault. It wasn't his fault at all! It was because of me that Mammy and Ellie died!'

Anne Marie and Stephen exchanged wary glances but said nothing. Roz was not going to allow herself to be interrupted. She seemed to be staring at something beyond their range of vision, something that had happened a quarter of a century earlier but was very much present to her now.

'I wasn't supposed to go to the party. It was going to be over too late, Mammy said. I should have stayed at home with Daddy. When I was twelve like Ellie, I could go and help hand round the food. I begged and pleaded and promised I'd be good and in the end she let me go too. But it was a grown-ups' party and I didn't like it. By midnight I was tired and cranky and wanted to go home. Mammy didn't want to leave so soon, but she had to. She was cross with me and I was sorry but I couldn't seem to stop. I made Ellie swap places with me though she was the only one allowed in the front seat, and even then I wasn't happy. I whinged and moaned all the way across town about the stupid present Clery's Santy had given me the day before and why did we have to have old Mrs Ferguson for Christmas dinner, it was disgusting watching her eating without any teeth and she was smelly and I hated it when she touched me.'

Roz's eyes began to fill with tears. 'I knew I was being obnoxious but I just couldn't seem to stop. I wanted to, but it was as though there was some sort of demon inside me that wouldn't let me. I remember my mother's face. She was frowning, trying to concentrate on driving and ignore my behaviour, but that only made me worse. I wanted her to pay attention to me so I kept on and on until she snapped. When we stopped at the lights, she turned and gave me a slap, which she'd never done before. It was a hard slap and it shut me up at once, but then she was upset and that's why she didn't look to make sure that the lights were green for us when they changed and she took off from them really fast and she didn't even see the other car coming from the right. And then it hit us and Mammy was killed because she was nearest and Ellie was killed because she had no seat belt in the back and I was left alive because I was bad and this was God's way of punishing me.'

Stephen went over to Roz and put his arms around her. He said nothing, but held her close and rocked her. Unnoticed, Anne Marie slipped away.

Another face revealed

In Vera Meaney's former bedroom, recently revamped by Brandon as a guest room, Professor Donald Garvey had enjoyed his first unbroken night of sleep since the death of his mother nine months earlier. It was such a surprise to wake and find the small hand of his old brass travel clock pointing towards the left side of its face that he lay still and stared at it until he was sure that he wasn't dreaming. Then he sat up, yawned and got out of bed to switch on the kettle for coffee.

He was glad he had come to Ireland. Even if he found out nothing about his true parentage, he would use his two weeks to travel the country, familiarising himself in particular with the counties of Cork and Galway, where his adoptive parents' families came from.

Perhaps that's all I need do, he mused as he scratched his beard and waited for the kettle to boil. The headaches that had plagued him in the early months had all but disappeared since his trip to Martinique, and last night when he had landed in Dublin, he had had a strong sense of being where he was supposed to be.

Don brewed his coffee and brought it back to the bed, happy that he had woken normally and that his body had achieved its quota of sleep for a change. He set the coffee on the bedside table and scratched his beard again.

What a nice house this is, he thought, glancing up at the elaborate plaster rose in the centre of the ceiling and at the marble fireplace on the other side of the room. Darina had given him the grand tour the previous night, ending with a visit to the landlord's quarters on the floor above. As a native New Yorker, Don had had no problem identifying Brandon O'Kane as an East Coast rich boy who had gone west and let California go to his head. In spite of their differences, they had got on well, to Darina's evident relief.

It was kind of Darina to come to meet him at the airport, though he had insisted on the phone that he would take a cab to her house on his own. He was glad that there was no awkwardness between them. From the way Darina had embraced him at the airport, he knew that for her, what had happened at Club Med was over and done with. Don was secretly relieved; he didn't regret their encounter for a moment, but it would have been embarrassing had Darina assumed that they were going to take up where they had left off. The fact was, for the past month he had been seeing a librarian whom he knew was the woman for him. Although they had yet to go to bed together, he would have felt as though he were being unfaithful to her had Darina been looking for sex.

Don drank his coffee and put down his cup. What next? Shower, then meet Darina for breakfast. She was going to take him to the Genealogical Office at the National Library so that he could talk to someone about the best way to look for a mother whose name he didn't know and who might not even have been Irish. What a forlorn quest!

He scratched his beard yet again, and this time he became conscious of what he was doing. What was wrong? Did he have a rash or something? It had begun to itch almost as soon as he set foot on Irish soil. He got out of bed and padded over to the tiny bathroom. In the mirror over the washstand, he examined his face carefully. No redness, but the itch was definitely getting worse. Maybe there was some cologne or something in the cabinet that would ease it. He opened the door. There was no cologne, but standing on the shelf, as though in invitation, was a shaving kit consisting of half a dozen disposable razors, a tub of cream, a bowl and a brush.

Donald Garvey had worn a beard from the age of sixteen. He couldn't imagine what he would look like without it. But he also knew that he couldn't tolerate this maddening irritation for a second longer. If he didn't shave, he would tear his face to shreds before the morning was out.

He opened the tub of cream and put some into the bowl. He used the brush to work it into a lather. He spread the lather on to his face and took up the razor. Well, here goes, he thought.

Thirty minutes later, he was ready for his breakfast date with Darina. He checked his appearance in the wardbrobe mirror one last time before he opened the door. How did he look without his beard? Should he have gone the whole hog? He looked at his reflection from all angles. No, it was better like this. He was not entirely naked. Smoothing his moustache with finger and thumb, Donald Garvey turned the handle of his door and stepped out onto the landing.

After leaving the house on the South Circular Road, Anne Marie cycled back to Belvedere Square in a bleak mood. Roz was not herself, but at the same time, Anne Marie couldn't help thinking that a lot of what she had said made sense. No matter how you looked at it, life was unfair. It took an awful lot of luck to get through it unscathed. Bad things happened to good people all the time, but poor Roz had had so much happen to her it was no wonder she was beginning to crack under the strain.

Of course, it was madness for her to blame herself for the accident all those years ago. It was just one of those bad timing things that no one could explain, like the lightning that had struck the tree that had killed Anne Marie's grandad.

Carrying her bicycle up the steps to the hall door, Anne Marie wished she could do something to alleviate Roz's suffering. Stephen had given up his job, so she wasn't needed for babysitting any more, but she resolved to call over every day to help with homework or cooking or whatever needed doing.

Just as well I've put some money by that I can use to live on for a few months, she reflected, and wondered in the next instant how Stephen was going to cope without any money at all coming in. With five children and Roz's medical bills, it would be no joke.

Head down, she trudged up the stairs to her room. Should she go up and talk to Brandon? Because he fancied himself as a bit of a guru, he liked hearing about people's problems and helping them find solutions. At the very least, she could ask him for some pot for Roz, she decided; he had said once that it was the only thing some cancer patients found useful for relieving their pain.

Near the top of the stairs, Anne Marie stopped and felt in her pockets for the key to her room. She was just about to take it out when she had the feeling that she was not alone. She glanced sharply up at the landing. There was a man standing there, outside Vera Meaney's old room. He was staring at her door with the strangest expression on his face.

Donald Garvey heard the footsteps on the stairs. He decided to wait where he was rather than pass the other person on his way down. It might be Darina's cousin, Anne Marie, whom he was told lived in the room across from his. She had been away for the weekend, so he hadn't met her last night. He should introduce himself now.

As he looked across at the door to the room occupied by Darina's cousin, Don had the weirdest sensation of déjà vu, the like of which he had never experienced before. He took a step forward, propelled by the insane urge to open the door and go inside. He knew exactly what the room was like, he could see it clearly in his mind's eye. Three long sash windows; a single bed with a cast-iron frame. A bookcase filled with books, all neatly ordered by author and height. At the back of the room, a basic kitchen. Everything immaculate. But how can that be? he thought wildly. I've never been to Ireland before, let alone to this house. He frowned and shook his head, as though to dispel the vision. He had almost forgotten about the steps on the stairs; it was only when he heard a sound like a sharp intake of breath that he turned to see who was there.

It was a young woman of extraordinary height. She had long fair hair and a round, pretty face. But there was something wrong with her. She was leaning against the wall, a look of blind terror on her face. Don saw the colour drain from her cheeks. He took a step forward and reached out a hand to steady her as she began to sway. She shrank from him. Her eyes rolled upwards and she began to slide slowly down the wall. He managed to reach her in time to prevent her head from bouncing off the skirting board.

Sally gets her story

Brandon was first on the scene. Anne Marie's scream after she came out of her faint brought him running down the stairs from his quarters wearing only a pair of loose cotton trousers tied at the navel with a drawstring.

'I'm sorry,' began Don, 'I don't know what happened. I guess I must have startled her.'

Anne Marie had backed away from him into the corner of the landing; as soon as Brandon appeared, she jumped up and ran to his side. Her eyes were still wild with fright and her breath came in gasps. 'It's . . . it's him! He's . . . he's come back t-t-to . . . get me!'

Brandon turned to face her. He took her arms and opened them wide.

'Breathe,' he commanded.

Anne Marie drew in a long, shuddering breath.

'Out,' said Brandon, bringing her arms down across her stomach. He manipulated her arms like bellows for three more breaths, then went behind her and put his hands beneath her chin. He raised her head so that Anne Marie was forced to straighten her spine. 'Shoulders down, let the tension go,' he ordered. Anne Marie dropped her shoulders.

When he was satisfied that she was calm once more, Brandon turned his attention to Don. 'You are owed an explanation. If Anne Marie has no objection, you should hear it in here.' He pointed to the door that had fascinated Don a few minutes earlier.

Anne Marie bent over the keyhole and fumbled with her key. It took her some time, but eventually she managed to open the door. She stood back to allow the two men to enter, averting her eyes when Don passed her.

The room was nothing like he had imagined it. Disappointed, Don gazed around the living room with its tasteful furnishings and the feminine touches of potted plants on the window sills, flowers on the table and throws on the backs of chairs. He shook himself. It was ridiculous to expect that the room would conform to his idea of it. And yet – those windows . . .

'Let us sit,' said Brandon, who seemed to be perfectly at ease in Anne Marie's room wearing a minimum of clothing. He adopted the lotus position in the centre of the couch, leaving the two armchairs for Anne Marie and Don.

'Anne Marie, this is Professor Donald Garvey, from New York. He is here as a guest of your cousin Darina. When he arrived last night, he was bearded, so I was not able to make the discovery that you made just now.'

Don put his hand to his cleanshaven chin and looked nonplussed.

'Of course, now that he has shaved it off, the resemblance is remarkable, is it not?'

Anne Marie nodded her head vigorously. 'I . . . I thought . . . it was the way . . . my room . . . I was sure he'd come back to get me!'

'I'm sorry, but could someone please tell me what's going on?' said Don.

'Sylvester Reed,' announced Brandon. 'The man who lived in this room. He . . . died here last year.'

But Professor Donald Garvey wasn't listening. He stood up, a puzzled frown on his face, and began to move as though in a dream. 'My bed, it was over there. There's a wall now. But there are only two windows . . . it must be inside,' he muttered, tapping the partition.

Anne Marie paled and opened her mouth to say something, but Brandon raised a warning hand to her.

'The bookcase . . . it's gone. I had the whole *Hornblower* collection, including a first edition. There was a trunk over there, by the window. I kept things in it. Private things. Things I didn't want anyone to see. I destroyed everything. My newspaper clippings. Pictures, too . . . there were always pictures. They were smiling in the pictures, like good little girls.'

'Stop! Make him stop, oh please, make him stop!'

Suddenly, Don clutched his head and reeled. 'Oh! Oh! Oh God, no, oh no!' Bowed down with pain, he sank to his knees on the carpet.

Nobody noticed the door opening. Darina came in and stopped dead. 'What on earth is going on? Don? You OK? What . . .? Oh! You've shaved your beard! But why are you . . . oh, your poor head!' She ran over and put her hand on the back of his neck, then turned and glared at Anne Marie. 'Well, don't just sit there – do something! Bring water! He gets these terrible headaches. Brandon, you must have some herbs or potions that would help. Why are you both just looking at him? Can't you see the man is suffering?'

Brandon smiled his knowing cat-smile. 'It is necessary. But do not be upset, it will end soon. And he will never suffer like this again.'

In fact, Don did seem to be recovering. He took his hands away from his head and looked about him, staring as though he had just woken from a dream and wasn't quite sure whether the people in the room were real or not. His eyes came to rest on Anne Marie. 'You thought I was someone else. I felt it too.' He looked around. 'I know what this room used to look like. Before. Just now, it felt like *my* room. I know he died here, alone. I know that that was . . . not his intention. Oh my God, I know what he did! He was a monster, and he got inside my head! How? Why?'

'It's uncanny,' said Anne Marie hoarsely. 'You look exactly like him.'

'Not exactly,' said Brandon. 'Sylvester Reed had less presence. He was a shadow-person, with a dark and disturbing aura. I'm pleased to say the Professor's aura is clear and bright; it belongs to a healthy, good and wise person. You have nothing to fear from our guest.'

Darina gasped. 'Sylvester Reed! Jesus Christ! Are you saying that Don looks like Sylvester Reed? Ooh, I wish I'd got a proper look at the creep before he topped himself! Does this mean he might have had a twin brother? An identical twin, even? Wow! You know what, it could well be true. Don, you were adopted, and you know nothing about your birth parents. Maybe there was another baby! He stayed here . . . and grew up to be the South Circular Strangler!'

Only Brandon was unfazed by the extraordinary story that Darina was unravelling. He seemed to think it quite unremarkable that Darina had won a holiday thanks to Anne Marie who had nearly been murdered by Sylvester Reed who had a twin brother who was sent to Club Med to get over his depression where he met Darina and was invited to Dublin and found himself staying in the room opposite the one where his evil alter ego had contemplated killing Anne Marie before he committed suicide.

'The Universe guided you here,' Brandon said with a benign smile. 'It is not extraordinary in any way. All our lives are strewn with signposts if we care to see them. What we call coincidence is merely evidence that the Universe is working on our behalf. For the Professor to complete his life path, it was necessary for him to come and face the other half of himself. Until he did that, he would never be free.'

'The headaches,' Don said with a frown. 'I thought they were connected to the death of my mother, but now I'm not so sure. If he died last October . . . it was just around then they started. Maybe this was meant to be . . . but how can I know for sure? Is there any way to find out more about this man called Sylvester Reed?'

Darina grinned triumphantly. 'There sure is. She's called Sally O'Shea, she has wild red hair and up until now, she has been one hell of a pest!'

Helpless male

Stephen Hunter tiptoed into the spare bedroom and stood at the foot of the bed. The shape in the centre was so hard to discern, it could have been made by a fold in the duvet. He knew that underneath, curled up like a newborn dormouse, lay the person who meant most to him in all the world. Roz – his wife, his life – did she have any idea of how dear she was to him?

Since the shocking diagnosis of breast cancer, he had done his best to be supportive. He had flown to London and held her hand when she woke after surgery, he had sat by her bed in the hospital, watching over her while she slept. He had spoken to the doctors and read books. Back in Dublin during the empty weeks before her return with the baby twins, he had gone onto the Internet and added sixteen breast cancer sites to his list of favourite places.

He knew that her chances of survival were good. She was young and fit, and she was tolerating the harsh régime of chemotherapy well. In another month she was due to have radiotherapy, which would minimise the chances of local recurrence of the cancer. But as he gazed on the almost smooth surface of the duvet, Stephen felt close to despair. It was four days now since Roz had removed herself to this stark room, bare except for the bed that was used by the occasional overnight babysitter and the computer desk in the corner that was the only evidence of the home office-cum-study they had planned to create.

So many plans! Stephen gave an involuntary shiver. He was going to have to forget about plans, learn to live for the here and now. Easy enough in theory, but who wanted to live like that in reality? Not he! The present moment had a bumbling idiot standing helplessly over his beloved, unable to offer her the comfort she needed. He longed to sweep back the duvet, take her in his arms and kiss every inch of her body. What did he care that she was scarred? The seams across her chest that looked like a child's drawing of a China-man's eyes; the Caesarean scar that was his mouth. He loved them as much as he had loved the tiny swellings of her breasts and the rose-pink nipples that had stiffened as his beard came into contact with her chest. She was dearer to him now than ever before, because for the first time, he had been forced to imagine a future without her.

If only she would agree to see someone. A pro-fessional, someone who had the skills that he lacked. He was useless, bringing her cups of tea that she didn't want, stroking her until she shrank from his touch. She had retreated to some faraway place where he couldn't reach her. This darkened room was like a womb, her tiny hairless body a foetus taking up the barest minimum of space. Foetus. Womb. Mother.

That was who Roz needed now.

More goodbyes

The two weeks of Don's visit seemed to go by in a flash. Although he had stayed almost a week in Dublin, Darina and he had ended up spending very little time together, just the two of them. In the evenings, Darina had been busy with the waitressing job she had taken to earn some extra cash for the summer, and during the day, Don had been taken over by the redheaded reporter from the *Evening Echo*. That was why, on the Saturday morning of his departure, Darina insisted on accompanying him to the airport. The taxi ride was a last chance for her to have a proper talk with him.

'So, are you glad you came?' she asked as they settled into the back of an ex-London black cab.

'Yes, of course I am. It's been an extraordinary couple of weeks; I shall be thinking about this trip for a long time to come.'

'You've no regrets – like not meeting your birth mother?'

'None at all.'

Darina was disappointed that the reunion had not gone ahead. She knew that Sally O'Shea had wanted to bring Don to see his mother, who was in a nursing home somewhere on the Southside, but Don had turned down the offer. He had no need of such a meeting, he had said, and he didn't wish to risk distressing an old woman who had had enough grief from her other son. He had agreed that Sally could inform her that she had met and spoken to the second twin if she so desired, but Don didn't want any further contact with his birth mother. Furthermore, he had made it clear that he did not wish to be identified in any book or article that Sally might bring out about Sylvester Reed. As far as he was concerned, he never had a brother, and his parents were the man and woman who had raised him as their son without ever indicating by word or deed that he was not their natural child.

So Don wasn't prepared to discuss the salacious details of his parentage as revealed by Sally O'Shea. That was too bad. But Darina knew enough to be able to regale Gerald with it when she went down home on Sunday. For now, she compensated by telling Don about her own adventure with Cleo aka Isolde Phoenix, formerly Martina Duggan of Cabra West.

This was another story that couldn't be shouted from the rooftops; she daren't mention a word of it to anyone in Dublin, for instance. Thanks to Brenda, the gang would never know that she had been working with the cops, but she would have to be very careful who she let in on the secret. She had never told Gerald about the lengths to which she had gone to pay back the criminals who had almost been responsible for his death, and she certainly didn't intend letting him know about the outcome. But Don was a safe pair of ears, and he was on his way back to New York. So she boasted to him about her part in the downfall of a major drug baroness, and he was suitably impressed.

At the airport, they embraced warmly. Don thanked Darina for her hospitality, which he hoped to return sometime soon. 'Take good care of yourself,' he admonished her, 'and when you go to Moscow, don't be tempted to take on the Russian mafia!'

Darina smiled and sat back in the cab. Moscow! Her flight was in three days. She had been back to Mountjoy to see Desmond Dunne and organise the transfer of money to his son in the Russian capital without letting John know where it had come from. It was exactly the sort of game of intrigue that appealed to Darina and she couldn't wait to get there. For once she didn't have to worry about repeating any exams, so she would be able to stay for all of July and August, then she'd have the month of September to earn a bit more money waitressing before term began again.

Life wasn't just good, she smiled to herself; it was bloody great.

Runaway

Early on that same Saturday morning, in the house on the South Circular Road, Ellie woke a fraction of a second before her alarm went off. She had put the clock under her pillow before going to bed so that the rest of the family wouldn't hear it ringing. She silenced it after the first bleep, then dressed quickly in the clothes she had laid out the night before. She straightened the duvet on her bed and smoothed the pillow. From her daysack she took the letter she had written and placed it on the pillow.

At the door, she turned and surveyed the tiny boxroom. It was little more than the airing cupboard and a bit of the bathroom that had been added together when the house was being renovated, but it was her own space and she loved it. Already nostalgic, she was expecting it to seem empty and forlorn at her desertion.

To her surprise, it looked complete. She had the strangest feeling that she had never occupied it, never played with the neatly stacked toys on the shelves, never lain on the bed staring at the glow-stars on the ceiling and dreaming girlish dreams. With a little pang of sorrow, Ellie realised that the room had forgotten her already.

She picked up her shoes and left them at the top of the stairs, then tiptoed up to the next landing to the room where the baby twins slept. Anna and Ben were awake but peaceful. Ellie knew that her father would have fed them at five o'clock; now they were content to lie quietly sucking each other's thumbs until the whole household was awake.

She leaned over the cot and rubbed the top of their heads. The twins turned and looked up at her. Ben kicked his legs and gurgled; Anna waved her arms and smiled.

Ellie put her finger to her lips. 'Shh,' she whispered. 'I'm sorry babies, I can't play with you right now. I have to go away for a while. Be good for Daddy, won't you? And if you see Mammy, give her lots of smiles, OK?'

The babies stopped as though to listen. Ellie let down the side of the cot, gave each of them a kiss, then raised it again and crept softly from the room. Out on the landing, she paused for a moment to see if they would cry. Part of her wished they would, so that the enterprise would fail before it could start.

But the twins were, if anything, quieter than before.

Ellie had told them about her plan, as she had told them all her secrets since the day they came home. Bathing them, changing them, playing with them, she confided in them as she had never confided in anyone before. She half-believed that they were quiet now because they knew what she was going to do and they approved.

No one else was astir. Ellie passed the closed door of the room that remained in darkness night and day, where the woman who used to be her mother lay empty-eyed and still. She passed the half-open door of the main bedroom, where her father, as though to compensate for the missing person, was sprawled across the middle of the huge bed, then passed the stairs to the attic, where the big twins had their new sleeping quarters. Pinned to the wall above the first stair was a red-lettered sign: *Strickly Privet, Keep Out.*

Down the stairs she crept, carrying her trainers and avoiding the creaky treads. In the hall, she slipped on her shoes and unlocked the hall door. Then she tiptoed down to the kitchen and picked up the lunch she had prepared and hidden at the back of the fridge the day before. Her bicycle was in the back hall; she lifted it up the three steps and wheeled it to the door.

Out in the street, she put on her helmet and cycled along the path in the direction of Kilmainham. It was a beautiful morning, the sky wincing blue, the air still and balmy. There were no cars about.

Now that the hard part – leaving the house – was over, Ellie began to feel elated. She had rarely gone anywhere on her own before. School was too far away to walk to and the roads too dangerous for cycling; the same applied to her swimming, gymnastics, music and horse-riding classes. The only time she got to use her bike was when her father took her to the park, or down in Kerry on the boreen that led from their holiday cottage to the beach.

It was exciting to be abroad so early on a weekend morning, when nearly everyone else in the city was still peacefully asleep and would be for another couple of hours. She knew that her father would wake up at around half past eight and go to check on the baby twins. He would go downstairs to make their bottles and get himself a cup of tea. Jake and Ruth were not early risers; they wouldn't be up before ten. So her father, after feeding and changing the babies, would probably go back to bed with the papers for another hour. Ellie had a moment's anxiety as she wondered if he would check her room to see why she wasn't up. Then she remembered that she had prepared for this possibility by yawning ostentatiously before bed last night and remarking several times that she was feeling very tired. Her father would notice that her door was closed and assume that she was having a lie-in. By the time they discovered that she was missing, she would be well on her way.

Heuston Station was deserted when Ellie arrived. The 7.10 train was not due to leave for another twenty minutes. Earlier in the week, she had rung the station to check the times and find out where to take her bike. If the ticket seller looked dubious about a child on her own wanting a return ticket to Limerick, she would tell him that her parents were separated and she was being met off the train by her dad, who was taking her for a cycling trip along the River Shannon.

In the event, the man behind the counter was chatting over his shoulder with two of his colleagues and barely noticed Ellie. He handed her the ticket and her change without a second glance. Heady with success, Ellie wheeled her bicycle to the platform where the train to Limerick was waiting. Now she had another stroke of luck. As she reached the car where the bikes were kept, a family of tourists came up behind her. Two parents and two children, all pushing bikes and speaking German. They smiled at her as they passed their bikes up to the guard. Ellie smiled back. The guard took all five bicycles and stowed them in the baggage car, and Ellie walked closely behind the German family as though she belonged to them until they were all safely on the train. Then she found a seat by herself and settled down for the journey. She had taken this train many times when she was younger and suffered from travel sickness on the long car journey to Killorglin. Ellie and her mother would go by train, while her father and eventually, Ruth and Jake, travelled in the car with all the holiday stuff. Those times, she went all the way to Killarney, but today she was just going halfway.

Looking out the window as the train pulled out of the station, Ellie fought the panic that rose suddenly like bile in her throat. Was she crazy? What if her mission was unsuccessful? She had told no one where she was going, except for the baby twins, and of course they weren't going to be any help if she got into difficulties. She was ten years old and travelling alone for the first time in her life. She had twenty-five pounds and eighty pence of her savings left in her purse, but no contingency plan. Was she asking for trouble? What if she was destined never to see home again? Ellie pressed her face against the glass and bit her lip to stop herself from crying.

Outside, the sun rose higher in the sky, dispelling

pockets of mist that clung to trees and bushes in dips and valleys by the canal. Once they had passed through the western suburbs of the city, Ellie concentrated on the fields flashing by, counting sheep, cows, horses and anything else she saw in an effort to take her mind off the enormity of what she was doing. Gradually, the motion of the train lulled her so that she relaxed and her thoughts became confident once more. She had done well so far. The train journey would take two-and-a-half hours; after that it was around five miles by road. Ellie had her map with her, and from close questioning of Anne Marie, she knew exactly where she had to go once she reached Limerick Station.

Some three hours later, as Ellie was cycling along a winding, tree-lined country road, it began to rain. The clear skies that had gladdened her heart on the cycle to Heuston station had given way in the Midlands to full-bodied rain clouds that mustered on the horizon, waiting for the right moment to release their pent-up load of water. Ellie had hoped to be at her destination before the deluge began. Surely it couldn't be far now, she thought as she began to pedal faster, trying to outdistance the downpour. She had been cycling for more than half an hour already and she had only stopped once, at a crossroads, to make sure she chose the right road.

The rain fell harder. Within minutes, it was pelting down with such ferocity that Ellie could barely see ahead of her. The bike wobbled and she almost came off. She began to feel scared. How much further was it? Surely she should have reached the gates by now? She couldn't take out the map in this rain to check. Besides, what if she had made a mistake? It had all seemed much less complicated in Dublin when she was sitting in her room with the map spread out in front of her and a ruler and a piece of thread to measure the distances. What if she had taken a wrong turn? Maybe she was going the wrong way entirely!

Ahead was an old stone bridge. That was a hopeful sign. She knew that there was a river she had to cross. Beyond the bridge, on the left side of the road, she thought she could make out a high stone wall. Her spirits rose. This could be it! If it was, then the gate was on a bit, maybe half a mile or so.

Suddenly, from behind, Ellie heard the sound of an approaching vehicle. The road narrowed at the bridge too much for her to risk cycling her bike. She got off and moved in as close as possible to the parapet to wait until the vehicle had passed.

From round the bend came a Land Rover. It had big wheels that swished through a puddle, spraying water over her. She caught a fleeting view of the man in the driver's seat. His face took on a look of surprise as he registered her presence.

She began to wheel her bike forward. When she was off the bridge she would start to cycle it again. But now she saw that the Land Rover was slowing down. The red brake lights came on, then went off, then white lights appeared. It began to reverse. Ellie stopped. She felt distinctly uneasy. What should she do? She looked around her. Down below, the river foamed and chattered over its bed of stones. On the bank, a willow dipped its long green hair into the water. Maybe she should abandon her bicycle and climb down. There were lots of trees and she could hide until the man went away again.

But even as she had the thought, she knew it was useless. Wherever she went, he would find her.

Besides, she couldn't move. She tried, but she was frozen in place. The Land Rover stopped on the other side of the bridge, a few yards from where she was standing. The door opened and the man got out. In his hands he appeared to have a blanket. He checked up and down the road, then he began to walk slowly towards her.

Once again, it was the wrong time of day for bad news when Anne Marie answered her cellphone that Saturday morning. She was half-expecting to hear from Dave, as she had given a dinner for him and Joe the previous night to repay the many evenings they had entertained her. He would be ringing to thank her and to extravagantly praise her humble efforts at *cordon bleu*.

But it wasn't Dave; again, it was Stephen, asking in a voice she scarcely recognised whether by any chance, Ellie was there with her.

Before Anne Marie could reply, another voice broke in. 'Anne Marie, it's Roz. She's gone – Ellie's gone! She left a note but it didn't say where. She's on her bike – she can't have gone far. We've tried all her friends but she's not with them. Maybe she's on her way to you? Look out for her, please! And ring my mobile if you think of anything, anything at all that might help locate her. We're going to phone the guards now.'

Anne Marie rushed downstairs to the basement flat. There was no way she was going to stay in the house twiddling her thumbs when her friends were in crisis. Darina had just returned from taking Don to the airport. Anne Marie left all the relevant telephone numbers with her in case the child did turn up in Belvedere Square, and ran back upstairs to get her bike from the main hall.

All the way to the South Circular Road, she was nagged by the feeling that she had the answer, but it eluded her efforts to bring it to the surface of her mind. She thought of Ellie, how different she was from the big twins and how her first impression on meeting the child had been of still waters running very deep indeed.

Where would she have gone? Poor Stephen; poor Roz – they must be frantic! Suddenly, Anne Marie realised the implication of the phone call. Roz was up! She was functioning! But what an awful way to be dragged out of the pits of depression.

At the house, she found only Roz and the baby twins. Stephen had taken Ruth and Jake out in the car to check the neighbourhood for any sign of their big sister. 'It's not as if we thought it would do any good,' said Roz miserably, 'but the twins were so desperate to do something to help that I told him to go. We've decided to wait until he gets back before calling the guards. I keep hoping the answer will come to me . . . I feel I should know my daughter's mind, but the trouble is – I don't! I've spent so little time with her; especially since the twins were born. The truth is, I've no idea who she would turn to at a time like this.'

Anne Marie could do little but be a sympathetic listener. While Roz paced up and down the kitchen, fluttering her hands agitatedly about her face or running them over her bald head, she read the note that Ellie had left on her pillow for Stephen to find. *Dear Daddy, Jake, Ruth, Anna and Ben*, she read, *I'm going away for a little while. Please don't worry about me. I want to do something to make Mammy better. I'll be back soon. XXX Ellie.*

'Oh God, just let her be all right!' Roz stopped at the French doors and leaned her head against the glass.

'Let her come home safely,' she pleaded under her breath. 'Nothing else matters. I can't believe how selfish I've been. I didn't notice . . . I was so caught up with my own problems, I didn't see what I was doing to my family!'

'No, don't say that! You can't blame yourself . . . it's not your fault. After the trauma you've been through . . . you needed time, that's all. It's just . . . Ellie probably didn't understand that; she couldn't see beyond the present.'

'The strange thing is,' Roz went on, continuing some train of thought of her own, 'it wasn't enough for me to have five kids to realise that I'm a mother. Imagine that! It's only when one of them is taken from me that I discover what matters in my life. I'll take the cancer, I'll take it gladly – if only she comes back to us safely.'

Anne Marie was in an agony of suspense. She longed to help, but unless she could discover where Ellie was, there was nothing of any practical use to be done. This was not a situation where cups of tea could be offered and soothing words spoken. The only thing she could do was concentrate on the elusive thought that she had the answer.

Maybe Ellie had said something to her? What did the child talk about, when she talked? Books, mainly. She devoured them, seeming to prefer the imaginary worlds they described to the real one inhabited by her noisy twin siblings. Was it something she read and later told Anne Marie about? Yes, that rang a faint bell. But what was it? Of late, Ellie hadn't been reading much. With Roz out of action, she had been busy helping Stephen after school every day. Every time Anne Marie had come over, the poor girl seemed to be changing nappies, feeding the twins or hanging out the washing. Because she never complained, everyone assumed she was all right. But was she? Her note had said she was going away for a little while. To get something to make Roz better. Where could she go? The chemist's? No, that was silly!

Anne Marie sighed. This was useless. *Where would I go?* She asked the question idly, but the answer popped into her head straightaway.

All at once, she knew that that was where Ellie had gone, too. Of course! It all fitted: the story of the holy well had given her the idea. She had met Nano in Dublin, so it was not as though she would be going to a stranger. And recently, Ellie had been asking lots of questions about Limerick and its environs, even asking Anne Marie to show her Riverwood on a map. The child must have been planning this for over a week!

Anne Marie ran to Roz. 'I have it!' she cried joyfully. 'I know where Ellie's gone!' Taking her by the hands, she began a mad dance around the kitchen floor.

At that moment, the telephone rang.

Mother and child reunion

The big twins didn't wait until Stephen had turned off the engine before tumbling out of the secondhand People Carrier that had become their new car after the baby twins were born. Flinging the doors open, they raced past a mud-spattered Land Rover across the gravel towards the house. 'Nano, we're here!' they shouted at the top of their voices.

Anne Marie was in the back with the baby twins.

'They're still asleep. Can I leave them for a minute?' she asked.

Roz was sitting hunched up in the front passenger seat. She seemed not to hear. Stephen glanced over his shoulder and smiled. 'Sure,' he said. He turned to his wife and took her hand. 'Ready?'

She nodded.

The door to the big house was open. Nano stood in the porch. A little behind her was Ellie. She was holding the older woman's hand tightly; as Roz and Stephen got out of the car and came towards her, she retreated behind Nano's back, as though she feared this meeting with her parents.

'It's all right,' whispered Nano, 'they're not angry, only relieved. Don't be afraid.'

'Hi Nano, hi El,' shouted Ruth as she dashed past them into the house. She stopped in the huge hallway. 'Hey Jake, c'mere and look! There's a real deer's head hanging on the wall! And two stairs! And the floor's brill for sliding on – whee!'

Her brother didn't hear. He had gone round the side of the house and discovered the orchard.

'Ellie?'

Roz approached her daughter tentatively, as though unsure of her reception. Stephen had stopped a little way from the porch, allowing his wife to go first. He smiled over her head at Nano, who acknowledged him with her eyes.

'Ellie . . . sweetheart, are you all right?'

The child looked questioningly up at Nano, who smiled encouragingly back and released her hand. Ellie took a few shy steps forward. Roz opened her arms.

Five hours later, all the grown-ups and Ellie were

sitting in the library. Although it was the end of June, Nano had lit a fire, purely for the comfort it bestowed. The wood crackled animatedly, giving off a pleasant scent of resin as it burned.

Ellie's story had been gone over many times. With each retelling, a different aspect was marvelled upon.

'What I can't get over is how she got so far on her own,' said Dermot, the neighbour who had found Ellie. He had gone away after meeting Roz and Stephen, but had been invited back for tea. 'Those back roads aren't signposted; you want to know them well to find your way about.'

'Eleanor's a very intelligent young lady,' said Nano. 'She taught herself how to use a map and compass by reading books from the library. Isn't that right?'

From her perch on the arm of Roz's chair, Ellie blushed and nodded.

'And like an eejit, I never realised that she was pumping me for information,' laughed Anne Marie.

'Ah, but it was you who guessed in the end where she had gone to,' Stephen reminded her.

'Only just before Nano's phone call.'

'All's well that ends well,' said Nano. 'A child was lost and is found.' She looked down at her hands for a second, then lifted her head and smiled. 'That is a gift to us all,' she said softly. 'And Rosalind has drunk water from the well. It may not have magical properties, but it is good water; we'll fill a big bottle for her to take back to Dublin. As for me, I've spent a very pleasant morning with Eleanor, and I've made some new friends who I hope will come and visit me here at Riverwood in the future.'

As though on cue, the door burst open and the big twins erupted into the room. They skidded around the furniture and, shaking with excitement, came to a halt in front of Stephen and Roz.

'This place's brilliant! We went down to the river with Mr Griffith—'

'His name's Matt!'

'—and he's got a boat!'

'It's a little rowing boat and he let us—'

'—We went fishing!'

'Shut up! I'm telling it!'

'No, I am too! We seen a – ow, Mam, Jake hit me!'

'Saw,' murmured Roz automatically.

Stephen put his hands on their shoulders. 'Jake, Ruth, slow down. One at a time. Jake, let your sister—'

Jake was too wound up to listen. Struck by a new thought, he ran to Nano and threw himself onto her lap. 'Nano, can we come and live here with you, please, please? This house is massive; I saw loads of bedrooms that nobody sleeps in! You could be our other grandmother. Oh can we, please?'

The adults exchanged amused glances.

All except Roz.

She knew what was expected of her. A smile as she shook her head fondly over her whirling dervish of a son. A gentle reprimand and an amused glance round. Oh, the things children come out with!

She couldn't do it.

Caught by the force of Roz's unspoken desire, Nano's head tilted back.

No one else noticed. Stephen pulled Jake off Nano's chair and tousled his hair. Ruth began her tale all over again, addressing herself this time to Dermot and Anne Marie.

Suddenly Nano stood up. 'Well,' she said, rubbing her hands, 'I don't know about anyone else, but I'm

ready for my tea. Only first,' she held a warning hand
out to the twins, 'some of us need a walk to work up
an appetite. Anne Marie and Dermot, I'd like you to
take the children down to the wet field. You can take a
few carrots for Esmerelda. You didn't know there was
a donkey, did you, Jake? Off you go now! You too,
Eleanor. You haven't been outside at all. And besides,
there are certain matters I need to talk over with your
parents.'

Reading Dostoevsky

The summer was a typical Irish one: weeks of cool wet
weather interspersed with glorious days of Mediter-
ranean blue skies and temperatures as high as the mid-
twenties.

Such true summer days were particularly hard on the
prisoners in Mountjoy. Incarceration was easier to bear
in winter, when the long hours of darkness and bad
weather made conditions inside the prison seem almost
attractive, especially to those men for whom Christmas
on the outside would only have been a day to be got
through, insensibly if possible. But in summer, when
daylight lasted until long after lock-up, and balmy
breezes wafted tantalisingly over the wall from the
Royal Canal, then the loss of freedom was keenly felt.

The exception to this rule was Desmond Dunne. He
didn't seem to mind being incarcerated, no matter
what the weather. During the lunch-hour lock-up on
this particularly delightful July afternoon, he was lying
on his bed reading a novel by Dostoevsky. His new
cellmate, a pasty-faced young man in his early twenties,

was sitting on edge of the bottom bunk, chewing his nails and sighing gustily. Dunne took no notice of him.

'Aw Jaysus, when are the screws going to finish eating? I swear their lunch-hour gets longer every day. I'm doing me nut stuck in here.'

Dunne made no reply.

'Fucking beautiful day, wha'? Wish I was on the outside.'

'So you could go to a park and get a tan while you shoot up, you mean?' said Dunne, turning a page.

'Aw Jaysus, give us a break! I've been off the gear for over a month now.'

'Which, funnily enough, coincides with the length of time you've been in here with me.' Dunne put his finger on the page he was reading and closed the book while he leaned over and gently swatted the young man on the side of the head. 'Can't you see you're better off locked up? When they brought you in, you were nothing but skin and bone; at night I couldn't sleep because you had the screaming heebie jeebies. Look at you now – you're almost human! Another few months and you could be sorted, like your pre-decessor.'

'Me wha'?'

'The headbanger that was in here before you. He cleaned up his act, showed willing and he's over in Pat's now, learning a trade. When he gets out, he'll be able to get a job, start over. You could do the same.'

'Nobody'll give you a job if they know you're after doing bird.'

'I will.'

'*You?*'

'Yeah, me. You sort yourself out in the next couple of years, stay off the drugs, learn to read and write.

When I get out, I'll find you a job. After I've written me memoirs and had a film made of me life, you understand. Who d'you think would be best to play me? I was thinking your man, Brian Dennehy, the Hollywood actor would've been good if only he wasn't so long in the tooth.'

'Are you serious? Are they going to make a film about you? Could I be in it?'

'Not unless you get up off your arse right now and tidy up your side of this place. After that, I might consider it.'

Just then there was a rattle of keys in the corridor. The cell door was unlocked.

'Censor's got some post for you, Dessie,' said the Class Officer who had opened up.

'Thanks, Mr Larkin. Hope it's those books I ordered.'

'Nah, it's just a letter. Got some sort of funny writing on it.'

Dunne's heart did a minor somersault. Maybe this was the letter that he had been awaiting in fear and trepidation since Darina left for Moscow.

Steady on, he told himself as the censor handed him a white envelope with a return address carefully printed in Cyrillic on the top lefthand corner. She might not even have met up with him yet, and if she has, he won't want to know about me. Especially not now.

Inside the envelope was a card and a photograph, blank side up. Dunne deliberately refrained from turning over the photograph at once. Instead, he concentrated on the card. The front of it had a picture of a man reading a book with a wild look in his eyes. Dunne glanced at it cursorily then quickly turned it over. He took a deep breath.

Howya Des,

Thought you might like the card – the painting's called Reading Dostoevsky. *If you've started on the book list I gave you, you'll understand it.*

Met John – he's not a bit like you. Pity, really. Public school accent and all – definitely not my type. I told him about seeing you. He won't admit it, but he is intrigued.

Sorted out the money thing too, and hinted there's plenty more for the asking back in Ireland. Fund-raising in September is a possibility. Meanwhile, thought you might like this photo – it was taken by a mate of his, Yuri, before I got to Moscow, but as I don't have a camera of my own, I swiped it out of their office.

That's all for now – I haven't been to language class for a while, so I'd better put in an appearance. You can write to me at the address on the envelope if you want. Otherwise, see you in a couple of months.

Do svidania, Darina.

Dunne turned the card round and looked at the picture again while he sorted out his emotions.

Darina had met John. She was disappointed that he wasn't like Dunne – well, that was what he had been prepared for all along, wasn't it?

The depth of his disappointment showed him that it was not so.

'Whass wrong? Bad news, is it?'

Dunne pulled himself together. Unclenching his fist, he forced himself to smile at his worried-looking cellmate. 'Nah, not really,' he said. 'Nothing I didn't know already.'

He turned over the photograph almost as an afterthought.

What he saw made him catch his breath. He ran over to the box where he kept his personal belongings and began rummaging through it.

'Whacha looking for?'

'You'll see in a minute. Oh, here it is!' Dunne stood up. He had another photograph in his hand. 'Pass us the Blue Tack from the shelf over there, would you?'

Handing a small packet of the sticky stuff to him, Dunne's cellmate peered at the photo in his hand. 'Is that the missus?'

'Get outta here! That's my mother, that is,' said Dunne happily. He stuck the photo on the wall above his pillow and stood back to look at it.

His mother was a thin woman with dark wavy hair and tired features. She looked as though she might once have been pretty, but life as Mrs William 'Wacko' Dunne had long since eroded beauty and hope from her face. She was half turned towards the camera, clearly not expecting the snapshot that had caught her wiping a wisp of hair off her forehead and frowning.

Beside the picture of his mother, Dunne stuck the photograph that Darina had sent. It showed a tall, good-looking young man with straight blond hair and a long, aristocratic nose. He too, had been caught unawares by the photographer.

The resemblance was not obvious. Physically, they were unalike, apart from an arguable similarity in the shape of the face. A stranger would never have connected them. But for Dunne, the young man's startled, slightly annoyed expression said it all. There was the cocked eyebrow, there was the furrow in the brow and the slight turndown of the lips, less pronounced in him than the lines etched onto the older woman's face, but unquestionably the same.

Dunne's cellmate was standing at his shoulder. 'So who's that then?' he asked, pointing to the young man.

Dunne smiled. 'That there,' he said with quiet pride, 'is my son John.'

Birthday girl

At the September equinox, Anne Marie turned twenty.

She found it hard to believe that only one year had passed since her nineteenth birthday. She remembered clearly how she had woken on that day thinking that in a couple of weeks, she would be starting her new life in Dublin. How full of trepidation she had been. How anxiously she had lain in her bed wondering if she ought not to put off the move until after Christmas. How forlornly she had wished that her parents would beg her to get a job closer to home.

How much had changed since then!

And yet, thought Anne Marie, frowning at her reflection in the mirror of her new room at Riverwood, I don't think I look any different to the way I did on my last birthday. Her hair was a little shorter than it had been when she came to Dublin, but it had returned to its natural colour and the perm had grown out. Her face was as round and childlike as ever.

But surely there must be some way of telling from my appearance all that has happened to me in the past twelve months, she thought, examining her eyes hopefully for some new depths that would reflect the wealth of experience she had acquired in that time.

Disappointingly, no matter how close she got to the mirror, she could perceive no light of wisdom shining out from her pupils.

Maybe it's all internal. I don't *look* any different, but inside I'm a more confident, mature and worldly-wise person than I was when I was nineteen, she said to herself. That seemed fair enough. Certainly, when she compared herself to the young woman who had stood staring helplessly up at the windows of the house in Belvedere Square after her arrival in the capital, she could see how far she had come. What a ninny I was then, reflected Anne Marie, smiling fondly at the memory of her first days in Dublin. I wanted so much for things to happen to me, but I was scared too. Well, I certainly got my wish!

She reviewed some of the major events of the year. One: she had almost been murdered. Two: she had worked directly or indirectly for two bosses who turned out to be criminals and were now doing time in Mountjoy Prison. Three: she had become good friends with a gay couple. Four: she had been adopted by the family of her best female friend, who was currently undergoing treatment for breast cancer.

As if that wasn't enough, on one fateful morning she had lost her lover, learnt that her father was not her father, and been told that her parents were going away and leaving her.

St Patrick's Day would never be the same again.

What was it that had marked her most? The answer came at once: Victor. Without a doubt, falling in love was the single biggest thing to have happened to her in the past year. She remembered with a pang how wonderful it had felt; how proud and happy she had been in the company of her African lover. Even now she could scarcely believe that she, mousy Anne Marie from Killorglin in Kerry, had had her first proper sexual encounter with someone so exotic and awe-inspiring. He was so incredibly handsome, she remembered wistfully. And so brilliant, and so dedicated to Human Rights.

And so good in bed, another voice in her head reminded her.

She smiled. Yes, there had been that too. Victor had awakened in her feelings she could never have imagined possible. Thanks to him, she had known passion. She would always be grateful to him for that. Of course, they had been worlds apart emotionally and intellectually; she realised that now. The wonder was that he had ever considered her worthy of his attention. Briefly, Anne Marie wondered if, in a few years' time when she would be so much more grown-up and sophisticated, they were to meet again . . .?

No, you will not go down that road, she told herself firmly. It's over, now and for ever. Besides, there are other fish in the sea, and one of them is bound to have my name on him.

Giggling at the image conjured up of a cod swimming around with a label reading *Anne Marie* hung about its gills, Anne Marie left off contemplating her twenty-year-old face and finished getting dressed. The day promised to be fine, so she took out the sundress Nano had given her as an early birthday present. Her grandmother had bought it on her latest trip to Italy, a week spent walking in the Apennines with Giorgio and shopping in Milan. It's lovely to see her so happy, thought Anne Marie as she fastened up the buttons on the back of the dress; after all the tragedy in her life, she deserves it.

She twirled in front of the mirror, enjoying the swirl

of the full skirt about her legs. It was a plain white dress with a heart-shaped bodice and a narrow waist. Sort of 1950s style, Anne Marie decided, and therefore not something she would ever have thought of buying for herself, but she recognised that it really did suit her.

Next she slipped the antique ring Nano had given her on to her finger. Getting it back had been one of the few pleasant surprises of the early summer, after Roz had been diagnosed with cancer and she herself had lost her second job.

She remembered the day well. Brenda, that nice woman garda, had come to the house to tell her that the ring had been recovered. Anne Marie had had trouble recognising her because she wasn't in uniform; if it hadn't been for the fact that Darina was with her, she wasn't sure that she'd have remembered at all.

It was funny how Darina had seemed much friendlier with Brenda than before; after explaining that the garda wasn't in uniform because she'd recently been transferred to Special Branch, the two of them had grinned at each other as though that was some sort of a joke. Then Darina had invited Brenda downstairs for a coffee. Strange, considering how hostile she had been to her on other occasions. Which just goes to show, Anne Marie told herself as she gave a last appraising glance in the mirror: you should never be too quick to judge people, because they'll always end up surprising you.

There was a knock on her door.

'Come in,' called Anne Marie.

Nano came in, carrying a vase of yellow roses. 'How's the birthday girl?'

'Grand,' said Anne Marie happily. 'Oh, roses! Are they from the garden? Thank you, they're lovely.'

'As are you, my dear,' smiled Nano, setting down the vase and kissing her granddaughter on both cheeks.

'How are the preparations going? Did the marquee arrive yet?'

'It's being set up as we speak. Your Aunt Barbara should be here shortly to drop off some supplies for the buffet, and Matthew has gone to get the trestle tables out of the barn. Roz rang to say they were just setting out, and the rest of the Dublin crowd will be picked up from the train at one o'clock. Meanwhile, Giorgio has some croissants warming in the oven and the coffee is on, so if you're ready, we'll go down and have breakfast before we start. I have my speech to work on; it's nearly done, but I'd like to try it out on you first.'

'Sure. As long as you remember what we agreed . . .'

'Yes, I do. This is not your birthday party, it's an Equinox party. And in return, you've agreed that we'll make it an annual event.'

'Correct!'

'Good. Are you ready? Yes? Then what are we waiting for!'

Cocktail sausages

Michael Griffith adjusted his dicky bow and surveyed himself in the mirror of the downstairs cloakroom. Not bad, even if he said so himself. He gave his reflection a last admiring glance, then went into the kitchen, where his mother and sister were busy taking vol au vent cases and sausage rolls out of the oven.

'Over there, Mikey.' His mother swivelled her eyes towards the table. 'The ones on the left are vegan, the rest are normal. Make sure you remember which is which.'

'Yeah, yeah,' said Michael, nonchalantly picking up the tray and balancing it on his upraised hand as waiters did in the movies. He went out through the back door, along by the vegetable patch and round the side of the house, swerving between imaginary tables and narrowly avoiding clumsy customers that only he could see.

At the end of the walled garden was the orchard; as he approached it, Michael could hear the geese making a racket inside. He stopped at the mesh fence to see what was disturbing them.

Inside the orchard, a small boy with a stick was circling the chief gander warily, trying to edge past him to a wheelbarrow full of windfalls. The gander allowed him to creep a little closer, then, just at the moment when the child looked as though he was ready for a final dash, it lowered its head, stretched out its neck and hissed menacingly.

Michael laughed as the boy dropped his stick and beat a hasty retreat up a ladder to the top of the wall, from where he could shout insults at the bird in safety. That gander had terrified him too, and he'd been a lot older than Jake when his family had come to live at Riverwood four years earlier.

Out in the front, most of the guests were dotted in twos and threes about the lawn, or standing in a cluster near the drinks tent. Michael went over to the nearest group, which included his father Matt and Dermot, the neighbouring farmer. There were two other men with them; Stephen, the father of the children, and a dark, foreign-looking young man whom he had never seen before.

'What's this you've got for us, Mikey?' his father asked, rubbing his hands in anticipation.

'Sausages – vegan or pork, take your pick.'

'Oh, definitely pork for me. What about you, Dermot?'

'I'll try vegan. Next time I have pork I hope it'll be from my own wild pigs.'

Michael offered the platter to the other two men, who were talking earnestly about bee-keeping and permaculture. They both chose vegan.

Wusses, thought Michael contemptuously.

Standing next to the drinks tent were Gerald and Darina and the other brother whose name he could never remember. They were talking with two young men whom he didn't recognise. One was short and powerfully built, the other tall and aristocratic in bearing. Michael pulled himself straight as he approached them, trying to disguise the shyness he suddenly felt in front of these sophisticated-looking young adults.

Gerald turned and smiled. 'Would you look who it is – young Mikey Griffith! God, but you've put on a spurt! How was France – did you pick up a *petite amie* while you were over there?'

Michael reddened and mumbled something about sports camp and having no time for anything like that. He thrust the platter into the centre of the group.

The youngest Davenport chose pork. The shorter of the two strangers hesitated for a moment, then speared a vegan sausage. *'Shto eto?'* he asked, holding it up to Darina.

Darina shrugged. 'Pig-free, by the looks of it. No good for you, Yuri. Here, have one of these.' She took a sausage from the other side of the platter and put it in his mouth, smiling into his eyes as she did so.

Michael blushed at the intimacy of the gesture. They were lovers! Darina, who up until a few years ago used to be quite plain and gave him wedgies when he annoyed her, was now a grown-up woman and a head-turner. A bit too thin and sharp-featured for his taste, he conceded, but definitely a looker.

Gerald helped himself to another sausage. 'Since Darina is otherwise engaged, let me introduce you,' he said, using his cocktail stick to point to the two men. 'This is Yuri Ivanovich Petrov and that there's John Sackville-Dunne. They're over from Moscow to raise funds for their charity, *Dom*, which helps kids living rough in Russia. I hope you've been saving hard because they'll be expecting you to break open your piggybank for them!'

Michael nodded, 'Hi,' to the two men, who smiled briefly before continuing their conversation in Russian. I'm just a kid to them, he thought, turning resentfully away.

Nano was standing at the steps in front of the house with Giorgio, the distinguished-looking Italian who had been a guest for the last week. They refused both kinds of sausage, saying they would eat from the buffet later on.

Next in line was the weirdo with long hair who had come down on the train from Dublin. American, naturally. Rumour had it he was a multi-millionaire. He certainly doesn't look like one, thought Michael, in that cotton pyjama suit and bare feet. He was walking with Daniel Davenport, who was wearing his monk's robes and sandals – yet another of the dramatic changes that had taken place while Michael was spending the summer in France.

Imagine deciding one day that you'd had enough of being a husband and father and wanted to spend the rest of your life singing with the monks over in Glenstal! If it was his dad, he'd die of embarrassment.

Daniel accepted one of each type of sausage; the weirdo smiled and said thank you but his body required no nourishment at this point.

'Over here, Mikey!'

Michael recognised Anne Marie's voice. She was reclining on a large rug on the grass with Roz and the baby twins. If his sister Cicely hadn't been so busy in the kitchens, she'd have been there too. He'd never seen a girl go ga-ga over babies the way she did over this pair.

'These ones are vegan,' he said, lowering the tray to within easy reach.

'Specially ordered for me,' smiled Roz. 'So I'd better have some.'

Michael had never met anyone with cancer before. It was strange the way she didn't look sick, he thought. She had stubble instead of hair, but that could almost have been on purpose; with her big dark eyes, she might have been going for the Sinéad O'Connor look.

'Michael!'

Anne Marie's aunt was beckoning him. She used to be plain old Auntie Barbara but was now Bibi Bracken and a force to be reckoned with. She was wearing a dark red woollen dress with an expensive-looking silver brooch at the neck and Michael had to admit that for an auld one, she was hot. She was also in charge of this afternoon's catering.

'How are we doing? Has everybody had something to eat? There aren't many vegan sausages left, are there? You'd better get your mother to do more.'

'I think there's another lot ready inside. That should be enough.'

'Well, get a move on so. Bring two trays next time and when you're going round with them, try to encourage people to come up for the buffet. Once the food is out, I want them to serve themselves quickly, before the flies get at it.'

'OK.' Michael glanced quickly round. Bibi was paying him six pounds fifty an hour for this afternoon; he'd better be seen to earn it. He'd offered his tray to everyone except for Anne Marie's parents, whom he'd seen heading with arms linked past the marquee and down towards the river some time ago.

On his way back to the kitchen he was nearly knocked over by the Hunter twins, who were being chased round the outside of the house by their big sister.

'Hey! Steady on there!' cried Michael, catching Jake with his free hand. He twisted him round and held him fast. 'I've got you now and I'm not letting you go until you've eaten at least three of these.'

His twin sister came over. 'What are they made of?' she asked, poking a pork sausage with a cocktail stick.

'Pigs, of course. Don't you townies know anything?'

'We're not allowed to eat pig sausages. They give you hormones.'

Michael laughed. 'They do? Well, in that case, you'd better stay off them for another few years. Have one of the other kind; your mam ate three so they must be allowed.'

The boy twisted out from under Michael's arm. 'If I eat three will you show me how to swing the geeses by the neck?'

'Oh, I couldn't do that! Only Nano knows how and

she only does it when they're really bad. Like when the gander's after eating a little boy.'

The children squealed.

'Tell you what,' said Michael. 'I'll make the three of ye a deal. If ye come with me next time and help round everyone up for the buffet, I'll take ye all down to the badgers' sett this evening. How 'bout that?'

'Yeah!' shouted the children.

Dream come true

'Mind if I join you?'

Anne Marie squinted up at the figure standing with the sun behind his shoulder.

'Oscar? Of course – sit down. Roz has gone to get something to eat; it's just me and the baby twins.'

Oscar lowered himself to the rug and bent over the sleeping babies. His black eyes melted as he gently stroked Anna's bare toes.

Anne Marie smiled to herself. Dilating pupils – that was what was supposed to happen to broody women when they looked at babies, wasn't it? Broody women and Oscar. Funny that she'd never noticed before how long and thick his eyelashes were.

Oscar turned his face to the sun. 'What a wonderful day for a garden party. And in such a setting! Riverwood is like . . . I don't know . . . a dream come true. I'm so glad to be here. It was very kind of your grandmother to invite me.'

Anne Marie smiled but said nothing.

'I met some very interesting people. The estate manager, Matthew Griffith, said there used to be bees here a long time ago, when the old owner was alive. He seemed quite keen to start it up again. I thought maybe . . . if your grandmother agreed, I could come down again sometime to give him a hand?'

'Sure, that would be brilliant. Riverwood will have organic honey to go with the organic veg, the organic fruits and the organic geese. And Dermot next door will provide organic beef and organic wild boar. We'll be the healthiest folk in the land!'

Oscar smiled, then asked hesitantly, 'Does that mean . . . are you going to stay down here for good?'

'No, no! I'm going back to Dublin tomorrow. Thanks to money from the fashion agency that used my photo, it's been a wonderfully lazy summer, but I've got to think about earning a living again.'

'Oh yes, of course. Have you anything in mind?'

'Sort of. Dave, who used to work on the magazine and was responsible for the photos that the agency bought – he and his partner Joe have got this idea for a business venture. They're designing websites. There's already a lot of demand for their services, apparently. They want me to do all the writing and take care of the business end of things. It sounds interesting, so I'll give it a try.'

'So you will be in Dublin then? Oh good!' said Oscar. Then he blushed and bent over the twins again.

'Your friends are lucky to have five wonderful children,' he said after a short pause. 'I love big families, but they're not in fashion any more. I suppose it's because women don't want to spend all their lives raising children. Not that I blame them,' he added hastily, 'but I look at my parents and I feel envious that they grew up with lots of sisters and brothers whereas

I am an only child and I have very few cousins on either side. I know it's selfish but I can't help it.'

Anne Marie nodded. 'That's OK, I know exactly what you mean.'

She almost added that her dream was to have a big family some day and be a traditional stay-at-home mammy, but she stopped herself. The last time she had indulged those fantasies had been when Victor had been on the scene, and it still gave her a twinge to remember how she had envisioned herself here at Riverwood with her African husband and their brood of beautiful mixed-race offspring.

Idly, she went on to wonder what Oscar's children would look like. He too was tall, dark and handsome, but in an Italian way. Judging by his attachment to Roz's kids, he'd make a great father. He was playful and affectionate, just like Seán had been with her. She smiled as baby Ben, who had just woken, looked up at Oscar and gave him a great toothless grin.

'Looks like he remembers you.'

'Yes, I'm the one who speaks to him in that strange language,' said Oscar. 'Eh, *bello bambino*?'

'Maybe I should learn Italian. Nano's started lessons, you know. She does it on the computer. She's even got into a chatroom in Italian.'

'I'll be your tutor – my rates are very reasonable,' said Oscar with a grin.

Anne Marie wrinkled her nose at him. He really was a pet. Her first impressions of him had been all wrong, she reflected; he wasn't melancholy at all. Dublin had been lonely for him, but now that Giorgio was seeing Nano, he would be able to visit Riverwood whenever he liked, check up on his bees and all that. They could come down together once or twice a month. It would be nice to have a travelling companion, and the great thing about Oscar was that she didn't fancy him so there was nothing in the way of them being friends.

Roz came back carrying a plate of food. She smiled at Oscar, who had taken Ben into his arms and was making strange noises that sounded nothing like Italian but delighted the baby nonetheless.

'Awake already? Little monkey! He does this all the time: naps for half an hour, then wakes up and looks around for someone to play with. If there's no one, he wakes his sister!'

'But they're such good babies. I've hardly ever seen them cry,' protested Anne Marie.

'Mmm, we are blessed this time round. Jake and Ruth screamed solidly at us for their first eighteen months. After that they fought each other. It was as though they were furious at having been born together. This pair are the very opposite; they can't bear to be parted. You're right – they *are* wonderful. All my children are wonderful.' Roz paused, then gave a wry little laugh. 'Now I just have to learn how to be a wonderful mother to them.' She fell silent and gazed around her for a while before turning back to Anne Marie. 'I'm so happy to have met your grand-mother,' she said. 'You've no idea how much it means to me.'

'Yes . . . well, she's very happy that you spent so much of the summer here. She has missed having young people in the house since her grandchildren grew up. I hope you'll continue to visit her at weekends during the winter. I know she'd love to see you.'

Roz gave her a strange look. 'Well,' she said slowly, 'funny you should mention that . . .'

'Oh look, here comes Daddy!' Oscar held Ben up to the approaching figure of Stephen.

'Last call for the buffet,' announced Stephen as he sat down beside Roz. 'You two had better get a move on before it's all whisked away. Here, I'll take Big Ben from you.'

Oscar passed over the baby and got to his feet. He gave his hand to Anne Marie and pulled her up. 'Let's go, I'm ravenous!'

Stephen watched them go, then turned to Roz. 'They make a nice couple, don't they?'

Roz smiled. 'Mmm. Even if they don't know it yet!'

Equinox

'Old friends and new,' began Nano, 'it gives me enormous pleasure to welcome you all to Riverwood on this beautiful, beautiful day. Officially, we are celebrating the autumn equinox, but there are many more reasons for having a party. Anne Marie's twentieth birthday is one, but I'm not allowed to talk about that.'

She smiled down at Anne Marie, who was at the front of the group clustered about the bottom of the steps. Anne Marie blushed and smiled as those around her patted her back or murmured birthday wishes.

'The other reasons for celebration I am going to share with you now.' She half turned towards the house and paused. Its old stone façade seemed to glow in the early evening light. 'I believe that there is a coming of age in the life of a house as much as in the life of a person. For this magnificent house, the time is now. I do not know what it looked like when it was built over two hundred years ago, but I cannot think it looked better then than it does today. It was never my intention to keep Riverwood for my exclusive enjoyment, and now that renovations to the house are finally complete, other people will be benefiting from it too. As it is now home to Anne Marie, I am looking forward to the weekends that she will spend here, bringing her friends with her to liven things up. You will all be very welcome. Next, I am happy to say that Giorgio has finally decided to retire, so when we are not in Italy, he too will be spending more time at Riverwood. I hope that means that Oscar and all the rest of the Bari clan will be frequent visitors.'

She smiled at Oscar, who turned to Anne Marie, hoping for and finding approval in her eyes.

'Through Anne Marie,' continued Nano, 'I have been privileged to meet many new people. These include Rosalind and Stephen and their five children. As most of you know, Rosalind has been undergoing treatment for breast cancer since the beginning of the summer.'

Heads nodded and some people turned shy smiles of sympathy on Roz.

'Having a serious disease almost invariably leads people to a reappraisal of their life. In some cases, it leads to a radical change. Such has been the case with Rosalind and her family, who have decided to opt out of the rat race. I am very pleased to announce that they have put their house in Dublin on the market and will be buying the coach house and old stables here at Riverwood. And, as six-year-old Jake pointed out on his first visit, there is plenty of room in the big house to accommodate them while the renovation work is being

515

carried out. I should add that I have my own selfish reasons for wanting Rosalind close by: I am hoping to persuade her to look at the diaries and letters of my friend and benefactor, Clarissa Stenbridge, whose life and words I would dearly love to see in a book.'

A few people clapped. 'Hear, hear,' called Yvonne, who turned then to Seán and whispered, 'At last! She's been pestering me to do it for the past twenty years.'

'Don't I know it,' her husband whispered back. 'Sure isn't that why we're fleeing the country and going to live in darkest Africa?'

'Among the new friends who came from afar to be here today, I am delighted to welcome John Sackville-Dunne and Yuri Ivanovich Petrov. They have come all the way from Russia to raise funds for their charity *Dom*, which I understand means "house" in Russian. We will of course contribute to their work with the street children of Moscow to the extent that we can today, and in a few years, it is possible that Riverwood will become a holiday venue for some of these youngsters. Darina, whose double first in her exams has made us all extremely proud, will be responsible for this worthy project.'

'Yeah Darina! We knew you had it in you!' cried Gerald as people clapped or raised their glasses towards his sister.

'And that, dear friends,' said Nano with a smile, 'brings me almost to the end of my speech. We are saying goodbye to Yvonne and Seán, but I know that they wish to make a quiet exit so I won't dwell on their imminent departure. I will remind them, however, that this Equinox party is to be an annual event and that we will expect them to return from Tanzania for it if they can.

'Now it just remains for me to thank all whose hard work has made today such a splendid occasion: Barbara, for her superb catering arrangements, Matthew, Cora, Michael and Cicely Griffith for the cooking and all the behind-the-scenes organisation, Giorgio and Anne Marie for lending a hand wherever it was needed—'

'And you, Nano, for everything!' interrupted Anne Marie. 'You're the one we should be thanking!'

Seán stepped forward and turned to the group. 'Let's hear it for Nano!'

They did three cheers, while Nano shook her head and smiled.

'All right, all right,' she said when they had finished. 'That has shut me up. We'll move straight to the toast. Michael has been quietly going round with the bottles, so I hope everyone has a glass with something in it. The toast I am proposing is quite simple, but I think it covers everything that we have found to celebrate. Anne Marie, it is your birthday after all, so I would ask you to come up here beside me.'

Pink with mixed pleasure and embarrassment, Anne Marie went up to the top of the steps and stood beside her grandmother looking down on the people gathered below. Her family and friends. They smiled up at her and she basked in their affectionate gazes.

I'm twenty and I'm one lucky girl, she thought.

'If you are ready, please, I would ask you all to raise your glasses.'

Glasses of champagne and mineral water were raised on high. Nano turned to make sure that Anne Marie was ready.

'To Life!'

'Life!' echoed her guests, smiling at each other with

eyes that were merry, excited, reflective, and, in one or two cases, tinged with sadness.

Anne Marie sipped her champagne and beamed. The bubbles tickled her nose, but she didn't mind.